"THINK BASEBALL— WRIGLEY STADIUM..."

Cedar whispered desperately—anything to distract himself from wanting her.

"You a sports fan?" Colleen splashed nervously in the hot pool.

"Actually," he muttered, "baseball is the furthest thing from my mind, so keep your distance, Sprite." Even as he spoke he absorbed the marble beauty of her arms, her white breasts misted and gleaming.

Then her thigh grazed his. She melted into him, and he cradled her, nibbling the sleek flesh curving from shoulder to throat. "Cedar," she breathed. "No...."

"Tell me plainly to let you go," he murmured. "Because it's not what I want."

"I don't want this—this craziness between us."

Abruptly he slid away from her firm body, her slim wet arms. "What *do* you want?"

"To be free, Cedar—for once. Please be on my side...."

Books by Louella Nelson

HARLEQUIN SUPERROMANCES
96—SENTINEL AT DAWN
128—FREEDOM'S FORTUNE

These books may be available at your local bookseller.

For a list of all titles currently available,
send your name and address to:

Harlequin Reader Service
P.O. Box 52040, Phoenix, AZ 85072-2040
Canadian address: P.O. Box 2800, Postal Station A,
5170 Yonge St., Willowdale, Ont. M2N 5T5

Louella Nelson

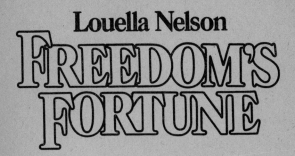
FREEDOM'S FORTUNE

Harlequin Books

TORONTO • NEW YORK • LONDON
AMSTERDAM • PARIS • SYDNEY • HAMBURG
STOCKHOLM • ATHENS • TOKYO • MILAN

Published August 1984

First printing June 1984

ISBN 0-373-70128-4

Grateful acknowledgment is extended to the following:
Randy Welch, for the quotation from "FAIRWEATHER TROLLER."
Used by permission.

For Danny Rear
and the Southeast Alaska Salmon Trollers
Let Freedom Reign

CHAPTER ONE

"*YOU* ARE COLLEEN?" The sturdy Alaskan choked out her derisive words. Shaking her head, she surveyed the slight young woman who hoped to assist her with this summer's salmon catch. In disbelief she added, "*You?*"

"Yes, I'm Colleen Conaughy."

"You expect to pass yourself off as my fish puller?"

"I'm here to do that job, yes." The sparkle in Colleen's blue eyes dimmed slightly, but she maintained the prideful tilt to her chin. "You must be Marion Brown. The mail-plane pilot said you lived in the gray house with the red window trim." Leaning back, Colleen observed the peeling paint of the porch posts. Finally she returned her gaze to her supposed employer. "I received a telegram. Was it from you?"

Wisps of Marion Brown's chestnut braids ruffled in the breeze blowing off Lisianski Inlet. Those tendrils did nothing to soften her disgusted expression. "Look at those skinny arms!" She gestured with a stout one of her own, admitting nothing but her incredulity. "Even under the jacket I can see there's nothing to 'em! Could they heft a forty-pound salmon over the side rail of the *Blue Sparrow*? Could those tiny hands rip a knife through its guts, get it into the hold without bruising it and bury it in a ton of shaved ice?"

Marion waved past the railed boardwalk where Colleen stood, giving her a brief review of what she'd seen from the air: wood-frame stores and cottages tucked at the base of alpine mountains still capped with snow; no roads, only the main boardwalk through the village; and paths leading up the hillside at the north end of town. About one hundred fifty boats clustered around the docks, Colleen remembered. She wanted very badly to go down to the harbor and get an idea of what it would be like, fishing on one of those red, blue or white boats. They looked like bathtub toys from the air, and the sight had allowed her to contain a quiver of fear that she might fail at this ambitious experiment.

But Marion was pointing toward the mountains across the inlet, or perhaps at the gleaming fjord itself, and again Colleen felt the woman's disgust. "What do you think run in Alaskan waters, Colleen Conaughy—minnows?"

Colleen shrugged and bent to retrieve her imported leather suitcase from Marion's weathered stoop. It was evident the woman would never hire her. Yet a spark of stubbornness made her hesitate. Impatiently patting back a strand of copper hair, Colleen once more stood erect and, with all the determination she could muster, held the gaze of the woman in the cottage doorway. "I'm strong," she said, her voice carrying clearly over the murmur of the stream flowing beneath the boardwalk. "And I'm not afraid of hard work. It's why I came here."

"All that strength and determination packed into five feet, huh?"

"Five feet four inches."

"All of that?" The skipper of the *Blue Sparrow* reached down and plucked at the all-weather jacket Colleen wore over jeans and a green plaid blouse. "There must be, at most, ninety-five pounds trying to make your clothes look like they're being worn by somebody."

"One hundred twelve pounds, to be exact."

"Don't look it."

"I—I've worked out in a weight room for months. Muscle is deceptive. It weighs more than fat. It's true," she added.

"Huh! Bet you'd blow overboard in the first wind that whistled down off Glacier Bay. Spit you right off the stern like you were popcorn!" Marion Brown shoved her fist into her waistline, pinching the weave of her heavy red shirt. "How old did you say you were?"

"Twenty-three. And I learn quickly."

"Still wet behind the ears, I'll bet. First time one of the men off the boats made a pass at you you'd faint at his feet."

Colleen glanced away, focusing on the bleached railing that neatly lashed the shops and cottages of the village to the base of the mountain.

"Right, wasn't I?"

Colleen swallowed. *There's no way I'm going back to Seattle,* she thought. *Back to father's steady stream of gold-digging women, the rambling rooms of Clifden Moor, the starched lives decaying under the weight of better years. No way I'm going back without first knowing what it's like to eat, sleep and work like a regular human being.*

Marion had turned away, saving Colleen an explanation. "Hey, Blue." She waved to a bearded man who clomped up the boardwalk in rubber fishing boots. "Ain't seen you in a while."

While Marion chatted with the heavy man about "needlefish spoons" and the benefits of her new green "hootchies" versus live bait—fishing jargon—Colleen stood with one tennis shoe on the porch, her green-and-brown traveling case looking conspicuous beside her. The conversation flowing around Colleen underlined her feeling that she was out of her element with these roughshod isolated villagers.

She hadn't been worthy of a man like Alec—her save-the-world Alec of college days. She had to change. She'd failed to help her father fight his drinking problem, she'd failed to keep Alec.... What good was she to anyone unless she could face life's tough problems and win? She was sick of failure, tired of a life without focus, disgusted by her own moral weakness. So she'd chosen the most rigorous proving grounds in the world—salmon fishing in the untamed reaches of Southeast Alaska. From here she could go anywhere, with anyone, and know she had courage and the fortitude to overcome hardship. She could write Alec in that lost village in the Amazon jungles and tell him she'd changed. To give him proof, to give herself proof, she had to have this job with Marion.

"Hungry as a bear," Blue remarked behind her.

"You're always hungry, Blue," Marion answered with a chuckle, going on with her discussion of fishing.

Colleen looked up at Marion's squarish face, envying the delicate crow's feet fanning her eyes. Years of peering past salt spray had etched that delicate webbing, Colleen decided. Marion had worked in wind and glaring reflections to earn those lines.

Five foot seven, she guessed, her gaze traveling over Marion's rounded shape. About thirty-eight. Beneath those stained jeans and the double layer of shirts, Marion could weigh anywhere from one hundred thirty to one hundred fifty pounds. And her hands—leathery from seasons of handling wet icy fishing gear—God, how she envied them! They were the reddened hands of a worker, not the porcelain hands of some china piece dusted by a maid twice a week.

Glancing at her own slim fingers, Colleen saw with satisfaction the ridge of calluses raised by months of lifting weights. The skin was taut, too, the muscles sinewy from tugging leather reins hour after hour as she rode through the blustery Seattle winter. She'd trained well for this season with Marion. All she had to do was get the flinty skipper to give her a chance to prove herself.

Blue cleared his throat, and Colleen glanced at the gray-bearded man. He gave Colleen a curious but friendly smile and said, "Well, Brown, I got my supper ahead of me." He waved to Marion and sauntered up the boardwalk toward the last cottages.

"Well," Marion demanded, pinning Colleen with a severe look, her pleasant mood evaporated. "What 'a you got to say for yourself, Conaughy?"

Colleen met Marion's direct stare with firmness. "Your ad said 'stable.' I've got a steady nerve, and I don't change my mind easily. Your ad said, 'Experience with commercial trolling gear preferred but not required.' I fit the latter qualification just fine."

"That ought to be worth several thousand dollars in lost weights and tangled lines," Marion said sarcastically.

At that moment a resonant male voice called from the interior of the cottage, "Bottom of the ninth and the score's tied, Marion. Better hurry."

The woman frowned over her shoulder.

Not wanting to lose her attention at this critical moment, Colleen squared her shoulders and spoke again. "I'd like to explain more about my qualifications, if you'll give me a chance. After all, I've come a long way on the expectation of being hired. I'd be disappointed more than I can say if we couldn't at least discuss the possibility."

"Disappointed, you say?" Marion's eyes snapped. "You're about the sorriest disappointment it's been my misfortune to consider as help aboard the *Sparrow*. If that seems harsh I can hardly apologize. We're talking life and death out there on the water. I've got responsibilities I can't afford to forget if we have a bad season, lose a ton of gear, or worse, get into a situation where you're too weak to hold your own. And I can't afford to have my puller running off with the first college boy who's trying to become a man in the fishing business. Your looks are a definite liability."

Marion gave her a contemptuous once-over that reminded Colleen of the buyers who used to come regularly to Clifden Moor, wealthy buyers who balked at paying the handsome fee her father demanded for his Connemara ponies. Used to demand, she corrected. Only Blarney's Blood remained, and she'd fought a degrading battle with her drunk father, at a public horse auction, to keep him. Strangely enough, the recollection allowed Colleen to bear Marion's degradation with a degree of hope.

The woman was taking a shoulder-raising breath, evidently preparing to sum up her opinion. "With all I said in my ad about hard work and harder conditions, I expected I'd made my point about the kind of puller I wanted. You're a sorry sight, Colleen Conaughy. I can't put it any other way.''

''Your ad said, 'Must be willing to work long hours under grueling conditions in all weather,' '' Colleen persisted, keeping the desperation out of her voice. ''I not only don't mind hard work, Marion Brown, I need it. I want hard work.''

That disapproving mouth seemed to soften.

''Your ad stated 'male or female,' '' Colleen said at once. She let a smile shine in her eyes. ''My letter to you explained I was female, in case the name Colleen left any doubt. And your answering cable read, 'Female okay. Season opens in one week. Come immediately.' Here I am.''

When Marion's lips tightened in what could only be a suppressed smile, Colleen took a steadying breath and plunged on. ''I'm easy to get along with. I don't take drugs, I'm strong for my size, I can cook but won't cost much to feed, I'm even said to read aloud effectively. And if you check very, very closely, Marion, you'll see I have all my teeth.''

Having obviously missed Colleen's attempt to revive an old horse-trader's joke, Marion scowled.

What did Colleen have to lose if she clarified the matter? She tilted her head, opened her mouth wide and pointed inside. '''Ee?'' she said. ''All 'ere. 'Trong 'ite 'eeth!''

''Bravo!'' said the deep male voice beyond the screen door. ''At the very least, Marion, she deserves a second interview.''

Colleen's mouth snapped shut. Embarrassed about the male witness and wondering if her behavior had confirmed Marion's low opinion, she searched the woman's brown eyes.

"Well," said the skipper, the remnants of a chuckle evident. "If you flew all the way to Juneau and jostled over here in the mail plane to work for me, the least you deserve is a cup of coffee. The best I can say, though—" her gaze roved once more over Colleen's trim figure before Marion turned to open the screen door "—is that you've got a sense of humor. After pulling fish and icing them down for twelve hours straight, you learn to appreciate a simple joke. Almost makes the money seem worth it."

As Colleen gripped the handle of her case and eased it through the creaking door, she heard the churn of the mail plane as it fought to lift out of the channel. She smiled to herself in satisfaction. The float plane wouldn't return until this time tomorrow.

For tonight, she thought, *Marion's stuck with me. I've got twenty-four hours to convince her I should be more than an overnight guest.*

CEDAR MCCLINTOCK HAD SET HIS BRIAR PIPE on Marion's coffee table and reached over to turn off the television. He didn't particularly enjoy baseball, not like Marion and her son, Mike, at any rate. And since Marion wasn't interested in the last moments of play, he had felt inclined to do without the distraction. Anyway, television reminded him too much of the traffic and pace of the cities where he'd spent most of his thirty-one years.

McClintock took up a great deal of space in Marion's front room. He dwarfed the easy chair he was reclining in. The tattered couch along the south wall and the scarred coffee table seemed scaled to fit in a doll house rather than to accommodate this broad-shouldered man. Yet he was so easy in his manner—retrieving his pipe, tapping out the burned tobacco, cradling the darkened bowl with familiar affection—that the furniture and not the man seemed out of proportion.

Other than the fierce Indian tribal mask on the wall over the TV, Marion's was a drab dwelling. By contrast, its inhabitant looked remarkably alive. McClintock's forest-green sweater, open-neck shirt and jeans were vibrant against the browns and grays of the room.

Ebony hair curled thickly over his right brow, and beneath this untamed mass, his eyes roved with a restless searching spirit. His nose was nondescript, plain and straight. This minor fault was easily overcome by a wide mouth that spoke of passion, and the ability to rouse it in others. The deep cleft in his chin balanced all that emotion, gave it focus.

While the television was on he'd been thinking that he came to Alaska every summer to escape city life. The theme frequently ran through his mind, yet he couldn't help wondering if Mack, his executive director, was making the right buying and selling decisions in the business. Sure, Mack was doing fine, he had told himself—that was what he told himself each time he packed up his stained sweat shirts and wool socks, leaving his stainless-steel-and-chrome condominium filled with three-piece suits and collections of conference papers on gemology. Sure, Mack had been running things smoothly for years.

Cedar would tell himself he was getting away from the bustle and exhaust fumes, taking that break he'd earned after traveling forty countries all winter. "Heading north to keep my youth," he'd grin at Mack as he stepped onto the airport tarmac.

He repeated the litany every spring, every May, because, dammit, no miracle was going to come along and make his life any rosier. At least in the summers his blood flowed, and he felt he was vital and struggling and alive.

And this year Marion needed him. He owed her.

Through an open window behind the couch had come the gurgle of the brook passing under the boardwalk near Marion's cottage, and with it the occasional cry of a gull. Above these sounds had come another, finally wresting his attention from the gem brokerage. He had begun to listen with interest as Colleen Conaughy presented her case.

Her voice soothed him, floated over his ears like a pulsing breeze. But a quality in her voice irritated him. He was reminded of the wealthy women he'd dated, women with mercenary claws sheathed in Bijon gloves... women like Alicia. There was an elegance to Conaughy's tone, a calm restraint that by no means revealed the desperation her words implied. "I need it," she'd said. "I want hard work." Yet she sounded as if she'd just left a French finishing school. All cool assertion and class.

The joke about her teeth had brought a smile to his lips, and impulsively he'd called out, "Bravo!", urging Marion to give the stranger a second chance. All tongue-in-cheek, of course; Marion couldn't afford to turn this applicant away. She was chomping at the bit to get off the docks.

He relaxed. The girl was human, after all. If Marion didn't so desperately need adequate help on the *Sparrow*, he'd enjoy seeing this sprite get her feet wet in the trolling business. Few women made it. Most were bred for the pleasures and plights of indoor living. The hardships aboard a cramped fishing boat reeking of fish took its toll on them mentally, and they soon returned to city comforts or the security of marriage.

He shifted impatiently, clamped the bit of his pipe between his teeth. Marion had alluded to the young woman's looks. It would be better if she had a beanpole figure or a beaked outsize nose. Anything to turn away the bold overtures of the summer fishing crew. Because the girl would be his responsibility for the next four months.

Over the winter he had decided that no matter who Marion hired, he'd see the crew stuck with her all season. Her puller would not run out on her. Not this season. Not with Marion's nineteen-year-old son lying mangled in that Seattle hospital. Mike's rehabilitation expenses hung over Marion's head in the wake of three years' bum luck with the fish. And now she'd saddled herself with a green girl for a mate! No question about it. He'd have to step in, watch over them both.

Marion was the only other woman he'd known who shared his mother's decency and devotion to family. He had been too young to do anything to stop his mother from working herself to death, providing for him, giving him a good Catholic education, buying new football and baseball uniforms when she wouldn't obtain adequate medical care for herself. He'd be damned if he'd let Marion kill herself needlessly the same way. She'd refused his money, but she'd get his watchful eye whether she accepted it gracefully or not. He owed Marion that much for giving him a break those many years ago.

McClintock sighed. There would be scant chance for his normal escape from worry this summer.

Still, he thought, setting aside his pipe and rising to his feet when he heard Marion invite the girl in for coffee, there might be something to be gained from being civil to her. If this newcomer was at all attractive, he'd enjoy taking her in his arms to comfort her after a humbling first fishing expedition. After all, few females both single and nice-looking could be found in the fishing fleets of Southeast Alaska. And it was going to be a long summer. . . .

Indeed he would enjoy seeing to this woman's comforts, he decided when he saw her. An aureole of red gold that could hardly be called anything as mundane as hair floated around her face, cradling delicate features. Her eyes shone with rich lights. They were startling in depth of expression, betraying a complex mind. Those eyes took in his form with a brief thorough look that stirred something half-painful in him. A little shaken by his reaction to her, he enumerated her other assets: slim legs and well-shaped calves beneath the snug fabric of sensible jeans, a hint of grace when she turned away to set her case by the wall and slip out of the bulky coat. An expensive case, he noted cynically, reminded of Alicia.

Then McClintock's breath quickened. Her narrow waist flowed into nicely curved hips. And outlined beneath the clinging tartan, her breasts were full, youthfully high and inviting. He instantly wanted her.

"YOU ADMIRING her teeth, Ced? Or giving her a dose of good old Alaskan male charm?"

"You can hardly blame me." He grinned at Marion, extending his hand to Colleen when she straightened away from her suitcase. "Cedar McClintock. I pull fish on the *Dart*."

Shaking his hand, Colleen found it warm and secure. His dark good looks disarmed her, charmed her. She smiled. "Colleen Conaughy. I hope you won't hold that teeth business against me. I'm sure having good teeth won't recommend anyone to a job pulling fish."

"Any strength comes in handy in this country," he said, winking at Marion. "But I suppose there are other assets more important."

"Such as strength in general," Marion remarked pointedly, brushing past Cedar, stopping to straighten a picture on the living-room wall.

Colleen felt the intensity of Cedar McClintock's interest, and shifted away to look at the framed print. It featured the primitive designs of an Indian ceremonial blanket, worn by a demure girl with two feathers draped down one side of her long hair. The metallic brown of a moon against a tan background was repeated in the pattern of the blanket. The garment's brilliant red edge made the print compelling. Captivated, Colleen murmured, "How beautiful."

"Mmm," Marion muttered. "Dust all over it." She rubbed a sleeve across the glass. "Jeanne Gamble would have a fit. She takes no small dab 'a pride in her work."

"Moon Maiden I," Colleen commented, reading the artist's inscription. "Silk screen, isn't it?"

"Beats me. She give it to me when I was down in Angoon a few winters ago. Eagles gave the Ravens a potlatch for helping 'em rescue one of their kin from a house fire. I went on down to say hi."

"A potlatch is like a party, food and gifts and all,"

Cedar said, his mellow baritone vibrating just above Colleen's head. He was like molasses, she thought—sticking to you everywhere you moved.

Marion craned her neck to look up at him. "What are you, my interpreter?" She glanced at Colleen. "I'm half Tlingit Indian, Eagle clan. How do you take your coffee, Conaughy?"

"One sugar, thanks." The Indian heritage explained Marion's dark features, she mused, interested in any scrap of lore about Alaska that would help her fit in. She felt excitement stir inside her. She was really here! And it was all so different, so exotic. Even Cedar, with his rubber work boots and husky shoulders, added a sense of the roughness of Pelican.

Trying to contain a smile of eagerness, she followed Marion into a cramped dim kitchen improved by tangerine curtains and canisters. Chintz pillows padded the maplewood chairs set around a table in one corner. "I'll fix my own coffee, if you like," she offered.

"I'll get the first round. It's up to you from then on. No sugar on the *Sparrow*, though. Honey keeps better in the wet."

"Then I'll try honey." Colleen crossed to the table and sat next to Cedar. She looked at him. "Honey's better for you, anyway. Not quite so disastrous to your system."

"You a health fanatic?" he asked, looking sincerely interested.

She resisted the impulse to mention her months at the health club, training for the fishing business. It would have been a routine topic of discussion with her friends in Seattle. "I'm not much of a fanatic on anything except good living."

"What do you consider 'good living'?" He folded his hands on the table and gazed at her, his expression wary.

"Having the things you want," she said, feeling in some way put down by his question. But because she liked the way his hair tumbled over his right temple, easy and uncaring, and the tapered strength of his body, she was reluctant to judge his nature too quickly. She wondered about his relationship with Marion. "I think freedom is the most important thing."

"Freedom from what?"

"From oppression."

"Really. Is that a political comment?"

"Partly. I'm speaking mostly of emotional freedom. Having choices. I imagine anyone who fishes for a living knows what I mean."

He looked at his hands, smiling privately. "Yes," he said slowly. "But freedom can mean so many different things to the fishermen up here. We each have personal interpretations."

"Such as?" He looked skeptically at her, as if she might be asking out of politeness. "No, really, Cedar. I'd like to know."

"Well—you know, breathing space. The chance to look back at where you came from and see if it holds anything of value."

"And perhaps to realize the past holds little of value," she ventured, speaking about herself, yet also sensing something untouchable about him.

"Yes...."

When Marion set three mugs of coffee on the orange checked oilcloth, the intimate moment splintered. "Black," she announced, pushing a cup toward Cedar's waiting hand. "And one with honey. How are things in Seattle these days?"

"Oppressed." Colleen laughed softly and wrapped her fingers around the hot mug. She breathed appreciatively of the fragrant steam. "Otherwise bustling as usual."

"You're from Seattle?" Cedar asked.

She nodded.

"What part?"

She took a careful sip of coffee, finding it sweet but tasty. She wished she could avoid telling Cedar anything of her background. It had paved too many roads in her life. Her family's former wealth and life of ease had become a barrier across the one avenue to her happiness: traveling as Alec's wife to the remote exotic regions of the world, where his training techniques were desperately needed. How she envied him his middle-class roots. Envied, too, his youth spent living and working with his father in the poor regions of the Northwest. Not that she'd trade the wonderful years before her mother died, when money had been plentiful but incidental to her parents' happiness. But most of all she longed for the anonymity that allowed Alec to fly off to the backwater villages of Brazil, free of typecasting, free of family responsibilities.

A flicker of pain swept her as she remembered him. She stared hard at the orange squares on the tablecloth. Alec. College romance. She drew in a soft breath, remembering his eventual withdrawal as he began making post-college plans. Then his rejection, sweet, regretful and final, that last afternoon she'd seen him.

"You're too soft for the life I've chosen," he'd said, taking her hand, stroking it as he would a child's. "A hothouse rose wouldn't last an hour in the Amazon.'' He'd tucked away his crisp new master's degree, brushed her lips goodbye and ambled across the quad, out of her life, with that slightly stooped walk of his. That humble gait he'd always said was his best asset, since it allowed him to "shuffle among the under-privileged without causing animosity.''

She sipped, remembering. Too soft, he'd called her. If only she'd known she was being tested! She could have avoided most of the parties, the ball games, the constant end-of-term social events she had used to hide her hurt over Alec's cooling affections. Instead, as he attended long meetings with intense strangers who talked of illiteracy rates and disease, she'd become the social butterfly Alec deplored. Of course, he hadn't in-vited her to but one of the meetings. He'd assumed, probably, that she wasn't interested. It was still hard to believe that a man she knew to be sensitive and caring toward the multitudes could have been so blind about his girlfriend's need for acceptance and worthwhile goals. He hadn't given her a fair chance.

In agitation she drank deeply, then jerked the cup away as she felt the bite of hot coffee. She set the mug down. Glancing up, she found Marion brooding into her own mug. Cedar was staring quizzically at Colleen. "Sorry,'' she murmured. "What did you ask? Oh, yes, Seattle.''

These two fishing folk from Pelican wouldn't likely be informed about Seattle's first families, she told herself, but her desire to be hired by Marion made her reluctant to chance recognition. Just as Alec had refused to take her with him, so Marion and Cedar might think her too soft to endure the rigors of commercial trolling.

"I was raised in one of the rural areas outside the city," she said vaguely. "I'd rather not dwell on that aspect of my life at our first meeting, though. I'm sure Marion has questions about my qualifications." She turned expectantly to her hostess.

"I'm only paying seven percent of my gross take for the season," Marion warned, her eyes coming alive again. "Otherwise I'd have been swamped with applications. The usual for newcomers is ten percent."

"I'll earn the seven and be happy with it," Colleen said.

"You're mighty small. It takes muscle to pull and gut all day when you're in the fish."

"I can imagine. Only vaguely, of course. I've fished for marlin and tarpin. Three years ago with my father, I hooked a two-hundred-eighty-pound tarpin that nearly cost me my right arm."

"You pulled him in?"

"Yes. It took me hours."

"That would have been on the East Coast?" Cedar wondered.

"Yes. Why?"

"I've been told marlin and tarpin are the sport of the wealthy."

"You've been 'told'?" quipped Marion, giving him a doubtful look. Cedar raised his hand in a silencing gesture that mystified Colleen.

"As my letter to Marion stated—" studying the faded blue flowers on the wallpaper, she made her voice quiet and sure "—I've fished my share of salmon and trout, as well. They don't necessarily require wealth to enjoy."

"But the time to fish often does, unless you do it for a living," Cedar said.

"Unless, of course, you sacrifice other priorities in order to enjoy what you like most," Colleen countered, her eyes shuttered to hide growing irritation. "And there are such things as vacations, Cedar. Washington State is ideal for both inland and ocean fishing, in case you haven't had the pleasure."

"But I have, Colleen, and I agree."

Her gaze jerked toward him.

"Seattle is perfect for many things. Including sailing. Have you sailed much in Puget Sound?"

Her gaze skittered to Marion. "Most of my life." Colleen was absurdly uneasy and wished Marion would divert the discussion to commercial fishing. Her voice cool, she turned back to Cedar. "Have you been sailing in the sound?"

"A great deal."

Yes, with those muscled shoulders and lithe, easy-movin' legs. Yes, you'd sail well. He seemed to recognize her, and she began to suspect he knew something about her family. He also seemed unusually worldly for a man who'd spent his life in Southeast Alaska. But unless she was willing to be more explicit about her own background, she couldn't really inquire about his. Besides, he wasn't the one she had to impress. She turned in her chair to give Marion her full attention.

"You call your boat the *Blue Sparrow*, Marion. How long have you been fishing her?"

"Nineteen years. My folks had her before that. We've caught a few fish, haven't we, Ced?"

"That we have. Two years ago I was wishing I was still with you. But, Ernie and I did okay."

"That's humble of you," Marion said dubiously, flicking a braid behind her shoulder. "If I recall, you guys did more than okay. Close to a hundred thou that season, weren't you?" To Colleen she said sarcastically, "Humility is a fisherman's best trait. He never wants you to think he knows where the fish are, just in case you might get it into your head to follow him around next time out. McClintock, here, knows I've got more pride than to follow him and Ernie around."

He laughed. "Marion, we haven't seen you off our stern in five years—unless we're heading to port, and then we're more likely to be off your stern."

"I taught you everything I know, didn't I?"

"Yep."

"Well, then, show a little respect in front of company."

"I think I'll have more coffee," Colleen said to hide a smile. "Anyone else?"

"I'll take a tad bit since you're up," Marion grunted, prompting Colleen to rise.

Aware of Cedar's dark gaze following her, she left the table and found an aluminum percolator simmering on the stove. She had replaced the coffeepot and was returning to her place when the wall phone rang.

"Get that, will you?" Marion ordered without sounding the least unpleasant.

Colleen lifted the receiver from a black dial telephone near the stove. "Hello?"

"Marion?" said a friendly male voice.

"No, this is Colleen—" She glanced toward the expectant faces at the table. "She's here if you need to talk—"

"No, just tell her the stuff's ready whenever she wants to pick it up. You the new hand she mentioned?"

"Well. . . we were just discussing the possibility. Just now, over coffee. Nothing's settled yet, Mr. . . . ?"

"Jerry. Jerry Tassic. Tassic Marine Repair. Well, Colleen, hope I see you around. Marion's the best, you know. The best to work for and the best cook on the water. She knows where the fish are, too."

"I'm hoping to find that out, Jerry. I'll give her your message. And thanks for the friendly welcome."

"Right. Anytime. Pelican's a friendly place. Who am I to give the town a bad name?" He chuckled and hung up.

"Jerry Tassic," she said when she returned to the table. "He said your stuff is ready."

Marion choked on her coffee and started to her feet. "Gotta go. Make haste while the sun shines, my pa used to say. Cedar, take Colleen down to the boat harbor and show her around the *Sparrow*. Then bring her up to the store. Now that Jerry's put the hydraulic pump back together, we can get ice, bait and groceries and pull out first thing in the morning."

"First thing...." Colleen watched the back of Marion's red shirt disappear into the living room. She heard the screen door slam.

"First thing in the morning," she repeated, looking with a dazed expression at Cedar. "Does that mean...?"

"You're hired," he said firmly. "Marion can't afford to lose the time placing another ad, and unless someone gets put off another boat around here, she'll have to make do with you."

"I'll see she doesn't have to make too much of a sacrifice where I'm concerned," she said, recovering from shock and feeling the sting of his condescension. "And I hope, Cedar, you'll choose to encourage rather than thwart my education. For Marion's sake."

He rose and looked down at her, his strange smile making her feel vulnerable. "For Marion's sake," he said softly, "I'll treat you like a babe in arms. All tenderness and consideration."

She stood up. Her chin lifting to his challenge, she met his gaze. Despite her bravado, his brown-black eyes reached inside her, connecting with her uncertainties, mocking her stubbornness. She knew then that Cedar McClintock would be one of the first hurdles in her path to freedom.

CHAPTER TWO

A CHILLY BREEZE lifted Colleen's reddish hair as she strolled with Cedar for the first time down the village boardwalk. His silence was companionable, and he gave her plenty of space on the splintered planking. She began to lose her resentment toward him.

He had shown her a carved black-white-and-red eagle mask in Marion's living room. He had explained that the deerskin rug on the back wall, by the stairwell, had been tanned by an old Tlingit woman in town. Now his silence gave her time to enjoy the wintry sun, the patches of snow, the salty scent of the tide marshes reaching raggedly into the channel.

The gray, evenly spaced boardwalk planks would have spanned a single car lane. Colleen touched the outside railing, running the tips of her fingers over the rough wood, convincing herself with every step that this beautiful town and its fishing fleet offered her a rare chance for success. All those painful months of lifting weights, worrying about being rejected, riding in the rainy Seattle winter to improve her wind—all of it paying off now. To be accepted so readily by the crusty skipper of the *Blue Sparrow* left her in wonder. She gazed toward the white peaks across Lisianski Inlet and sighed happily.

"Pleasant, isn't it?" Cedar commented, his eyes flicking in her direction.

"Mmm. Reminds me of Washington, in a way. The spruce forests. All this water. There's just more of it here."

"What sent you up our way?"

She looked quickly at him, but he was still walking with that easy stride, studying the stores and cottages ahead.

"Oh...." She made her voice nonchalant. "Just needed a change. I love to travel, especially to out-of-the-way spots. And trolling appealed to me."

"You don't seem the type for it."

"*Type*...now there's an oppressive word. Describe a trolling 'type.'"

"Tough. Strong. Somewhat driven."

He smiled, but she wasn't disarmed. "Like you?"

He shrugged, kept walking.

"Marion looks strong, but I wouldn't call her burly, or anything."

"She can hold her own in a nasty southeasterly." Again the dark gaze flicked over her. "I just wonder why you're really here."

"Instead of tending tea roses and sailing in Puget when the sun shines?" she asked with an edge of contempt.

"You could be setting the business world on its ear, or something," he admonished, flashing a smile. "What did you study in college?"

"What did you study? Psychology?"

"Economics. You?"

"Liberal arts." She sighed, feeling bested. Frustrated, she added, "French! My mother insisted it would come in handy someday."

"When you traveled to the continent."

"Yes." She didn't add that she'd already been. Twice.

"Français," he said musingly. *"Voulez-vous charmer les poissons? En français?"*

"No, I don't think charming the fish with my French would be any more effective than showing them my teeth— Oh, look," she blurted out, stopping him with a touch on his jacket sleeve. "I'm here because I feel I have to be, all right? Among other things, I had a falling-out with my father. I'm escaping his—his wrath, or whatever. Okay? Anyway, what's a man who speaks French and touts an economics degree doing trolling salmon?"

Cedar rocked back slightly, studying her. In that moment she knew she'd never seen so striking a man, and she felt a rash chemistry flaring between them. Now, while their gazes locked, she came alive with impulses she knew instinctively she could never master—not if he touched her. Kissed her. The resentful line of her lips softened. She felt the widening of her eyes, as if to look at him required all of her. Color flamed her skin.

When he spoke again it seemed the timber of his voice bonded them in some way—intimately, perhaps—yet she quickly discarded the notion, forced herself to hear what he was saying.

"Might be here for the same reasons as you," he said. "Who knows. There are lots of different kinds of oppression in this world. Maybe when we know each other better we can compare notes."

Her tongue seemed reluctant to respond, though she did force out a non-word. She marveled that he didn't notice her reactions, merely took her elbow to start her walking again. He was silent. Perhaps he *had* noticed, then. Was he giving her time to compose herself?

Embarrassed at these entirely unprovoked symptoms of arousal, Colleen turned her face toward the channel, keeping a guiding hand on the railing. Someone thumped by on the boardwalk, calling a greeting to Cedar as he passed, but Colleen glimpsed only a heavy green shirt and rubber boots like Cedar's.

Obviously the way to get Cedar off her back was to fire questions as quickly as he did, she thought, resenting his power over her emotions. He'd been deliberately provoking her before that spark of intimacy arced between them.

After a stretching silence, she began to feel the weight of memories stirred by their exchange.

She hadn't lied to him about her father, Sean Conaughy. Following Alec's departure last June, she'd immersed herself in the social life she'd always known. Because of her months with Alec, she'd suffered a little guilt about the excesses of her crowd—the lavish parties, thousands spent on summer wardrobes, richly outfitted sailing sloops. She'd kept her own expenditures to a minimum, not in memory of Alec but out of necessity. Still, it was like slipping on a comfortable old shoe to be with her friends again. Their warmth and acceptance eased her hurt over Alec's rejection. Besides, she had chastised herself during that lost unhappy summer, how could she possibly have considered going off with him when her father needed her?

Strangely, it was her father, not Alec, who finally forced her to look at her future. His drunken speeches, his reminders of how much she was like her mother had been cruel toward the end. The embarrassing calls from the sheriff's office, the restaurant scenes and belittling comments from his lovers—all of it had degraded her and enraged him when she complained. *You grow through pain,* she thought, remembering the moment she'd decided to leave, that last emotion-charged scene in the stable at Clifden Moor.

As she'd put away her light English saddle after a morning ride, her father had stumbled through the stable door, his tan corduroy blazer stained and lopsided. She had admonished him. He had patted her shoulder and said something vague about it not mattering how he conducted himself. "It's beyond caring I am, lass," he slurred.

She turned saddened eyes to her father, to plead. "Daddy, you must stop killing yourself over her. Mother's gone, gone these three years. Can't I help you at all?"

He pushed her roughly away, then grasped her arms with the steely strength of the horseman he'd been. His green eyes blazed. "Help me to do what? How can I forget her, lass? She of your blood, who gave you breath and beauty, gave me reason to breathe—forget her?" He wiped viciously at his liquor-loosened mouth. "She lives yet, my colleen. She'll live here among my things and in this place until I'm in the grave...."

He turned, stumbled from the stables, flung back, "Get ye to your man, daughter. Every living moment with you is a dark bleeding memory of the one who gave you life!"

Colleen fell against the saddle rack, too deeply hurt to cry, her face ashen. Before the alcohol had taken control, her father had zealously protected her, screening her friends, choosing her schools, escorting her and her mother to the "right" vacation spots of the world.

Now, with a two-minute, brandy-soured speech, Sean Conaughy had cast out his only child.

In those minutes of anguish Colleen hated everything about herself. She belonged nowhere. She was an idle socialite, unwilling, until then, to face the fact that the Conaughy millions were rapidly dwindling. Properties and businesses foreclosed, horses gone, spirit gone—and the heiress without a shred of training in anything but French and the arts.

All of August had remained, and by the end of the month Colleen's fit tanned body had gleamed with health. Alec had planted the seed, the idea that being tough allowed you to go anywhere, do anything.

Colleen knew from the start she wouldn't choose salmon fishing as her life's work. But if she could hack one of the toughest occupations in the world, no one, anywhere, would ever be able to tell her, "Sorry, can't take you on. You're too soft." She longed for that secure inner strength others saw in her, that shield of feistiness that no one saw through...she'd use it as raw material in her own transformation. By the end of the summer she'd be morally, mentally and physically as tough as anyone coming out of the state of Alaska.

Maybe she'd run a company someday, as Cedar had suggested. Perhaps she'd convince Alec she was a perfect helpmate for him. Kids, married life—they were a hazy dream in the back of her mind, the image half-scary. To see her father so ravaged by grief...well, whatever she chose to be after her twenty-fourth birthday in October, she'd be ready for it. Certainly by then she would have some inkling of what she wanted.

The May breeze brought the crisp tingle of salt, and she studied the tide marshes reaching out here and there from beneath the boardwalk. On one grassy spit, a collection of large birds milled around at the waterline. Colleen stopped suddenly in amazement. Her companion retraced his steps to her side.

The largest bird was perhaps fifty feet away, his plumage mottled brown and white. The eagle bent intently over a mussel clutched in one talon. He tore at the mollusk for several seconds, then raised his flat, snowy-capped head and glanced around. Briefly his hooded eyes regarded Colleen and Cedar. A gull lunged for the unattended mussel, and the young bald eagle wheeled away on mammoth wings. His flight caused the gaggle of gulls and eagles to scatter, screaming, but they soon settled again and began to squabble among themselves.

Colleen was thrilled to encounter this symbol of her country so near at hand. The sight filled her with keen pride and an immediate sense of belonging. Expecting to find Cedar equally impressed, she turned to him.

She drew in her breath at the expression in his dark eyes, eyes that were intent not on nature's wild creatures but on her. She recognized an avid quality about his gaze not unlike that of the feeding eagle. Forgotten were his probing questions about her background, which could hardly be important now that Marion had hired her. She could only marvel at his attractiveness, and especially at the unmistakable invitation of his lips.

Locked for a time in emotional upheaval, Colleen stood very still, her nerves strung taut. She knew he wanted her. His signals were pulsating very clearly in her direction. And she knew if he so much as touched her arm, now, it would be difficult not to lean into that broad chest, turn and accept that promised kiss.

Without meeting his gaze, only glancing briefly at

him, she turned toward him and said, "Do you always see eagles along the shores here?"

"Frequently. Pelican has only four hundred permanent residents, so local predators feel free to hunt without too much interference."

His answer seemed oblique and double-edged, she thought. "Without being shot, you mean?"

"Yes, except when they're a hazard."

That brought her gaze sharply to his. "They don't shoot the eagles!"

"No, they're protected." He laughed. "Otherwise Marion would be camped on the steps of the capitol building in Juneau. She takes her Indian heritage pretty seriously. I meant the bears, mainly. They nose around in the trash dump on the north side of town."

She looked beyond the main dwellings and saw that the cottages on the outskirts, surrounded by timber, were, at most, half a mile from where she stood. "I've heard brown bears are plentiful in Southeast Alaska," she said uneasily. "I wouldn't want to meet one face to face."

"Blacks roam in small numbers, too. It's not wise for a *chechako* to travel silently or alone through the woods here."

"I give up—what's a *chechako*?"

"Newcomer."

"Oh." Labels again. She supposed he couldn't help it, being part of a water-locked community that was obviously snowbound in the winter. Anyone who wore tennis shoes instead of those rubber treads of his probably got labeled an outsider. At least it was a relief to be chatting normally with him again. "Anyway, I was looking forward to hiking," she said. "And berry picking later in the season. I mean, after the fishing's over and before I head home. Bears could put a crimp in my plans.''

"You like to pick berries?''

"Uh-huh. Friends and I used to ride out and pick berries and eat them all before we got back home. It's a nice way to see the country, you know? I'd sure like to take in something of the Southeast before I leave.''

"Don't worry, you'll have your chance. The winter storms are still with us. During a blow you'll have to anchor up in a handy cove. There are forced closures, too, usually ten-day intervals during the trolling season when Marion and all of us will have to quit fishing.''

"Why?'' she asked, wondering again about his relationship with her boss.

"Why the closures?''

She nodded.

"Oh, just the fisheries' way of limiting the number of salmon taken each season. The numbers have been declining drastically for years. The fisheries limit the licenses issued, as well.''

"Aren't the closures rather hard on people who survive by commercial fishing?''

"Exactly. That's why the governor of the state appoints someone among us to testify before the legislature and various government fishing agencies that regulate the business. That balances things a bit, puts a check on the environmentalists. Not all of them, of course. Just the rabid ones who'd like to take over completely and destroy the local economy. The battles get pretty nasty sometimes.''

"Are you the appointed rep?''

"Nope. Fisherman by the name of Dan Rear has that tough job.''

"I would have thought you."

"Why's that?"

"Well...." Her composure restored, she ran her hand along the rough railing and leaned against it, looking up at him. "You have an easy way of speaking about these matters. And you seem concerned about your community and its economy—about Marion's well-being, for instance."

He laughed. "You're confusing a lot of issues, I'm afraid. First, Marion's my friend. Certainly I care about her, and because I'm fishing each season I care about regulation and a decent income for Ernie, my partner. But Pelican isn't 'my' community. I'm a transient like you."

"But—I thought you were a resident."

"No."

"Where, then? Where do you live?"

"With Marion when I'm fishing out of Pelican." When her cheeks burned suddenly from consternation—she would virtually be living with him!—he added lightly, "My winter residence is in your own hometown."

"Seattle?"

"Seattle. If a good proportion of Alaska's fishermen didn't hail from the same place, I'd say that was an amazing coincidence, wouldn't you? I'd say we even know some of the same people. Johnny Strange, for instance?"

Her breath whistled as she turned abruptly away. He knew Johnny, the skipper of the yacht *Green Bay*, the man who had been the most successful in breaching the protective screen her father had created around her before her mother died.

Johnny was a good-looking gold digger who had gambled away his fortune in Las Vegas, then roamed through the watering holes of the rich in half a dozen states, looking for a new stake to the gaming tables. Colleen had been Johnny's object long enough to make her care about him, until he'd found someone with a larger fortune. There had been weeks of waiting to hear from him. She recalled how hurt and embarrassed she'd been when her father showed her a society clipping from New York.

On Independence Day, her father had explained, Johnny Strange had announced his engagement to the daughter of a wealthy, aging, British arms manufacturer. It was Johnny's kind of joke, really, choosing that date for an alliance with a British girl. But it was a joke he was still living with as he waited for his wife's inheritance to come due. Evidently the old man had a constitution as reliable as his guns.

"I know Johnny," she slowly admitted to Cedar, her emotions settling. Her chin rose as she turned to face the man who seemed bent on needling her. "I wouldn't call him a friend."

"No," Cedar said complacently. "I suppose you wouldn't. Shall we comply with Marion's orders and get moving? I should find Ernie and give him a hand getting the ice and gear for the *Dart*."

What had he meant by mentioning Johnny? And by closing the subject the moment she admitted knowing the playboy? She glanced at Cedar's crisp profile, watched his gaze sweep restlessly over the water, the town, the distant boat harbor. She liked and resented him all at once, she realized, walking in silence. But she would not be bullied by him.

Stopping briefly at Channel Flying Service, Cedar picked up her extra suitcase. Only a few more minutes and they were standing above a picturesque collection of fishing boats. They made their way down the gangway to Pelican's harbor.

The entire town seemed to be loading provisions into vessels of every color and size. Peering upward for signs of bad weather, the men carried boxes of groceries and warm clothing. An eight-year-old in braids tore down the dark stained floats and leaped nimbly across the decks of boats tied three deep. Women coiled ropes or aired blankets, their wool shirts and rubber boots adding earthy charm to sturdy bodies. Colleen observed a towheaded Swede and, laboring shoulder to shoulder with him, a dark-haired Alaskan Indian.

Faces of the North, Colleen thought appreciatively. Faces lined with weather and hard work, rosy with fresh air. One man was old and bent, yet he went on sanding a newly patched hull, cheerily calling out that he was pulling out at dawn. His ring finger was stubbed short, but useful nonetheless.

After being urged by Cedar to admire the clean-cut lines of countless craft, Colleen began to feel tiny shocks of anticipation about the *Sparrow*. She couldn't concentrate solely on the boats, however; male owners and crewmen stopped often to stare at her, to call out a friendly challenge or to greet Cedar. Soon he transferred her case to his other hand so he could take her lightly by the elbow, and once he slid his arm around her shoulders, thereby warding off the attentions of an overzealous giant of a youth.

Almost immediately Cedar withdrew it. He pointed out a forty-two-foot crab-fishing boat whose decks gleamed dully, painted steel gray. And next to it—the *Dart*, a fifty-foot salmon troller carrying four trolling poles astride her wheelhouse deck. White and sparkling, her prow curved gracefully out of the water. Stern and bow lines were displayed in neat coils, and the stern deck was inlaid with narrow strips of highly polished wood.

A dory painted the same chalk tone lodged above a canvas tarp. The tarp served as a roof over a collection of pulleys and gears at the back of the boat, presumably the controls for running the fishing lines. The wheelhouse and living quarters were no doubt as pristine as the rest of the *Dart*, Colleen speculated, but these areas were protected from the elements by a closed door with a small window.

"Ernie must be out kibitzing on one of the boats," Cedar remarked as he walked away from the *Dart*. They passed a low-slung catamaran, its double hull and sailing rig looking frivolous next to the practical lines of neighboring trollers. And there were boats of such dark sinister character that Colleen shuddered inwardly at the idea of crewing on them. But these were few.

Following Cedar, eager to see her own place of employment, Colleen was gazing at boats far down the float when she stumbled into Cedar's back.

"Here we are," he announced, bringing his arm around her waist to steady her. "The *Blue Sparrow*, a thirty-five-footer with a horseshoe stern and plenty of beam. Place of my apprenticeship, and now yours."

Speechlessly Colleen stepped forward, her hand stretched ahead as if to wipe out the pitiful sight of the *Blue Sparrow*.

"But—" she choked at last. Her throat went dry. No

words would follow. The gulls' screams were cries of derision.

The ancient troller was blue—in places. It seemed every other board in her beamy hull was black or orange. A trolling pole on either side of the salmon-pink wheelhouse reached into the sky, the lines and snaps tinging in the breeze. Black paint peelings hung from the doweled poles, leaving patches of blue intact. Rope, buckets and an upended orange skiff tumbled over the cramped deck. Grimy tools lay scattered near the winches in the stern. There were windows around the wheelhouse, but the visor installed to cut reflective glare had lost great sections to corrosion.

In her shock, Colleen would have overlooked the throaty rhythm of the engine but for the dank choking smell of diesel fuel from the exhaust. The entire craft vibrated in the water. Even as she stood near the side rail, her feet planted on the dock, Colleen's eyes and throat burned from the fumes. Marion had probably been conducting some last-minute checks, though the red shirt and braids were nowhere in sight.

Colleen felt anchored to the swaying platform beneath her. She was unable to force the cries of eager inspection she had planned. Inside the dark wheelhouse, she could see rolled navigational charts held against the bulkhead by fishing line. She could see the dull gleam of the wooden wheel and the shine of stainless-steel-trimmed gauges. Those were meaningless details to a mind numb with foreboding. She had prepared herself for hard work, for learning a difficult new trade. But she hadn't prepared herself for living in squalor. She refused to imagine what the belowdecks quarters were like—no, couldn't imagine them. Nothing in her background even remotely compared.

Cedar's voice cut through her stupor, low and mean with sarcasm. "I was wondering when you'd fly your true colors."

"Wh-what?" She pivoted from the repulsive craft, intent on grasping his meaning.

He stepped quickly in front of her and cupped her chin in an uncomfortable grip.

"Thinking of quitting already, Red?" His black eyes glittered close to hers. Before she could twist away in outrage he said, "Forget it. You'll stay. Marion's son will die unless she earns enough money to keep him in that stateside hospital. If you left tomorrow she'd be out on the water alone, and driven the way she is about Mike, she's just apt to do something foolish. You're going to see she doesn't, Colleen. It would have been better if you'd been a man, but since you're not, you'll have to do. You're her guardian angel. Mike's, too, for that matter. I could make it mighty uncomfortable for you and yours in Seattle if you left unfinished business up here."

She was too stunned to move. If he'd let go of her, she probably would have fallen into the channel. "Mike?" she whispered.

"Her son."

"What happened to him?"

"He was mauled by a bear. Had serious complications. His chances look pretty grim." He added this with a small hesitation in his voice, as if he cared for Marion's boy. Then he said with more force, "It's Marion's place to tell you the story, not mine."

"When did this happen?"

"Late last August."

"Sweet Mary."

Perhaps regretting his harsh treatment, Cedar loosened his grasp, rubbed gently on her chin. "Another thing," he added more kindly. "Marion will ride you hard. Not just for the money—the money your mistakes will cost her. But because Mike was with her last year, has always been with her, even when I was aboard. He was born on the *Sparrow*. Now that he's gone, every wrong move you make will remind her of how good Mike was at your job. She'll resent you. Resent it if you learn to run the gear half as good as Mike. Hate you, sometimes, because you're whole enough to reach over the side rail, hour after hour, and gaff the fish. She'll even resent your beauty."

Her eyes stung as she pictured a young man immobilized with injuries, the son who had been Marion's partner just last year. But why would Marion resent the way she looked? She asked Cedar to explain, not minding that he'd placed his hand on her shoulder.

"You know what your looks do to a man," he chided, not disagreeably. "Every strapping seaman who sees you will be trying to wed you or bed you." His eyes were telling her that he, too, would try the latter. The thought of courtship from so striking and confident a man sent a mild quiver through her body.

"I know Marion was worried I'd run off with the first college apprentice who set eyes on me." Her dry tone belied her erratic reactions. "None of them has the slightest chance of success. I'll be working much too hard for Marion." She remembered his warning about those close to her in Seattle, and her expression hardened slightly. "By the way, Cedar, that's my decision, not yours. Threats mean nothing to me."

"No? Then think on this while you're settling in, while I'm rustling up Ernie. Marion won't be plagued by a string of sex-starved fishermen parading across the deck of the *Sparrow*, or through her living room. It would be cruel this soon after Mike, would remind her too much of his helplessness. She won't be tortured like that. Ask me to explain, Colleen."

"All right, Cedar. Explain."

"Because I'll prevent it. There's little time for court-ship out on the water. And when you're in town, I'll be with you." As if to be certain she received the message clearly, he bent close, his eyes narrowed. "We'll stop by Rosie's Bar and Grill when you feel the inclination to party, we'll go to the chapel on the hill when you want to pray, and when you want to sleep...I'll be right there in the next room to make sure you sleep soundly."

Suddenly understanding why his hand was on her shoulder—to stake his claim on her—she jerked violent-ly away. The stifling life-style she'd left in Seattle rose like mist from the channel, enclosing her, infuriating her. Her face flushed, and when she had finished sput-tering on her own indignation, she drove her gaze into his with all the fury she felt.

"McClintock, you black Irish swain, keep—keep away from me! Just stay clear! You haven't felt a woman's thorns until you've felt mine. I warn you, if you try to make good that preposterous intent to escort me day and night, I'll find a way to prick that balloon ego of yours."

"But think of the benefits," he protested, mocking her wrath. "I'll protect you. I'll keep those lonely men from going berserk at the sight of that wild red hair and perfect body."

"I'll do my own screening! You keep to your side of town, I'll keep to mine. I tell you, I'm not above rash means to protect myself from being smothered by the likes of you. I came here to be free, and I will be free!"

"It's too late. You're too late for arguments." His expression closed abruptly, his mouth thinning in suppressed anger. "I've made a pact, and I'll stick by it. Now unload your gear and get settled in. I'll be back for you in twenty minutes." He pivoted and stalked away, his boots thudding loudly on the wooden float.

Made a pact? With whom? Colleen shook slightly as she looked after him. *Conceited boor! Thought I'd submit willingly to his "protection."* He would protect her from others, she fumed, only because he wanted her for himself. *Whistle Dixie, McClintock! I'll have my freedom!*

The pinging of the *Blue Sparrow*'s rigging finally roused her, beckoning her to the shadowed quarters Cedar McClintock had once shared with Marion Brown. Casting a look of trepidation at the cluttered deck, she dragged her suitcase over the side rail and stepped aboard.

CHAPTER THREE

THE WESTERLY DELIVERED a witch's slap that burned Colleen's face and numbed her fingers as she struggled to lash the last safety line to the starboard stays. It was dark, perhaps 4:30 A.M., and the beam of the work light above the aft door didn't reach around the wheelhouse to aid her progress.

If you could call a snail's pace progress. Marion couldn't have picked a meaner chore than tying damp rope to icy stays in the dead of night. "Get these safety ropes up around the deck," she had ordered as she headed into the wheelhouse to warm up the engine and pull off the docks. "We're putting lines in the water at first light."

No need to test me like this, Colleen thought resentfully, trying to force the line through a corroded metal eye. She lost the rope, grappled for it. No use. The line slid into India-ink water, flapping wildly.

Angrily Colleen leaned over the side rail. The rope snaked across her palm, biting, rough.

The *Blue Sparrow* heeled slightly, and Colleen slid forward toward the water. Desperately she clamped her thighs against the side rail. Her heart hammering, she grasped the flat slick rail, hung on, hauled herself and the rope back against the tilting bulkhead. She squeezed her eyes shut in relief. When she again took in her surroundings, her breath steamed into the starlit night. Her thoughts wheeled. "She'll resent you...hate you sometimes," Cedar had said of Marion.

Wood grated behind her. "Hey!" Marion's voice sawed through the wind and the chugging of the diesel. "You rigging the whole boat out there?"

"Just about done!" yelled Colleen.

"We're hanging a left at Cross Sound. Wind's gusting to fifteen knots. Hold on!"

"Right!"

The wheelhouse door slid closed.

Obviously Marion was concerned about losing her fish puller, Colleen reasoned. *Ridiculous to accuse her of trying to do me in. She needs me. Sufficient sleep usually cures a suspicious mind.* Gritting her teeth, Colleen shoved the line through the metal loop, brought it around, tugged it into a knot. Immediately she put her fingers to her mouth, sighed at the meager warmth, then straightened. Ahead was blackness and the bitter wind. She feared the dark sea. Turning, huddling into her coat, she saw a faint gray smudge on the eastern horizon, the lower edge glimmering with salmon rose.

She wondered if Cedar was up yet, back on shore. Or if he was still tucked in that enviably warm bed next door to her room. He was a strange mixture of male heaven, she thought. So handsome her heart twisted when she looked at him, but infuriatingly in command, even when Marion ordered him around. "Marion orders everyone around," he had whispered out of the side of his mouth when she told him to hang up his jacket. "Got it from raising her younger siblings when she was barely thirteen."

Cedar had buried his macho come-on act by the time

they'd all gathered for supper, and it was difficult to remain cool toward him when his probing gaze went relentlessly to her face. And other places, Colleen admitted, her face warming from the memory. Yes, a bit of heaven in those dark-eyed looks.

He'd gone out for a while, and by the time she and Marion had finished the dishes he'd returned, his cheeks bright from the crisp night. He had grabbed Marion around the waist and kissed her loudly on the forehead, earning a shove and a scowl, before he'd laughed and said, "It'll be great to get off the docks tomorrow, won't it? Get the *town* out of our blood."

"If you were harboring any plans to beat me off the docks," Marion warned, jerking her head toward the stairs, "you should have hit the hay two hours ago. You need more sleep than a newborn baby."

"When you live good you sleep good," he'd returned, winking at Colleen.

They had all turned in at once. Thudding up the narrow oak stairs, Marion and Cedar called dibs on the bathroom, pointed out assigned rooms, issued challenges about who would bring in the first fish. Colleen had been given the bathroom first, after all, and been told to make it a quick shower. Afterward, wrapped in her thick mint-green velour robe, she had padded to her tiny room. Only after what seemed hours of restlessness, she had closed her eyes.

Heading northwest out of the needlelike Lisianski Inlet in the predawn darkness, the *Blue Sparrow* had slugged through a rough chop, and now Colleen felt the deck shudder slightly as they wheeled to port. The wind pressed against her back, whistling down her collar.

Enough, she decided, stepping into the lee of the cabin.
She slid open the door.

After a sideways inspection, Marion grunted, "You
look like you've drank a fifth of whisky."

"Refreshing breeze out there." Colleen touched her
cold nose.

Ghosting a smile, Marion glanced at a circular screen
to her left. The flasher's red light blinked at a mark Colleen recognized as thirty fathoms, one hundred eighty
feet to the bottom. By Marion's elbow, the wheel ticked
rhythmically to port and starboard as the automatic
pilot guided the boat. Marion resumed reading a chart
spread over the instrument panel.

Colleen read "Cross Sound" on the map, and
"Yakobi Island." Shaped like a wedge of pie, Yakobi
was tucked into the northwest shoulder of the larger
Chichagof Island, with Pelican serving as a cornerstone
where interconnecting waterways linked the two islands.

Like many of the islands in Alaska's Panhandle, bor-
dering western Canada, Chichagof looked as if it had
been dropped from a great height to shatter on a stone
surface. A long shard pointed south toward Seattle.
Centuries of storms had frayed the outer edges of the
islands into lacy coves and inlets.

But it wasn't the broad, relatively calm waterways of
the Inside Passage that locked Colleen's eyes to the
map; it was the open sea. Out of the wide mouth of
Cross Sound stretched the blue Gulf of Alaska, the
northern reach of the Pacific. A nerve jumped in her
stomach. She'd sailed rough water in Puget, and she'd
felt the roll of steep cerulean waves outside Nawiliwili
Bay off Kauai, Hawaii. Sure, she'd done some sailing.
But she'd never faced the open sea in the throes of a

storm. The unpredictable deep could take a few knots of wind and whip it to wicked fury in no time. She'd heard about Alaska's storms.

"We heading outside?" she said, keeping her voice level.

Marion was silent at first, reading. "Mmm?" she mumbled absently.

"Where are we headed?"

"Down along Yakobi Island. If nothing's happening, we'll head toward the west bank of Chichagof. Ever been? Nice hot springs there. Warm you up some." Marion glanced up, straight faced.

Colleen laughed. "Can't say I've had the pleasure, though if May stays this nasty you could tempt me at a moment's notice."

"This is nothing." Marion waved her arm toward the windshield, indicating the small whitecaps visible from the *Sparrow*'s reflected glow. "We'll see some rough weather before summer rolls around. Trick is to out-guess old Mother Nature and stay out of the worst of it."

The skipper reached behind them and snapped off a switch. The outside work light went out, and darkness surrounded the tiny cabin. Uncertainty swept through Colleen. She had handed her life to Marion Brown, she realized. Cedar's warning threaded through her mind. "Driven the way she is about Mike, she's just apt to do something foolish.... She'll resent you...hate you sometimes."

Colleen shivered, wrapped her jacket close.

"I could stand a cup of hot coffee. How 'bout you?" Marion said, one braid shading her cheek, her expression hidden.

"Sure thing."

The woman is psychic, Colleen thought as she stepped down into the forecastle to rummage for the light switch.

BACK IN THE WHEELHOUSE the VHF radio crackled softly with voices and static. A red halo from the fathometer framed Marion as she hunched over the wheel. Although the map had been rolled and tucked with the others overhead, the dim map light spilled yellow over the gauges on the dash. Colleen set Marion's mug into a shallow caddy.

"Take a look behind you," Marion directed when she'd taken a drink. "On the wall, there. Flashers, spoons, hootchies—all used to catch salmon."

Colleen turned. Silver, brass and gold lures gleamed in the cab light. She'd seen salmon lures before in her father's tackle box, though not in such variety. She touched them; they felt slick and cool as wet pipe. They were expensive shiny trinkets used to tempt salmon to the hook. Stainless-steel hooks with a curve the length of her crooked forefinger were snagged in neat rows along bars of cork. The barbs looked wicked.

"Those are snubbers," said Marion, pointing.

"Which?"

"Those lengths of rubber in the tray below the spoons you're lookin' at. The snubbers connect the leader and spoons to the fishing line. They take the stress off the line and keep it from snapping when a big king salmon hits the hook. Kings are what we want. Good-sized king can bring in sixty, eighty dollars. One fish like that could go a long way toward offsetting our expenses for the day." Marion glanced out into a rosy dawn. "If we don't lose a ton of gear."

Colleen turned away to hide her foreboding. She knew what Marion meant. *I can meet expenses with one fish if my green puller doesn't lose the damn thing bringing it aboard. Or worse, lose the whole set of gear—weights, lures, all of it—by some stupid move.* Colleen hadn't any idea what she might do wrong, because she didn't know the first thing about operating the power winches in the back of the boat, unloading wiggling forty-pound salmon at the same time. She was a sport fisher, one line, one pole, not a pro salmon troller. Yet. But Marion had a boy in the hospital and, by the looks of the boat, a heap of expenses to meet. Colleen was supposed to be their guardian angel. She didn't need Cedar's reminder to realize that a lot was riding on her untrained shoulders.

"*Blue Sparrow*, this is Ernie on the *Dart*," barked the radio, issuing call numbers to identify the vessel. Marion adjusted the squelch and turned up the volume as Ernie continued. "Come in, *Blue Sparrow*. You clear up to the Pole by now, Eagle Woman?"

Marion grabbed the mike. She lifted it to her mouth and growled, "*Dart*, this is the *Sparrow*. I see you're operating from the hot end of the earth as usual, Ernie. When you've got something intelligent to report, such as where the fish are, call back. Over."

This was an interesting development, Colleen thought. A little fire war between Marion and Cedar's skipper.

A static-peppered chuckle floated over the air waves. "Hey, Marion, that Injun blood of yours sure makes a guy glad to be back at sea. Nothing like your temper to make a long boring run worthwhile. Where are you, anyway? Ced wants to stop by and give you a hand taming that little sprite you got tagging your shirt tails this year. I hear she's a redhead with a disposition second only to yours. Over.''

Colleen grumbled indignantly. Marion met her gaze, smiling faintly. ''You're wasting good air space,'' she said into the handset. ''Why don't you put that fancy long-range gadget you got to some good use and find your own way out to the fish?''

''Aw, Marion. You're the only one in these waters who knows where the fish are. The fleet's counting on you to lead the way.'' He chuckled again. ''You out in the sound somewhere?''

''This ain't like you, Ernie.''

''How's that?''

''Well....'' Marion smiled as if she had a mouse pinned under her boot. ''You know, Finn—comin' right out an' courtin' a gal on the open seas. The whole Pacific tuned in.''

''Marion, now what'd you have to say that for?'' Ernie sounded a touch on the angry side.

''What'd you do, lose your virginity on your last trip out of town? Give in to sin?''

''Marion, knock it off. Nothing like that happened, and you know it! It was a trip to visit the Greenings, down in Ketchikan. They're trying to work out some problems and needed a listening ear!''

''So you say, Finn. So you always say.'' She chuckled to dig the barb a little deeper.

Evidently Ernie was as straightlaced as a high-top boot. Colleen listened with amusement as the two bantered for another few minutes. Then Ernie snapped, ''Look, Squaw Woman, just tell me where you're aiming that barge of yours. I want to make surefire I'm not headed in the same direction.''

''Just running to the old YB-two,'' she relented, mouthing, ''Yakobi Island, second trolling drag,'' to Colleen. ''About fifteen minutes and I should have the prince and all his court dancing right on my deck.''

''What're you running on, jet fuel?''

''Gotta get up early to catch the fish, Ernie.''

''I hear you, Pocahontas. You hear that, Ced?'' He called something to Cedar about getting up on time. Colleen would have loved to be standing next to Cedar, sharing this comical skit and seeing his reactions—if she hadn't been crisp around the edges herself, after hearing that ''tagging Marion's shirttails'' business.

Then Ernie came back on the line, his voice more serious. ''Uh, Marion?'' Pause. ''Uh...I was still in Ketchikan when you got back from Seattle. How's the boy?''

The breath went out of Marion. She lifted the mike, let it sink, then picked it up with more determination. ''Same, Ernie. The first fifty kings are for Mike. Check you later. Out.'' She hung up, snapped off the radio, took a long swallow of coffee. Disengaging the autopilot, she clasped the gleaming wood wheel in a tight grip.

Colleen forgot her mild irritation. She watched Marion's stony expression, feeling awkward and sympathetic.

''Go below and rustle up some breakfast,'' Marion said harshly.

''Sure. Eggs? Bacon?''

''Whatever. Time's a wasting.''

"More coffee first?"

Marion stared at the wind-whipped swells.

Slipping below, Colleen returned in seconds with the aluminum percolator. She poured. Marion's gaze flickered her way, but the pleasant features were set in hard lines of self-control.

As Colleen backed down the companionway, she paused to gaze through the rusty visor at a deep rose sunrise layered with gray clouds. The dark forested mountains of Yakobi Island, so different from the manicured paddocks of Clifden Moor, flowed by the port windows. It was a grand view, too magnificent to waste on bleak thoughts. *Swallow your fear, Colleen,* she told herself. *Cedar's right. No matter how tough things get, you can't run out on Marion. On Mike.* Alaska was too raw and wild to pay sympathy to mere human need. Sheer determination to make a profit would have to tip the scales. It would have to.

As she pulled out a black skillet and set it on the cast-iron stove, she added her own will to Marion's effort— and knew the summer could go either way.

CHAPTER FOUR

THE ONLY VESSEL heading into the overcast morning, the *Sparrow* cruised a mile offshore, skirting the western bank of Chichagof Island, where the surf pounded in a pale ragged line. Day three, Colleen thought, waiting for Marion to come aft to supervise the confusing process of getting the spreads of tackle into the water. Day one and two had been cold windy disasters. She'd never been all thumbs before. Now she was two left feet, as well.

From forward, near the cabin, came the humanlike groan of winches; the trolling poles lowered like the arms of Father Gregory when he gave the benediction in the old stone church near Clifden Moor. She had been thinking more and more about home: how wonderful it would be to climb up on Blarney's Blood and hie to the hills and woods. Anything to avoid Marion's curt comments and the backbreaking, confidence-destroying work of fishing without any luck.

The skipper made her way aft, buttoning her blue corduroy coat and throwing the collar up high around her neck. Beneath a wool knit cap her braids flapped in the wind. Holding on to the horizontal boom mast that swayed and creaked above her head, she peered down at Colleen. "Where's your hat? You'll catch your death."

Colleen dug into her pocket, fitted the cap over her loose chignon.

"This isn't California, Conaughy. Keep it on when the weather's grim."

"Will do, skipper."

"Climb on out, and I'll show you once more how to set the lines."

Colleen clambered out of the gloomy sunken cockpit. The *Dart* had a nice roomy trolling cockpit, she thought enviously. As the *Sparrow*'s deck gently rolled, she grabbed the edge of the dory Marion used to shelter the work area.

The ribbed flooring where Marion stood vibrated from the whirring of the propeller, and water churned away in a diminishing froth. Colleen was willing to bet the *Dart* had a better dampening construction, too. In this boat you'd probably eventually get water on the knee or throw out a joint if the waves hit just right.

Oh, what was she complaining about, she scolded herself as Marion realigned the cannonball weights secured in rusty clips by her thigh. She was here, wasn't she? Learning to be tough?

She ducked into her collar to escape the biting wind. A silver coat of dew shone on the decks and hatch cover and gear. The ocean had been gentle with them as they drifted with the current through the nights. She was free. Free and learning to live on her own. *Cheer up.*

Marion fiddled with a tray of tackle she'd wedged onto a shelf between two galvanized pipes rising out of the deck. The pipes angled overhead supporting the dory, and a gaff hook clanged near Colleen's right elbow. Creaking on salt-pitted fittings, several metal spools swung from the horizontal sections of pipe. Guy wires ran from the tips of the trolling poles to the trolling cockpit, where the wires were attached by oversized bronze clothespins. In front of Marion, power winches already carried stainless-steel line.

The skipper ran some of the line up through one dangling spool, then through one of the clothespins. "Hook up the tag line first thing," she said, showing the clothespin and heavy wire to Colleen. "But always remember to secure the tag when you're through running the line back in. Otherwise we'll have to hoist up the pole again, try to get it back. It would be just like trying to catch a strand of wet spaghetti in a whirlwind."

She glanced at Colleen. "All right. What's the tag line for?"

"Holds the fishing line running straight behind the pole," Colleen recited.

"Why's that important?"

"So the line won't run off at some cockeyed angle—or worse, in toward the propeller."

"There's hope for you yet, Conaughy." Marion reached for a lead cannonball weight, attached it to the line, lowered it over the side. It looked easy. The line pulled taut.

"How much did that one weigh?" Colleen asked.

"Thirty-five pounds. I'll put a float on this outside line before I'm done. That will keep it trailing out a ways from the inner line that you'll set. Now what am I supposed to do?"

"Gurdie?"

"Right. Run this power winch here." Marion threw it into gear, paying out line. "I'll run it, like I said, stopping every fifteen feet to snap a spread of tackle onto the fishing line. It's a cinch once you get used to—"

The wind snatched away her words as Marion's

square coordinated hands set out spread after spread with increasing speed. Finally, after Colleen had watched intently and was still feeling a little uncertain of the procedure, Marion climbed out beside her and said, "Your turn."

IT HAD BEEN an exhausting catastrophe, Colleen mused seven hours later as, alone on deck, she huddled in the lee of the pilothouse, feeling disgraced. She'd painstakingly tried to get the "rhythm" Marion hounded her about. But all she had seemed to do was tangle the spreads and run the line out too far, so that she had to hang dangerously far over the side rail to hook on the spreads.

To give Marion her due, she hadn't shouted in frustration until Colleen caught the tip of her coat in the power winch—an unnerving experience, as if she were rope being dragged through the eye of a needle. Marion had swiftly reached down and flipped the motor into neutral. Wiping her forehead, she had untangled the frayed coat, alternately yelling at Colleen about safety, complaining about people who took two hours to do a thirty-minute job and asking whether her puller was hurt.

Embarrassed at the memory, Colleen shook her head. On top of everything, after they'd finally set all four lines into the water, there had been no strikes. Nervous and frustrated, Marion had cruised south to a new drag, changing to live bait. At least Colleen had known from past experience how to hook the oily ten-inch herring so it traveled naturally through the water. Not that Marion had mentioned how easily she caught on to the small chore. And still no gleaming salmon had littered the deck.

"Heck of a way to start the season," Marion had grumbled at last, sending Colleen a dark look. "I'll rustle up some sandwiches."

"Shall I do that?"

"I want some more spreads baited up. 'Sides, my hands are itching, or something. Fiddly. You got anything against salami and cheese?"

"Nothing," Colleen had said quietly.

"Time."

"What?"

"Takes a little time to get the hang of it."

Colleen had pulled off a blue rubber glove and glanced at her small, hard, reddened hands. She had nodded. Heading for the galley, Marion had flung back, "Chow in half an hour."

They had eaten lunch, including a tasty potato salad with quarters of hard-boiled egg and coffee brewed with egg shells for flavor, and then Colleen had come topside to read. Inside the wheelhouse, Marion was watching the paper that rolled out of the sea-floor recorder, looking for "patches of feed" that might also indicate salmon were in the area.

Colleen closed the small book in her lap and absently rubbed the chipped gold leaf that had once spelled *Pilgrim's Progress*. Before coming to Alaska, she'd combed the library at Clifden Moor and found a collection of undersized classics. Her mother's. The one she was reading bore no copyright but an editor's note dated 1821. Someone had given the volume to Colleen's grandmother, three times removed, the Lady Sarah Lines Bowles of Yorkshire. Colleen wondered if Lady Bowles had been in any urgent need of fire-and-brimstone religious instruction, to be given such a book.

In any event, with salt tang in the wind and purity in the cold green sea, Colleen wasn't inspired to keep her eyes trained on the tiny print.

She squinted at the starboard pole. Marion had told her that since she preferred the chilly deck to the fo'c'sle or the wheelhouse, she could listen for the peal of one of the bells mounted on the pole tips; that would signify a strike on one of the lines. At the moment only the throb of the engine, the thrash of the wake and the cry of a gull filled the wintry air. Again Colleen felt lonely. "Joan," she said softly, speaking to the saint who had been her patron since her confirmation at age thirteen, "I don't know where you got the courage to lead those armies. The fishing business is going to take everything I've got."

"Coffee?" said Marion from the open window above Colleen's head.

Colleen glanced up. "Sounds good. Be right in."

"Company's coming."

"Here?"

"Off the stern to port. Ernie's trying to horn in on my trolling drag."

Her day suddenly much brighter, Colleen whirled and spotted the crescent-shaped *Dart*, plowing like a ghost through the pearly mist. *Cedar, at last,* she found herself thinking. Half the time while she was trying to read, Cedar's dark eyes and clean-jawed face wavered on the page. Half the time that she spent lying in that dank fo'c'sle trying to will herself to sleep, her mind conjured up Cedar: Cedar laughing; Cedar giving Marion a good-natured hug; Cedar standing three inches from Colleen, his gaze making her pulse ragged.

"Maybe they brought the fish with them," she said to Marion.

The skipper scoffed in disgust. "Ernie called a while ago. Got big plans, he says."

"I didn't hear you on the radio."

"I imagine not. It was just about the time you were chasing that cannonball around the floor of the trolling cockpit."

"Oh." Colleen turned away, the dig hitting home. She glanced at the approaching *Dart*. "What are their plans?"

"Says the fish are bitin' on down toward the tip of the island, if you can put any store in what that white-haired, preachy-mouthed Finn has to say. Which I most times doubt."

Colleen chuckled. "You must mean Ernie. He sounds like a real character."

"Right outta Moses's flock." Marion sighed. "Well, I'm up for that coffee, how 'bout you?"

"Mmm? Oh, yes. I'll be right in." Once Marion had ducked back inside, Colleen was free to lean against the wheelhouse and watch the pretty white boat cut a path off the *Sparrow*'s port side. *She* is *pretty,* Colleen thought—*and Cedar looks like Ben Hur riding backward in his chariot.* She giggled.

Cedar, his yellow sou'wester whipping in the breeze, stood at the baiting block, his hands busy with herring and hooks. A navy-blue seaman's cap confined most of his unruly hair as he bent to his task. A silver flasher winked from his hand.

Colleen answered Ernie's wave from the pilothouse as they passed, diesel exhaust trailing from the *Dart*'s chimney, the engine purring, the wake churning white. Just as she was fighting disappointment because Cedar didn't realize she was watching him, he looked up. He smiled, saluted with a herring.

A current of pleasure spread through Colleen. Smiling, then grinning, she waved vigorously. *There, now, I've seen you. You're safe. You look happy in your yellow cape. Now I'll have that coffee.* But she waited until Cedar's yellow slicker disappeared and his own grin was long diminished by the fog.

Inside, Marion handed her a chipped brown mug filled with coffee.

"Thanks. I'll take the pot back down. Think I'll have a dab of honey in this." Elated, she smiled to herself as she went below.

"You always look like you've had a pull off the rum bottle when you come in from the cold!" Marion called over the clatter of the diesel engine. "Saint Nick would be jealous of that nose and those rosy cheeks."

"Mother called it strawberries and snow. My complexion, I mean. I used to hate it, with my red hair. But—" Colleen stowed the honey jar in the locker and climbed the steep companionway. She pulled off her cap and tucked it into a pocket, unzipped her coat. "I came to accept it. Along with this curly hair that wants to do its own thing."

Marion had taken the controls and was moving the troller in a wide sweep that would put them back on the northbound drag. "Don't imagine you've had too much to put up with in the looks department," she commented, sarcasm thinly veiled.

Surprised and insulted, Colleen opened her mouth to retort, closed it. Had Marion noticed her interest in

Cedar? Was she jealous? Thinking of Mike? Realizing that Marion had built a wall of mystery around her and that she had better see what was on the other side before she tangled with her skipper, Colleen took a quieting sip of coffee. She strove to bury her anger and self-pity before saying to Marion's profile, "My looks were nice sometimes, you know, Marion. But the way I look has cost me, too. Cut me off from things—chances. People look at you in a certain way, imagine things for you. They never bother to ask if you have what you want."

"Sometimes there aren't any choices."

"You mean for you? Cedar mentioned you raised your brothers and sisters—"

"Hell, those kids deserved a meal or two and some clean clothes." Marion waved with her mug. "I didn't mind that. What did they have to say about being dumped into this fog bank some people call a life?"

"'Dumped'? You were abandoned?"

"That's one way to look at it. The folks took the bunch of us out on the boat most of the time. All five kids, even Alexandria, who was born in that forward bunk below decks."

"Alec...." The similarity in names brought a scenario to mind for Colleen, the image of a wild jungle and a sandy-haired man shuffling through it, set on teaching children to read. But Marion was still talking, a rare occurrence, and Colleen set aside that worn mental picture of Alec.

"Bright baby girl, Alexie," Marion sighed. "The only one of us who showed that Swede blood of my dad's. Cute as the dickens, too." She chuckled affectionately. "I had big plans for that little Einstein."

Marion turned her head seaward, sweeping her gaze

over the shivering lace on the water in her habitually watchful way. Colleen could feel the wall between them, crumbling a bit at the top but still impossible to scale. Should she probe into the hurt she sensed beneath Marion's gruffness? The skipper had lost Alexandria, her parents, her son Mike, at least temporarily, and a husband nobody had mentioned. And her back was still straight as a spruce. How much pain could one person stand in a lifetime? Her respect for the skipper jumped a notch. But questions. As much as she wanted to see the wall between them crash down, questions could make things worse. Unbearable.

"This guy we knew took the folks and Alexandria to Juneau one day, in his boat," Marion said in a dry crisp tone. "Bad weather hit. Took that baby right down into the emerald sea and never brought her back to me. The three of them—four of them. All lost. It just happens, that's all. No choices."

"We've got to make our choices, Marion. I hate the feeling of no control, and I've learned that if I want to be in charge of my life, *I* have to make the choices."

Marion gave her a surprised look. "Well, go on, Conaughy. Don't stop there. What kind of choices have you had to make in your short life?"

"Well. . .take this fishing season, for example."

"I hate to say it, but if you hadn't decided to answer my ad, maybe someone a little more right for the job would have."

Colleen squared her shoulders and met Marion's gaze head-on. "And maybe no one would have, Marion. Maybe you'd be out here trying to watch for patches of feed, driftwood or whales in front of the prow and schools of herring splashing up the surface—and baiting hooks and putting out gear and making the coffee. Then what would you do when you found the fish?''

For a long moment Marion stared silently at her. Then she nodded and took the wheel in a busy-looking grip, her face averted.

The bell on the port pole tinkled.

Marion twisted so fast in her chair, Colleen jumped. The woman's brown eyes blinked excitedly at her mate, as if she couldn't quite believe the bell for round one had just struck. "It could be a halibut," she said, half to herself. "We could bring up all that gear, take in both lines, and it could be a halibut on the very last spread.''

"Wonderful," Colleen breathed.

"Not wonderful. We'd throw it back."

"But why?"

"Out of season."

"You mean nobody would buy it? A perfectly good restaurant fish?''

Another bell tinkled, and the pole rattled.

"Well—'' Marion hesitated "—we'd keep the first one. Haven't had me a good halibut steak since last. . . .''

This time the pause was emotion charged. *Since Mike's accident,* Colleen finished for her. A hard look closed off the excited flicker in the brown eyes, and Marion began clipping out orders. "We'll wait. See if there are more strikes. Go below to the drawer on the left of the oven and bring up the gutting knives, the whetstone. And rinse out the coffeepot. We won't be needing it for a while.''

Colleen slid down the steps just as the radio barked, "Marion?'' Static. "Come in, *Blue Sparrow*. You ought to head on down this way, take a look at the royalty. Or are you already holding court?''

''A couple jesters is all that showed up, but I'm still waiting on the prince,'' Marion said in code as Colleen stopped in the dark galley, her hand poised over the light switch.

She had no clear explanation for the erratic pounding in her chest—except, of course, that after this long tiring day with its frustrating failures the tinkling bell was like a small wavering light to a skipper of a skiff lost at sea. It wasn't possible to feel so happy, Colleen told herself, simply because she heard Cedar's voice on the radio.

''Don't suppose that redheaded puller of yours has a sec to grab the mike?'' Cedar asked in a casual tone.

''Sorry, Ced. Work to be done.''

''Okay, right. Glad to hear you're keeping her busy. Best way to get the bills paid.''

Marion hesitated, then Colleen heard her say, ''Tell that no-good Finn skipper 'a yours the salmon aren't impressed by a pretty hull. Only thing they get excited about is something flashing by that looks like a meal—over.''

As Cedar depressed the button, Colleen could hear Ernie grumbling in the background. But Cedar said calmly, ''I'll tell him. Say, Marion....''

''Yeah, Ced.''

''Once the weather clears up we're all heading out to White Sulphur Springs—kind of get the kinks out of our legs. After fishing hours, I mean. You want to go along?''

''Depends.''

''On what?''

"On everything. I don't know. We'll see."

"Okay, then. Tell your puller to keep her gloves on. I'll check you later. That's an over, Marion."

Marion clicked off the mike, and Colleen flipped on the light switch, certain at any moment that Marion would yell down at her to hurry with the gear. But with one hand full of gutting knives and the other reaching for the whetstone, Colleen paused, a big smile on her face. *Keep my gloves on? Nighttime picnic at White Sulphur Springs?* She was absolutely crazy to be so happy about such inconsequential things!

CHAPTER FIVE

THEY WERE LATE getting to shore. Colleen glanced over her shoulder as she pulled on the oars, guiding the skiff through the swells. Fishermen moved against the orange glow of a campfire. Cedar.... Somewhere on that dark beach, Cedar waited for her to arrive. She knew it.

Excitement at the prospect of seeing him made her careless and the oar slipped out of its lock. The molded plastic dory swung sideways into the current, rocking crazily.

"Watch it, Conaughy!" Marion leaned over, set the oar in place.

Ten days, Colleen counted. Ten days since she'd seen those lively dark eyes and that tumble of hair over his right temple. Cedar's face and lean frame were etched in her mind like engraving on a silver coin.

"Even her up, or we'll be broadside in nothing flat," Marion demanded irritably, even as Colleen adjusted the bow toward the rocky, spruce-lined shore.

"Got it, skipper. Glad...the wind died down," Colleen said pleasantly between deep breaths. She leaned forward, dragged the oars through the shiny water. "Nice night for a picnic."

Marion peered at her through the moonlight. "You winded?"

Colleen shook her head, saving her breath for the chore at hand.

"Yeah, well." Marion settled against a red blanket in the stern. Dispiritedly she nudged a box of groceries with her boot. "Good night for trolling, too. If I thought there were any fish out there."

"I thought sure. . . you were going to keep trying."

"Your heart wasn't in it. Not that I blame you."

"What do you mean?"

"Wore out."

"I am not, Marion. Who's pulling these oars?"

"Come on, Conaughy. You're near stir crazy."

"You'd be a little antsy, too, if—" she gulped air "— if you'd gone from a full-time landlubber to a permanent barnacle on the hull of your fair ship. Fishing's like breathing to you."

"You've grown a few scales yourself, girl. Don't tell me you weren't enjoying that run of kings we had yesterday forenoon. Pitiful small they were, though. Watch that shoal to your left, now."

Colleen let the orange skiff drift down a rush of foam as a small breaker came in, tamed by a reef at the entrance to the bay. Lugging hard on the left oar, she skirted a black mass that gleamed with tendrils of seaweed. The night was calm, the seas gentle. From behind her, the moon shot crescents of silver across the water to the west, where the boats rocked at anchor, port lights glowing red against a navy-blue sky.

Four hours earlier Cedar's deep voice had said over the radio, "Hey, *Sparrow*, time to party! Let's hit the beach!" But Marion wouldn't waste the light, not while a breath of a chance existed to fill her hold. So the others had begun the party. Her stomach jittery with anticipation, her eyes skimming the sky as the blue deepened, striated with magenta, Colleen had set out new gear on the starboard pole. At first she'd been loyal to Marion's cause, glad to clean fish for Mike.... Yet as twilight descended on this almost summery evening, without a hint of a strike on the poles, she had grown restless. Sure, she was here to work, but she had spent too many years enjoying the good life to erase it from her nature. When it was time to party, she was ready and able. And so, evidently, was Cedar.

"Aw, hell, pull it all in," Marion ordered at last, pacing the deck, her face pinched with disappointment. At dusk they had set out on the run to the hot springs, Colleen hiding a tired grin.

As they neared the beach, she caught the fresh-scrubbed scent of pine, the nutty smell of charcoal-grilled hamburgers and the breathless languor of the tide. Waves whispered. The moon's silver lamé trailed away from the dory as they bumped and grated to a stop.

A shadowy figure came down the beach to catch the bow line Marion tossed out of the skiff. Panting, Colleen stowed the oars, then slipped over the side and sloshed through ten inches of water. Turning, she steadied the skiff while Marion clambered out, carrying the blankets and food.

"Give her a hand with this washtub, will you?" the skipper directed the tall man behind Colleen. "Stow it good in those rocks yonder. Contrary to what that Finn has to say, nobody I know walks on water, and it's a damn long swim to the *Sparrow*." Marion crunched away toward the fire.

"Welcome ashore, Sprite," said a laughing resonant voice that made Colleen's insides lurch. "Looks like your skipper needs this party more than the rest of us."

"Cedar." Colleen smiled, tugging the boat with his help, her head bowed to the task. Satisfied that the skiff was safely wedged among the rocks, she stood still, hoping the world would stop tilting, wondering if her sea legs were permanent, or if his closeness had caused the riot in her legs. "I'm still aboard the *Sparrow*, it seems," she said, taking a tentative step, stumbling slightly. "It's funny—"

His hands came out of the darkness in a blur. She felt him grasp her elbows, pull her upright, steady her against his chest. Her breathing quickened. She put both hands to the rough fabric of his bulky white sweater, pushed slightly. Nothing happened. And so she brought her gaze up past the crew neck of the sweater, over the pointed collar of a plaid shirt, beyond the shadowed cleft in that jutting chin. Here she stopped, maddeningly shy.

"Hey...."

Finally she looked at him.

The lightning was still between them. Much worse. Better. The current arced directly from him to her, and down with muscle-weakening speed to her lower body.

A smile of welcome curved her lips. The smile moved across that sizzling thread between them and found its way to his mouth, his eyes. Each feature was lit by lantern and fire and moonlight.

Voices, laughter drifted to her, but somehow she couldn't focus on the sounds. The current intensified between her and Cedar, and she was only just thinking it had been illusion, the invisible line joining them in that moment, when his shadow fell across her face. He leaned close, said against her lips, "I missed you," and kissed her, gently, with a restraint that made her heart turn over.

Her lips were soft in response, but wonder, surprise, kept her from melting on the spot or returning the caress.

"I missed you, Red," he whispered again, and kissed her with a feather-light seduction that sent awareness spiraling through her.

He was rushing things, even if everything he'd done in the past few seconds felt completely right and natural. And she had so much to tell him. "You really have no need to seduce me with those velvet kisses, Cedar," she chided softly, chuckling. "You don't have to con me into staying in Alaska. You couldn't *drive* me back to Seattle."

"What's this? A convert in less than two weeks?"

"I would never have run out on Marion, anyway, but now I've breathed this white air up here, I think it's become a part of my blood." She laughed. "I swear, there's more oxygen in the air here! Oh, Cedar, I wish you'd told me how wonderful it would be out on the water. How...alive you feel in this country. Deer bounding along the beaches of the islands—thousands of islands! No bear yet, but I saw seals. I saw a whale, Cedar. A blackbird dive-bombing an eagle that had flown into its territory...."

His chest rumbled beneath her fingers, and at last the laughter broke from him and floated up the beach to mingle with the voices at the campfire.

"Hey," she said with mock reproach. "It's true. I saw so much I could write for *National Geographic*.

And worked. Sweet Mary, how I worked. Look at these hands." She held them up to his face, noticing that she'd lost the leverage between their bodies; he'd tightened his arms around her back.

But he was peering at her palms and at the cut, brown in the dim light, that angled down her little finger.

"Hurt?" he asked.

"Not much."

"Battle scar."

"Yes, isn't it great?" She put her hands firmly against his chest and broke the embrace.

Draping his arm around her shoulders, he urged her toward the shadows flickering behind a break of alder. "Who would have believed you'd be won over so soon," he mused. "Careful. Watch that log, there."

"Why are you so amazed?"

"This turn of events is more puzzling than ever."

" 'Turn of events'?"

"That cut. Surely Marion told you the salt and fish slime keep cuts infected all summer sometimes. You've seen Marion's hands."

"Oh, yes! They're beautiful. Full of character."

"Full of—they're a mess," he said with a hiss of disgust. "What are you going to do with hands like that, back where you're from? Wear gloves twenty-four hours a day?"

"Of course not, Cedar. Don't be a frump! I'm going to work. At whatever I choose. No more prissy this and prissy that—" She rubbed her palms together, her brows knitting as she felt the calluses and small nicks in her flesh. "Oh, well, *hands*, Cedar. They don't make the woman, do they? Any more than clothes make the man."

"Still, Red. You ought to take a few precautions."

"Stop calling me 'Red,' will you? It makes me feel like a moll in some old Sinatra movie."

"Sprite, then."

"Colleen," she insisted.

"Hey, Cedar!" someone yelled in a slurred voice as they rounded the rustling saplings. "You gonna let us pay our respects to the new girl? How come it took you twenty minutes to show her how to put the skiff in dry dock!"

As they came into the firelight, Colleen, blinking in the bright glow, felt Cedar remove his arm from her shoulders and walk across the camp. She had only a moment to miss the warmth, and then a hulking fellow of about twenty-two shouldered his way past his companions around the fire.

"My name's—" The blond man stumbled over the flap of a carton of beer. "Ugh!" Righting himself, he scowled at his laughing companions, then lurched toward her, and she wished Cedar's arm was around her again.

"Name's Josh." He was nothing less than fullback material for the Jets—his shoulders layered in muscle, his neck like the trunk of a spruce. Oblivious to the crisp night, he'd torn the sleeves out of his gray sweatshirt, bearing bunching biceps to the crisp night.

She'd forgotten to hold out her hand in greeting. Josh righted the matter by grasping hers and pumping vigorously. She tried not to wince as he pinched her sore finger. "Colleen," she managed as lightly as she could.

"Don't I know it," he said. "Have a beer."

"Not just yet. Think I'll say hello first—"

"Ernie's the only teetote'ler allowed in camp." Josh

winked, still gripping her hand. "Geez, girl, you're really tiny. Bird wings for wrists. No wonder Marion don't let you pull fish. McClintock gets all the luck, don't he, Doc?" Josh glanced over her shoulder. Through her flaring anger Colleen glimpsed a middle-aged man with dull gray eyes and a putty face. The man grunted a reply and drank deeply from a mug.

Did Josh's opinion stand for the whole group? Did they all know she was still gutting fish while Marion pulled them aboard? She could feel skepticism emanating from the men at the campfire, and she realized their respect was something she wanted. She'd chosen their country for her proving ground. Their rules were centuries old, rules for surviving in a brutal land. Shoring up her courage, she told herself she would be as tough as they required her to be.

Josh's fingers still clung like octopus tentacles to her wrist, but she cooled her resentment, looking for a graceful way to end the interview.

"Should'a beat Ced down to the beach, that's what I should'a done." Josh chuckled. "Doc had this story goin', though, see. 'Bout talked my ear off while you and Cedar were stowin' that skiff."

Doc didn't look to be the talkative type, but Colleen said nothing to Josh as her gaze quickly swept the other shadowed faces. Firelight wavered over weathered skin, rough coats; work-curled hands clenched bottles of beer and cups of coffee, and most gazes slid away. The dark forest enfolded them like a cape. A cave scene. Early *Genesis*. Apprehension shook her, and Colleen tried to gently extricate her hand, without luck. Josh laughed and pulled her toward the fire. It was a joke, a silly drunken joke, but too much of Josh's behavior rang a bell, too much of it reminded her of her father stumbling in from his favorite tavern, blind drunk and groping for his brandy bottle.

Josh studied her face, her green coat, her rubber boots and jeans. As his blond hair and deep-set eyes filled her vision, at least his leering scrutiny reminded her he was not her father.

"Wine, then?" he asked, the beer on his breath wafting to her nose. He swayed. "What'll it be, beautiful lady? You name it, I'm yours."

She smiled and finally pulled free. "I'd heard you Alaskans were friendly, Josh. Now I'm certain. Where's the coffee?"

Still he stood over her, his bare arm snaking around her waist as he turned to the group. "This is my kinda lady, y'know? Prettier'n a sunset and quick as phosphorus on a black wave." He grinned down at Colleen. "C'mon over and meet the guys." Again he dragged her bodily forward, around the fire, beyond which she glimpsed Cedar, Marion and the blur of strangers.

Josh said names like Blue Harry—she recognized him from her first day in Pelican—Al, Jim, but the faces faded into a confused image of toughness. Colleen felt a moment of anger that Cedar didn't come to her aid. But she'd seen him glance worriedly toward Marion, and she suspected there was a protocol here she didn't understand.

"Really, Josh—" she protested.

"This here's Doc, my skipper," he said, leaning heavily on Colleen's shoulder. She staggered. Josh lurched after her, caught her around the waist again.

"Doc." She nodded toward the dull-eyed man slumped against a log.

"And J.T. He runs the *Dolphin II*."

With what seemed like disgust, J.T. ran a hand over his high forehead. "He's harmless," J.T. said to Colleen, reaching out his thin hand to shake hers. "Just been partying awhile longer than the rest of us. Josh likes to party."

Gratefully she moved away from Josh, shook hands, began to turn toward Cedar and Marion.

"Hey!" Josh swung to her, grabbed her arm. "Have a sit-down with us. Make room, Doc! The lady wants a seat!"

"Give her a break," J.T. said placatingly.

"You trying to tell me my manners?" Josh's voice was suddenly low. Likely without meaning to, while he stared at J.T. he increased his grip on Colleen's arm. She flinched. "What about it, J.T.? What the hell's your problem if I want to make this gal comfortable? Huh? Ain't every day we get a looker like her in the fleet."

"Colleen."

Cedar had spoken from across the small camp, only her name, but with a command buried in the quiet word. All of them turned to him. He stood by the fire, shadows dancing across his tight features, and he held out a steaming mug. A small pale man stood like an apparition at his side.

Josh's fingers loosened slightly.

With a nod of thanks to J.T., Colleen slipped from Josh's grasp and came across the clearing to Cedar. Their eyes met. Surely she wasn't seeing reproach in his glittering gaze. Taking the hot cup of coffee, smiling questioningly, she said, "Thanks."

His glance went back to Josh, remaining there a telling moment. "No problem. Come and meet Ernie."

The white-haired apparition stepped forward, touched Colleen on the arm and grinned. Ernie was small-boned like Colleen and at least an inch shorter than Marion. His hair bristled with a life of its own, giving his lined face more youth than it deserved.

"Bible-totin' Finn and proud of it," he announced in a booming voice. His fine features were alight with the first warmth she'd seen from anyone here.

Colleen smiled. "I feel I already know you."

"By reputation or ESP?"

"Your radio calls. The way you and Marion nip at each other, I pictured someone. . . well, more like—"

"More like Satan himself," Marion called smugly from her perch on a stone.

Ernie spun toward Marion, his aquiline nose and carved cheekbones stark in the changing light. "You've been at it all night, woman. Give it a rest!"

"Like I said," came the smooth reply. "Satan."

"You're just asking him here, you know. Just asking him right into camp!"

"Aw, g'wan, Ernie. Don't seem like I'd be conjurin' up anything that ain't already here, if you think about it." She eyed Josh and his companions ten feet away, engrossed in a discussion of beer labels. She said to Colleen, "Ex-preacher."

"Who?" asked Colleen.

"He is." Marion pointed to Ernie. "Don't like to be reminded, though."

Colleen glanced at Ernie, who had gone stiff as a front door. She looked at Cedar. He shrugged as if he'd been dealing with this cat fight for centuries and had learned to keep out of it.

"We all carry crosses, Marion," Ernie said stiffly.

"Don't know what you mean, Finn."

"No, it doesn't suit you at the moment, that's why. But I know you...." Ernie coughed delicately. His face ruddy, he scrubbed his head, then whirled to Colleen and Cedar, his hands beseeching. "She does it on purpose! Courts my temper, just courts it! The woman is mad!" Laughing, Colleen and Cedar led a sputtering Ernie to the rocks near Marion, and by the light of a lantern they began unpacking containers of food.

Through the next hour everyone toasted hot dogs, gaining a measure of comradery in preparing and eating the food, tossing out gibes about their neighbors' fishing ability. Josh had settled against the log between J.T. and Doc. Colleen caught the hulk's gaze, and through the screen of campfire smoke, smiled at him, letting him know she wanted peace. He tilted his beer at her, grinned, drank.

Colleen began to enjoy the jokes and challenges tossed around the camp. She enjoyed the way Ernie went out of his way to win Marion's favor, although the skipper of the *Blue Sparrow* was caustic in return. But Marion was caustic with everyone except Cedar. Like the other fishermen, she held him in some kind of special regard, her demands tempered by chuckles or a brief smile.

She issued commands to all of them. Once she was so engrossed in a fish story with Ernie that when J.T. bent over the fire to pour himself some coffee, Marion simply held out her cup for a refill. J.T. complied, bowed with mock humility, swept his domed forehead with a palm and crossed the camp to hunker with Doc, Josh and the others. It amazed Colleen, when she wasn't sidetracked by Cedar's long silent gazes, that these

rough men would give a woman any other kind of recognition than the sexual attention she had just received
from Josh.

Occasionally one of the men, lantern swinging from
his hand, wandered up a path to the woods. Then the
low campfire conversations would be shattered by
splashing and loud whoops as he sank into the cleansing
hot springs.

Two men had returned so far, hair slicked back and
faces shining, and now J.T. wove toward the baths, his
light wobbling along the trail. Colleen envied him. The
grime of physical labor that clung to her skin began to
magnify in her mind until she felt unfit for company.

A blue towel hung over the edge of the carton Marion
had hauled ashore; wedged between the half-empty bags
of bread rolls and potato chips was Colleen's plastic bag
full of clean clothing. She eyed the box longingly, eyed
it again and again until she could no longer even focus
on Cedar's friendly comments as he sat on a rock next
to her.

Never in memory had she gone so many days without
immersion in a bath or shower. Sure, she'd washed her
hair and as much of the rest of her as she could manage
in the galley sink, and the cool sea air had kept perspira-
tion to a minimum, yet she felt nearly inhuman. She
tried to urge Marion to the springs as companion and
guard, but Marion retorted that she wasn't interested in
catching pneumonia in the prime of her life. Laughing
with chiding approval, the men called her an old salt.
Worried about a scene between herself and one of the
men, a situation that would be all but impossible to control in the woods away from camp, Colleen sighed in
frustration.

Cedar propped his elbows on his knees and glanced at her. "Tired?"

"Dying for a bath," she whispered, desperate enough to be honest.

He nodded. "I was waiting until the rest had finished."

She glanced suspiciously at him. His comment spurred the memory of his threats to keep tabs on her, that first afternoon on the docks, but she gave him the benefit of the doubt. He, at least, had more polish than liquor-soaked Josh, and she *was* desperate. "It's getting to you, too?"

"What?"

"The grime. Being out on the boat so long."

He laughed quietly. "It's not quite so bad for me. The *Dart* has a few more modern conveniences."

"Well, in my cheerleader speech back there on the beach, I forgot to mention how I feel about the restroom facilities. Prehistoric isn't my style."

"What, the bucket-behind-the-curtain routine getting to you?"

She fought the urge to blush. "Please. I don't need to be reminded of the gruesome details. I live there, remember?"

"So did I."

"Touché."

"Wait a sec. Let me just tell the boss lady what we're up to." He leaned over Marion's shoulder and spoke softly.

Up to? Colleen felt her pulse jingle. He made it sound secretive and lascivious. But if she wanted the bath, she would *get* the bath. And no more.

She heard Marion's snort of derision. "Better make it

quick, McClintock," she said. "I'm about ready to call it a night."

Cedar's answer was too low to hear. Grabbing a small canvas duffle bag and a lantern, he turned to gently grip Colleen's elbow, pulling her to her feet. She picked up her own plastic bag. In minutes they were making their way over tree roots and stones, ducking through branches that felt like wire brushes. Colleen heard Josh make a loud comment about Cedar's luck with the women, and then from ahead came a crunching sound. J.T.'s thin face appeared, lit grotesquely by his flashlight. He stepped aside to let them pass, massaging what little hair he had with a yellow towel.

"New man." He grinned. "Feel like a new man. Rebuilds tired blood, this place does."

"In that case," Cedar said pleasantly, "try to keep Josh nursing a beer in camp."

"I see what you mean." J.T.'s pale eyes flicked over Colleen. He saluted the two of them, made his way down the trail, his light bobbing until it disappeared.

In the moonlit clearing a few yards farther on, a dark wooden structure rose from the grass and bushes. Colleen was delighted. The springs were enclosed, and she could bathe in private. They stepped into a short hall sheltered by a roof and open to a small field, and in the light of the lantern, steam heavy with the odor of sulphur drifted in threads. Their boots hit the concrete floor with a glassy thud. The bench along the wall was convenient, she thought. Cedar could wait for her in some comfort.

"Just inside," he said in hushed tones, guiding her once again by the elbow. "The rocks are slick, so be careful."

They went through an opening in the wall. Flat rocks lined a pool encased in mist. She felt the heat and the dampness float against her face, clinging. As patches of steam drifted out through a windowlike opening in the seaward wall, she could see only blackness. Shiny black pool, dark slick rocks, the fetid smell of sulphur.

"I didn't realize...." she began, and faltered.

"Once you get used to it the smell doesn't bother you."

"No, I mean...it's so black. I can't see the bottom."

"In the far corner it's about six feet deep, a bit shallower on our side. We can kind of ease down and hold on until you get the feel of the wall. And relax. No wild creatures could survive the temperature."

"'We'?" She looked at him for the first time in a long while. The smoothly shaved face with that vulnerable cleft and the dark gleaming eyes froze before her vision. The electric current skimmed between them for an instant, and she drew in her breath. "'We,' Cedar?"

In a swift stroke he turned out the lantern. His chuckle echoed across a blackness more total than any Colleen could remember.

"Cedar."

"Marion's in a hurry, Sprite. And we both want a bath. Look ma, no hands. Okay?"

"You set me up!"

"Set you—come off it, Colleen. This is back country here. People share the resources without making paranoid innuendos. I'll give you an example. People in the small bush communities in interior Alaska build central bathing and laundry facilities, because piping water to individual homes is next to impossible. The subzero temperatures freeze the pipes, and there's just not much water in some areas, anyway. There are steam baths all over the state, too. It's a way of life here. Are you so damned modest that you can't enjoy the hot springs like the rest of us without making this into a tawdry incident?''

''That depends,'' she said in a low angry tone.

''On what?''

''On how much of my modesty you're willing to leave intact. I have no illusions about the difference in our strength. And you've got to admit, if you took advantage and I screamed, my chances of rescue from that crew down there aren't great. Those men aren't much more of a bargain.''

She felt him brush against her. His breath pulsed softly on her cheek. ''More a bargain than what? We haven't really struck one yet, have we?''

''McClintock—'' she stepped back ''—I'm getting conflicting vibes from you, so just let me get my bath, okay?''

''That's exactly why we're here.''

He moved away from her, and she felt a moment of panic. The control was nearly all his. He knew the pool, the path through the forest. He even knew where he'd set the lantern. Too much to fight, she thought, submerged in the claustrophobia she had felt at home. The odds were too great.

''Damn you, Cedar,'' she said softly.

And she began to remove her clothing.

CEDAR HEARD THE PURR of the zipper on her green coat, and the tenseness went out of his shoulders. He'd managed to get her through most of the evening with those liberty-starved fishermen without any serious mishap.

And as long as Marion was swapping lies with Ernie and her cronies, he hadn't feared upsetting his former skipper; she wouldn't have seen the brooding looks he cast at Colleen. He wouldn't want Marion to worry about her fish puller's devotion to the job at hand, not with Mike lying in that hospital bed. Yet he'd had to choke back the rage when Josh practically dragged Colleen down with his sloppy-drunk bulk. And the rage had nothing to do with Marion. No, he had to admit, his feelings were entirely selfish on that score.

He shrugged out of his sweater and shirt, kicked off his boots, slid out of his jeans and heavy socks. His mind registered the sounds of Colleen undressing, and his body reacted in a way that would have infuriated her if she'd known. Perhaps his response might even have embarrassed her. Who knew, with a riches-to-rags princess like her?

The thought cooled his senses. His speeding mind conjured up Alicia, her furs and ringed hands, her imperious voice as she announced his father's death. "Oh, him, Cedar. I heard your father finally fell from one of those buildings he was so fond of. Loved walking the girders, got high walking the steel—as if he was proud of the construction business! I do hope you don't end up like him, Cedar, a handsome boy like you."

The shrill quality of his aunt's voice grated on his memory, knotted his guts as it always did, and his fists curled.

"Cedar?"

This voice was melodic. Angelic. He almost laughed at the contrast between Alicia and Colleen Conaughy, next to him in this dark cave. How could he ever have imagined Colleen was like his grasping dark-hearted aunt? There was a world—and several decades—of difference between the two women.

"Cedar, are you there?"

More insistence this time. That slight edge of imperiousness that did remind him of Alicia. "Yes," he said more shortly than he'd intended. "Yes, ready. You?"

"I—I have to admit, it's a little scary in here. I think I'm suffocating."

More of an edge to her voice this time, but it wasn't domination; it was the beginnings of hysteria. How had he read her tone otherwise? He must be edgy. "Here, Colleen," he said with gentle firmness. "Stretch out your hand."

Her first touch was electric; sensation shot through him. He half shook his head, dismissing the sudden tightness in his chest, and clasped her cool hand. "I'm stepping down to the first level of rocks," he said, his voice raspy. "In a moment I'll guide you down."

"Is it very hot?"

"Mmm. Pure luxury. The Clift has nothing on this joint."

She laughed nervously. "The Clift Hotel in San Francisco?"

"Yes, a favorite spot when I'm in the city."

"It is lovely. All that wood in the dining room."

She gasped in surprise as she edged into the swirling water, and he felt the small exclamation dive into the pit of his stomach. He was losing his mind. Half of him had wanted to bring her here so the others wouldn't lay hands on her, cause problems that might upset Marion, so shaken up already over Mike. The other part of him wanted to know how available she really was. With some women protests didn't mean "No"; they meant "Try harder." For the first time he felt uncertain about this woman. But he definitely felt challenged.

"Oh...."

It was a purely feminine expression of contentment. Sensuous. Feline. His senses soared, and he knew if she touched him he would find her warm body, crush her against him, taste her fire. *Think of baseball,* he told himself as she splashed in the water to his left. He sank to his chest, feeling the sting of hot water, the bite of stone on his naked skin. His senses sharpened. Colleen was washing her hair. He heard the tap of a plastic bottle as she set it on the rocks. He imagined all that golden-red hair turning a deep rust in the water, the soap bubbles sliding down her shoulders. They must be lovely shoulders, he thought, feeling like a spring wound tight. Pale and sculpted. Dear God, he had to divert his mind.

A breath of sharp, salt-laced wind blew the mist away from the window, allowing him to study the bobbing lights of the trollers a quarter mile out on the water. He was reminded of the facets on that eight-carat brilliant he'd traded last winter in Morocco. He'd gotten an Australian blood ruby in trade, but even better...a tiny, perfectly faceted, oval-cut blue diamond, a rarity. He'd kept the blue for his collection, and now he transferred the image of that glittering gem to the blue of Colleen's eyes. He would never forget the force and sparkle of her anger when she'd said, "McClintock, you black Irish swain. I came here to be free, and I will be free!" Lord, this woman had fire. Sheer guts.

Imagine a tiny creature like Colleen, he mused—red hair and clear blue eyes and that slim rounded body a man could worship in the heat of passion—a woman like her working a fishing boat. A fight with her father, she'd told him. That was why she'd come here. There was more she hadn't explained. He wanted to know.

The moon brightened, and from the corner of his eye, with the mist cleared away and the moonlight pouring in, he saw the marble grace of Colleen's arms as she bent back to rinse her hair. He turned to her. Pale perfect breasts gleamed and shimmered on a delicately formed torso. Her neck rose gracefully to an angular, tilted-back chin. He sucked in his breath and turned away as she came up out of the water, the mist drifting across her like silver gauze. The pain he felt now, wanting her, wanting to consume her, ground into his loins.

In desperation he whispered, "Wrigley Stadium. Chicago...."

She murmured, splashing, oblivious to his desire.

"One time in Chicago—" His voice sounded hoarse. He cleared his throat and tried again. "I'll never forget that right fielder pulling in that long ball off the wall, then turning and throwing a perfect strike to home plate. Caught that guy coming down from third—hell of a throw!"

"You a baseball fan?"

"Just a remarkable throw!"

"Cedar...?"

"Actually," he muttered, "baseball's the furthest thing from my mind right now."

She laughed nervously.

"Keep your distance, little sprite...."

"There was a musical with words like that," she said softly.

"What?"

"You know, the musical about the wife of a South American president. Only she said it—" her voice drifted "—the other way around. Something about 'don't keep your distance'...."

The water sloshed as she continued her bath, and it was physical agony to know the water caressed that narrow waist and those white full breasts. His hands, his body ached to know her.

And then her thigh grazed him.

She cried out, the sound mingling with his low groan as he found her, slid his arms around her waist and cradled her against him. His heart pounded; Colleen trembled. His head bowed, and his lips found the sleek flesh curving from her shoulder to her throat.

"Cedar...Cedar," she breathed, and he moaned with the delight of hearing her own desire expressed against his ear. "Cedar, Sweet Mary, no...."

The sound penetrated his whirling brain. There was no anger or accusation in her tone, only pleading. For what? Somehow it was important to know what she wanted. Because he wanted her with him, completely, in this maelstrom of longing. He wasn't an animal who took a woman because he was too swept away to think of her needs. Shaken by his desire for her, he drew her tightly to him and murmured, "Tell me to let you go. Tell me plainly, because it's not what I want. How can a woman turn a man to such desire, such pain, in so short a time, Colleen?"

"I don't know."

She was letting him hold her, and he felt like yelling with happiness.

"Cedar? Cedar, we have to live in the same house. With Marion, remember? We can't hurt her."

"God, how I wish that weren't true."

"And—and, I don't want this."

"Don't want what?"

"Us. This. Cedar, I want to be free. I've waited so long to be on my own. You understand, part of the freedom thing is to be unattached. Completely free."

"Then you do admit to feeling this...this craziness between us."

"Yes, but—"

"You feel it, too," he insisted, his body tense with longing.

"Yes. From the first day. But, Cedar, it's not what I want."

Unable to refrain from touching her, he slid his palms, his fingertips, from her delicate shoulders down the hollow of her back to her buttocks. She shivered, floating against him in the swirling current. Thrilling to the scent of her shampoo, the glow of her slim wet arms, he pulled her firm body against him. "What do you want?" he whispered, kissing her on a soft earlobe and along her damp neck. Her head fell back, and he knew her eyes were closed. "What do you want, my Colleen," he said as he trailed his lips along her delightful throat to her chest.

Uttering a small cry, she slipped her arms around his neck and held him still, preventing further caresses. "I want *freedom*," she said, the usual melody of her voice choked with emotion. "Please, Cedar, don't you be against me, too. Be on my side. I need someone to care, for once, what *I* want."

Frustration rose to choke his own words. "I'm on your side. I want what you want. But I also have to deal with what I want."

"Please...."

"I don't know if I can promise you restraint." He hugged her close, pressing her wet cheek against his shoulder. Her rapid breath cooled his skin. "Not when I know you want this, too."

Her fingers tightened in his hair, sending a pulsing heat through his already taut thighs, and she firmly, gently pulled his head back until he knew she was staring hard at him. The moonlight caught a glimmer in her eyes, traced a pale cheekbone, her jaw, her shoulder. Their breaths drew tight in the same moment.

He strained to kiss her, but she held him back. "We don't even know each other. It's not right, Cedar—not for me. Yes, it would be good between us. Don't you think I know that?"

"Then...?"

"I've made mistakes. Lots of them. With you, I don't want another. You don't care about me as a person, what I want, what I'm trying to do. We feel this heat between us. Passion. Desire. It's beautiful, so very beautiful. It would never be enough. Not for me, Cedar. Never, with you."

Anger stirred in him. "You're being puritanical. What do you expect, a proposal just because we want to make love? Come on, Colleen. This is the 1980s, and we've both seen the world."

He was guessing at her sexual experience. She was alive with sensuality. Her body throbbed with it, like his. Her fingers tightened in his sleek hair, and he knew he'd struck a vulnerable chord in her. Well, what did she expect? To drag him to the altar first? His thoughts ran bitterly to Alicia... and the weak man who had been his father. Neither of them had cared about breaking up the family and destroying Cedar's mother.

Marriage. It was for weaklings who needed the public's blessing to do what was natural and right. Colleen was one of them, another like Alicia with her airs of wealth and propriety. Worse than Alicia, if he got down to facts. Alicia had married her first husband—and at least two others after his father—for money; Colleen had already tasted the pleasures of wealth. Did she think he didn't know her father was verging on financial ruin? All of Seattle knew. And now without a fortune to continue her easy life-style, she'd make deals first...hold out on providing the other pleasures. Well, he wasn't buying in to the proprieties. His lip curled at the distaste he felt, and he set Colleen away from him.

"Get dressed," he said as calmly as he could. "Marion will send someone for us if we don't get back to the fire."

"So you're refusing to be my friend, Cedar?"

He thought her voice sounded choked again. He could feel himself relenting, softening—how did she get to him so easily? "We'll table it," he said abruptly. "Where you're concerned, I'm not refusing anything, not after feeling the way your pretty little body fits mine."

"Is that all?"

"I'm not made of stone!" Frustrated, he groped, found her hand, rubbed it vigorously against his arm, his chest. She trembled even as his own body reacted. "Arm, chest, stomach. A man, Colleen. A man who wants you. I don't think I've ever wanted any woman more." He dropped her hand. "Don't ask me why, but I'm beginning to care about you already. You don't have to ask it of me. But I have all the instincts of a healthy man in his prime, so no promises, okay? This isn't going to be easy.''

''For either of us. Oh, Cedar, let's make it work!''

Her words probed that soft spot inside him, but he was wary. He said nothing.

''Let's get to know each other's traits and needs,'' she said eagerly. ''Put aside our desires for a while.''

''I *said* we'd table it, Colleen. Let's get moving, shall we?''

''All right.'' She climbed out of the water, groped through her things.

Her silence meant he'd hurt her, but his frustration warred with memories from years ago. He slipped his jeans over his wet body, perversely liking the cold discomfort, then searched the damp stone for his lamp.

CHAPTER SIX

"MIKE! MIKE, ON DECK! NOW!"

At the sound of Marion's shouts, Colleen froze, the skillet in her hand. She heard Marion slow the boat, dash outside toward the stern. The bells on both poles were tinkling in rapid succession—fish hitting the line, another and another—until the faint ringing was like sleigh bells on a long winter ride, merry and insistent.

Colleen had been worrying about Cedar, her reaction to him in that pool two nights earlier. Thinking back over that thrilling but unsettling incident, she'd decided she was wrong. He would be dangerous to her bid for freedom. She was a fool even to ask for his friendship. He was too predatory, too virile, and he reached too deeply into her own hidden sexual reservoir; she would have to put space between them. He would ruin her plans.

As she dropped the skillet into the dishpan and shrugged on her coat, she heard the winches already whining above the thrum of the engine. Clambering out of the fo'c'sle, passing the rows of spare lures in the wheelhouse, she tore out the door onto the windy deck. A banner of her hair fluttered across her face, and she hurriedly jammed on her knit cap and tucked in the streamers.

"Gutting knife better be sharp," said Marion,

laughter in her voice. One hand ran the gear while the other toted the gaff hook like a rifle. "My, oh, my, we're in for a run, aren't we, son? That old Finn was durned tootin' when he said there's fish on this drag, just waiting for us to—" And then she looked up with a stunned expression, her mouth slack, her body still. Distractedly she slipped the gurdie into neutral.

At the same instant, Colleen met Marion's look and stopped to stare. Mike? Marion had called her "Mike," and from the look on her face she was having a terrible time coming to grips with the fact that Colleen, not her son, stood on deck waiting for orders. Here was proof that Cedar was already jamming a wedge between her common sense and her duty; she had heard Marion call her Mike, but that hadn't even given her pause.

She looked sorrowfully at the skipper. She would have given anything, in that moment, to be Marion's son, healthy and ready for work. Mike's mother looked like she'd died standing right there in the trolling cockpit, her mouth twisted with grief.

"I—I honed the knife on the whetstone yesterday," Colleen stammered.

The brown eyes grew narrow, shuttering the pain. The square chin dropped an inch or so. "Okay," she murmured. Marion glanced at the lever that would run in one of the lines. "Fish on board in two minutes. Fill the washtub."

Marion jerked her hand forward, engaged the gurdie, and the line began to hum at full speed.

"Conaughy, what the hell are you standing there for?"

Colleen jumped, looked at the gray sky. "Sorry, skipper. Still asleep, I guess."

"Move! We gotta have this catch iced and back to the cold storage in Pelican by this afternoon."

Colleen's face lost color. Cedar. She would see him so soon again, without sufficient time to erect fortifications. Because now her emotions had declared war on her quest for freedom, and she was vulnerable.

"*Conaughy!* What's the matter with you?"

"What? Oh. Nothing, Marion, moving right away." Forcing herself to forget Cedar so her performance wouldn't suffer, she snugged the hose coupling to the galvanized oval tub used to wash slime from the fish. She jogged over to the through-hull fitting to open the valve. Seawater poured into the tub, gushing and splashing.

"Marion," Colleen asked. "Why the rush? Why do we have to sell the fish today?"

"We've been out the maximum—ten days—a fish can stay fresh in the hold. Starts to deteriorate after that."

No wonder Marion had been an ogre the past few days, Colleen mused. Only one side in the box-shaped hold was packed with ice and fish. Two other compartments were empty, the third packed solid with shaved ice. Marion was losing money, and she had to save the few fish they had. Colleen returned to wedge the tub along the narrow gangway beside the hold, close to the cleaning trough. She pulled on blue rubber gloves.

"Fish on!" cried Marion. In a smooth sweep she struck the first fish right between the eyes, hooked it under the gillplate and landed it in the holding box near Colleen's knees. With the point of the gaff, she clipped the hook and spoon from its dark mouth.

Marion had a way of dancing the fish aboard, Colleen noted in admiration. Every movement fluid. No awkward jerks or wasted time. Envying Marion's grace, wondering when she'd get a turn at the important work, she watched Marion drop the spread into a carton and spin to the rail, gauging the downed fish over her shoulder.

"Eighteen-pound king," Marion growled, unable to keep the satisfaction hidden. "Another one on. Get out the knife."

Colleen hauled the gaping king salmon out of the box. Nerves in the fish trembled for a moment, and then the black-spotted tail relaxed, draping over her forearm. She slid the king to the V-shaped wooden cleaning trough and began the messy process of gutting, saving the eggs of the females in a plastic bag, and slipping the catch into the wash bucket for desliming.

Last time she'd asked, she'd been told curtly that Marion would do the pulling until Colleen got the hang of cleaning. Less chance of waste that way, Marion had concluded. Well, Colleen consoled herself, it was all work. She had cleaned enough fish in her lifetime to be good at it, and her contribution to the trolling process still helped pay the bills.

In twenty minutes both holding boxes were full of shiny bluish fish with silver sides and bellies, and Colleen was hurrying to finish cleaning her sixth king. She felt a nudge of pride. She'd never dressed fish so fast in her life. Gray-and-white gulls screamed, dived, hovered around the stern. A brave fellow balanced on the rim of the entrails bucket, dipping his long beak for a morsel.

Colleen smiled at the bird. As she worked, she began to feel loose and easy of limb. She wouldn't likely see Cedar in town, anyway, she reasoned, slicing cleanly along the belly of a fish Marion called a "brown bom-

ber''—worth only two bits a pound, but still market-
able. The *Dart* probably sported a freezer aboard. That
gear Colleen had spotted through Ernie's wheelhouse
door looked fancy. Ernie and Cedar probably didn't
even have to ice their fish down or run to town to sell the
catch every ten days. They had been calling on the VHF
once or twice a day, but they hadn't mentioned going
into town.

"Holy dynamite!"

Colleen glanced up. Bent far over the starboard rail,
Marion struggled with a fish. Splashing mingled with
the diesel's chug. Colleen leaned over to look, and
gasped. The smug grin of a shark paralyzed her. Her
father had loved the power and grace of the scavengers.
Colleen had always hated them, feared them. They represented the kind of terror, dark terror, that sometimes
seized Colleen at night.

The shark was perhaps five feet long, crescent mouth
clamped over the spoon and the leader, which ran in a
straight line to Marion's jiggling fist as he flailed the
water. Marion tried to get the gaff close enough to his
mouth to break the tackle free.

"Dammit," Marion puffed, "he won't hold still!
Slow the boat down, and then go below and get the billy
club, Conaughy. See if we can stun him a little so I can
get the hook out."

"Why don't you just gaff him?"

"The club, Conaughy, the club! Don't want to cut
him! His own kind would tear him to pieces."

Mystified and a little ashamed that she'd been willing
to kill the shark just because she disliked them, Colleen
went below. When she returned, Marion told her to
reach over the side and tap him sharply above the nose.

Grasping the short billy club and leaning over, gritting her teeth against the fear of falling in, Colleen swung, missed, had to grab the rail to steady herself.

Marion took her arm, easing her farther over the side, where she swung with the motion of the boat, her club poised, the blood rushing to her face. The cold gaze of the shark, the jagged jaws, chilled her. The old darkness of fear hovered. She shoved it back and panted, "He's salable, isn't he? Why not sell him in Pelican?"

"Salable, yeah.... Wait, I'll drag him in a bit. Bad luck to kill a shark, though. My uncle's a member of the Shark clan south of here."

"'Shark clan'?" Colleen swung. The shark dived against the line, forefins and dorsal stiff, tail slashing. Colleen's hand shook.

"The Tlingits are comprised of the Raven and Eagle tribes, with subclans belonging to each. The Eagles are my people."

"That wooden mask in your living room. It's a Tlingit tribal mask, then?"

"Yeah. Hey, forget the club. Go down to the fo'c'sle and look in that forward locker under the bunk. I've got another gaff down there."

Marion pulled her back aboard. Colleen turned away to hide her fear. She had a feeling the word wasn't in Marion's vocabulary, and the skipper already doubted Colleen's worth on the boat. She didn't need proof she had a hothouse rose for a mate.

In minutes she had returned and handed Marion the second gaff hook, taking the line herself. She liked the distance better. The skipper managed to wedge the hook into the shark's mouth, and with the other she jimmied the spoon free. As the shark flipped its tail and dove deep into the sea, the spoon spun through the air, struck Colleen's cheek a stinging blow and clattered to the deck in a tangle of leader. Colleen rubbed her cheek.

"You okay, Conaughy?"

"Fine." Shoving her hand into her pocket, she bit down on the pain.

Marion reached for the tackle and turned it over in her hand. "By the looks of this spoon, that shark's still wearing the hook in his jaw."

"Maybe it'll keep him off our line next time."

"Doubt it. Sharks are instinctive creatures. When they're hungry, they eat. Let's get back to it. Time's a wasting."

The skipper of the *Sparrow* resumed shucking salmon off the hooks, resetting the lines, and running to the wheel periodically to set a new drag or in checking for patches of feed that showed up as dark clouds on the rolling paper of the recorder. Salmon filled the boxes, spilling onto the deck beneath Colleen's feet, until her boots and gloves were red with blood and her back and arms were aching from exhaustion. Hours later Marion cut off the engine, dropped anchor and joined her at the cleaning trough.

"I'll take over while you break loose some of that ice in the hold," she said, elbowing her way in front of Colleen and taking the bloody knife. "Rinse off those kings you had to take out of the tub, will you? Ice 'em down clean."

" 'Clean'?"

"Clean fish looks better, sells better at market. People don't take my fish and cut 'em up and freeze 'em and ship 'em to Arizona, where nobody knows the difference."

Colleen nodded. Wearily she trudged to the tub, unhooked the hose and sprayed the kings covering the deck. She'd never seen so many fish. Forty, maybe fifty of them, speckled bluish-gray and silver, a gleaming carpet of king salmon. The few brown bombers and red snapper looked insignificant. "The first fifty kings are for Mike," she remembered Marion telling Ernie. So why wasn't the skipper smiling for a change?

Crawling down into the hold, Colleen chiseled and scraped at the ice with a rusty shovel until it was broken up enough to pack around and inside the bellies of the fish. Climbing topside, her hands numb beneath the blue gloves, she picked up the nearest king by its mouth and dropped it into the hold. She was reaching for another when she felt a grip on her arm.

Braids whipping, Marion swung her bodily until they faced each other. The brown eyes snapped with anger, and Colleen felt a rush of resentment. How dare the woman handle her this way? She attempted to free herself, but Marion hung on doggedly, her face butted up close enough for Colleen to see the leathery skin and dark pupils.

"Haven't you learned anything by watching me, Conaughy? What do you think those fish will be worth, handling them like that?"

Colleen sighed angrily. "Like what?"

"Like they were gunnysacksful of corn!"

"Marion, I don't know what you're talking about, but my back is bent, my hands are raw, and I don't see you have call to lay hands on me. Let go of my sleeve, please."

"You cost me one fish, Conaughy—just one—and I'll more than grab your sleeve."

"Get off my back, Marion!" She felt tears of frustration blur her vision, and hated her weakness. She yanked away. "Dammit, what's the matter with you?"

"That's it! You don't straighten out and straighten out quick, you're off the boat!"

"Don't be silly. You can't do this work alone. You know you can't."

"I might as well be solo, with you takin' three hours to do what should be done in twenty minutes."

"What do you want, miracles? I can hold my own. You'll see. I will!"

"Not soon enough to suit me!"

Rage and the fear of losing sight of her goal made the blood pound in Colleen's temples. "It's not me," she said hoarsely. "It's Mike. Isn't it?"

Marion's face whitened. "What the devil are you talking about?"

"You'd rather—" Colleen felt the first pangs of remorse, but she had tipped over the edge of common sense, was consumed by exhaustion and the hatred of trying to fill a role that wasn't her own. She waved and blustered, "You wish I was him!"

"That's insane!"

"No. No, Cedar told me. He said you'd hate me, that I'd remind you Mike's not here anymore. You—you're taking everything out on me. But I'm here, Marion, here to learn. *And I'm not him!*"

Her face contorted, Marion paced back, slipped, cursed as she grabbed the lip of the hold and slid down. She landed on her rump in the fish. Fuming, she tried to stand, and slipped again.

Her anger dwindling swiftly, Colleen looked out to sea, trying to stifle hysterical laughter. But it burst from her. She looked at Marion, blue gloves shoving salmon off her lap.

The woman glowered at her. And then she laughed. It was a cough, really, a few hiccups of mirth that sounded foreign from the harsh woman. She looked at a salmon lying half across her knee and sighed.

"You've gotta *ease* 'em down into the hold, girl." Marion caressed the salmon. "Landing them on their tail can bruise the meat. I like to sell clean fish."

Colleen, smothering her giggles, came to Marion and offered her a hand. Once she was standing, Marion bent and picked up a fish. "Look, you take the fish by the jaw or under the gills, the other hand kind of cradling the tail. See?"

Colleen nodded.

"And you lean over the hold, like so." The skipper bent into the cold opening, voice echoing. "Then you sort of get a rhythm—that rhythm I was talking about. Everything in this business has a kind of music to it. Row, row, row the boat. Know what I mean?" She gracefully slid the fish from her hands to the ice below. It landed with a slither. Straightening, she looked at Colleen. "Like body language. Rhythmic. Nice and easy."

"Got it, skipper. I think I can do that. Say, are you hungry yet? I could fix a quick peanut-butter-and-jelly sandwich."

"Not a chance. Latch on to one of those apples in that pocket in the hatch cover, and next time stick a wedge of cheese in your pocket. It'll tide you over when we're in the fish. C'mon, the sooner we get these fish in the hold, the sooner we can head for the cold storage."

Colleen felt tension rush through her. Her hands

curled into fists, and she turned away. There was only one way to know whether Cedar had already docked in Pelican.

"What's the problem, Conaughy? You look like you seen another shark."

"No, skipper, just a little bushed. Gotta get those fish sold while they're still worth something. Gotta...get back to town."

BY THE TIME she had soaped and hosed the decks, coiled the lines and locked up, it was dark. Rain misted onto Colleen's cold cheeks.

Marion had gone to pick up the mail and some groceries, leaving Colleen to walk the swaying floats of the Pelican boat harbor alone. They'd sold the fish. Colleen's cut of the catch made a paper pillow in the breast pocket of her wool shirt. She hadn't counted it yet. It was enough, and comforting at that, to know she'd earned the cash by forcing her muscles to go on and on with the painful task of lifting, bending, slashing. The fishing business. As she thudded along the dock in her knee-high rubber boots, too numb with cold and exhaustion to care whether she ran into Cedar, she adjusted the blanket-wrapped sack of laundry more comfortably on her shoulder, surveying the silhouettes of the boats as they rocked in the light wind. Stay wires and poles crosshatched in changing patterns against the dock lamps and the night sky.

A kitchen pot clattered; a hazy glow through steamy windows indicated some of the fleet lived where they worked. At least she was spared that monotony. Loving the sea life as she did, she was still enough of a Conaughy to feel closer to the land. She felt a stab of regret, thinking of her family. Family? Other than an aunt or two and a few cousins in England and Ireland, most of whom she couldn't remember, she had only her father now. And she no longer had even him. Her throat burned; she cleared it softly.

Ridiculous to wish Sean Conaughy could see her now, to wonder if he'd be proud of the twenty-dollar bills wadded in her shirt. He must have felt the same pride when he'd come to America and begun to build his empire. Her chin went up. He was too soaked in cognac to care. "Get ye to your man, daughter!" *Indeed, father. The very last thing I need is another keeper like you, or any keeper at all.* And yet in a part of her heart, she ached for her father's gentle hand on her red curls and that lilting Irish brogue saying gently, as in years gone by, "Lass, you're the spittin' image of your mother. Lovely like her and as feisty as me own sister when we'd be dumpin' th' sugar in her porridge!"

His stories. She missed his stories. She missed him. Seeing him in his jodhpurs and those slick black boots, "talkin' soft as roses" to a jittery mare or a leggy colt. Lord, she was maudlin. And Cedar yet to face, if he was in town.

She didn't see the *Dart* anywhere in the dock area. Relieved, she climbed the ramp to the boardwalk, her legs straining and sore, and headed past two quiet taverns, the tiny library and a clapboard building with a sign that read, Health Clinic. It was closed. The doors of the cottages along the boardwalk were closed, as well, some of the windows dark, others with the light projected through bright curtains, looking like stained glass. Finally she stumbled up the step to Marion's gray-and-red porch. Keeping the bundle of laundry balanced, she wiped the rain from her eyes, dug for a key.

The door burst open. "There you are! Where the devil have you been?"

Colleen jerked away in fright, before she realized it was Cedar who stood with the light pouring around him, his shoulders practically brushing the molding on either side of the door. She lost grip of the blanket. Laundry fluttered into the rainy night.

"Oh—darn it, Cedar!" She bent to collect the muddied clothing—befuddled, weary, half angry and refusing to admit her senses were out of control again. "You must have been the kid on the block who leaped out of the bushes at people on Hallowe'en."

"Sorry, Red. Here, let me give you a hand."

"I can *do* it. Really." She grabbed one of her bras from his fingertips. "Whipping the door open like that!"

"What took you so long, anyway? I expected you before noon."

"We were clear down to Khaz Peninsula, for crying out loud. The prince showed up along the way. We were in the fish—" She was snapping a towel out of his hand when his words finally registered. " '*Expected*' us?"

"Well. . . ." Cedar, cleanly shaved, his hair damp and his shoulders outlined by a red knit golf shirt, studied Colleen's eyes. He looked as if he wanted to ask if he could trust her with a secret, she thought, staring at him. Worry rippled his brow.

"Well, what?" she said softly. "How did you get here? The *Dart* wasn't tied up."

"Ernie's over getting fuel and supplies."

"How could you be expecting us, Cedar? I don't recall your reaching us by radiophone since yesterday afternoon, and you definitely didn't hear Marion say we were heading in. I didn't know it until she was pulling in the lines today."

"She still running the gear herself?"

This time Colleen hesitated. When *would* Marion trust her to pull fish, anyway? She wrapped up the last of the laundry, slung the weight over her shoulder and tried to stand up. Her legs were rubbery. They refused to respond.

"Yes, she's still running the gear. I'm cleaning the fish, and today I iced them for the first time. Here, take this blanket, will you? My sea legs are misbehaving again." She shoved the laundry into his arms and pulled herself up with the aid of the gray post near her elbow.

They stepped into a living room glowing with lamplight. Something wonderful was boiling loudly in the kitchen. Cedar's pipe tobacco scented the house with a manly woodsy smell that welcomed Colleen in a profound way. A quiet peace settled over her. Just tired, she averred, wanting to disown the notion that Cedar was terrific to come home to, wanting to collapse in sheer relief on that shabby brown couch. But she had to think of Marion. She'd worked all day, too, with only breakfast to keep her vital. She would want a meal and a clean kitchen afterward and probably the laundry washed, dried and folded.

"Be right back." Cedar headed for the back of the cottage where the washer and dryer were kept, the blanket bundle tucked under one arm. But he didn't return immediately. Colleen stood listening with detached wonder as the dials clicked and water rushed into the machine. The man was washing clothes. It seemed an incongruous and somehow touching act of consideration. Perhaps...it wouldn't be so terrible to care about him, just a little. From behind her own wall of reserve, that is, a wall best kept in place as long as Marion was out of the house. More distance seemed the essential thing at the moment. With the energy of sudden decision, she marched across the living room and up the narrow wooden stairs.

No shower for this weary body, Colleen told herself as she sank into the hot tub water. She soaked her sore hands for a while. Then, reaching languidly for a bar of fragrant soap she had brought with her from Seattle, she slid it over her skin, closed her eyes and sighed. Pure luxury. Her eyes opened wide. "Pure luxury," she murmured.

Suddenly she was back at the hot springs, feeling the swirling sulphur water wring the tiredness from her muscles until she was limp and tingling...and very aware of her male companion, in that dark, dark sanctuary....

"Cedar," she said softly, remembering the warm hungry hands and the timber of his voice, urgent and compelling against her flesh. Now. Now she would build the walls. Alec had taught her about walls, about distance, but he had taken the lesson too far, closing himself off from her completely. Whereas she would steel herself against her own physical desires. She must never again fall into that state where sexual gratification took presidence over the spiritual oneness she longed to share with a man. *This man,* a voice said within her. *This is the man, Cedar McClintock, with whom you want to share every trial and joy of your life.* But no. To end as Sean Conaughy had ended, sodden and empty, without the one he loved. No, it was too great a risk. Later in life, when she had traveled on her own, seen suffering and deprivation and perhaps experienced some of that herself, when she'd built a strong character within this shell she knew had been formed from idleness, then—a slim chance—she would be ready for marriage.

A steady stream of hot water poured into the yellowed porcelain tub. As she had done in the rocky hot springs, she tipped back and let the liquid reach to the roots of her hair. She lathered shampoo, scrubbed vigorously, then rose and closed the aqua shower curtain. She let the water cascade over her shiny skin until every trace of life aboard the *Blue Sparrow* had vanished down the drain. After tidying the tub, she wrapped herself in towels. Standing before the steamy mirror, which reflected back a hazy image she at last recognized as her own, she pulled a comb through her long dark red hair. With a portable dryer and her brush she tamed the curls into glossy red-gold flames around her face. *Cedar,* she thought in silent approval, *I am restored to my former power. Stand clear!*

He was at the stove when she came down, fully dressed. Stirring a meat-and-potatoes stew with one hand, he sprinkled in pepper with the other. He sniffed, evidently unaware of her presence a few feet behind him. "Better keep your distance," he said without looking around.

He was so smooth. "Why?" she laughed. "You working on a secret weapon to balance our arms deficit?"

"Nope."

She grinned. "Well. Why?"

"Because...." He dropped the spoon; the pepper bottle clattered to the top of the stove. He spun quickly. Cedar caught her around the waist, lifted her off the floor. "I warned you," he said, laughter in his eyes.

"I kept my distance," she reminded him, giggles threatening to burst through her words.

"It would have taken at least five hundred yards, maybe a mile, to save you from this." He kissed her, a smacking-loud kiss on the lips, and set her down.

She tried to pry herself from him. He held her for a moment longer. Bending close, he kissed her gently. Then he stood away.

"You taste good," he said. "Smell good. Look yummy in that green sweater and blue jeans, even if you do have a bruise on your cheek. Another war trophy?"

For reasons she refused to acknowledge, the incident with the shark receded to insignificance. She smiled.

"Well, most of all, you kiss like a goddess born to it."

"Poetic, you are, rogue. A thespian lurking in your background somewhere?"

His smile faded. He turned to stir the bubbling stew. "A food server, a bartender and a laundress. No thespian."

"Which was your mother and which your father?"

"They were all my mother."

He stirred the stew vigorously, his face averted. It seemed an evasive move, though she couldn't say why she knew that. Giving him a moment to settle down, she glanced around the old kitchen with its bright spots of tangerine. Three thick-stemmed glasses lined the counter near the stove. They were filled with a ruby wine. "What vintage?" She picked up a glass and sniffed. Not an expensive wine, but a hearty dry wine nonetheless.

"You're a sweet man for all your faults," she said, picking up the other glass. She held one out to him. "You think of nice things to make a hardworking girl feel—" She switched away from soft comments. "Well, here's to you, Cedar, for being a thoughtful roomy."

He took the glass, clinked with hers, drank. "You're welcome," he said, meeting her gaze, sparking a flash fire somewhere in the region of her thighs. She felt like honey clear through. To divert trouble, she took a deep swallow. The wine bit her tongue, but quickly mellowed and traced a warm path to her stomach. Alcoholic signals flared through her shoulders, arms, thighs, a caress as physical as Cedar's ebony gaze.

"So your mother did all three," she said, sipping again.

In answer, he tilted his glass at her.

"And. . . what about your father?"

He set his glass on the counter, took a stack of plates and bowls to the table, placed them around. Colleen pulled paper napkins from the cupboard and advanced around the table, too. He followed, silent, setting down silver. Spices, butter, oven-toasted rolls beneath a cloth with orange flowers followed, but still Cedar didn't answer.

"Right, Cedar, we'll drop that subject for now. Why did you expect us today? How did you know we'd be here for dinner?"

He leaned against the counter, watching her put glasses of water at each place, his gaze moody. "My mother raised me."

She glanced at him in surprise. He was certainly losing his mellow-roommate glow. His lips were set. He ran a rough hand through the waterfall of black hair over his right temple.

"I watched my mother—" again the distracted sweep at his brow "—watched her work herself to death for me."

"Cedar, no mother ever looks at it that way."

"*I* saw it that way. I watched her leave at five in the morning to run washers full of other people's clothes, then report for the noon shift at a greasy spoon down near Lake Michigan. That wasn't enough. Nights, she tended bar in one of the seediest taverns on the waterfront. Oh—" he waved with a kind of bitter lightness "—she had a pleasant view in the daytime: sailboats idling by, beautiful people lolling against the rail with a—" he lifted his glass "—in their hands. Laughing and joking and carrying on as if the whole world were their oyster!" He set his goblet down with a crack.

Colleen glanced uncertainly at his profile. "That's where you learned to sail, Cedar? On Lake Michigan?"

"Yes!" His violence startled her.

"Cedar, you don't have to tell me this. I—I'm sorry. If it's something painful—"

He laughed harshly, interrupting her, his shoulders hunched as he turned away to grip the counter. "Painful? I'll tell you pain. Pain is the life draining out of you while you still have a son to raise, while you still have a son to finish educating in a 'proper' Catholic university. It's dying while you still feel the urge to see to his every need, his ball games, his sailing classes, his every youthful whim. Oh, pain was lots of things in those days, Colleen. It was having her ignore every guilt-ridden denial I faced her with, telling her I didn't want all that." He stood up and turned around, and involuntarily she drew back from the blistering look he gave her. "What the hell would you know about pain? With your horsey set and your wealthy college studs!"

Her chin rose.

"There," he accused, his arm outstretched. "Look at you. Poor little rich girl got her nose out of joint. I can read you like a road map!"

"I'll warrant at this moment you'd fail miserably."

"Try me." He turned, picked up his glass, saluted her with it and drank.

"Against every instinct, Cedar, I think I will."

"All right. You're filled with revulsion at the seedy picture I've painted, my mother working her guts out for a son who believed her when she said the good life was his birthright."

"You're punishing yourself. 'Wallowing in self-pity,' I think is the phrase."

"Rubbish."

"Where was your father?"

The lines deepened around his mouth. "That subject is closed."

"Is it? Still blaming him for putting her through that hell? For not absolving you of your own guilt?"

"Leave it alone."

"Leave it alone? You were guessing about my feelings, weren't you?" She stepped forward into his shadow, sensing the danger but ignoring it. "What else do you suppose I was feeling, Cedar?"

Holding his glass in one hand, he reached around her waist and pulled her tightly to his chest. She drew a sharp breath and squirmed against him.

"What do you know about pain," he murmured bitterly as his mouth touched hers and pressed there, moving and rough.

She struggled, gained a matchbook of distance between their faces and whispered, "Cedar, you're wrong about me! Don't do this, please. Your pain is so great you could destroy others with it. Let it go, let it go.''

Briefly he closed his eyes. "You're right, of course. I—I don't know. It struck me, flew at me." He shook his head, loosened his grip on her waist. "It's never been. . . never gotten so out of control."

Slowly she brought a palm up to his face. A thrill went through her. She ran her fingertips gently along his cheek and jaw and teased, "If I didn't know better, I'd think you were scorning me for rejecting you at the hot springs."

"Perhaps I was."

"I don't think so."

"No?"

"No way, Cedar."

"Look, I'm sorry about my. . . ."

"Rude outburst."

He hugged her and set her away from him. "Yeah. Say, do you want a little more wine?"

She glanced at her glass and found her hand was trembling. Quickly she set the glass on the counter. "Great. And I'll have that explanation, too, if you don't mind."

He poured from the bottle of burgundy, handing her a full glass. "Hey, let's forget my rude outburst for now, okay?"

"No, I mean explain how you knew Marion and I would be here tonight. What gives?"

"Ernie and I just counted the days from her first catch. The reason we did that should be obvious. You wouldn't have to be a detective to figure it out."

"For the sake of argument, let's say I'm not following you yet. The trail's cold. Give me a clue."

He gave her a satirical smile. "Ernie and I are in cahoots."

"I know that, Cedar."

"More than mates, I mean. We're ghosting your ship, blue eyes. Keeping tabs."

"Cedar, no. We discussed that my first day on the docks. I won't stand for your harassing me, following me around, choking me with some kind of macho—"

"Whoa!" He held up his hand. "We're not ghosting you. It's Marion."

Her expression was doubtful.

"Haven't you noticed she's tense, constantly grouchy, given to strange moods?"

"Well, yes, but I figured that was her nature. Isn't it?"

He shook his head. "Not to this degree. We think she's tipped over."

"Over the edge, you mean?"

A footfall sounded outside, and Cedar lowered his voice. "She's fishing after sundown, racing in a crazy fashion from one drag to another, looking bruised under the eyes. She getting any sleep?"

"Neither of us are, and no proper meals, either. It's appalling."

"You see? And she refuses to joke around as she's always done. She was the life of the party for years."

The screen door squeaked. Marion bustled into the kitchen, and Colleen snapped her mouth closed. She had been about to tell Cedar about this morning, when Marion had called her "Mike." But Marion's arms were full of damp grocery bags, and Cedar went to help her, asking Colleen to serve the stew.

"Surprised to see you in town, Ced," Marion said,

shedding her wet red jacket and rinsing her hands under the tap. Hungrily watching Colleen fill the bowls with stew, she added, "Oh, by the way, Conaughy, be ready to pull out at eight in the morning. That ought to give you time to write a letter or do whatever."

Colleen restrained a groan. Nodding, she replaced the heavy pot on the stove. Cedar crossed the kitchen, brushing against Colleen's sleeve as he picked up Marion's goblet. The touch went through her. Glancing quickly at his face, she read in his expression a signal for silence.

"Hope Ernie's got that pump fixed," he said conversationally, handing Marion her wine.

She took a long swallow. "Bilge pump went out?"

"Mmm."

"Rotten luck."

"Really. It's much too early in the season to be hanging around the docks with time on our hands."

"Don't I know it," sighed Marion, scraping back her chair and collapsing heavily into it. "This first run barely paid expenses. I'll be damned if I'm going to settle for that." Her broad face set in lines of fatigue, the skipper picked up a soup spoon and began to shovel in the food.

Colleen and Cedar, still standing near the table, frowned at each other. Though Marion was rough and sometimes crude, not once in the days she'd spent with her had Colleen ever seen the skipper display such a complete lack of manners. Marion broke up a dinner roll, chewed off a mouthful and pushed it down with more steamy stew. Colleen observed her with concern.

"Dinner bell already rang, didn't it?" Marion asked, downing her wine.

As if to compensate for his old friend's behavior,

Cedar pulled out Colleen's chair and bowed briefly at her side. "Be seated, ma'am. Shall I pour the coffee, or would you like more wine?"

She gave him a quiet smile. "This terrific-smelling concoction of yours will do nicely, thanks." She eyed the skipper. "Marion will probably have another round of the grape, as well as the stew. In fact, I have a feeling we'd all better eat hearty while we have the chance."

"Now you're talking, girl," said Marion, handing her glass to Cedar. "This venison's gonna have to do you for a while. Running short of cash, so I had to cut back on supplies. Herring's up another three cents a pound. It'll be scrap fish or a sandwich from here on out. If there's time."

It was a moody supper, the food delicious but the family atmosphere strained. Afterward Marion sat watching television, the laundry stacked in neat folds around her chair. Ernie telephoned Cedar just as Colleen started up the stairs to write a letter to her father, and she heard Cedar say lightly, "So we're all set, then, Ernie? Pulling out at the usual time tomorrow morning? Great. I'll see you on deck."

He hung up the telephone and walked to the landing to stand gazing up at Colleen. In a voice Marion couldn't hear, he said, "Guess we'll see you out at the Fairweather Grounds tomorrow. I gave Ernie the word that's where you two are headed."

"What's it like out there?"

"It's open water opposite the most awe-inspiring mountain range you've ever seen, situated about forty miles off the northern leg of the Panhandle. The Fairweather Grounds is a good fishing spot, actually, right at the edge of the Continental Shelf, the last of the underwater mountains before the shelf drops thousands of fathoms to the ocean floor. Should be other boats around."

"I'm sure Marion won't do anything silly," she whispered. "We'll be fine."

"Except that Ernie says a southeasterly storm just hit the coast of Oregon. Maybe it'll die out as it comes up the Panhandle, maybe it won't. The weatherman predicts heavy seas at the very least."

"I see." The fear jerked inside her. "Where's the nearest sheltering cove?"

"That's just the trouble. You get caught out there in a southeasterly, then try to run for Lituya Bay or something, you're liable to end up at the North Pole. And Lituya has a dangerous sandbar, like a sword lancing out from the land. Tide's got to be flooding or you can't make it inside, even in calm weather."

"Hey!" Marion called from the living room. Her expression suspicious, she turned down the television and glanced over her shoulder. "You two were quiet as mice in a tomb at supper. What's all the confab about now?"

Cedar stepped back from the stairs. Feeling censored, Colleen, too, moved away.

"Discussing the weather, is all," Cedar said, running a hand through his hair. "Storm churning up the coast."

"Aw—" the woman waved "—Prince Rupert's about all the distance it'll come. Little rough water, no big deal. Besides, the *Sparrow*'s got plenty of beam."

"Won't hurt to allow yourself time to hole up somewhere, though. Maybe fish the Inside Passage, or something."

"Huh! Waste of good bait. If I thought the fish'd

done anything different than they have for the past five years, I'd fish the sound, now, wouldn't I? You won't see me in those waters, having to throw back ninety percent of my take. I got no stomach for catching shakers.''

" 'Shakers'?'' Colleen asked.

"Undersize salmon," Marion replied. "Those guys who stay in a school of shakers all day just to catch a few big ones—hell, ruins it for the whole fisheries business. Except for the inside drag around Yakobi, and maybe a dinky little spot here and there in the sound, it's fished out inside. Those salmon would be nothing but shakers. I got more pride.''

Cedar leaned against the stairwell, the lamplight gleaming in his black hair. "Fish can't bleed much," he explained to Colleen, talking with his hands. "They die easy. You lose a big percentage of them just shaking them off the line." When she nodded, he glanced at the woman reaching for the TV volume control. "Marion, those seas'll beat you something awful if you try to fish outside in the next few days.''

"You telling me where to fish, McClintock?''

"Nope. I can see you've got no more sense than Ernie. He's bound for the grounds, as well, and nothing I say will change his mind.''

"For once that preachy-mouthed Finn is showing his education." Marion turned up the sound and dropped back into her easy chair.

Cedar raised his hands in defeat. Colleen felt the moment was right for her exit. "Well, you two don't tell fish stories all night, or you'll never be awake in time to earn your living. Me, I'm going to write that letter and go to bed.''

"You do that, Red," Cedar said lightly. Then he put out a hand to stay her. He turned toward the easy chair. "Say, Marion, do you get the feeling we have a house mother in our midst? Since when did you and I need a keeper?"

"You, Ced," Marion remarked, scowling at him. "You better pay her some mind. You're the one needs all those zees. Me, I don't sleep all that much anymore."

Cedar's touch on her arm woke Colleen from her trance. She looked at him, down at his tanned fingers where they dented the soft green knit and sent spirals of warmth through her. The storm working its way up the coast and the storm brewing in her heart—she felt caught between forces that would crush the life from her.

"By the way...."

She met his shadowed gaze.

"Colleen, do you know how to work the radio on the boat?"

"Yes."

"Good. You know how to reach me, then, in case—"

"Yes," she whispered, cutting him off. "I know how to reach you."

He squeezed her arm. For an eerie moment Cedar looked at her as if she might disappear off the face of the earth, as if he were very worried about her.

"What is it?" she whispered.

For another space of time he looked as though he would lean close and kiss her, but with a distracted glance over his shoulder at Marion he said, "So sleep well, blue eyes. Ernie and I won't be far away."

Perplexed, she nodded and headed up the stairs, every nerve dancing because he'd held her.

CHAPTER SEVEN

THUNDER TORE at Colleen's fragile sleep. She woke with a nervous start. White light shimmered through the windowpane, blanching the narrow bed, the scarred six-drawer dresser, making her hands, clutching the soft cotton of the patchwork quilt, seem skeletal. When the lightning faded, she rubbed her eyes.

The melancholy she had felt while writing to her father had trailed into her sleep. It wouldn't do. After about forty tries, rest had finally lost out to worry. Now she listened to the rain drumming on the roof, hitting like scattered stones on the boardwalk below her window. Perhaps it was late enough in the night to be considered morning, and time to put the coffee on.

Wrapped in her velour robe, she padded down the dark hall past Cedar's closed door. She disliked being in darkness; it reminded her of death. Her mother's death in the night, lying right there beside her husband. The terror of finding one's mate dead went skittering through Colleen, and she paused to lean her forehead against the wall until her breathing settled.

How awful for her father, waking to all that stillness beside him. Death meant you were never free again, always trapped in darkness. She tried to think of Joan, her brave fighting spirit, and of the sainthood her church had given her. Deep in her heart and her mind,

Colleen knew there was light; they called it "eternal light." Yes, she believed. But somehow there was a terrible darkness between the earth and heaven, and it was this place she sometimes dreamed about. She hated being awake in darkness, hated even more the time some people called peaceful: the few soft-edged moments preceding sleep. Feeling silly at the morbidness of it all, Colleen forced herself to move along the wall toward the head of the stairs. Marion's door stood open across the hall, and she could hear the woman's light snoring.

Cedar's door creaked behind her.

Surprised, she gasped and turned. Lightning speared through the doorway, freezing his naked body, outlining his wide shoulders and narrow hips and the smooth curve of muscle on his thighs and calves. Thunder rumbled. She knew the light glanced briefly over her own amazed features, yet she stood with his beautiful image etched in her mind, and her heart pounding crazily.

"Colleen?" he whispered. "Colleen, for the love of God, it's four-thirty."

"Is it?" Magnetized, she moved toward him. "Cedar, you sleep in the buff? How strange that I, that is—what are you doing up?"

"Trying to figure out who's prowling around the house."

"In the nude?"

"Very funny. I'm a light sleeper. I heard a noise."

"We always seem to be whispering, you know? I bumped the dresser. Sorry."

Lightning wavered behind him again. Cedar's body reminded her of the marble sculptures censured by religious fanatics at the dawn of the Dark Ages. The grace and strength of the Greek in his form. The humor and passion of Ireland in his blood. Perfection. She wanted to blend her own inadequacies into that presence in the doorway, lose her fears in his sureness, lift her frightened spirit with Cedar's confidence.

"Go back to bed," she said softly, for wanting him was a path to weakness. "I'll try to be quiet."

"Are you up for the duration, as they say? Heading downstairs?"

"I was thinking something warm to drink sounded good."

"Can't sleep?"

"No."

"Wait a sec." He disappeared. She leaned against the wall, waiting, wondering why she was suddenly so relieved to have his company. And wondering how many weeks it would be before she could stand a few feet from him without feeling the earth was shaking. Aeons, probably.

His door creaked. "Where are you?"

"Here. Right next to—"

He came up against her, naked chest pressing into her face. He smelled warm and musky. His arms circled her shoulders at the same instant she reached to his waist to steady herself. He wore jeans without a belt. She quickly lowered her hands and waited for him to do the same. He did not. She felt him nuzzle her neck, and a fire leaped through her, quick, burning, weakening.

"Cedar, let's get downstairs," she murmured a little desperately. "Have some coffee. Breakfast. I'll start breakfast, all right?"

"Busy little bee," he said softly, nudging aside the collar of the bathrobe. He kissed her again and again, his lips traveling slowly up the valley between her jaw and throat. The wall at her back, she wedged her hands against the washboard ripples of his solar plexus, and the feel of his flesh turned her objection to a searching caress.

The rumble and crack of the storm outside came like liquid glass into her senses, merging thunder with the thrumming of her heart, downpour with the rush of longing, lightning with the brilliant flash of desire as his lips found hers and the kiss became the center of a raging world.

Everything about his touch became essential. She needed the creative dance of his tongue as he mapped her mouth. Needed the undulating pressure of his lips as, together, they learned how to taste each other. Needed, most of all, the glorious molding of her soft curves to his boldly formed planes and hollows.

His hands slid low, pressing until he felt the shape of her hips and thighs, roving until the kiss he was evidently reluctant to lose prevented further exploration. At that moment his hands came to her jaw. He tilted her head gently back, tasting her deeply. Again his hands grew restless, and she instinctively followed the path of desire he traced on her body. She had known; yes, she'd known their sexual natures would be perfectly matched. This one area of her life was right. His lips and hands and body were the natural mates of her own.

Behind her closed eyelids light wavered, red blending to heat, heat to fire, a deep piercing fire that darted through her body at the moment she felt his hand touch her breast through the thick robe. He found her softness, and she pressed against the forming loving caress, letting the velour drape off her shoulder until the cool night bathed her skin.

Tracing her curves, tender yet urgent, in a graceful motion he parted the garment and drew his mouth from her lips to the crest of one breast... and on down to the firm flesh of her stomach. She trembled. The moment his lips left her breast, his hands warmed her, but the cold air came against her slightly parted lips, and an unconscious sigh floated from her.

She was dreaming. Surely dreaming. Head tilted to her shoulder, body resting languidly against the wall, robe open, Cedar's hands possessing every contour while his lips traced and his tongue sent fire through her thighs as he slid lower... surely dreaming—not the nightmares of darkness and death, but a joyous love song of romance.

"I was dreaming about you," he murmured as if he, too, shared the dream. "And here—" Chuckling intimately, he kissed her navel, making her breath whistle with pleasure. "Here you are. You taste so good, so much better than my dreams of you."

"Then it's true," she said, her voice a whisper, the beauty of the moment shattered.

He stood up, took her face in his hands. "Every muscle in your body is toned to perfection, Colleen, yet you're like satin all over." He kissed her again.

"Cedar, why? Why every time we meet? Like this, wanting each other, touching as if we were starved. Oh, God, I don't want to feel this way!"

"You're trembling, Colleen," he said huskily, still aroused. He drew her robe around her, up to her throat, belted it and folded her close against his chest. "Shh. You'll be warm soon. I meant to find out why your face looked stricken in the dead of night, and here I've—I've...."

Shaken by her need of him, she struggled to inch away. "I don't know how I could have—" She sighed impatiently. "We'll wake Marion." Her head jerked sideways; she stared down the hall.

"Be quiet and lean against me," he coaxed.

"No."

He pulled back at last. " 'No'?"

"Do we have to get into a clinch every time we meet?" she demanded in a terse whisper. "You're the one who didn't want to hurt her, remember?"

A great snore shuddered out into the hall. Bed springs squeaked.

"Let's get downstairs if we're going to have a fight," he said with a hint of indulgent laughter, taking her into the stairwell and guiding her down.

Growing irritated with his self-possession, when she was jagged glass all through, she growled, " 'Fight'? What fight?"

"What I wouldn't give to have you switch places with Ernie on the boat. You want me, too, only you won't admit it, so we'll fight about it until one of us gives up."

When they reached the landing, she backed away. "Okay, Zeus. You want to throw lightning bolts? I've had a lousy night so far, and I'm in just the right mood to throw them back."

"Hey, Red, relax. I was kidding."

"I told you, call me something else. My name, for instance."

"What do we have here, another Marion? You giving orders, too? C'mon over here. I want to hold you."

"Go back to bed, Cedar."

"C'mere."

"No!"

" 'No' again. You see why we fight?'' He reached for her, his arms sliding around her back.

"You don't listen, McClintock. Let me go.''

Suddenly his arms relaxed. He turned from her and went to a lamp, snapped it on. She shaded her eyes, glanced at him, wanting the anger to keep them apart. He straightened, and the light gleamed on his shoulders and arms. His eyes crackled with warmth. She swallowed.

"You're ice-cold, Angel,'' he said. "Tense as window glass. I felt it when I ran into you upstairs. I admit it was easy to want to hold you, but in my arms you felt as if you desperately needed to be held. What's troubling you?''

"I need to be alone.''

"I don't believe you.''

"Was that one of your lightning bolts, Zeus?''

"Talk to me, Colleen.''

"Like you talked about your father?'' she snapped, the words lost in a long heavy rumble of thunder. He was lying, she thought as the cold pine floor vibrated beneath her bare feet. He had only wanted her in his arms because it felt damned good—yes, it felt good to both of them—but he didn't have to build this elaborate framework, lies that speared through her. He would only hurt her. Alec had left scars, and they weren't yet healed, at least not the wounds to her pride. Was there no place on earth where she could hide from unhappiness until she was whole and strong?

In his arms, said a voice inside, but the drumming rain put rhythm to the silence in the room, distracting her. Rain splattered the window. The stream beside the cottage gurgled and gushed as if it would tear out the boardwalk. Feeling caged and wary, she paced to the television, turned, paced to the deerskin rug on the back wall.

He'd evidently smoothed away the brief wave of anger after her remark about his father. He spoke evenly. "You studied mythology in college?"

"Enough to know the Greeks used to say, 'Zeus made it rain. Zeus made it thunder.' Eventually they believed he controlled everything—men, gods, the earth and the elements of nature." She swept her hair back, irritated. "Like all men try to do. Like you would if I let you."

Cedar flexed his shoulders, relaxing a little. A smile flirted around his sensuous mouth. "He was supposed to be quite a guy with the women, too, right? Lots of wives, good bod and all that?"

She shrugged. It was true. Writers of the time said Zeus married many times, fathering Athena, Apollo and other mythological heroes. Sculptors and potters often portrayed Zeus as both slender and robust, the virile balance of the warrior physique, possessing great warlike abilities. "He was always ready for combat," she said with insinuation.

"In the end, Zeus brought peace, order and wisdom. You flatter me."

She blushed. Again he was correct. "I'll put coffee on."

A grin sprang to his lips. He bowed gallantly, his arm sweeping toward the kitchen. "After you, Hera, my one true wife. Legend has it, behind every great god there's an ambitious goddess."

She walked straight to the coffeepot and filled it, set it over the flame and took out honey and mugs and spoons. She kept very busy. After watching her for a while, Cedar scraped back a chair and sat down.

"What's this?" he said behind her.

"I haven't any idea," she responded sharply, still un-accountably irritable. She brought napkins to the table, saw the dawn and the living-room light glowing on the waves in his hair as he bent over an envelope in his hand, and quickly moved back to the stove. The pot began to bubble; the barklike smell of coffee filled the kitchen. Even that reminded her of mornings at Clifden Moor.

Her mother's slim form, she remembered... looking graceful when she read the View section of the paper, while her father couldn't help glancing from the sports page to watch the ripple of sunlight in his wife's honey-blonde mane. Ophelia Bowles Conaughy wore her favor-ite chocolate satin dressing gown on those last mornings, and Sean would call her his "chestnut palomino," wink-ing at Colleen as if she were the only other person in the world who understood what he meant. Everything in his life was tied up with horses. It was his highest compli-ment to refer to someone in equestrian terms. Funny, thought Colleen as she poured the coffee. She never dwelled on those cherished moments that had been safe and full of love. They brought too harshly into focus the emptiness of their homelife after her mother's fatal stroke... the sheer helplessness of watching her father kill himself with alcohol and grasping women who cared nothing for him. Why remember now?

With a small shake of her loose hair, as if to shut out the pain, to keep it locked away, she brought the mugs of coffee to the table and said, "Well, here you are, Zeus. Perhaps this offering will induce you to still the forces of nature long enough to give Marion the calm seas she so desperately needs."

"I anticipated your sacrifice and already put in the order." He grinned.

She glanced out the smoky-looking window over the sink. The rain had lessened. "So you did," she said, and sat down near his elbow.

"Your hair looks great, kind of wild and sassy. I like it in the morning."

God, he's a smooth one, she thought, sipping coffee, her gaze locked on the rim of the cup. *Next he'll be saying how nice it would be to run his fingers through my hair. . . and I'd want him to. . . .*

"This was on the table." He handed her the letter. "I can't imagine why Marion didn't give it to you right away."

"She was pretty upset last—" As Colleen took the white envelope, she instantly recognized the letterhead, Clifden Moor Connemaras, the classic black logotype and the embossed pony that was Ireland's own breed, imported and raised in the States by her father. She had never expected him to write, not even to answer her own questions about his health and well-being, the worry edited out, of course. She felt hollow inside. The envelope had been typed. But her father didn't use a typewriter. What was wrong at Clifden Moor? Perhaps it was Gates, the family attorney, writing about some accident. . . .

Her heart began to pound. She looked blankly at Cedar; his concern registered only dimly. She must get hold of her emotions, not turn everything into a dilemma. Fumbling, she tore the letter, tore it right through the delicate embossing of the Connemara stallion and, with trembling fingers, brought out the single folded sheet. She read. Stunned by her father's announcement, her voice quavering, she whispered, "He—he *can't!*"

"Hey, easy, Colleen." Cedar touched her arm.

She jerked away, stood up, slopping the coffee in both mugs. She clenched the letter with white fingers, searching Cedar's face. "After all I've gone through with him! He lied. He said to leave him to his misery, his memories of her. He lied to me, and I believed him."

"Believed what, Colleen? What's happened? A lover, a lover jilted you?"

She laughed shrilly. " 'Lover'? Is that how your mind works?" She shoved the letter violently into his hands. "Does this look like the signature of a lover? No, it's the scrawl of a brandy-soaked man who fooled me completely. Read it." While she shook with anger, he read the letter. The words still seared her mind.

I've decided to marry, Colleen. In the months while you were training, preparing to leave the farm, and especially, lass, after you left, I realized how empty my life had become. To my gratitude, Esther McMillan will marry me, for all my faults. The bottle has been my companion too long, has cost me nearly everything, perhaps even you, and the widow McMillan has laid her terms before me—her companionship, or an early hell in spirits. It's a struggle it'll be, but she's of a fine temper. Not mean like an ill-bred mare, or so fiery she'll fight the bit. Just steady, like me ponies. Clean of line, too—you know I always had me eye on the bones and way 'o going of creatures. Puts me in mind 'o the easy gait I liked in your dear mother. Well, anyway, lass, Esther likes to till a garden patch, she does. And Blarney's Blood is kicking his rails down, ye know, so we'll be building up the stock together. We've gone to Father Gregory for his blessing. Do I have yours?

Daddy

"Well?" Colleen demanded, snatching the letter back when he'd finished reading it. She flung it to the table. "Can you believe he had the gall to write me in one of his drunken moods and declare his intention to marry one of his women? Garden patch, indeed!"

"Sounds to me like congratulations are in order, not recriminations," Cedar said blithely, moving her chair and indicating she should sit down.

She did so with an angry lurch. "Congratulations? He was drinking when he wrote this, you can be sure of that. He must be totally wiped out—brain-drowned. He's never gone so far. I'll call Gates, have him go out to the farm and check on him, take Doc Middleton along, too. Garden patches, fine lines!"

"She sounds nice," Cedar said softly.

"Don't patronize me! You don't know what I've been through. It's betrayal, I tell you. Outright insult, after the years I've begged him to forget her."

"Forget who?"

"My mother. She died one night, and he was so in love with her he stopped living. It's there, in the letter, how much he's lost because of drinking." *Because he loved,* she wanted to shout.

And then she realized she was shouting. Marion would have to be tranquilized not to hear her. The cottage closed around her; Cedar's shadowed face and wide shoulders filled the kitchen. All the air seeped from her lungs until her chest heaved. She started to get up. The years of loneliness, grief and terror caught her...

stayed her. A cry of desperation tore from her throat. She found her footing, banged into the edge of the table, held to its edge so the world would stop tilting. *He didn't need her anymore. Had never needed her.* Her father had been indulging his weakness for women and alcohol and lying about his terrible loss...lying to the daughter who had tried time and again to draw him from the abyss. And she'd failed. As she failed at everything. He had ordered her to leave, that time in the stable, because she was in the way.

The weight of the realization bore down on her, and a strangled sob rushed from her throat. She bit hard on the grief, clutched harder at the smooth cold maple. But she lost the battle for control. She began to shudder.

The world enfolded her in a merciful embrace. Warm bare arms wrapped around her shoulders, easing the steel grip she had on the table. There were soft murmurings in her ear, tender caresses against her cheek and hair and back. The shudders racked her, the sobs fell from her in echos, and she gave in to the anguish with gratitude.

Her face was wet, as if the rain had found a crack in the ceiling and deluged her. That seemed not to matter to the man who held her so tenderly. The warmth around her shifted—changing patterns that eased the grief, loving strokes that brought the warmth inside. That cold ache of failure melted away; her skin burned. When she lifted her lips, it was to quench a growing ache that was entirely different from desolation. She cried out softly as his lips came over hers, cried out again as the desire in her climbed like flame to every cell of her body.

The passion of her grief became the passion of need,

the first fully awakened sexual need she'd ever known. Her hands ran over the muscles in his naked shoulders, grew frenzied in the exploration. His breathing short- ened, and a low cry surged through Cedar. She respond- ed like a wild thing, her fingers twisting in his hair, her breasts pitched tight against his bare chest, her hips be- ginning a sinuous rhythm. Someone needed her touch, her body, needed something of her that cried out to be given. She felt the heat and arousal in his loins sudden- ly, like the shock of snow in summer, and she pressed to him until the heat burned completely through her. Their bodies lost their distinct form. Even his hands were blurred, leaving halos of heat in a thousand swirling patterns, without the barrier of velour, for the robe had fallen low on her hips.

Cedar's strong hands knotted in the kitten-soft robe and used it to bring her thighs closer against him. He trembled. Even that sent Colleen's senses spiraling. She knew an instinctive joy that this man needed her as much as she needed him. When he lowered his lips to her breast, such fierce love went through her that she whimpered, shaken. She felt a new wetness on her face, and there came a moment while he tasted her flesh when she knew she was crying again. It was a welling, con- suming feeling—she couldn't name it—that twisted with a bittersweet ache deep inside her.

He left her, breathing raggedly, too soon, much too soon—then crushed her close. He simply held her.

Her first impulse was to whisper thanks to him. Joy was still with her, sealing off the hurt, filling her heart. *A miracle,* she wanted to say. *Don't end this miracle, not so soon, not when so many other feelings could take its place....*

"I'm sorry, Collie," he whispered, and it took a long moment for the phrase to reach her brain.

"For what?"

He shrugged. "Aw, dammit, Colleen, my intentions were not this. Not, for once, this."

"In Marion's kitchen, you mean?" She laughed awkwardly, the pleasure and ache of need still mingled in her voice. Marveling at the bittersweet joy that had created them, she dried her tears.

He touched her shoulder blade, and her body quivered. "God, your body's alive. I can't leave you alone, even now."

She shifted in his arms. "His letter devastated me."

"I know."

"I wanted to help him, all those years. He never let me. Never let me, and it wasn't my fault she died. Oh, I know he didn't blame me for losing her. But I should have been able to *do* something, you know?"

"Yes, I know. Exactly."

"Oh, Cedar, why? Why does the past have such a hold on us? We're bright lively people trapped in the deaths of our parents. What's wrong with us?"

He nuzzled her shoulder, and she caressed the thick tendrils of hair at the back of his head. He kissed her gently. Spasms leaped along her arms. "Maybe nothing's wrong with us," he whispered, and the tremor in his voice made her catch her breath. "Maybe nothing that wouldn't release us if we allowed ourselves to heal each other . . . be together."

She stiffened. He felt it, and tightened his arms around her waist. "Easy, Colleen. Is it such a bad idea? The two of us spending a little time together? You said yourself I didn't know you. Let me. Completely."

"Cedar," she said with a rough sigh of exasperation. "Have you forgotten Marion?"

"Discretion is the better part of—"

"Of valor? No, thanks." She twisted out of his arms. Wrapping herself up, belting her robe, she thought, *He'll use me.* She felt cheapened by his proposition. When she reached for her mug, it was cold. "I told you, Cedar, I don't want an involvement right now." She dumped the coffee into the sink and refilled the cup. She tasted it, made a face, added honey. Stirring, she said crisply, "I want to be free."

He followed suit with his own coffee mug, and when he'd sipped a moment he said, "Your dad has his woman now. You are free, Colleen."

She glared at him. "Cheap shot. Really low."

"Think about it."

"It doesn't deserve thinking about. It's not him I want to be free of." *But it is,* a voice taunted. She ignored it, turning toward the window and the gray dawn.

"Isn't it?" He followed her. When he touched her arm she firmly disengaged herself and looked at him.

"It's not," she insisted. "I want total freedom. I've...got some things to work out."

"Such as?"

"Getting away from smothering by overbearing men," she tossed back, staring defiantly into his black eyes. "I've got a thing about that, okay? So let me work it out alone."

"You're denying what we could have together."

"After three weeks?" She lowered her voice to rid it of the edge that had crept in, but for some odd reason she felt indignant again. She tossed back her hair. "Sex. We feel a beautiful sexual attraction for each other,

Cedar. I don't want to do that with my life, can't you understand? I'm not ready. And I want more, when I— that is, we don't know the slightest thing about each other, and you're trying to tell me we have some great love or something!''

"Don't *do* that, will you?" he erupted. "It drives me nuts!"

"Don't yell at me! What drives you nuts, for crying out loud?"

"You! That—that way you have of sticking your chin in the air. Can't you have a discussion without sounding and looking like an imperial bitch from the queen's court?"

"Oh! You're—you're disgusting. What kind of man touches me like you did a few minutes ago, then turns into a fire-breathing dragon? Drink your coffee, Cedar. It's getting cold! Again!"

He looked at the mug tilting in his clenched fist, gave her a hateful frown and said, "Yes, ma'am. Anything to please the countess! *Ma'am!*" He drank the whole mug down and set it on the counter with a crack that should certainly have woken Marion up. . .if she hadn't already been listening to the strange argument ensuing in her kitchen.

Colleen gestured toward the stairs. "Now you've probably woken her."

"It's time for breakfast, anyway," Cedar said coldly.

"Fine! I'll get it," she snapped, turning to the fridge and pulling out eggs, bacon and some boiled potatoes that had mysteriously appeared on the wire shelf.

"Here, let me." Roughly he took the potatoes from her and rummaged for a knife. Clattering a black iron skillet onto the stove, he began cutting the spuds as if they were dangerous enemies.

"Talk about *my* bad habits," Colleen said, getting out a second frying pan and laying in the bacon strips. "That just drives me up a wall!"

He ignored her, angering her further. "That." She pointed as if he'd asked what bothered her. "That nasty temper of yours."

"Sounds like you two are best friends," said Marion from the kitchen doorway. She buttoned the cuff of her red plaid wool shirt. "Hell of a ruckus to wake up to."

"I *told* him to keep it down to a dull roar," Colleen said, fork in hand, viciously poking the bacon. "He's so *sensitive* to those around him, though."

"Seems you're the one being cruel to your fellow man," Cedar commented with heavy innuendo.

Marion filled a mug with coffee and sniffed appreciatively. "What're you two fighting about?"

"Nothing," Cedar and Colleen said in unison.

"That nothing is pretty much something, seems to me." The skipper wandered into the living room and switched on the TV to hear the weather report. A metallic voice predicted winds gusting to twenty-five knots and intermittent rains, adding a caution to small boats. That wouldn't stop Marion.

"You're some friend," Colleen whispered, swatting a ripple of copper hair out of her eyes. "You're practically flaunting us in her face."

"What 'us'? You categorically deny...us."

"I don't deny anything. I merely said I don't *want* it. And you're vindictive, you know that?"

Leaning so close she felt his breath against her hair, he said softly, "You're right. Keep your distance, little sprite. Because I've changed my mind. Courtesy is the better part of valor."

"Oh?" Warily she lifted her gaze to his.

"Do you recall much Tennyson from English Lit?"

"Not much."

" 'For courtesy wins woman,' " he quoted, " 'all as well as valor may.' "

"I'm afraid you're being obscure...."

"Tender pursuit, Colleen. Friendly persuasion."

She shook her head.

"Yes." He quickly traced a thumb along her jaw, his touch as hypnotic as his eyes. "Pursuit—gentle pursuit—is by far the better part of valor."

CHAPTER EIGHT

EVEN WHILE COLLEEN worried about Cedar's threat, she couldn't refute the chemistry between them. He sat on her right during meals, and this morning he took every opportunity to remind her of their attraction.

"Pass me the pepper, will you?" he would say, brushing her elbow. Or, rising, he would pour Marion a mugful of coffee, refill his own, then wedge his hand between the chair and Colleen's back while he refilled her cup. His gaze caressed. In sunlight his pupils were black nuggets in very dark brown irises, but inside the dim kitchen his eyes shone with inky warmth. He knew it; he played on his looks with a little-boy charm that said he had big-boy appetites. He cracked jokes, directing his gaze to Colleen for approval. She gave it; she laughed. The gentleness of his courtship simply weakened her anger. By the time they left for the docks they were chatting about hootchies and needlefish spoons as easily as Blue Harry and Marion had been the day Colleen arrived.

The wind gusted, its temper nasty. An overcast hung low against the mountains, refusing to be driven away. At the harbor, fishermen strode to bow lines and cast them off, complaining of "sixty-knot winds on the outside." Neither Ernie nor Marion could "hang a left at Cross Sound," ultimately. They were forced to travel,

not north up Lisianski Inlet, but down through a connecting strait by the same name, the strait that separated
smaller Yakobi Island from Chichagof. Here, at least,
they could catch fish with some degree of protection. A
good number of the fleet took this route, so the *Sparrow*
had company in the tree-lined channel.

The crew of the *Sparrow* wove drag patterns in Lisianski Strait for two days without success. Time and
again Colleen heard Marion swear under her breath at
the shakers she was forced to throw back. "A
seventeen-incher!" she'd shout above the knife-edged
wind. "Another!" She'd pull in the gear, run forward
to the controls and slog the *Sparrow* through the whitecaps to a new spot.

The *Dart*, the *Sparrow* and the *Dolphin II*, a blue-
and-white forty-footer skippered by tall balding J.T.
from the hot springs, finally escaped the rough weather
by trolling inside the mouths of small inlets. Here, to
Colleen's relief, the towering mountains shielded the
deep-running tides of the Inside Passage. Only Marion's
bark of command kept Colleen from lingering at the
side rail, her gaze lost in the mist and mountains, her
mind trying to sort out what to do about Cedar. In saner
moments she thought of Marion, and watched with apprehension as the woman grew more desperate to have
fish in her hold.

It surprised her, too, that Marion didn't realize the
Dart was shadowing the *Sparrow*. The regularity of
Ernie's radio calls to Marion, at mid-morning and mid-
afternoon each day, was obvious to Colleen. She wondered how she'd failed earlier to notice the jokes and
encouragement that barely camouflaged Ernie's concern.

Today, as usual, he eased into the topic of Marion's fishing plans. "Guess we'll all be sticking it out another few hours. Probably get a break tomorrow morning, though. Those heavy seas outside can't last forever."

Marion's crusty nature rose to its prime against optimistic statements like that. "About now I fully expect you to read me some verse or other from Luke, Finn. Tell me how merciful your Lord is in this weather!"

"Now, Marion...."

"'Now Marion' nothing. Conaughy! Conaughy, get out there and pull in that inside line on the starboard pole. Move, girl! See you shake loose those fry in something less than a century!"

And in the next half-hour, with rain clouds shrouding the white peaks behind the *Sparrow*, Colleen became the fish puller she'd come north to be. She grinned. She was ready. She had memorized Marion's skillful handling of the gear until the technique was emblazoned like a sign in her mind. Clambering into the trolling cockpit, she grabbed the gaff. Starboard inside line first, she remembered, watching the pole clatter with another hit. Her heart slammed with excitement. She could already feel the weight of those salmon pulling at the muscles in her shoulders, already feel the jerk of calf muscles as she bent over the rail. *Dance,* she thought, going up on her toes. *Get to dancing those fish aboard.*

She sent a look of appreciation toward the peeling black paint of the deck, the poles spread like wings, the skipper behind that smoky window in the pink wheelhouse, the diesel exhaust luffing to port. The *Sparrow* lost its humble details and became a thing she loved for the opportunity it gave her to prove herself. A thousand storms had battered this troller, and yet, like Marion, it charged through the season as if it had important business to do. She glanced proudly across the water— and her smile faded.

She would have preferred to pull in her first line *without* Cedar watching from the cockpit of the *Dart*. She felt her stomach grab. Why did she have to have an audience, now, while she might get the gear tangled or lose a fish? The yards and yards of slop between the boats seemed like inches.

Disconcerted, she jammed the gurdie lever forward, secured the tag line and extended her hand toward the fast-moving fishing line, waiting for the first spread to surface. An unruly band of red hair fluttered across her eyes. Chancing a moment away from the lever to tuck it back under the hood of her army-green slicker, she cut Cedar a quick look.

He wore his yellow sou'wester, the hood down and billowing. His skipper's cap looked like a blue sailboat heeled to the wind, riding the black waves on his head. He stood tall against the white paint of the *Dart*, as if the boat were that chariot drawn by blooded horses, lunging toward a stadium of spruce and gray clouds. Ben Hur. Zeus.

Across the widening space between them, Colleen could feel the electric pull of their natures—always that tight knot of heat in her chest, the tingle through her limbs. And memories now. Again and again she had re-called the gentle insistent way his mouth closed over the crest of her breast, and remembering, she felt the telltale surrender of muscles in her thighs. Nor could she forget his restless dark eyes probing for answers about her tumultuous feelings. Answers she couldn't find. Instead of losing herself in the work and rugged weather of

Southeast Alaska, instead of healing her shattered confidence, she was caught in a gale of new uncertainties,
confusion, bitterness. She couldn't even answer her
father's letter. He'd never listened to her before, and
now what good would her protests do? She felt buffeted
like a scrap of bark in a river. Cedar's presence only increased the tumult.

But it was dangerous to be tucking in curls and thinking of Cedar McClintock when she was about to pull in
her first salmon. She whipped her gaze to the line bead-
ed with water. The line hummed smoothly up and
around the corroded spool overhead. Here, at least, was
duty.

Her first fish surfaced in a splashing arc from the
gray-green water. A shaker. She wouldn't need the gaff.
Oh, well, he was a beginning. As she grasped the spread,
she flipped the gear lever into neutral, giving herself
time to struggle with the fish. A small jerk on the leader
set the young salmon free and angling away toward deep
water. Colleen looked at the wire in her gloved hand,
searched the chop for a trail of blood—she found
none—and then, slinging the leader into a wooden box,
she turned back to the gurdie.

A smile ghosted her lips. What was all the fuss about?
Pulling fish was a cinch. Pulling shakers, she corrected,
feeling pleased as she threw the lever forward. She
glanced over her shoulder at Cedar, but the *Dart* was
now a silhouette against steely cliffs, its caped
charioteer only a yellow daub in the distance. The feeling of success was entirely her own.

A BREAK IN THE WEATHER came on the fourth day. J.T.,
Ernie and the heavy-set fisherman Blue Harry joined in

a radio conversation with Marion that was peppered with colorful language. Excitement ran through their crackling voices. All four boats would soon head into open water.

The previous afternoon Colleen had watched disappointment groove new and deeper lines around Marion's set lips. Hollows darkened beneath the woman's eyes. The catch had been pitifully small, but when they stowed the *Sparrow*'s anchor and headed into a weak June sun, Marion began to talk of the Fairweather Grounds—the time she'd filled her hold twice in three days and had to sell to a tender in the area because the fish were still running. Normally, she chattered on, she preferred to bring her catch back to the Pelican Cold Storage, keeping the revenues of her hometown flowing. Or at least she'd sell her fish in Elfin Cove, a small boardwalk village in Cross Sound. Colleen could almost believe the skipper had forgotten whom she was talking to in that happy gruff voice.

They swung by the docks to unload the one large king and the handful of other species they had iced in four days, and after topping off the oil tank and taking on more ice, they cruised out of Lisianski Inlet into the Pacific, heading northwest. Having run slightly ahead of the *Sparrow* in this procedure, with the wind nudging astern from the southwest, the *Dart* was already a good hour up the coast.

The weather would hold for at least a week, according to the forecast. But on the fifth day, while the *Sparrow* trolled the East Bank of the Fairweather Grounds, Colleen suspected the weather bureau had miscalculated. Cold, moisture-laden gusts again plagued the boat.

The bells on both poles rang intermittently. The inflow of salmon to their decks was sporadic but steady, and in an open sea unencumbered by dangerous shoals, Marion ran the trolling gear while she taught Colleen to steer the boat in a smooth drag that didn't snap or tangle the lines. Executing this tricky chore well in spite of the gusting winds and strong currents, Colleen felt a keen satisfaction. Her years of sailing weren't wasted here. Yet she tensed when she looked at the darkening southern sky.

The sun should have been climbing overhead at this time of day, she thought as she flipped on the autopilot and leaned back in the skipper's wooden chair, listening to the tick of the wheel and the soft stutter of the VHF radio. But then, with Alaska's winter weather lasting clear into summer, you could never be sure a sun still existed. You had to rely on common sense to tell you it did. Without the sun or any land in sight, you felt cut off from the world. For instance, she mused, they were trolling thirty-five miles west of Cape Fairweather. But to Colleen the world included only the *Sparrow* rocking in rough gray seas and a curtain of steely overcast. It was a miserable day to fish. Things felt ominous.

She had learned Cedar and Ernie were somewhere out on the West Bank, trolling in waters that dropped clear off the flasher's screen to a depth of six thousand feet. She glanced at the round screen near her left elbow. The red flicker indicated twenty-five fathoms. Knowing the bottom was only one hundred fifty feet down, she felt vaguely comforted—but only just. Safe harbor was still thirty-five miles away. It seemed months ago that she'd discarded Cedar's joking wish that she crew aboard the *Dart* with him. Yet the notion grew in appeal every time she glanced at the sky—or watched Marion get that desperate gleam in her eyes.

A look over her shoulder through the window showed her Marion's braids pulled straight back in a stiff gust. She was setting a line. Her lips were pinched, her eyes narrowed against the wetness and cold. Five or six salmon were waiting to be cleaned.... Colleen rose from the chair and resolutely zipped up her coat. Much as she wanted to, she couldn't keep warm in the wheelhouse while Marion did all the work.

She glanced reflexively toward the recorder, where paper about a foot wide rolled through a mechanism that drew a picture of the peaks and ledges beneath the boat. At that moment the marker began tapping out a series of ticks.

Colleen swung around and pulled open the door. "Marion!" she yelled, shivering in the blast of cold air. "Come and look! I think there's feed under the boat! Needlefish or herring or something!"

The wind howled. Colleen pulled up her collar. She'd have to go aft and ask Marion to come inside, confirm the recording. The feed patch was large, if Colleen was interpreting the reading correctly. Very large. But one detail worried her. If they found a big run of salmon, there was no telling when they'd head for shelter. The day before at least forty boats had been trolling in the vicinity of the *Sparrow*—now there were none in sight.

Marion responded to a sharp jiggle on one of the poles. The gaff already in her hand, she waited for a fish to break water. Quickly Colleen glanced at the loran, jotting down position numbers in the Empty Log Book as Marion had shown her, numbers Marion could later locate on her chart. They kept a record of where they caught fish. That chore complete, Colleen turned toward the door.

But the intermittent low crackle of conversation from the radio drew her attention. She heard the *Dart*'s familiar call numbers, then a scratchy version of that voice she always stopped in her tracks to listen to. Cedar. She half resented the relief she felt.

Twisting around, she adjusted the squelch and filled the cabin with his voice so she could catch his latest message. "Marion Brown aboard the *Sparrow*? Come in, *Blue Sparrow*."

Colleen spoke into the hand mike. "I read you, *Dart*. What's up?"

"Colleen?"

"Marion's running the gear, Cedar. I'm on my way outside right now."

Static disturbed part of his message. "Head for Lituya."

"Didn't catch that. Say again?"

"The boats are pulling out. It's too nasty to fish, and the seas are building up. See if you can persuade Marion to head for Lituya Bay."

She frowned. She'd heard his voice often enough to recognize the note of warning it contained. Again she depressed the button on the black mike. "I'll try, Cedar. But you know how she is about staying till the last minute. We're in the— I mean, the prince just came to court, you know?"

"I hear you, but you've got to let her know the swells are rising out here off the West Bank. Repeat. Seas are getting steep. It won't be long before you'll be in a nasty blow, water everywhere. Head for cover, repeat, get out of there while you can still make it into Lituya on the flood tide. Colleen, if the seas reach that sandbar before you, or if you try to come in on the ebb tide...dangerous. Do you read? Over.''

She spoke past a tremor of fear. "All right. Thanks, Cedar. I'll do what I can."

"*Blue Sparrow*, this is J.T.," interrupted a calm male voice. Colleen imagined J.T. rubbing his bare scalp as he spoke. "Colleen, is that you taking up air space?"

"Check, J.T.," she confirmed.

"Just the person I wanted to reach. I'm about three miles west of your position."

"Having any luck out your way?"

"A few, a few. But it's looking mean out here. Wind's blowing pretty bad. I'm heading in."

She paused, wondering why he was letting her know. She sensed his relief in reaching her instead of Marion. Before she could question him, however, Cedar cleared up the confusion.

"J.T., this is Ced McClintock. I was just explaining to Colleen the need to remind Marion of the dangers crossing the bar."

"Then she knows we've only got a few hours when the timing's right. Colleen?"

"I'm here, J.T."

He asked for the *Sparrow*'s precise position, then said he'd sound two short blasts of his horn when he was passing to the south.

Cedar broke in. "We may have a little trouble getting the *Sparrow* headed in. I'll hang around until we have confirmation of her intent to quit the area."

"Don't be too patient, McClintock. This wicked sea won't forgive errors in judgment."

A chill spread over Colleen's skin.

"I read you," said Cedar. "Safe trip, J.T."

"Same," offered the quiet man. "Out."

Static filled the cab. Then Cedar said, "I'll check back in an hour, Colleen. Give Marion the word."

She noticed her fingers were cold. She grasped the mike with both hands. "Thanks, Cedar, I will. Uh... safe trip."

He chuckled. "Same, Sprite." But she was not reassured.

J.T.'s SAFETY HORN blasted through the wind; Marion didn't so much as look up from the cockpit. At this, Colleen's stomach knotted like fishing line. They'd hit only one edge of the moving patch of feed, evidently, and Marion was determined to drive them right smack into the middle of it. "Pay dirt!" the woman had shouted. "We want pay dirt for Mike!"

Soon rain sheeted so thickly that midday looked like twilight. At Marion's insistence, Colleen headed into the storm, preparing to turn left at the bottom of the drag. At that moment the salmon hit. At the same moment a crosscurrent shifted the bow of boat.

Through the open door of the wheelhouse Colleen heard Marion's scream of fury. The rain poured through holes in the rusty visor, pounding on the windows, and when the glass cleared momentarily, Colleen saw the lines angled almost straight under the boat. She tried to smooth out the turn. Her hands hooked on the shiny wooden wheel. Marion would kill her if she lost a line full of gear and salmon.

The bells tinkled wildly; the poles shook from the strikes; Marion scrambled to get the fish aboard. Abruptly the boat bucked in a gust. Colleen heard a grinding sound, then a zinging *pop*. Something cracked like a mule-skinner's whip against the wheelhouse wall. The propeller had severed a line.

In seconds Marion barreled into the cabin, her slicker dripping rain. "Dammit!" the woman shouted. "You just cost me a grand, an easy grand! Get the hell out of the way!" She dragged Colleen from the chair and took the wheel. The clipped stainless-steel fishing line snapped against the window, and Colleen ducked as if Marion had struck her.

The radio barked. "*Blue Sparrow*! Come in! This is Cedar. The *Dolphin II* reports your lines are still in the water. What the hell are you doing fishing in this gale?"

Colleen reached for the mike, but Marion snatched it away and growled, "No one on the other side of my deck has anything to say about when I fish, McClintock. I got no time for your opinion. Out!"

Before Cedar could argue, new call numbers sounded. "What're you trying to do, Brown?" Blue Harry thundered into the tiny cabin, "Hit the beach!"

"Go to hell!"

"I got no hankering to head that way," said Blue. "Come on, call her quits. Set in on a hand of poker this evening. May change your luck some."

"Hasn't done much for yours," she retorted, one hand gripping the wheel, her eyes squinting through the windshield. Colleen cringed at the insult.

"Marion...." Cedar's voice held that note of authority Colleen had heard him use with Josh at the hot springs. It gave her courage. "Marion," he said quietly. "You remember the *Courageous*? They were late getting to La Chaussee Spit two seasons ago, tried to cross into Lituya just as the tide was changing, seas breaking.... All hands lost, remember? Hold full of fish...."

Colleen watched Marion deliberate. The woman held the mike crushed against the underside of the wheel, two fingers wrapped over the jerking curved wood as she fought the wind. Colleen's own shoulders ached from hours of fighting the wheel.

The wind moaned, the deck pitched, and she had to find a new grip on the dashboard.

"Marion," Cedar said in exasperation. "What the devil are you trying to prove?"

Marion glanced toward the stern. She was thinking about the salmon still on the lines, Colleen knew, about the worsening weather, the danger, the possibility of missing the flood into Lituya. It hadn't been necessary to explain all that to her skipper. When she'd tried to express Cedar's warnings, when she'd told Marion why J.T. hooted that signal, she'd seen by Marion's closed look that she knew the odds.

"Marion," said Cedar in a low tone, and Colleen knew it cost him to keep the anger out of his voice. "Look, Marion, we're not leaving without you. Blue... Blue, you still out there?"

"Yo."

"*Dolphin II* still standing by," said a quiet voice Colleen recognized. Her heart thumped. J.T., Blue, Cedar and Ernie—they were thwarting Marion's drag. Risking their own lives....

"I'm about eight miles east of the grounds," added J.T. "Things are a little calmer out this way, but it's no tea party."

"It'll get worse," Cedar said grimly, and Colleen's breath halted. Were they all going to die in this alien place? "Marion," he said carefully. "I hope to hell you're tuned in. Otherwise.... Marion, I can't believe you'd risk Colleen's—"

Something cut him off. After a silence when the rain and wind and tinkling bells seemed like the crescendo in a brilliant symphony, an angry voice broke into the cabin. "Squaw woman, you listen to me! You've got no call to take your own misery out on that girl you have aboard there! It was David, said to the Lord, 'Put thou my tears into thy bottle....' Get that barge of yours pointed east before you bring the lot of us to an early grave!"

Marion's breath came hissing into the tenseness. Slowly she turned to look into Colleen's eyes, and Colleen read remorse and a kind of despair in the look.

Colleen tried to smile at the skipper. She reached out, touched Marion's green slicker. "Maybe," she said over the lump in her throat and the fear in her gut, "maybe they'll still be here when the storm dies out. I—I wrote down our position. We could...find the fish again."

Still Marion looked at her with those hollow eyes. She shrugged, a small, absentminded movement. Almost an apology.

"They'll be here when we come back," Colleen said again, softly.

"Marion?" Ernie's tone had risen with concern. "Come in, *Blue Sparrow*. You still out there? What is your location?"

Something cracked against the window; both women jumped. The loose fishing line, flailing around in the wind.

Marion slowly raised the mike to her mouth. She cleared her throat. "All right, boys, what's all the ruckus about? A body would think the fishing business is a group effort, or something. You hang around here much longer, this green puller of mine is liable to think I don't know what the hell I'm doing. Get lost, will you? I'll be right along."

A burst of static. Then, "Eagle woman, you radio me soon's you get the decks cleared. I'll be standing by. Over."

Marion's face reddened. "Look, you bible-totin' Finn, I got more to do than hang around this mike while you hand out permission slips. Conaughy!"

At the shrill command Colleen felt the sweat pop on her forehead. She came to attention. In her anger Marion still held down the button on the mike, and to Colleen's embarrassment the whole fleet heard her next words. "Conaughy, what in tarnation are you standing there for? Hustle your skinny behind outside and get those fish out of the water! They don't land themselves!"

As Colleen jammed the woolen cap on her head and pulled on rubber gloves, she heard Marion spout to Ernie, "Don't crowd me, Finn. I got a line to tie down and fish to ice, and until that's done I'm not budging. If you're in the area when my chores are done—and *if* I feel like gettin' that permission slip, which will happen when hell freezes ov— Well, you just tend to your vessel, and we'll see who rides whose wake, crossing the bar! Out!"

"Believe me," Colleen heard Ernie bark as she was stepping into the downpour on deck, "the Lord's got more in store for me than to breathe my last in this watery hole. If you can still manage a few knots out of that diesel-choked barge, we'll just see who limps in last!"

As it turned out, Colleen caught the renegade fishing line—just after it slashed the underside of her jaw. Half blinded by the pain, she lashed the line to the safety rope. Marion roared out of the wheelhouse. Colleen looked up in surprise and saw the guilty tinge in Marion's expression.

"You're bleeding," was all Marion said. Then she staggered across the pitching deck and slid into the trolling cockpit. She began landing salmon with record speed. Colleen wiped the back of her glove across her jaw. It came away bloody, but not dangerously so. She could tolerate the sting. She wove unsteadily to the cleaning trough and began gutting fish.

They worked feverishly. When the lines were secured, Marion dashed around to ice the fish, and by Colleen's best estimate they were done with the entire job in close to forty-five minutes. Surely a record. If the seas hadn't been so rough, the wind so biting, she would have liked to collapse on deck and feel darned good about the teamwork they'd developed over the weeks.

After a terse discussion with Ernie, Marion and Colleen learned that all but the *Dart* had gotten a slight head start on the return journey. For the sake of argument, the real race was between Marion and Ernie, and no one bothered to mention that the *Dart* spotted the smaller boat a good deal of power. That seemed unimportant.

While Marion marked the chart with their position and plotted a course to Lituya, the *Sparrow* charged full out at eight knots an hour. The *Dart* drew ahead. Colleen knew Marion had compensated for the crosswind, knew with luck they'd make safe harbor in four hours. She went below to brew the coffee that would keep them alert during the grueling run. Fishermen fell asleep at the wheel in exhausting situations like this, and that's what put them on the beach.

As the coffee perked, she took a look at the extra tide booklet Marion had chucked into the silverware drawer. "High tide at 6:45 P.M." Good Lord, they'd come mighty close to crossing the bar on the ebb tide! Cedar had said it was nearly impossible, that a few had tried crossing on the ebb, but it was risky. Marion had deliberately put their lives in danger. For Mike's sake? Or because she harbored a desire to die?

Chilled, Colleen held to the edge of the kitchen counter, bracing herself as the *Sparrow* tipped down a wave and rammed against another. The seas were rising. Would waves be breaking over the bar by the time they needed to cross? You couldn't cross La Chaussee Spit when the seas were breaking. That was another thing Cedar had said.

Colleen forced herself to slap together cheese sandwiches. It was the best she could manage during the jarring ride—the best her stomach could handle in the diesel-choked claustrophobic fo'c'sle. As always, she had to control the urge to get topside, in spite of the storm, and clear her lungs. Her arms and legs ached as they always did after a hard day on the boat. But her mind was the difficult thing to control.

She thought of Cedar, his loyalty, his concern for her. It meant nothing, of course, nothing special, because Ernie had also reminded Marion to think of her fish puller. Yet it was Cedar's half-finished statement— his words laced with emotion during that tense confrontation with the fishermen, and the impact of what he'd been about to say to Marion that she felt now. Why did it mean so much to her, his half-spoken concern?

Yet the fear edged into those few moments of pleasure. Both of them could die—all of them—mere human need buried in Alaska's richest resource, the sea.

CHAPTER NINE

"AHOY the *Sparrow*!"

Her stomach queasy from the rough ride and the tension, Colleen sighed inwardly. Ernie again. Ernie and Marion had chiseled at each other for hours. Reluctant to be pitched around on her bunk in the fo'c'sle, Colleen had resolutely stood in the wheelhouse, sipping coffee and asking questions about navigation. When Marion fell silent to listen to the weather report or check their position, Colleen gazed into the storm and thought about Cedar.

She felt herself wanting to rely on him when her own fear of darkness and death made her tremble. It was her weakness again. Her weakness being drawn to his strength, his confidence. *Fight it,* she told herself during a lull in the background conversation. *Stand on your own.* She'd come north to find courage and principles— and the first storm wiped out all her growth. She felt helpless, unreliable, skittery as a colt. How did these fishermen stand the pressure of pending death, year after year?

She listened as two tugboat operators farther west joked about ninety-mile gusts and twenty-foot seas and weather reporters who played last summer's recorded forecasts instead of telling the real story. Not a spec of fear in those calm voices. She envied them.

Ernie called Marion again, nagging her to hurry on, until Colleen was certain the two were in love...and fighting it.

"*Sparrow*, this is Ernie. Where are you?"

Smiling slightly, Colleen glanced at the woman crouched over the wheel. Marion's gaze flicked across the water, briefly assessing the pitch of the next wave, and then she raised the mike. "Yeah. What is it now, Ernie? You got more determination to hassle than a salmon swimming upstream to spawn."

"That's pretty provocative language for a gal who's crawling along in my wake."

"This bird isn't built for speed, Finn, 'case you forget. She's built to fly true as a swallow in an updraft, when the seas look like they do now." The boat lurched, and she corrected for the next swell.

"We can argue that later," Ernie griped. "And I'm not calling to discuss the spawning habits of salmon, either. I'm calling, if you'll put a muffle on that mouth of yours for one sec, which is asking a lot, I realize...to tell you to kick a few more horsepower out of that barge. The seas are starting to form up outside La Chaussee Spit."

Marion's mouth tightened slightly. "The bar's breaking? You're inside?"

"Not breaking, woman, not yet. Geez, don't put words in my mouth! I *said* the waves are forming a curl now and then, definitely not breaking solid clear across, or anything. But the tide's about to change, too. I advise all haste."

"I'm burning out this Jimmy diesel as it is!" Marion looked grimly at Colleen. "But I'll check the chart and my numbers, make sure I get a straight shot through the bull's-eye. Bay pretty busy?"

"Looks like a convention of dentists come to see Donny and Marie Osmond. I'll have to ask some of the stragglers to step aside, case you take a mind to come crashing in on a breaker."

"You do that, Ernie."

Electrical interference. Then Colleen heard Ernie say gruffly, "If you see it's breaking too much, Marion, don't come across. Better to let the wind push you on up to Cape Fairweather than—" static "—life. I... uh...wouldn't want anything to, uh, take out my best sparring partner."

Marion laughed, that dry coughing laugh it almost hurt to hear. Colleen thought Marion was being unusually callous, tromping on Ernie's feelings after he'd practically admitted in public that he was worried about her.

"Sparring," Marion said, still laughing. "Your best sparring partner is yourself, Ernie. Me, I got my pagan heritage to fall back on when things get tough." She said "pagan" with sarcasm, and Colleen wondered if she was putting down her own mystic convictions or mocking Ernie's. But the skipper wasn't finished chipping away at Ernie. "All you got is that human side of you that *feels* things and *wants* things, Ernie...warring with the side that says you shouldn't."

"Geez!" he snorted, obviously stung. "And you have those legends that date, what, before Christ, right? Have they shored you up any this past year? Have they brought you the inner peace we talked about?"

"Has your God brought *you* inner peace, Finn?"

This exchange told Colleen Ernie was facing some kind of personal battle. Evidently all the bickering between the two fishing cronies skirted buried pain. Only when tempers flared did they cut close to the sources of that pain—and they knew each other well enough to cut cruelly.

Finally Ernie said simply, "Don't take any chances tonight, skipper. I'll see you inside in about half an hour, *God* willing. Emphasis mine, I realize. Out."

He cut the connection so abruptly, Marion looked at the mike in surprise. "Well, he don't have to get so touchy, does he?" She snapped the mike onto the radio and turned down the volume.

"You weren't exactly gentle on him, Marion," Colleen pointed out.

"You don't know him. He can bite pretty hard himself."

"Why, do you suppose?"

"His nature. He's like one of those devil's club bushes you run into in the woods around here. You see 'em from across a clearing, tall as porch eaves, with the sun making those huge green leaves look like a Disney fantasy movie, and they're fine. But run into 'em coming around a spruce—the spines burn like acid."

Colleen felt like holding a mirror up to Marion's face. If Ernie had spines, Marion had sword points. Colleen still simmered from the woman's abrasive treatment earlier in the day. But what was the point of easing her pride by airing that incident? Marion was the one with the emotional problem. So Colleen dropped down into the galley and brought back the half-empty coffeepot.

"More?" she asked.

"A tad, I guess."

After filling the mugs and returning the pot, Colleen came back to lean on the dash of the cabin. The vibration of the engine and the dipping, climbing of the boat made her voice uneven. She spoke over the sonorous drone. "What makes Ernie so bristly?"

Marion glanced sideways at her. "He thinks he failed his Lord."

"In what way?"

"Supposed to be a preacher. Couldn't hack the pure life, though. Temptation, he said. That was his downfall. Temptation kept getting in the way."

So he buried himself in the remote life of the salmon-trolling business, Colleen decided.

Marion's expression was sardonic now. "Got saved during a rock concert in the sixties down in California and then had a big identity crisis or something. Cutting loose of wine, women and song was supposed to be easy, once he found the Lord." Marion shrugged. "He quit the ministry, and he's been tryin' to say he's sorry ever since."

"Why do you bug him about it, especially if you know it hurts him?"

"Aw—" she rotated one shoulder as if to dismiss the topic "—he gets under my skin, is all. Same as I do to him. We don't mean nothin' by it. Nothin' lasting."

"You've been friends...."

"Fourteen years and some months."

Colleen had a feeling Marion recalled to the day how long she'd known Ernie. She had a feeling this tough female skipper was a little sorry for scraping Ernie's vulnerable spot, too. But apologies weren't part of the woman's makeup.

"Besides," Marion broke in, warming to the discussion. "He's taken it on himself to save *me.*"

"From what?"

"Suffering, I suppose." Marion pursed her lips

thoughtfully. "Ain't nobody can do that, though. Been strong all my life. Had to be. What's mine to bear. . . is mine to bear."

Colleen said tentatively, "You mean Mike?"

Marion squinted out the windshield. "Mountains out there, snow like a virgin's throat all over the tops. But you can't see 'em. Not now. Not with the rain an' all." After a pensive moment when Colleen noticed Marion's knuckles had grown pearly as she gripped the wheel, the skipper rasped, "That's how it is to have a son. . . and not have him."

"I think I know."

"Do you, now."

"Yes."

Marion turned, and Colleen saw the woman's bitterness. "How would you know what the hell I mean? That boy of mine was born right down below—" Her square tough index finger pointed into the dim passage beyond Colleen's right hip. . .pointed, then began to waver. "Born in that bunk of yours. And after eighteen years of trying to raise him without too much anger, in spite of his father, and to give him ways to feel he could *do* things with his life, raisin' him to hunt and do with his hands and tread proudly on the trails his ancestors used thousands of years before him—teaching him to be strong and to care about living things as if they were his own body—" She drew a breath that sounded asthmatic, and her wavering hand curled tightly in her lap, protectively.

Colleen wanted to close her arms around those shoulders that seemed about to buckle with grief. Marion's sharp gaze stayed her. "What would you know about a son?" she said in that awful rasp. "Oh, maybe making one, sure. Them colleges is full of the makin's—high spirits and low morals and mistakes all over the place! What would you know about my son!''

Colleen gestured, searching for words that would express the kinship she knew they shared, the loss. ''I...know, that's all, Marion. How empty you feel, how useless. Utterly, blackly useless. You can't fix things, can you? You can't fix what's wrong with Mike, and it makes you feel helpless.''

Marion turned away, the movement sharp. She studied the red flash on the depth indicator. She reached blindly for the coffee mug, slopped it a little and brought it to her lips. Before she swallowed, she set it down.

''Mike was always a big boy, like his father,'' she said, her face still averted. ''At ten he was pulling cohos. Rowing the skiff to the hot springs. Bringing the groceries from town in that red wagon with the loose offside wheel. When he was fifteen he—'' she cleared her throat ''—he, uh, found his father behind a grocery store in Ketchikan. Drowned, he found his father. Death by drowning in a rain puddle, they called it, but I knew it was murder. Art was a taker, see, a taker. Money, cars, businesses. Other people's wives. Oh, hell—'' she waved ''—I hadn't seen him in twelve, thirteen years, but I remembered he was a taker. But the boy, Mike. He wanted to see his father, the way kids do, you know. They like to see where they came from. Gives 'em a better picture of who they are, who they're going to be or not going to be.

''So the two of them set it up. I couldn't stop that, could I? The boy went on down to the motel where Art was staying at the time, and when his father didn't show up, Mike went looking. And like I said, the boy was big. He was strong." A ragged sigh, a nod. "Mike brought him to me. All two hundred thirty-eight pounds of Art Brown, dead of drowning."

The story stopped quietly, the way the wind sometimes settles down to a stillness.

"Good Lord," breathed Colleen, shaken by the stark facts.

"Said tongue in cheek, I presume?"

Colleen smiled. "I've got to wonder . . . what did you do with him?"

"Who, Art?"

She nodded.

"Well, Mike was crying some. Kinda silent, his nose all blubbery. He was my main concern. I let him set there on the deck of the *Sparrow*, just holding his dad, until dusk. It was prime fishing season, then, so there weren't many folks about. We buried him in Ketchikan and came on up to Icy Strait—it was still fair fishing on the Inside in those days—and we fished hell out of the rest of the summer."

"I'm sorry."

The wind and thrash of the seas drowned out Colleen's soft comment, and Marion said loudly, "What?"

She raised her voice. "I'm sorry!"

"'Bout what?"

"Mike. The accident. I really am."

"Yeah, well. It ain't easy, I'll tell you."

"What's that, Marion? What isn't easy?"

"Havin' kids. Don't ever do it unless you're ready for them to tear out your guts. Because they do. Any parent'll tell you that."

Colleen swung away, her thoughts filled with the

thousand times her father had held her, had run his broad palm over her curls, cupped his hands for her to use as a lift to mount her horse. But as she pressed her forehead against the glass, staring blindly into the rainy twilight, she was forced back to the business of getting into safe harbor.

"Look at that!" she cried, pointing toward a flashing light and the rolling comb of ocean surf.

"I know," Marion said so darkly that Colleen turned to look at her. Marion's face was squared at the jaw with tension. She squinted, muttered something, wiped irritatedly at the glass windshield as if she could clear away the poor visibility. "It's breaking over the bar," she said.

As if Colleen needed to be told. Her heart froze, surged, dived. Marion began to parallel the beach, back and forth, looking for a miracle, Colleen supposed, a way through the wall of water. Everything roared: engine, surf, wind, rain, blood in Colleen's ears. Outside, the range markers glimmered. Suddenly the white curls of surf broke open, revealing a narrow tunnel. Marion headed the boat toward it. "Get aft!" Marion shouted. "Watch for big white water!"

Colleen pulled open the door. The wind and all the pounding, growling sounds of the sea tore at her. She was drenched and without a hat, but too terrified to hunt for it. Leaning into the maelstrom, she capped her eyes with a palm and strained to see any shape that could be called a breaker. *Breaker.* The meaning became clear, suddenly, the way Marion's talk of being a parent bore down into her and reminded her of her father's love. *Breaker.* Colleen was a pillar of fear, looking into the terror of dying.

Marion had cut the speed of the boat way down, and the tide was just beginning to ebb from the bay, so they were making, at best, only trolling speed. Colleen could have screamed from the agony of slowness. The roaring increased. They were close to the surf now. Very close. Would the tunnel close on them, come pounding down on her and the deck, maybe flipping the entire boat into the white frothy champagne of the sea? "Mary, Mother of God—" she felt her lips form the prayer "—please let Marion's barge get through this!"

And then she saw the breaker.

It glowed. Grew. Roared. The roaring was close on both sides of them now, and from the corners of her eyes, when she threw her head violently from side to side, panicked, she saw that the tunnel had not closed. White water rose on both sides and behind the stern. *Bull's-eye*, was her ludicrous thought. And then, a few hundred yards astern, the breaker climbed, closing like a white freight train.

Colleen screamed, "Breaker! Go, go, go!"

She sensed Marion's terrified glimpse backward, felt the surge of full power as the *Sparrow* shot through the wall. A light winked to port. The breaker loomed, hurtled...and broke behind them. The stern rose sharply as the diluted wave pushed them inland. A lump of land shadowed by, but Colleen clung to the doorframe, panting.

Where was her heart? Her courage? No wonder Marion missed Mike so much. The skipper had known all along that Colleen had no guts for the really dangerous work of fishing. Colleen felt the hours of fear begin to flake from her like ice floes. She'd been afraid all day. Afraid of dying. Afraid of the dark.

And they must not know. Somehow she must get through this season without any of them knowing how afraid she'd been, this close to death. Not even Cedar must know, she thought, clinging to the wood, bent double with fear. Especially not Cedar. His opinion mattered the most.

CHAPTER TEN

SHE WOKE TO THE SOUND of Cedar's voice. Her hair lay across her face and tangled in the zipper of her heavy coat, which she'd thrown across the wool blankets for extra warmth. The morning sourness of sea salt and dampness and diesel clung to her. Her mouth tasted foul.

She could barely fuse the opposing facts her brain forced her to gather. He was on deck; an occasional faint thumping sound told her that. People moving around.

"Crazy stunt like that," Cedar was saying, the deep pleasant voice comforting to Colleen as she dragged herself off the bunk and stumbled toward the galley sink to wash. She ached everywhere. But Cedar's voice comforted her, and she felt the world was at last safe.

From the looks of the army-surplus blankets tucked like skin around the skipper's bunk, Marion was topside, too, arguing like a wolverine with Cedar.

There was an old-fashioned hand pump at the sink. After two clanking tries that produced a dribble of fresh cold water, Colleen stopped pumping to hear the increasing pitch of the conversation coming from the work deck.

"Don't want your charity, McClintock!"

"Pride won't buy you sanity," he said shortly to Marion.

"No, and your money won't, either! There's fish out on the grounds, I can feel it. Fish is the only thing I know besides misery and that boy of mine. What d'you think Mike would say, you payin' his way in life? You think he'd stand for it?"

"He wouldn't know! He's in no condition to know, Marion. Face it!"

An uncomfortable silence passed, during which Colleen realized Mike was very, very ill. She closed her eyes on a jolt of sorrow for Marion.

Cedar said more gently, "A few thousand, Marion. It would ease things, is all. Pay me back in the fall, if you've a mind."

"Thanks, but no thanks, Ced. I'll do it on my own."

"Yeah, and everybody'll be on pins and needles till you do, too. Hell. You'd look a gift horse!"

Colleen wondered whether Cedar's motivation had been love for Mike, or concern for Marion, or concern for herself. Embarrassed to be putting labels on his generosity, she pumped the creaky handle. The argument continued, and she thought surely they realized everyone in the bay could hear them.

"Change the subject," Marion finally snorted in disgust.

"That pride your mother taught you does more harm than good," Cedar retorted, and then he lowered his voice. Colleen lost the thread of their discussion.

It was true, she mused, filling the sink and reaching for soap. The Tlingit ways Marion had learned permeated her life. Yet she couldn't agree that the influence had hurt the skipper. In spite of the tragedies the woman had suffered, she still walked with a back stiff as deck planks. Colleen respected that kind of durability.

It was decent of Cedar to want to wear down that pride so he could help with the hospital bills. She wondered if he'd planned to contribute to Mike's cause from his own fishing wages or from a business account in the States. She recalled his threat the previous May to make it rough on her family in Seattle if she tried to walk out on Marion. Perhaps Cedar had political ties. Maybe he owned a bank. That would certainly give him power over her father's affairs! Her thoughts gave way to a growing curiosity about Cedar. She wanted to know a lot more about him.

The floor of the fo'c'sle tilted back and forth, the wind rang in the rigging and surf ground at the sandy bar at the entrance to the bay—all of which meant stormy weather. It wouldn't be half-bad to rest for a day. . . to get to know Cedar a little.

From a purely friendship point of view, she added, thoroughly cleaning her face, shivering from the chilly water. She had given up the notion that she didn't need his friendship. Life on the water was lonely, and she was used to a yacht club full of friends. A whole campusful of them. She'd wanted a clean break from those old friends so she could focus on her growth without falling back under their influences, but she still wanted someone to talk to. About everything but the fear.

"Ow!" Colleen sank back from the sink and held her jaw. Tentatively she ran the wet washcloth over the cut on the underside of the bone. The flesh was puffy and sore, downright ugly, she saw when she gazed into the cloudy mirror attached to one of the compartments. Her hair haloed her face and shoulders, wild and tangled and dark red in the gloom. "Colleen," she said softly, regretfully. "What a changed woman you are."

Only the bold blue of her eyes and the chiseled cheek-bones looked familiar. Where was the natural blush her mother had always remarked on? The smooth creamy complexion? She had aged. Well, she had wanted to age, hadn't she? She had wanted the character she so admired in Marion, and she was getting it. But why did Marion wear seasoning so much better?

Feeling let down by her body, she finished cleaning the cut. The rich lotion she smoothed over her skin cooled the sting somewhat. And then in a moment of defiance, perhaps because she couldn't bear the effects of wind and salt and poor diet, she brushed her hair and tied it with a length of narrow green ribbon. Her curls fell like russet maple leaves from the green bow, spreading over her shoulders and down the green-and-black plaid of her cotton shirt. She slipped into jeans. Instead of the heavy work boots, she laced up her white tennis shoes. Finally she rummaged in her satin makeup kit until she found a rust-rose lipstick. "There," she whispered when she had highlighted her lips. "I can live with you now." *Well, why not make the best of this rugged dirty world,* she reasoned. *Because you fish for a living doesn't mean you have to look like a gutter wren.* She smiled, consoled.

She started up the steep ladder to the wheelhouse, then dropped below again. One second up there, and she knew she'd have to sacrifice style for warmth. She pulled on her heavy green coat, zipped the collar high over her cut and went out on deck.

Marion and Cedar were just finishing a chore under the hayrack in the back of the boat, restringing the broken fishing line. Backs turned, shoulders hunched, they chatted amicably about that mainstay of a fisherman's conversation—the trolling trade.

"Tried a new green hootchie out on the grounds, and it works better'n that dark green one I used last year," Marion commented. She wiped her hand on her red shirt. Evidently their flare-up was over.

Wearing a brown cord jacket, tan shirt sleeves showing as he held the line while Marion threaded it through the brass clothespin, Cedar chuckled. "I was baiting herring yesterday morning. Pulled in sixteen kings. How'd you guys do?"

"Prince and half the court tryin' to jump aboard. Them new green hootchies is somethin'. I sure hated to leave the party. I just might have to see if I can rustle up a fish skow instead of selling in Elfin Cove or Pelican. Hate to waste a second if I don't need groceries or fuel."

Colleen shook her head. The skipper never let up. She stepped around the wheelhouse to peer out at the bar. Cenotaph Island lay like a caterpillar with green bristles in mid-bay, and beyond, huge breakers crashed onto the spit. The thunder of the surf vibrated and echoed across Lituya Bay. They wouldn't be heading back out to the grounds this morning, at any rate.

Colleen glanced over her shoulder toward the overcast mountains at the head of the bay. The clean smell of the forests mingled with the sour scent of churned-up tide flats, the mixture familiar and pleasant to Colleen.

"That oughtta do her," Marion said, whisking her hands together in satisfaction. She climbed over the holding bins and came toward Colleen, Cedar following with his head bent in thought.

Marion spotted Colleen. "Hey, Conaughy." She propped herself on the hatch. "Get enough beauty sleep?"

"Sure did, skipper."

From inside the port runway Cedar glanced at her, grinned, picked up his pace with his arms stretched toward her as if he wanted to hug her. She wouldn't have minded, not at all.

But a side-glance toward Marion changed his mind, and he summoned her toward him instead. He grabbed a handful of side rail and sat down.

"Hey, Sprite, you survived the bar." He laughed.

Colleen checked her first reaction just in time. She couldn't tell him how frightened she'd been the night before. "Marion pulled us through." She grinned, trying to settle the craziness of her heart as Cedar reached for her hand and pulled her next to him on the side rail. Brushing lightly against Cedar's brown cord jacket sleeve, fighting the urge to lean against him, Colleen said to Marion, "How on earth did you know that tunnel was going to open for us, anyway?"

"Didn't," said Marion, gesturing past the low island to the solid wall of breakers sealing off the bay. "Wasn't entirely closed off when we arrived."

"Only about as close to entirely as you can get," Cedar remarked with friendly sarcasm.

"Aw, g'wan. You think I wanted to stomach another two, maybe three hours, rolling north to the cape? Maybe have the wind change on me and run us aground in that miserable anchorage? Night coming on, wore out, eyes redder'n tomatoes? P'shaw! A little weather on that bar, was all. Tide hadn't hardly even changed yet."

"Ernie and I are using the official tidebook from the Pelican Cold Storage. What are you using, Marion, your own?"

Marion sniffed in mock indignation.

Again Colleen felt drawn to Cedar. *He looks so good in the morning,* she thought. *So confident.* "Where's Ernie?" she wondered aloud. "Not awake yet, I guess."

"Ernie?" Cedar shook his head. "Ernie was up before me."

"Mad," said Marion.

Colleen gave her a glance. "Pardon?"

"Oh, he's got his nose outta joint. Got a lousy disposition sometimes."

"Why's he mad?"

Marion rubbed her nose. "The usual. I can't do nothin' to suit him."

"Such as quitting the grounds when a storm's nipping at your heels," Cedar pointed out.

"I was *comin'* in!" Marion snapped. "You guys were just rushing me before it was time! He's got no call to be telling me when I head for cover and when I don't. I've got enough salt under my nails to consider my dues paid in full."

"Seems to me," said Cedar, "I paid a good share of them for you last night."

"What's that supposed to mean?"

Cedar reached over and tucked a strand of red hair behind Colleen's ear. She kept her gaze riveted on the crush of white breakers, afraid he'd tell Marion he'd been anxious over her puller's life. That would put their romantic struggles right in the skipper's face. It would remind Marion of the risks she'd taken yesterday, which would hardly improve their working relationship. It would get everything out there for Colleen to look at again, too, all the touchy feelings she'd carefully buried in the past week. So she ignored the gentle touch on her ear.

"It means," Cedar continued at last, "*you* don't have to live with Ernie when he's mad. His hair never stood so straight off his scalp as last night."

"He's got no call—" argued Marion.

Cedar looked right at her, cutting off her words. "He *had* call, Marion, and you know it."

Disconcerted, the skipper pulled at the brown plait bouncing on her shoulder, skipping to the wind.

Colleen felt a return of compassion. "She only did it for Mike," she offered. Cedar looked down at her. Marion's mouth curved open. No one spoke for a time. Evidently it was taboo to mention the reason for Marion's insane race for the fish, but Colleen thought it was high time everyone, including Marion, faced up to the issue. There had been one close call too many the night before. The cards had to be shown for what they were.

"Well," sputtered Marion, color showing in her cheeks. "Well, for the love of Pete, what kind of notion is that? I did what I did because the fish were out there and I run a fishing boat. Sure, I got hospital bills clear to the bulkhead. But if you think I'm letting the boy's condition color my judgment, forget it. Stick to your books and your job, and we'll get along. Forget we ever talked about Mike last night!"

"Look, Marion, there's no point in getting angry at me," Colleen flared. She straightened away from the rail and stepped around Cedar's long legs, moving toward the work area. Turning to face them, she spread her arms wide for a moment. "Did I complain once about last night? Yesterday? Did I? Did I get angry when you jerked me out of that chair because a line snapped?"

"I had good reason, Conaughy. You lost a fortune in fish and weights and flashers. And my new green hootchies."

"I'm not new to steering a boat, Marion, in case you thought I just picked it up fast. Even you might have had a little difficulty making that turn, the wind blowing the way it was."

"I'll grant you, you did fine up till then."

"You'd bite your tongue off before you'd admit someone did a good job!"

"I just don't hold with you dragging Mike into this, that's all. Look, Conaughy, what I let on to you last night was said private. I want to tell the world, I'll tell. Not you. It ain't your place."

Thinking that over, Colleen lowered her chin. "I suppose you're right, Marion. I—I just thought— Well, the truth is, I enjoyed our talk last night. After, you didn't seem nearly so. . . ." She shrugged.

"Yeah, well." Marion gazed across the bay, studying the *Dart*, the *Dolphin II* and the other boats as they rocked in the chop. "I never tried to win no personality contests," she conceded.

"Here, now," soothed Cedar, standing up and patting his jacket pocket. "I rowed all this way on an empty stomach. Least you can do is quit squabbling and offer me some coffee. Let's see. . . ." He dug into the pocket and pulled out a pound of bacon folded in half. He grinned. "I don't believe this side-back will fry itself. You still got that big black skillet, Marion?"

"Nervy kid, ain't he," she grumbled, sliding off the hatch and heading toward the door. She turned, snatched the bacon, swung away again, still complaining. "Everybody's on my case. Falsifying my intentions. Busybodying. Talkin' nonsense...." She disappeared, leaving Cedar and Colleen chuckling together on deck.

THEY WERE LAUGHING, and Cedar felt good, watching the lights dance in her eyes. Eyes like that blue diamond. Some color came to her cheeks. Her copper hair stood out like a Rubens against the grays and greens of the bay. Feeling the familiar rise of desire she inspired in him, he gripped the railing. He had had to curb his urge to embrace her, seeing her beside the wheelhouse this morning, looking like one of those Irish country girls on the postcards. Now the need to touch her shot through him again. The smile faded from his lips.

She saw his seriousness and fell silent. She glanced warily in the direction of the busy kitchen noises from belowdecks, and he knew she was fighting something internal again. Loyalty to Marion? The memory of sharing breakfast with another man? Lord, he transformed into one giant libido every time she was around. Right now, while his senses pulsed and his body grew warm, he was exhibiting all the traits women traditionally accused men of—cave-man instincts and a sex-tracked mind. Well, she was that kind of woman. Fiery spirit that made him want to tame her. Kitten-soft skin with a toned body beneath that turned to liquid lightning when he touched her. Remembering, he pressed his fingertips into the damp cold wood until his knuckles hurt. *Lord.* Did they have anything in common, anything they could *talk* about?

"Ever seen the Hope Diamond?" he asked quietly.

She turned quickly, as if he'd startled her. "What? Diamonds?"

"In the Smithsonian in Washington. Ever seen the Hope Diamond?"

"No. No, I never have. You?"

"Mmm. But I was disappointed."

"Why?"

"I guess I expected more. There's a topaz there that weighs close to one hundred fifteen pounds, though. Really something." He wanted to say her hair reminded him of that topaz with a sunset behind it, gold-and-red fire. Instead he added, "The Smithsonian's gem-and-mineral collection is magnificent. You really ought to see it next opportunity."

She smiled indulgently. "I'll book the trip the minute we get back home." The smile turned embarrassed. "I mean, to Pelican."

They needed to be off the boats and away from other people. He knew that suddenly, with a lurching feeling in the pit of his stomach. It was crazy, but he saw a brief flash of his future, and his arms were around this woman. They were laughing, leaning close to each other, embracing. He couldn't believe it. His image of the future had always been gray, shadowy, unpeopled. Colleen had a disconcerting way of drifting into his mind a hundred times a day, not only reminding him of his celibacy the past weeks, but also stirring fantasies of what it would be like to see her on a more regular basis. It was a new experience, thinking of the future as something he could enjoy.... What the devil was so special about her? He had to know. So he asked, "Want to see the glaciers after breakfast?"

"Glaciers? Oh, that'd be great!" She gave him a relieved smile. "I'm not used to being cooped up this
long." She frowned and ran a hand through her hair. "I
don't know, though...Marion might want me to stand
by in case the seas calm down."

"No chance, Sprite. We might not sail out of the bay
for days."

"Days? Really?"

"Don't look so thrilled. Boats have stayed bar-bound
in Lituya for twenty, thirty days at a stretch, waiting for
the weather to break."

"Cedar, right now that possibility sounds as good as
ye olde semester break. Last night just about did me—"
He caught the flicker of wariness, the quick switch in
her conversation as she moved to rub a fingertip in the
dew on the hatch cover. "That is, Marion's been working herself far too hard, Cedar. In fact, we could both
use a rest, even if it means a few days penned up in
Lituya Bay. Did I ever mention I'm an avid explorer?"

"No. Are you?"

"Absolutely!" She walked the deck as far as the
wheelhouse, where it rose a foot higher to form a roof
over the living quarters. She stepped up. Grasping the
rusty visor over the windows, she leaned against the
pilothouse and gazed toward the mountains misted in
fog.

"I love to hike!" she called to him. "And there's
nothing like a long ride on horseback into the most
isolated countryside you can find. I wish Blarney's
Blood were up here."

He saw her in his arms again; then the image shifted.
They were riding pack horses into that remote Burmese
mining area he'd read about in one of the journals, the

spot where they'd discovered a new cache of rare, blood-red rubies....

Colleen seemed to be breathing the tidal breeze as if it would bring her the image of what lay beyond the mist. She looked very tiny and vulnerable against that peeling blue paint. At the idea that he could have lost her last night his desire returned full force. And his anger. Marion's sanity couldn't be bought, damn her!

Colleen's magnetic hold on him moved him away from the cap rail. Crossing the deck, he came to stand by her side, one hand resting on the rail, the other propped behind her on the housing. Her shoulder grazed him because of the height she gained from the raised decking. He could swear she swayed toward him, but it was probably the wind.

Without looking at him, in a voice slightly high with tension, she said, "My favorite thing in Washington, D.C., aside from the marble stonework on the buildings, is the Freedom statue."

A scent of almonds and roses drifted to him. Teasing. Tempting. His own voice sounded like a saw grating through cordwood when he said, "I've never heard of it."

"I found her when I was reading a magazine years ago, while my father met with some lobbyist or other about opening horseback riding trails from coast to coast. Most people don't hear about her, Ced."

She turned her head, staring at him. Her shocked expression told him she hadn't intended to use his nickname, but the knowledge that she had made his stomach lurch. Desire rose again. He was filled with a need, strong and insistent. He had to force his hands to stay where they were.

She couldn't seem to look away, and he refused to release her from his gaze. Her lips moved. "Something—something's changing about us, Cedar," she said haltingly. "Something I can't exactly see."

"What gave it away?"

"Your face this morning, the way you're talking with me now. I don't know, I feel like I want to run from you, but you won't let me. It's a little frightening."

"I'm crazy about you."

"Oh...." Her voice trailed away. She swept a nervous hand through her hair, and it streamed across his cheek.

In that instant he brought her close to him, tight against his pounding heart, and when her hair fell around his face, he lowered her body until he found her lips. It was like bathing nude in the sunshine to taste her again—unknown depths, a sudden warmth igniting him. Yet even when he knew instinctively she felt the same submersion in pleasure, she resisted.

Though he wanted to lock their souls with this kiss, he restrained himself. He'd kissed her wildly in the hallway that night of the storm, and afterward she'd told him again that she wanted no ties. Well, neither did he, not formal ones, at least. But instinct told him he'd have to go slowly, or she'd bolt. That was the one thing he couldn't permit. He suspected if she got away he'd be sorry until he was as white haired as Ernie.

He had never been so moved to passion and protection and caring in his life. He could feel her giving in to his kiss, bending her body in surrender, and then he felt the resistance, as if he'd floated to the bottom of a cove with his eyes closed and felt the sand nudge his body. It was slight, so subtle he could easily ignore it. Yet he reluctantly drew away from her lips. "Sweet, sweet woman," he murmured.

"I...." Her voice faded, coming back strong with determination. "I never finished telling you about *Freedom*, the statue I liked."

"By all means...." He nuzzled her cheek, following the hollow below her cheekbone until it led him back to her mouth.

"Well, she's seven-and-one-half tons—"

"Good Lord!"

"Yes." She nodded, her breath sweet against his lips. "And six inches short of twenty feet tall."

"Amazon."

"Well, similar. She wears an eagle on her helmet and a long flowing dress, and a plaster original of the real bronze stands in the Smithsonian. My father took me—"

Her glistening lips invited him. He swept her softness in a kiss, and thought of the contrast to a cold bronze woman. He'd known a few, touched them as he'd touched Colleen, but never with this inner caring that made him pull away after a feather-light caress. "This bronze," he said against her lips. "What about her appealed to you?"

"You kiss me so gently, Cedar.... I—she stands for the entire nation, you see. And above the nation, at least figuratively. Can you guess where?"

"My mind's a blank. I don't think I could even recall the details of that game in Wrigley Stadium."

She giggled. "Easy mark! The *Statue of Freedom* graces the top of the Capitol Building, and at her feet are the words, '*E Pluribus Unum.*'"

"Out of Many, One."

"Very good, Cedar! Not only French, but Latin, too. Are you sure you studied economics?"

"*Oui, ma petite,* and right now I'd give anything to translate that Latin phrase even more literally." Forcing himself from the depths of desire, admiring her ability to divert him, he sighed. "Couldn't most of the boats and all but two of the people in this bay disappear for a week or two?"

"Not a chance! How dare you blaspheme America's motto? Have you no pride?"

At that moment she had everything he admired in a woman: beauty, wit, charm; the music of laughter in her eyes as she leaned against him, warm and feminine. Hugging her tightly, he growled, "I'll show you pride, my gem. I'll show you pride!"

"No, you don't, blasphemer!"

Giggling, she twisted out of his arms and scrambled to the foredeck, where she disappeared around the front of the wheelhouse. Ducking under the guy wires, he followed.

"Freedom!" he shouted with mock anger, hugging close to boards stippled with peeling, salmon-pink paint and moisture. He hurried, bent double, around the far side. Colleen had already gone aft. "Freedom!" he called again, reversing direction and planning to trap her as she came around behind him. "I demand you show yourself."

"You don't have your attitude down right," she argued.

"Nonsense! Women should display proper obedience! No notions of standing above mankind, no ideas above their station!"

"Standing above the U.S., silly. And she's been there

since 1863, so I doubt a woman in her 'station' would give your theory or your attitude much credence." Her laughter rippled behind him, and he whirled in time to see a reddish blur where she had crouched under the starboard windows. A small boat didn't offer a man his size much opportunity for crafty maneuvering.

He slid beneath the stays and straightened up, peering toward the trolling cockpit. Aha! A patch of green coattail showed behind the far side of the hatch. Creeping as quietly as his rubber boots would permit, Cedar neared her hiding place. She was crouched like a beetle, her knees jammed to her chest and her head down, probably holding her breath. He lunged for her.

Colleen squealed when she felt his hands on her waist, and she shot straight up and whirled. She threw him off balance. Still clutching a scrap of her coat, one arm flailing, he fell to the deck, dragging her across his chest. Their laughter shook them.

"What in the name of Allah is going on out here!" Marion screeched, then came running up.

Still laughing, Cedar squinted up past mud-colored rubber boots, faded jeans and two broad mounds that were probably Marion's breasts, although from this angle they could be almost anything animate wearing red wool. Colleen was struggling to untangle herself; he held her still. When she hit him in the solar plexus, he grunted from the impact and wound his arm around her neck, pinning her face to his belly.

"We're just having a polite discussion, skipper." He grinned at Marion. "Little friendly disagree—"

"Ga-a-rumph!" Colleen wiggled. She was a wiry little thing.

Inclining his head toward the woman writhing on his

belly, Cedar mocked, "What's that, dear? Decided to accept woman's role and get off this nonsense of *Freedom* statues and the like?"

"Ma-a-r-arumph!"

"Marion," he said patiently, carefully tightening his grip on Colleen as he gazed upward, "this crazy fish puller of yours is telling the most ludicrous tales!"

"What kind of tales is that?" said Marion. "Luda-what?"

"Ludicrous, skipper. Ludicrous. Some nonsense about a woman standing on top of the Capitol in Washington, since 1863, I think she said. What red-blooded American male is going to buy that?"

"Can she pull fish?"

"Well, skipper, I'm not quite sure. She's had more than a century in the wind and rain. Now, the *Sparrow*, here, too. She's been taking the elements, what, almost eight decades?"

Marion glanced around the decks, then bent to look into Cedar's face. "Almost. What're you tryin' to say? What're you doing to my fish puller?"

"Nothing, skipper. Just having a friendly discussion about woman's role."

"M-m-mphr," Colleen grumbled, finally tiring and lying still. "Sheedr," she lisped.

"Ced, your brain's salted. Let that poor girl up, a'for you ruin her for work."

"Why certainly, skipper. Breakfast almost ready?"

When he released his hold on Colleen's neck, she sprang to a sitting position and slugged him hard in the stomach. The wind went out of him. He doubled up, hugging himself.

"She's a statue on the Capitol, and she's a woman!"

Colleen cocked her head sideways and rubbed her jaw. "God, you're a bully!" She stood up, sighing in disgust.

"Come and grab a plate," Marion said as she turned away, shaking her head. "And for heaven's sake, wash up beforehand. Wallowin' around on deck with the fish scales. Squabblin' about statues and ludicrouses and junk like that. P'shaw! Salt on the brain!"

Cedar gazed after the two women. Colleen's supple body struggling against him had had a rousing effect. He'd better wait a moment or two before going below. "Heck of a left hook on that woman," he muttered, slowly getting to his feet and straightening his tan cord coat. "Heck of a woman, period."

CHAPTER ELEVEN

IT WAS A MATTER OF CONTROL, Colleen decided. You could like a man—in regard to Cedar, that was putting it mildly—and still keep your goals in front of you. If he was the kind of man who made every pore in your body want to open to him for sustenance you simply had to remind yourself that if you fell for him, gave yourself to him physically, you lost any real chance of freedom. But a brisk hike with him, maybe a little handholding on the slippery parts of the trail and even a few light kisses—it all seemed very controllable. She would hardly be slipping into her former easy-livin' state, would she? The minor risk to her emotions was offset by the bliss of enjoying herself with a strong, fun-loving, good-looking man. She had worked hard. She deserved some fun.

For the first time since she'd come to Alaska, she was alone aboard the *Sparrow* for a solid hour, taking the time to sort through her impressions and feelings. She never would have imagined appreciating that small block of time so much. Offering both to prepare a lunch for their hike and to invite Ernie along, Cedar had returned to the *Dart*. Marion had refused to go hiking once Ernie's name was mentioned; she had rowed out to Blue Harry's boat, *Diversion*, to "chew the fat." She had a dent in her reputation to mend following yesterday's fiasco on the grounds.

Colleen made short work of the dishes. After she'd straightened the fo'c'sle, scrubbing the cast-iron stove, putting books and pencils and odd articles of clothing away, half an hour still remained of her precious solitude. She used it to reassure herself that it was safe to spend time in remote country alone with Cedar...in case Ernie didn't go with them.

After all, she'd become adept at holding off amorous male friends in college and during those summer parties and sailing excursions. Other than the brief courtship with Alec, after her father's protectiveness had waned, she'd talked her way out of more potential disasters than the UN Security Council. She got them sidetracked with a story; the most impressive, used for serious cases requiring several minutes for the cooling-down process, involved her father's being hit over the head with a garbage can while he was trekking Paris during the demonstrations in '68.

It had worked with Cedar, too. Her exposé on the *Statue of Freedom*, all of which was true, every word of it, had turned both of them away from desire. She had been a little shaken by his kiss, she had to admit, and had had to force herself to put together enough detail to divert them both. She'd been successful, that was the important thing. And she hadn't just awakened from nightmares and loneliness, either, like that time in Marion's hallway when she had needed Cedar's arms around her—even if she had denied it. Today had been easier. Cedar didn't seem the sex-starved fisherman she had first thought. He seemed controllable.

What was it she had admitted to herself a few minutes earlier? That she more than liked him? True. She was crazy about him. When had that happened? One moment Cedar had been tucked neatly into a category, "interesting but aggravating." The next, after weeks of telling herself he was dangerous to her plans for freedom and self-growth, her world was glorious because he seemed to want to be with her—on her terms.

He had said he was crazy about her. He was bright, sensitive and well educated. He was affectionate. He'd probably saved her life, urging Marion to give up on the fish for the time being. Reasons. Reasons to care about him. He knew how to play, too, and she liked that in a man. But there was something else: the dangers of the fishing business called for reliance on other members of the fleet, sometimes for survival, and so the fleet's respect had to be earned. Cedar carried their respect in a hip pocket. Those men on the grounds yesterday seemed to fall in behind him like soldiers when he'd said he wasn't leaving without Marion, soldiers so in tune with Cedar's plan that he hadn't even issued a command. Even J.T. had been about to head for shelter until Cedar hinted there might be trouble with Marion. Reasons.

Colleen pulled snippets from her memory and her feelings, trying to form a picture of Cedar, trying to figure out why she suddenly cared so much what he thought of her and why she felt so vital when she was with him. It was important to know so she'd have ammunition for controlling her emotions, because she wanted to be worthy of a man like him someday. Right now she'd be of no real value to him; she was of no value to herself.

Ten minutes later she heard the echo of a diesel engine and knew Cedar was coming for her. Throwing on her coat, she climbed topside. On deck she halted, staring at the mountains. The overcast had risen from the water and hung in wreaths along the ridges and snowy peaks of the Fairweather Range. She'd seen Marion's chart of the bay, deciding Lituya's shape approached that of a halibut, with the head flattened by La Chaussee Spit, a deep gouge across its middle marking Cenotaph Island and the tail fins extending into two inlets along the Fairweather Fault, beneath the mountains. Around the steep hill to Colleen's right, Crillon Inlet ran southeast to a glacier. To the north extended Gilbert Inlet, nearly filled with another ice field called Lituya Glacier. Between these, Cascade Glacier poured straight down a mountain pass into the water, at just about the center of the halibut's tail.

"Sweet Mary," Colleen breathed, thrilled by the sight of the jagged peak that rose probably twelve thousand feet behind Cascade Glacier.

Then sorrow temporarily blinded her to this scene. She remembered Switzerland...her mother wearing a fitted black-and-white ski suit, trim body skimming the snow slightly ahead of Colleen, blond curls streaming as she knifed gracefully over the moguls and buried herself waist deep in powder. Their mingled laughter, the hugs of excited warmth at the bottom of the run—the memories burned, ached. She turned away.

Dammit. No one had the right to be that happy as a child, not when it was so empty without either parent later on. Close friends couldn't fill that much of a void, and she had deeply resented, in recent years, having no brothers or sisters, no close relatives at all. No one who understood the loneliness. No one she could tell about her failure to help her father with his problems, because she couldn't bear to degrade the family name.

And yet she'd shared her father's letter with Cedar and blurted out her pain over his alcoholism. She even hid that kind of embarrassment from her friends back home. Her candor with Cedar made no sense.

Glancing toward the throaty sound of the *Dart* as it plowed toward her, Colleen was surprised to see the troller as though through a foggy glass. She rubbed the back of her hand over her eyes. Its staying sail furled to the boom mast and its poles locked upright, the *Dart* came sharply into focus, green eddies swirling back from the prow. What *was* this nagging nostalgia? She'd come north to build a new life!

The engine roared for a moment, then settled into neutral, gliding without power. The boat drifted toward her. When the *Dart*'s white beam nudged the *Sparrow*, dwarfing the humbler boat, Cedar ran out on deck and threw her a line. She tied it off, hearing the squeak of the rope as it checked the forward sweep of the *Dart*. It gave her time. She composed herself. She would forget the memories; she would build a new life, one without loneliness and that terrible feeling of inadequacy.

"All set?" Cedar called, grinning, reaching over to grasp a length of black wood rail, steadying the two boats.

With a single short sigh, she set her mouth in a smile and faced him. And suddenly the smile was genuine. "Cedar, thanks for this chance to get ashore. I can hardly wait." Climbing to the cap rail, she took his hand and leaped aboard the *Dart*. She laughed eagerly. "My first glacier. Where's Ernie?"

"Out visiting."

"Oh?" She glanced toward a cluster of boats. "Are we picking him up on the way?"

"Nope."

He took a second to sweep back the right side of his black Windbreaker and prop his knuckles on his lean hip. He wore the tan shirt and jeans the way good gloves are worn, barely a wrinkle, tastefully fitted, a complement to his own brand of vibrancy. His eyes serious, he added, "I did my best to discourage him from coming with us. I wanted this time alone with you."

Apprehension coursed through her. How quickly her confidence fled, her certainty that Cedar was controllable. If she could paint, she would choose as her subject this man and the graceful *Dart* against those rugged mountains. She would win prizes if she could capture Cedar's raw attractiveness: body of the warrior Zeus, ebony waves lifting off his brow, dark eyes saying he wanted the world and would do with it what he wished. It was more than his looks, though. Any woman would feel secure, wrapped in those steel-banded arms. She must remember her goals, she thought, a little dazed by his intensity, his virility. Freedom, time to mature. . . .

"Did I ever tell you about France?" she said, feeling as if the seas had drenched her and left her breathless.

He took an awfully long time to shake his head.

"My father . . . went there during the revolution. . . ."

"Did he?"

She nodded. The details were getting lost inside her head. "A trash can . . . hit him."

Cedar laughed, breaking the mysticism. "During the student demonstrations?"

She nodded. This time the diversion hadn't worked all that well. She'd have to think of something else. While he wound up the stern line, she looked around the roomy deck, noting the scrubbed planking, the neatly coiled lines, stacked buckets, canvas tarp over the trolling cockpit. From the size of the hatch cover, she thought someone could shove a Chevrolet nose first into the hold. Everything was immense and clean. "Wow," she said.

"Nice, isn't she?"

"A beauty. Ernie has good taste."

"He'd like to hear you say that. The *Dart* is his pride."

She turned to him. "But you thought maybe I should get to know him some other time."

A slight sheepishness wrinkled his brow. "I'm only earning the pleasantry you called me that first day."

"What's that?"

"And I quote: 'McClintock, you black Irish swain—'"

She chuckled. "Maybe I did misjudge you then. Don't earn it today, though, okay?"

Looking mighty pleased with himself, Cedar took her through the wheelhouse and down two companionway steps to the belowdecks quarters. Again Colleen sighed in envy and appreciation. "This is how a work boat should be rigged," she said, running her hand over gold plaid bench cushions. "Roomy, everything chemically treated for easy cleaning, easy-care counters, stained-wood lockers, gas range, built-in coffee maker. And no diesel smell! Gee, are you sure this isn't one of the Onassis-family yachts?"

"Ernie'll love you. But wait till you see the sleeping area." He led her through a door. Standing with his arm resting lightly across her shoulders, bringing back that magic link between them, he pointed to two narrow twin bunks flanking an aisle, and a last low door in the bow section. Fuzzy brown blankets with orange slashes across top and bottom covered the bunks. The wood frames of the beds matched stained bookshelves and lockers above the pillows. Above the left bunk, among a collection of pencils, cassette tapes and papers, she saw a large leather-bound red Bible.

"Ernie's bunk?"

"His side of the gym. He's got the gospel tapes; I've got Mangione and Jareau and Tchaikovsky." He waved to the starboard bunk, indicating his books and tapes.

She saw a tattered orange volume by McCullough: *The Thorn Birds*. That surprised her. She would have thought he'd be the type for thrillers, something throbbing with action and intrigue, nothing so sensitive as unrequited love between a girl and a priest and the attendant battles over power and carnal desire. It would be interesting to hear Ernie and Cedar discuss such a book.

His cord jacket lay crumpled across the bed. "Marion would kill you for that," she said, pointing.

Picking it up, he hung it in a wardrobe at the foot of the bed. "There. Nothing to tattle. My guess is that you'll be more impressed with what's behind door number three, up forward." He gestured toward the bow.

Glancing at him, she walked the length of the small compartment and opened the door. She looked inside at the chrome-and-gold fixtures. "A bathroom! You and Ernie don't even have to rough it!"

While his low laughter filled the cabin, Colleen leaned into the minuscule bathroom. In addition to the usual fittings, a tiny shower was sectioned off by a stiff curtain that ran on tracks in the floor and ceiling. The chrome showerhead and faucets gleamed. "Oh, Cedar...."

"Ye-s-s-s, my darlin-k-k," he growled in a voice like Bela Lugosi doing Dracula. Coming up behind her, he nuzzled her neck until her skin prickled pleasantly. "Make yourself kom-for-t-table, why don't you? A shower to purify that be-o-o-otiful skin, eh, my sweet? What will you trade for such a privilege?"

"My body, my body," she panted, laughing, twisting around behind him, backing down the aisle. "Anything for a shower. You've found my weakness!"

"Then you vill surrender! Now!" He lunged, tackled her, cradling her weight as they sank together onto a bunk. Beneath her shoulder, the bed gave and wallowed strangely.

"Cedar!" She met his playful gaze. "A waterbed! Oh, now you've really ruined the image of suffering fishermen. This is too plush. No one stateside would ever believe it."

"Believe, my dar-l-link-k-k, believe. It is all yours for one small favor...."

"Not on your life. Marion would disown me. I can't believe she even knows about this, or she'd never let Ernie live it down."

"Aha!" He kissed her on the nose. "Ernie made me swear never to tell. It was my idea. When he wasn't around, I converted to reduced-motion waterbeds with special baffles in them. Foam wedges and a shallow depth of water over more foam make them comfortable without rocking you out of your bunk in a storm. Neat, huh?"

"But how can you keep a thing like this secret? In a fishing fleet?"

"If I tell, will you—" he nuzzled her ear and growled with exaggerated sensuality "—capitulate?"

"No way!" Giggling, she pushed him away. "If you don't tell, I'll let this slip at the next picnic."

"She-devil! Irish leprechaun! Never trust 'em, me mother always said. I smuggled 'em in in me luggage, lass. Filled 'em up with water and bottled purifiers and ran the wiring for the heaters. Did it secretlike, and Ernie clammed up about it. I've got something on him, don't I?"

The warmth of his legs beneath her thighs seeped through her jeans, reminding her of her weakness for him. She shifted nervously. "It's a wonder he ever lent you his boat today," she said, making sure her tone was still teasing. "Next you'll bring home a bear and keep it in the bathroom as a surprise."

"I'd like to keep you here as a surprise." He kissed her jaw. Pulling back sharply, he stared at her cut. "Hey, it's much worse. How did you do this, anyway?"

"That loose fishing line caught me. And you, I might point out, did the cut no good whatsoever by mauling me to death this morning."

"Colleen, for the love of Caesar, this is nothing to treat lightly. At breakfast I saw an edge of it, and it just looked red. Now it looks infected."

The concern in his voice and his serious investigation of her injury ended in a session with medicines and the application of a wide skin-tone adhesive strip. When she was nearly a walking basket case, unnerved by his touch and the soft whisper of his breath on her throat as he cleaned the cut, she talked him into setting off for the glacier. The mountains loomed above them as they motored into the northern inlet.

After tying the boat bow in to a ledge of rock, they jumped down from the prow. Cedar slung a big-bore Winchester .375 carbine into his left hand, explaining that you couldn't have too much protection in the event an Alaskan brownie sow and her cubs wanted the right-of-way on the trail. Colleen couldn't agree more. He led her across an upward sloping bed of gravel to the jagged ice pack.

Runnels of milky water rustled among the rocks. Having carved away the trees and grasses, the glacier flowed like a shattered highway down through a gorge to the inlet. The temperature dropped several degrees beneath cliffs layered like a frozen birthday cake—gray frosting cementing thicknesses of white and pale dove and cream. The top icing gleamed sky blue.

Intrigued, Colleen ran her hand over the dripping lower edges, finding the texture porous. Great hollows and caves of ice echoed their voices, and the cry of sea gulls made the atmosphere eerie. She thought of saber-toothed tigers and mammoth woollies.

"You've heard about the shock waves of Lituya Bay, haven't you?" he asked in a tour-guide tone as he led her over the fringes of the ice cap where they wouldn't likely slide into a fault. He leaned the gun against a steep sliver of blue. "In '58?"

"That would have been ten years before my father went to France, I think. What happened?"

"Well...." He turned to gaze back down the inlet to a granite bluff denuded of vegetation. "Experts say a quake triggered a rockslide along the eastern edge, causing a splash against that bare mountain you see there. It reached up more than seventeen hundred feet and wiped out every tree, bush and bird on the face of the bluff.

Huge wave rolled through the bay then, a wave they say averaged one hundred feet in height and traveled about a hundred miles per hour. A troller called the *Badger* was anchored just inside La Chaussee Spit...." He paused.

He really did have the most impossible sense of humor. He cast her a half look without lowering his chin, and she said urgently, "Cedar, for heaven's sake, what happened to them?"

"Ever been surfing?"

She shook her head.

"The Swansons hadn't, either, I don't believe, not until the *Badger* was picked up by that wave and taken about two boat-lengths higher than the trees that used to grow on the spit. Then the crest of the wave broke, throwing the *Badger* pretty hard at the bottom the ocean, and the Swansons had to abandon ship."

His story touched her fear. She said quietly, "And?"

"Couple hours later an angel of mercy in the form of another fisherman picked them up. The crew of a second boat that July evening wasn't so lucky. They were swamped inside the mouth of the bay, all lives lost. A third troller inside rode out the whole thing, only lost an anchor and got tossed around some. Amazing."

The horror of the event traveled straight to Colleen's stomach, where waves of apprehension radiated. She could imagine only too easily the power of that shock wave, the terror of its victims, the awful blackness and cold of drowning. "Let's talk about something else," she said uneasily, running her hand over a cold chunk of ice.

"Hey, Freedom," Cedar chided, taking her hand and wrapping it up in both of his, massaging away the chill.

"That was more than twenty-five years ago. You're not adopting the superstitions of the Fairweather fleet, are you?"

" 'Superstitions'?"

"Some notion that the bay isn't safe, predictions that shock waves like that occur every twenty or thirty years. What if it is true? Look at the beauty around us. Wouldn't it be a shame to shun this place? I just don't think you can live your life in fear of natural catastrophe, Colleen."

She looked into his dark eyes. He seemed so confident. "No?"

"Uh-uh. If you know a freight train's coming at 4:45, sure, you stay off the tracks. But natural disasters, no, you can't let them rule your life. You'll live in a cave."

"I never wanted to live in a cave. I only want—" She couldn't tell him about the fear of dying the night before. Nor could she tell him she wanted to be safe from the darkness that had claimed her mother.

"What, Colleen? What is it you want?"

"To be happy, Cedar." She pressed his hands with her own. "To feel like I'm of some use to somebody."

"Colleen," he said in surprise. "You of all people, with your pride and your way of tearing into the world with both sets of claws, surely you don't feel useless?"

"Don't I? What special skills do I have, Cedar? If I couldn't even be a proper daughter to my father, how can I hope to be any good to anyone?"

" 'Proper daughter'. . . ?" He bowed his head for a moment. Then he slid her hand to his forearm, picked up the rifle and headed into the forest, his brow wrinkled in concentration. The peal of gulls faded as Colleen and Cedar left the salt marshes. The cry of chickadees and the caw of crows took Colleen back in time to the primeval rain forests of Hawaii. The plants were different here, more bristly, but the green mosses, the drip of moisture and the feeling of oppression remained.

Cedar stepped carefully as he made way for her to skirt boulders, clumps of fern and spruce trees. They walked past intricate fans of roots from fallen trees, the ground beneath ruffled with orange mushrooms. White shelf fungi clung to withered bark. Moss humps higher than Colleen's waist smelled moldy and shone with pearls of dew. She waded through waist-high blueberry bushes just beginning to pop out in green fruit.

Cedar put a cautioning hand to her sleeve. She stopped, glanced at him. He nodded toward a small clearing.

The buff fur of a deer's back moved behind a clump of bushes; twigs snapped. Colleen sighed. What was wrong with her—how could she let old insecurities ruin this beautiful walk? The animal's head came up, slender nose trained toward them, dark eyes blinking. The long full ears quivered, pink in the centers from backlighting. And then the deer leaped sideways, graceful on slender legs, and bounded into the woods. "Sitka black-tail doe," Cedar announced, and continued ahead of Colleen.

The wind sifted through high branches; the cool air brushed her cheeks with dampness. Eventually her body warmed as they wound along the narrow deer trail, climbing deeper into the woods.

Had she revealed too much of her fear? Or could Cedar distinguish between her love of adventure and her fear of catastrophe? Worried that she'd chipped away his respect for her, she said quietly, "Back there at the glacier, I didn't mean that I couldn't do anything, Cedar. I mean, I know French and can read the literature. I remember most of the foreign history and culture I've ever studied because it fascinated me. I can catch on to just about anything I study, and I feel perfectly at home in most social situations. Riding, hiking, swimming, sailing—they're all easy for me. I can run a power boat." She shrugged. "Fish."

Cedar stopped and leaned the gun against a gray boulder. He pulled her to his chest, his back resting against a spruce and the green branches draping just above his head.

"Hey...." He stroked her cheek. "Babe, you're the strongest, toughest, new little fish puller I know. You worry too much."

"And in case you've forgotten my interview," she went on in a distracted whisper, "I have strong white teeth."

He took her chin gently in one hand, and with the other smoothed back the curls on her forehead. "You," he said softly. "You are about the most exciting woman I've ever met. Your body excites me. Your mind is fluid and interesting. Most women wouldn't have stuck by Marion under the conditions you have. You're loyal and tough. I respect you, Colleen."

"Cedar, you don't know—"

He closed his eyes in mild exasperation, hushing her. "Your voice is like velvet, your eyes like a certain blue diamond I've seen, your hair...." He stroked her. "Like blood rubies in sunlight."

"Oh, Cedar," she admonished. "That's too beautiful."

"Not for you, Freedom. Your smile, when you show it, lights your whole face, and you look like happiness itself. And your will—your will is a track of pure gold." He paused, and her heart ached with an emotion she refused to believe was happiness.

Brushing her lips in a respectful kiss, Cedar said softly, "Colleen. . .Colleen, I'm falling in love with you."

CHAPTER TWELVE

SHE DREW a shocked unsettled breath. Cedar wasn't the kind of man to love someone from afar. If he cared, he put his life on the line to prove it. He meddled and hovered, and he protected those he loved. Smothered them, practically. He made pacts in Marion's best interests, attempted to pay Mike's medical bills, took Colleen for walks to hot springs and glaciers. Frightened by the possessiveness his words implied, she arched against the circle of his arms. "You don't mean that," she protested.

"Colleen." Emotion edged his voice. "Shall I tell you again? Did you even hear? I'm falling in love with you."

"But...when? When did this happen?"

"Well, yesterday, I think I realized it. Yesterday, yes. When I was so worried—"

Disbelieving laughter burst from her. " 'Yesterday'?" She spun away from him, her pulse jumping. He couldn't love her. Couldn't be beginning to love her. Oh, God, not yet. Too soon, far too soon. She wanted him, yes, and felt the attraction, but she wasn't ready for love.

" 'Yesterday'?" she repeated in a high voice as she reached toward a mossy stump and put her weight on one hand, sinking to her wrist in the damp carpet.

"How could you even know what I'm like, Cedar? I mean, inside? And—and yesterday is only twenty-four hours ago! How can you not love somebody one day... and love them the next?"

A stick cracked behind her; his fingers wrapped over her arm. He pulled her roughly close. His chest rose and fell against her breasts. His black eyes snapped.

"What is it with you?" His voice low and tight, he snugged her closer. Her arms bent under the strain as she tried to hold herself away. "What kind of game are you playing?"

She glanced at the ground. "Game—no game, Cedar!"

"Then why the warmth and sparkle one moment, and this virgin's paranoia the next? You asked me to care about you, remember? Well, I could throttle Marion for risking your life. Believe that!" He shook her a little. "Believe that you strike something dangerously soft inside me, woman, and I don't know any other name for it but love."

She felt trapped. He was a force like the ocean, storming around her, cutting off oxygen, blocking out the sun. Her hands twisted in the loose sleeves of his Windbreaker, pushing him away, and her respiration grew erratic. "Cedar, you barely know me!" She willed his obsidian gaze to soften in understanding, and then she said what even she did not believe: "We're strangers!"

"What does it take, Colleen? You tell me, because I don't know. What is love?"

Their gazes held. His energy sapped her will, and because she couldn't answer, tears of frustration temporarily blinded her. Closing her eyes, shaking her head bleakly from side to side, she choked, "I . . . don't know what love is."

That wide sensuous mouth closed over her own. Her murmur became a soft moan of surrender, and her arms circled his neck. *This is love,* something deep in her brain intoned into the misery. *These uncontrollable feelings of happiness mixed with sorrow, with despair, because you can't accept his love. But love him. You can grow together.*

His kiss made the ache inside her well up until she shook. Stretching to reach around his shoulders, she returned his caresses, pressed close to him, relishing the flat steel of his hips against her stomach and the searching play of his hands on her back and hips. Was love this kind of pleasure? Was Cedar's personality a part of it—his laughter, loyalty, humor, integrity—reason to love him?

They were learning the pleasure of tasting each other again, building on the knowledge of that first deep kiss. His teeth were perfect rows exciting to explore with her tongue. His lips moved, delicately at first, then with an increasing pressure that made her tremble.

Was this the way it had been between her parents?

And there, suddenly, was the reason not to love him. It struck her full force, black fist in her stomach. Between her and Cedar existed every nuance of love she'd seen her parents share, and more that she'd never seen. But she knew, clearly, that to call this love would be to hurt terribly if she ever lost him. Pictures of her father stumbling around his study plagued her; his tormented yelling and the shattering of glass had floated up the wide stairway to her bedroom, where she suffered with the fear that her father, too, might die. For weeks, months her father raged and drank. Colleen withdrew into nightmares, and the hopelessness and terror of those years made her shrink from Cedar now.

His breathing sounded ragged, and his hands moved wildly, stoking fires in Colleen's center while her mind lay like a frozen lake above her body. She struggled to free herself, but Cedar mistook the movements for frenzy, and he arched against her, groaning with need. The blackness hovered in her mind. Her breath began to rasp. All that stood in Cedar's way was her will, her own desperate need to flee.

Steeling herself against a driving impulse to bend to him, she waited through a torment of feelings. . . waited until he moved his hands over her shoulders and into her hair.

With all her strength Colleen shoved against his chest and twisted out of his arms. Free! Run! She hesitated as he stumbled backward. Half-crouched, she stood a few feet away, legs apart, panting, and watched him sprawl across a decaying log. A pain of regret twisted inside her. He grunted. Chips of gray bark and pine needles showered his jeans, but he wasn't injured.

Colleen spun around. Heading south and slightly downhill, she sprang into the bushes.

"Colleen, what the devil—?"

She heard Cedar shout, the sound swallowed up by the moisture-laden forest and her sprinting, leaping, careening escape. Light and shadow flickered around her. Sunlight poured into a shallow clearing, turning the tiny flowers of the forget-me-not into a blurred carpet of blue as she sped past. Gnarled roots crawled like snakes over the russet pine needles, and pale mushrooms sprouted from the chocolate soil. She leaped these. A small bird swooped into Colleen's path; she veered without breaking stride. The years of riding, the months of lifting weights, the weeks of fishing—all paid off now. Her wind, though growing labored, held.

Clutching a low hemlock branch, the soft needles cushioning the sting as the branch burned across her palm, she skirted the tree and zigzagged around half a dozen more.

The stomp and thud of a running man followed her for perhaps five hundred yards, but within two tearing breaths the sounds faded. Cedar called her again from somewhere behind her right shoulder. *He'll trap me,* she thought, *and I'll let him do it.* She cut farther south, her breathing coming raggedly.

The air changed, grew cooler, and she knew she'd crossed the mountain to the glacier. Now she whined with the effort to breathe. Her heart jumped like dancer's feet, but the fear drove her to a ridge where the thick forest ended. She plummeted down, down, the gravel rattling like wooden maracas.

She paused on a chunk of granite to loosen her coat. In that fleeting moment she saw the caverns and spires of the ice field. Backed by a frosted peak, the glacier poured between cliffs of granite that supported neither brush nor trees, and she could hear the wind sighing in those lonesome reaches. An eagle circled in the thin air. But below Colleen, the heavier salt-rich breeze rose off the ice to cool her cheeks.

Gravel and bleached timber littered the sloping bank. Milky runoff splattered over the polished stones, gleaming and gurgling until the creek dodged beneath a million pounds of ancient ice, to murmur quietly away.

Bears, wolves—God only knew what creatures lived

in this prehistoric place, she thought as she bent to ease a stitch in her side. Her heart still drummed in her ears. Just get back to the *Dart*. Follow the ice downhill to the bay, then turn right at the beach. He'll be furious and hurt, but at least he'll be there. And now he would understand she wanted to be free.

But sorrow ebbed and flowed through her determined thoughts, and she felt the rapid stroke of her heart more acutely. Heading toward a silt-dusted ledge on the ice field, where she could rest and cool down, she repeated, "I will be free. I will—"

A sound disturbed her—like someone beating a tennis racket against sand—and she whirled to scout the hill behind her. A golden shape scurried toward her, and her body lurched instinctively. She cried out as she pitched backward. Falling downhill, she rolled several feet, clutching ineffectually at the loose shale, until she crashed into the ledge. Instantly the stream soaked the seat and one leg of her jeans. A sleeve of her coat dripped ice water.

"Sweet Mary," she murmured. Wiping a wet hand on her pant leg, she pulled herself upright. She leaned against the iceberg, chilled hand at her throat, and searched the bluff.

The golden blur turned out to be a porcupine. The fat animal crouched on its haunches, kangaroo-style, long spines glistening in the sun, paws propped on its chest. Its black nose wrinkled. Tiny brown eyes strained toward the shadows of the glacier, trying to register Colleen. Then the animal's head jerked sideways. The creature glanced toward the woods, chattered and tropped to all fours, scurrying across the gravel and into the brush.

Something had frightened the porcupine into the open,

Colleen speculated, glancing nervously along the ridge above. She leaned forward and studied the spikelike trees to her right. "Oh, dear God...."

Cedar stood beneath the pale green lace of a hemlock. Feet braced apart, rifle hanging loosely from his left hand, he gazed down at her. His chest pumped with exertion. Though he was sucking in air with a vengeance, he managed to smile. But it was a very, very angry smile.

He leaped halfway down the bank, and by the time she realized he intended to capture her, he was already half the distance to the ledge.

She bolted. Stumbling into the creek, she came up out of it and jumped to a narrow path of stones. The gravel gave to her steps, dragging at her, and she panted, "Damn you, damn you!" as she doubled back and forth down a ravine.

In the open she retained no advantage, though she covered ground like a lumberjack working logs in a river, dancing, twisting, leaping.

Cedar's boots crunched behind her. She could hear his breath, labored, rasping. He'd been running a long while, and she sensed his fury. Beneath that fury, she told herself, was a will to dominate her. *Leave me alone,* she screamed inside. *Let me breathe!*

The glacier, she thought in panic. She cut through the stream and followed a stone-paved canyon. The ice caves echoed back her footsteps...and then Cedar's. Her knees shooting pain through her thighs, she ducked down a lavender-tinted passage. The trail branched at least five ways. She slid behind a wall of ice. Her heart lurched in exhaustion. Holding her hands over her mouth, she concentrated on easing her breath to silence.

A gull's scream pierced the sunlit maze.

"Where are you?" she heard him pant softly outside. Breathing hard, he trotted down a canyon, scattering pebbles.

Colleen withdrew her hands and clenched them to warm her fingers. The silence was broken by the bubble of the brook somewhere under the ice. She looked around.

Light filtered through a half-moon, a thin spot in the roof of the cave, carving an arc of blue light on the gravel floor. On the uphill side, craters pocked the cave wall. Water dripped from the curved outside edge of the roof, but inside the gravel was barely damp.

The crunch of stones made her hold her breath. Cedar retraced his path and paused outside her cave, and she knew with a leaden feeling that he'd found the indentations of her footsteps.

He stepped around the wall. She watched his eyes widen. Cedar stared hard at Colleen. "Damn you," he whispered, his chest heaving. "You could have been lost!"

She faced him with her hands at her sides and her chin tilted. "I have a right to be here, a right to some breathing space. As much right as you or Doc or Blue."

"You have a *right* to die in this ice field? The caves and trails and hundred-foot drop-offs go for miles!"

She swallowed. "I wouldn't have died."

"Colleen!" He gestured with the carbine. "These things collapse all the time!"

She whirled and looked around, then spun to him with a glare. "I asked you to be my friend! You have no understanding, do you? You take, take!"

"What do you want from friendship, woman? A Ken

doll who can't move his arms or head without your say-so?''

"No!" She lifted her hands in frustration, then let them slap against her thighs. "No, Cedar. Friends go places together and help one another and listen to troubles and...and let the other person be what they want to be. They understand. They tell each other things—why won't you talk about your father, for instance? I mean, if we're such *good* friends?''

He slapped the rifle against the cave wall. "My father is dead, and he'll damned well stay that way!"

"Great. Dead-end topic. Where do you go in the winter, or is that classified information, too...friend?''

"You want an itinerary?''

"Yes!" she shouted. "All right, an itinerary!''

"Fine! When the season closes I'm heading up to Kotzebue, north of the Arctic Circle. I'll meet with the heads of the local Eskimo corporation to arrange to export some of their jade artwork, okay?'' He tromped across the cave and swung around, ticking off dates on his fingers. "November 24...Düsseldorf, West Germany, for a world conference on corundum, sources and methods of extraction.''

She didn't have even a remote idea what corundum was, but the timing of the trip took her off guard. "But... that's Thanksgiving.''

"Who cares? My mother? My father?'' He took a stride toward her. "December 5 through 17...a tour of the old sluicing sites in the California gold-mining areas. December 21, Australia; December 24, flight to Brazil—''

" 'Brazil'?'' Alec, she thought. Alec, buried in the jungles, teaching people to read and write. But she didn't care about Alec. She didn't care. Her gaze flicked back to Cedar. "On business? But—that's Christmas time."

He came closer, stepping right in front of her, his face four inches away. "Colleen," he said with a hollowness that rang through her, "who cares?"

"Oh, Cedar...."

His eyes burned her, challenging her to go on. She bit her lip...and moved out of his way toward the back of the cave. She paced, *spur spur spur* across the gravel. "I care, that's who cares," she murmured distractedly, wringing her cold fingers. She whirled. "*I* care, damn you!"

His face jerked with the violence of her cry.

She looked away. "But I can't love you. I—I don't love *me* yet. I'm running. Searching. Trying to *be* somebody, Cedar. Not this—this hothouse rose who wilts at the first sign of stormy weather."

She stopped, her back to the wall of ice, and raked her fingers through her hair. Across ten feet of gravel he stood with his hands held out toward her. A pain went through her. *He wants to come to me, to give,* she realized. *He wants me to give back.*

But she was that rose Alec had named her—only the petals were wrapped in a tight bud that wouldn't bloom for anyone, not even this man who looked at her as if she were a whole field of full-blown roses.

Sighing desolately, she turned and pressed her face to the ice. "I'm a failure. I can't love you." She whipped around, her hair flying. "Do you want a failure for a lover?"

"Whom have you failed?" he boomed, approaching her.

"Myself! Others! My father!"

"How?"

"He's a drunkard!"

"That's not your doing, Colleen, not something you can fix."

"Oh!" She threw her hands high, clapped once. "Right, friend McClintock. Oh, but I tried."

"Colleen—"

"Years of it, Cedar, begging, pleading, 'Daddy, don't drink today, don't go out with what's-her-name. Daddy, please, *please* come riding with me.'" She choked and was surprised to feel tears in her eyes.

Cedar tried to take her in his arms, but she held up her hand. "But you know why he couldn't, Cedar."

"No, tell me—"

"I'll tell you why," she interrupted, laughing, the high sound reverberating. "Because, Ced, the horses were gone, sold at auction for a pittance of their value. My father staggering around the stands of the auction block—" She wiped the irritating dampness from her eyes. "He was weeping, my father, watching his blooded stock dance and shy around the square. Sawdust over everything." She appealed to him. "I had Blarney's Blood at the halter, and he was snorting and dancing, tossing his head and dragging me off my feet. So then Blarney's Blood whinnied, and the auctioneer shouted something about spirit, and a bid came in. Then they came thick and fast, the auction man yelling and people getting to their feet...." The images came forcefully to her—the red of the auctioneer's shirt, the chips of sawdust flying, her father.... "And my daddy was still crying," she said, her voice thin. "Crying and moving toward the ring, dragging that woman in her spike heels with him. Both of them drunk as sin, Cedar."

She gulped a breath of damp air; it shuddered back out in a moan. "He—he tripped, or something, toppled into the ring on his face, and the woman down, too. Blarney went up, just exploded, throwing me against the back wall. I lay there, breath knocked out of me. I could hear Blarney whinnying, thudding around the ring. And then he nuzzled me. He's a blood-red sorrel, Ced, with a nose soft as roses...." She put her hand to her forehead, sighed, collapsed to her knees. Both arms hung limply as she stared at the gravel, remembering.

"What happened?" Cedar asked softly.

She drew a breath. "The police came. They closed the auction until the ring was cleared. Gates, the family attorney, arranged bail so daddy wouldn't have to spend the night in jail—it was his seventh offense—I don't know how Gates managed it. But I kept Blarney's Blood." She glanced over her shoulder and whispered to Cedar, "I kept him."

He nodded. She turned away and looked at her reddened hands.

Cedar draped her coat over her shoulders. He knelt beside her and put an arm around her. She leaned against him, drained.

"Have you written your father yet?"

She shook her head.

"You should."

"Why?" she said bitterly. "So I can give him my blessing for something he's been doing for years without it?"

"So that's it."

"'So that's it,'" she mimicked.

He patted her shoulder. "You have this jaded view of men," he said with apparently dawning understanding.

"You think we're all womanizers. You think I'm going to drink myself into the arms of every loose woman in sight."

"Don't be silly." She knuckled her eyes again. "I know you're not him."

"Do you? I wonder."

"Don't waste your time on that track, Dr. Freud. It's a dead end. It's true I failed to help my father. It's true I have a confidence problem and I'm working it out up here in Alaska. But it's not true that I think all men are worthless drunks and womanizers. I have a friend in Brazil, since you mention that country, and he's about the purest, most unselfish, high-minded man I know. He gives Ernie a run for his money."

"Hey, Freedom," he admonished, hugging her. "No more temper tantrums, all right? Just relax. You forget, I still think you're the best thing that ever walked into my life, shouting at me." He chuckled.

She looked into his face.

"Okay?" he said, still smiling.

She watched him check an impulse to kiss her. His caring reached down inside her. "Okay," she said softly. Feeling drawn to his comforting arms, she snuggled against him. "No more temper today."

He held her wrapped in the jacket for a long while, rocking her slightly, pressing his chin into her hair. She grew aware of his heartbeat, his breathing, the cocoon of warmth his thighs made for her hips as he cradled her.

"This cave could collapse at any moment," she said tentatively, listening to the water drip to the ground.

"I thought about that. But if it didn't come down while we were screaming at each other, I guess it's safe enough."

"I wonder what Marion's doing."

"You should write to him, Colleen."

"I can't."

She turned in his arms. When their eyes met, she watched the color in his deepen as if a storm had blown clouds across the sun. Midnight longing in his gaze. He, too, felt desire again.

"Cedar," she pleaded softly.

His lips parted; the lowering afternoon sun made them russet. "My love," he whispered huskily. He lifted a strand of hair from her cheek and smoothed it back into place. Her lids trembled, and she fought to keep them from closing in anticipation of his kiss.

"If love, is a kind of terror at losing someone," he said gently, "I love you desperately. Shh." He shook his head to silence her denial. "Listen to me. . . ."

She lay against him, her jeans drying in the shaft of sunlight through the cave opening, her ear catching every tremor and sigh as he spoke to her.

"Pure gold will," he said as he slid his fingers through her hair, untangling the waves. "You were very brave to come to a harsh world like the Alaskan salmon trolling business just to prove you're worthy. You're wrong, Collie, wrong to think you failed your father, wrong about your inability to help others. You had to be scared, out on that boat last night, but you never uttered a peep about it. Pure gold will, huh?" He tilted up her chin.

She smiled, shrugged.

"And another thing," he added while she watched his eyes and his mouth and listened to the coaxing timber of his voice. "Your father is helping himself, *must* help himself."

"But he won't," she protested.

"Well, I think you might be wrong."

Colleen opened her mouth to argue, but Cedar shushed her again. "I'm not finished yet." He took their jackets and spread them on the ground, then eased her onto her back and stretched out beside her, an elbow propped on the coat. "As I was saying, you ought to write him back and give him the okay. This woman— Esther McMillan, isn't it? Maybe she's different. Maybe she drew him out of his—" He glanced outside and said softly, "That empty feeling that sometimes grips a man." He turned, searched her face, and the warm light returned to his eyes. "Maybe she gave him hope."

"I don't see how—"

"Give him your blessing, Colleen. Let him go... and then, you can learn to love me."

She gave him a strained smile. "It's all so beautiful, the way you paint it, Cedar." She traced his lower lip with her forefinger and laughed when he took the tip between his teeth and shook it gently.

"You know, Cedar...."

"Umm." He released her finger. "What?"

"If love is a kind of terror at having this wonderful man love me, even though I think it'll never work, then maybe...."

"Oh, babe." He buried his face against her neck, holding her tightly. "Babe, say the words."

She caressed his hair. "Maybe, Cedar, I could love you... someday."

He sighed and relaxed against her. She knew he was disappointed that she was so hesitant, but they passed a close moment holding each other. His left hand moved in small circles on her belly, tracing the slight hollow, then slid over to explore the curve of one hip. Mesmerized, she closed her eyes. His right hand touched her shoulder, traced down her arm. At his circling touch, she found she had a sensitive area inside her elbow and down the protected side of her forearm.

"Will you tell me about your father?" she asked languidly.

"Someday."

"When?"

"Colleen, love me," he urged in a husky aroused voice. He nuzzled her breast. "Let me love you with all the tenderness I feel for you now."

"I need time," she sighed, but the sweetness of her denial invited rather than deterred him, and Cedar gathered her into his arms.

When he kissed her on the lips, urgency arrowed through her. She held him. Gentle as he was, Cedar was nonetheless direct; his own need stirred rapidly. She heard him moan as he explored the inside of her mouth, searching, mapping, kindling. Trailing his hand from her hip across her chest, he caught the collar of her blouse and parted the front, capturing a breast in his palm.

She cried out softly. She was full aware of the rituals preceding lovemaking, and she fought her body's signals. It was hellish to be so torn. She murmured, "I do want you Cedar, but—"

"Yes," he answered, and lowered his head to her breast.

She gasped. He was direct, too direct. As he traced a nipple, his tongue and his warm breath and his loving hands made her writhe. She felt the warning signals slipping back into her subconscious. She lost the will to roll away from him.

A hot languor sealed her muscles; her brain disengaged. The crescent of blue in the ceiling of the cave faded behind her closed lids, and she responded to the rising forces in her body by sinking her fingers into the luxuriant dark hair against her breast. Images of their bodies floating together at the hot springs, of him trailing kisses over her thighs, the night of the first storm...each memory made her long to give more to him. Each dart of heat through her thighs made it a matter of necessity that he continue his loving journey down her body.

He slid low, worshipping the pale flesh of her rib cage, her stomach, the curve of her hip, and below, as he unzipped her jeans. There was a part of Colleen that died then, and though she knew it, she grasped the knowledge as if through layers of gauze, layers of ecstasy. She murmured.

Cedar's hand found hers, twining her fingers securely in his. She moved, lifting her hips, and his low call of gratitude brought a veil of tears to her eyes. A subtle sob slid from her throat. Reviving from the floating plane of pleasure momentarily, she tried to grasp the meaning of the cry. Cedar kissed a soft inner thigh, his lips tender, caressing. Again her soft cry. Instinct and reason were at war in her, tearing her apart, even as her gentle lover healed her loneliness and despair. But he was unaware that anguish mingled with the waves of pleasure.

His free hand slid across her stomach, warm and searching. Finding her breast, he again sighed his satisfaction, the loving murmur blending with the drip of water and the faraway rush of a stream. This time, aware of her mind's betrayal, Colleen swallowed her hot salty cry, unwilling to stop him, refusing to play the wanton tease. Trembling with tension and the rippling sensations Cedar coaxed from her body, she fought to surrender her mind to the pleasure. *Yes,* she thought, beginning to move against the pressure and probe of his lips, tongue, hands—and still a sob echoed against the walls of the ice cave, primal with anguish, guttural with aborted desire.

Cedar stilled instantly. He kissed her thigh and shuddered. "Colleen?" he asked in a voice like wind.

The tears ran, and she held her breath, embarrassed, tremulous, wanting to hide the shame of failing him. *My mind has betrayed my body,* she thought. She wanted him desperately. Yet she rejected his presence in her life. She had let him make love to her. She squeezed his hand so hard her fingernails bit into his flesh, yet he returned the pressure lovingly—making her rejection of him even more painful.

She gasped then, the torrent of tears unleashed from a parched throat. "I'm sorry," she said in a watery voice. "Sorry, Ced, so sorry."

"Hey, babe, easy," he murmured, concerned, sliding up her body and wrapping her in his arms.

"I'm—I just can't, Cedar." She tried to stop the tears by pressing her face against his tan shirt, her body a rigid line of unspent arousal.

His own arousal had to be equally painful. Her guilt deepened. His flesh through the shirt trembled, and his legs trembled against hers. She squirmed in self-disgust. "I'm sorry," she whispered again.

He brought a set of knuckles beneath her chin. "Sorry, nothing," he said, making her look up at him. The perfume of her body surrounded them. "Hey, Freedom." He smiled encouragingly. He kissed her nose.

"Don't cry, heart. We'll take time. It was selfish of me, and I'm sorry, too. I was just in this great rush to show you I loved you. I've never been the calculating type—degree in economics or not. I live through my emotions, and this time they gave me the wrong signals too fast. Okay? Dry your tears? We'll start over, love. We've got lots of time."

"You promise you don't think I'm some kind of tease leading you on? I wasn't, Cedar. This wasn't expected."

"You know what I think?"

"What? I need a shrink?"

"Nope. I think you need a decent meal and some time to relax. You're trying to take on too much at once. We'll talk at lunch. What do you think?"

"I think...you're about the most gallant frustrated lover a woman ever had. If I had the slightest control over the situation, I'd love you this instant."

"Freedom, I'll only ask one thing of you, and then we'll leave."

She looked worriedly at him. "What's that?"

"Right here." He pointed to his cheek.

She peered at him. "Where?"

"Here. I want a kiss, right here."

"Oh!" Catching on, she cuffed him lightly on the arm. Then she leaned close and pressed a kiss of grateful affection on his cheek.

CHAPTER THIRTEEN

"ERNIE WON'T MIND if you borrow a clean shirt," said Cedar, his hands busy on the sleek wooden wheel and his eye on the depth gauge as he maneuvered the *Dart* away from the rock ledge. "There are towels in the low cupboard by the galley sink. Sorry I didn't remind you to bring a change of clothes."

She glanced at her black-and-green plaid blouse. "This will do. I'll be out of the shower in time to help with lunch. Sure you don't mind if I leave you alone to find a mooring?"

"No problem, darl-link-k," he said, slipping into Dracula. He winked at her. "Perhaps I vill see you before you dress again, eh?"

"No chance, Dracula. One slice on this pearly-white throat is enough." She pointed to the cut on her jaw. Then she teased, "You have a lock on the bathroom door?"

He smirked and said nothing.

"Depraved, sea captain, depraved...." As she was turning toward the companionway stairs, she shook her head in mock disgust. "One-track mind."

She heard him say, "When it comes to you," but she ignored the comment and ducked down the stairs to the galley. "You can use my robe, if you want!" he shouted when she'd reached his bedroom door. "It's in my locker!"

Smiling, she pulled open his wardrobe compartment. The faint scent of woods and manly exertion reached her. Wools and cottons in bright green, vibrant red, plaids, solids—she enjoyed a private glimpse at the simple garments Cedar wore in the fishing trade. A few of the wool shirts had a tailored, expensive look, patterns matched at the shoulder seams and hems turned by an exacting hand. It was silly, she knew, but she felt something very personal, seeing the neatly hung shirts, jeans, sweaters. Even if she passed by him on a street in some foreign city years from now, she would remember this small intimacy.

She sighed. At some time in the future, she'd want another chance with this man who said her hair reminded him of blood rubies in sunlight. And that was the problem. When she'd told him "someday" maybe she could love him, she hadn't meant in the next week or two. He wasn't the type to wait around. He was too full of life, living too close to the edge of the present. And she was still stuck in the past. Regret teased her thoughts as she took his thick kelly-green bathrobe from a peg.

As she was closing the door, a cream-toned scrap of paper tacked to the wood caught her gaze. She read the simple blue-ink printing:

Live now in splendor, for tomorrow lacks wealth.
Live with dignity, for your memory survives you.
Live with exuberance, for this moment is life.
Celebrate life.
Tomorrow is empty.
Tomorrow is only a dream.
Tomorrow can be nothing until you live it.

Something possessed her to press her face into the soft green robe, and she inhaled the male scent of Cedar McClintock as if she had little time left to breathe.

THE HOT STING of the shower let her forget, for a time, her inadequacies and problems. Standing in the tiny cubicle, head bowed and eyes closed, streams of water beating on the back of her neck, she felt her muscles loosen and relax. The water sheeted from her arms and thighs. Mist swirled, cleansing her pores, heating her skin. The faint vibration of the *Dart*'s engine lent the ritual an exotic mood. She thought of the creaking hand pump in the *Sparrow*'s galley, the kettles of water she'd boiled to take the chill off the sinkful of bathwater she used as often as time permitted. She luxuriated in the change.

Beginning to soap her body, she chuckled in pure delight. There had been some changes in her life, all right. Her private bath, off the bedroom at Clifden Moor, had never meant that much to her. She had taken for granted the soft pink towels and the brass repoussé sink with its patterns of swans. Now she felt pampered because she could shower in a three-cubic-foot enclosure aboard a fishing boat. Quite a change, indeed.

But remembering where she was urged her to hurry. Even a troller with four poles astride and chemically coated bench cushions didn't carry the Mississippi River in its water tank.

When she'd finished her shower, she found a small portable hair dryer on a metal hook near the mirror. It was so steamy in the tiny bathroom she couldn't see her hair, so she dried most of the moisture, borrowed a man's brush that hardly penetrated her mane and settled for a damp, semismooth hairstyle. At some point in the hour Cedar had anchored up. The deck swayed without the throaty rumble of the diesel. Spices filtered into the bathroom; Colleen's stomach growled. Wrapped in Cedar's robe, she opened the door and stepped into the bedroom to dress.

The far door stood ajar. She could see a long jean-clad leg and half of Cedar's tan shirt. His pectoral muscles bulged against the cotton as he leaned across the table, evidently distributing place settings. Silverware clinked against glass. He was the most domestic male she'd ever known, she mused. Probably got it from living with a mother who worked twelve hours a day.

She realized she knew next to nothing about Cedar. Evidently in that regard she had adopted the habits of the fleet. Fishermen were a cliquish, private lot. They never asked questions about your background, but if you wanted to offer a tidbit, they were all ears. Cedar had made love to her in an ice cave, and she didn't even know how he spent his winters, except for the hectic travel schedule. That was carrying fleet etiquette too far. She'd have to ask him more about his family, discover what a conference on corundum was like, find out why he hated his father. She wasn't the only one dealing with skeletons in the closet. Cedar had a few rattling at him now and then.

Silently she moved toward the door.

"How was it?" Cedar popped his head inside the room, a grin spreading across his face when he saw her. "Wow, angel, you look yummy in green. And I'm starved."

She came to the door, started to close it. "Degenerate!" She smiled.

His arm snaked through the opening, and he pulled her toward him.

"Cedar, c'mon, truce."

"Don't get excited, now. I'm just kissing you hello." He gave her one of his smacking kisses on the lips, then turned her loose.

The contact still managed to put jets under her nerves. She gave him a cocky look. "What's this hello business? What are you going to do for ten days at a stretch when I'm out fishing?"

"Go nuts." He grinned again as if it wouldn't be a terrible hardship. His light mood made it easy to play his game.

"You can call me up, then."

He ran a light finger down her chest to the valley between her breasts, making her shiver. When he glanced at her, knowing she reacted to his touch, he said softly, "Oh, angel, I'll want to do a hell of a lot more than call you on the radio. I'll go crazy waiting till the first closure."

"That black-out you mentioned. When?"

"The season closes for ten days starting July 1."

She nodded. "It's going to kill Marion, but to me the idea of ten days of free time sounds heavenly. Too bad the salmonberries aren't ripe in early July. I can't go home without picking some of those huge berries I've heard about."

"There'll be at least one more closure later in the summer. Let's don't waste this first closing, huh? We'll see some country, you and I. Cruise over to Juneau, maybe swing down to Ketchikan? How about—" He stood up, emphasizing the difference in their height, and his voice fell and rose, resonant with enthusiasm. "Freedom, we could fly to Seattle for a few days. Yeah! See your dad and meet his future missus—I'm positive that's part of what's bothering you—and once you see what a great gal she is, why, you and I could have a regular vacation together. I want to show you this special diamond, this marquise cut with the sky in it, Colleen, and maybe see a ballet or something. God, I haven't seen a play or a ballet in, must be seven years. What do you say?"

She stared at him, her mouth agape. He was presumptuous and charming and so perceptive that she could feel her own transparency. She wanted to hug him... and to slap him. "Cedar, we can't just go traipsing off on a vacation together!"

"Why not?"

"Because! We've just been through all that—back at the ice field. And you don't have to wait for me to go fishing...you're already nuts!"

His merry belting laughter filled the quarters and made her ears buzz. Smiling quizzically, she watched him, liking the way his wide mouth tilted, liking the boyishness of one hand pressed against his chest, as if he were trying to hold the hilarity inside. When he finally settled down enough to talk, he sang, "I'm going to make you love me," and closed the door. She could still hear him singing as she began to pull on her jeans.

IT WAS WHILE DRESSING that she found the financial papers on the *Dart*.

In a careless gesture she swung her green plaid shirt over her shoulders, and the sleeve swept the nest of papers above Ernie's bunk, sending them floating to the floor. She bent to gather them. As she buttoned her shirt one-handed, hurrying because she was starved, she scanned the top sheet. It was a promissory note spelling out principal-and-interest payments on an enormous sum, and she quickly turned to stack it with the rest on the shelf. But a firm black signature jumped into sight. Cedar Cleary McClintock, legal owner of the *Dart*. The fine print said Ernie Esau would take possession of the vessel once he'd paid the final balance, which was due the coming October. Feeling ill at ease for snooping, she replaced the contract.

Again she felt a nudge of curiosity. Unless Cedar had saved his earnings from several years of fishing, he'd never be in a position to swing such generous financing. But what right did she have to ask him questions about his business, she chastised herself. What right—when she wasn't going to be involved with him?

She joined Cedar in the galley and helped him serve steamed jumbo Alaskan shrimp, which he'd obtained from a passing boat out on the grounds. Colleen could hardly restrain herself from sampling the musky-smelling, pink-veined succulent-looking—she'd better get a handle on her manners, she told herself, glancing out the wide window behind the table. Another glacier and the thick rain forest barely registered. Cedar set a bowl of carrots julienne on the table, bright, sweet-smelling orange slivers in sauce. Colleen's mouth watered. She turned to Cedar and said urgently, "What can I do to help?"

"Take this platter of brown rice, then sit down, if you will. I've got everything pretty much under control."

While she complied, trying not to gaze longingly at

the food, he opened two bottles of beer and poured them
into glasses before seating himself next to her at the table.
She shifted uncomfortably when his elbow grazed her rib
cage. His touch quite miraculously drove food from her
mind.

There was a lot they should discuss, she knew. As
friends, of course. Cedar had been a major part of her
life for weeks and she didn't know even the basics
about him, even what he liked to do for fun. In addition, she had promised to tell him a great deal. She
realized she wouldn't be able to leave this luncheon
without his insisting on an explanation for her behavior in the cave. That little fact kept her appetite further at bay.

As he liberally peppered his rice and carrots, she
glanced out the window. The *Dart* lay abeam the Fairweather Range, directly across the water from a glacier
that reflected like a wavering ghost in the inlet. To the
north, mountains ran like whipped meringue into the
distance, towering over the boat. Clouds still wove
among the peaks, leaving small patches of blue sky scattered overhead. The white moisture of Alaska was so
different from the blue haze of Seattle, with its thousands of wood fires.

"It's the most gorgeous country I've ever seen," she
said, reluctant to dwell on personal issues. "No wonder
Ernie gave up stateside cities for this."

"Hmm." Cedar bent to kiss her cheek. "Eat hearty. I
ought to get the boat back to him before he sends out a
search party."

She willed him to look up at her. "Cedar? By mistake
I found a loan document back there in the bedroom."
She sampled the carrots, hoping he wouldn't be angry.

The sugared sauce jolted her taste buds, and she took another bite.

Cedar paused briefly on his way to a drink of beer. Then he took a swallow and set down the glass. He wiped the corner of his mouth with a napkin. "No big deal," he said, picking up his fork. "Keep what you know to yourself, though. I don't advertise our setup."

"The fact that you own the *Dart*, you mean? I'm sorry I snooped. It was accidental. . .Cedar Cleary."

He gave her a chastising look. "Nobody uses my middle name, love. Ced's fine. Or Cedar."

She smiled. "You hardly limit yourself to Colleen."

"That's because you're too many kinds of wonderful for one name to do you justice." His grin was charming.

Too close to personal issues, she thought. "Why do you keep your deal with Ernie quiet?"

He shrugged. "He's so attached to the *Dart*. I knew him from my days with Marion, and he and I went to Seattle together after the season one year. You get to looking at boats, you know—sizing up the lines, figuring the hold capacity, arguing about the benefits of one pole style over another. The *Dart*'s a Finn-built boat. Ernie just flat fell in love with her the minute he saw her."

"And the money was tight?"

He chewed a shrimp; she tasted one of her own. Heaven! The sweet meat reminded her of lobster with the slightly crunchy texture of a cucumber. She devoured another while Cedar explained about the finance contract.

"I needed a tax shelter at the time. We worked out payments." He glanced at her. "Besides, it guaranteed me a good boat and a steady skipper for the fishing seasons, without the responsibility of maintaining her during the winter. Ernie's a fixer-upper guy, smart about diesel engines. And he matches Marion for knowing where to find the fish. It was perfect.''

"The deal left you free to do your own thing in the off-season?"

"Uh-huh."

He forked half a prawn into his mouth, effectively curtailing her questions, so Colleen devoted herself to the pleasant task of eating the best meal she'd had in months. They sustained an easy silence for a while.

Swallowing the slightly bitter beer, Colleen again wondered about the side of Cedar McClintock she didn't know. He had made light business of the loan to Ernie. Yet she realized he had given Ernie a rare opportunity to make the most of his fishing abilities. Many of the boats in the fleet showed far more age than the *Dart*, and while some of the trollers plying southeast waters had more length, the comely *Dart* took your breath away when her poles were down and the white mountains and a bit of blue showed through the rigging. Any fisherman would be proud to own the *Dart*. It was no wonder Cedar expected Ernie to send a rescue party if they were late getting back.

If they had to hurry, she mused, finishing off her rice and shrimp, there was no reason to fear a long discussion with Cedar. That brought her confidence up a notch, more in keeping with the adrenaline pumping through her body every time he brushed her hand or challenged her to look at him. She finished her beer, thinking fast.

She had no illusions now about the difficulty of keeping her emotions in line where he was concerned. She forced herself to reflect on that embarrassing incident in the ice cave. With the distance of time and a good meal, she realized Cedar had nearly prevented her from continuing her tough uphill trek to maturity and moral strength. She had nearly slid back down to temporary gratification. Then some inner question had blocked her giving.

She had given freely to Alec, but she had learned by losing him that relationships had to have more than fun and pleasure to make them long lasting. She'd come to Alaska to learn to be strong—in every way. She was a grown woman with goals, not a college deb with parties on her mind. But being tough, she realized, included more than the strength to heft forty-pound salmon all day.

She glanced at Cedar as he lifted his napkin to his lips. Being tough also meant shoring herself up so she'd be fresh and strong for a man like him someday, a husband like him. It wouldn't be easy. She couldn't control what he said to her, coaxing, loving, playful comments full of innuendo about their physical future together. If she survived this single day with him, she thought, turning away, it would be a miracle. She began to plan to ask him so many questions, he would find it impossible to quiz her about her emotional frigidity.

"Delicious," she pronounced, pushing back her plate and smiling at him. "So you fish every summer with Ernie, do you? Plan to continue with him after the boat's paid off?"

He pulled at his chin in serious thought. "I don't know," he said slowly, leaning back and taking a swig of beer. "His last payment is due, let's see...."

"October," she supplied.

He gazed into her eyes. "October."

"Sorry. I wouldn't ordinarily have remembered, except it's my birthday month. And that neat signature of yours had me intrigued." To keep the mood light, she gave him a roguish look. "Locked my eyes right to the page."

He slid his arm around her shoulders. "A martin couldn't be more crafty."

"What—" Her exhilaration at his touch stalled her for a moment, but she hammered out the next question. "What will you do next year, Cedar?"

"He'll still need a puller. I'll probably stick with Ernie. What about you? Coming back to Marion?"

"You know, I wouldn't mind. But maybe Mike will be well by then."

"No chance."

She looked quickly at him, her own problems forgotten. "What do you mean? Is he dying?"

Cedar nodded reluctantly. "It's possible. He's pretty torn up, Colleen. He faded out on us twice, and they brought him back. Yet every time they think he's strong enough to withstand surgery, he gets pneumonia or some kind of infection. He was a strong kid, but that bear just about did him in. It was awful."

"Poor Marion," she said softly. When he remained silent, gazing at the mountains, she slipped out of the booth and began clearing the table. She filled the sink with sudsy dishwater. Cedar sighed and stood up. He came to the sink, took up a cotton towel and waited beside her until she handed him a rinsed dish.

"Marion ever mention the incident to you?" Cedar asked.

She shook her head. "She talks all around the incident. It seems to me she's trying to accept the loss of her family by telling stories about how great they were."

"What kind of stories?"

"Oh, like talking about her life as a child, when her baby sister, Alexie, and her parents died, and Mike finding his dad drowned in Ketchikan—things like that. She's almost eulogizing them, as if to remind herself they're really gone. Trying to face the fact that she's really alone, maybe. But she doesn't talk about the accident."

"She thinks she caused the accident, that's why," he said, stacking the plates into a wood cabinet. "Feels to all intents and purposes she killed her own son."

Colleen stiffened. Turning to him, she said in a low voice, "What are you trying to say?"

"Just that she'd unloaded the rifle before he took it into the woods. Went walking, I guess, looking for wood. I don't know. Mike had no protection when that sow tore into him."

She whispered, "Why, Cedar? Why did Marion do that?"

"She'd cleaned it, is why. And when she realized he'd gone off with ammo in his vest and none in the gun, she ran into the woods to find him.... " He leaned on the counter for a moment, tense, gazing at his knuckles, then finally looked at Colleen. His face was grim. "She shot the bear with her own gun, shot the cub, too, out of hysteria, but it was too late. The sow and Mike were all wrapped up together, Mike crushed under the bear, blood everywhere—aw, God, a mess!"

Her eyes wide, her shoulders rigid, she stammered, "Were you—did you hear the shots?"

He flung the dish towel into a corner. "No, dammit! No, she and Mike were loners, Colleen. They didn't need anyone else once he was capable on the boat. That's why I left the *Sparrow* and went with Ernie. I bunked with Marion and Mike when I was in town, but that was it. She—" Cedar's eyes seemed to bore holes in the cabinets. He said through clenched teeth, "She brought him down out of the woods by herself. Had to load him in the skiff, then run him back out to the boat and get him up the ladder before she could call for help. There were no planes in the area, so she tried to hold the boy together until one arrived. A pilot finally brought them to the hospital in Juneau. From there it was on to Seattle and pretty much a hopeless situation. It damn near killed her, too. You can see the damage to her personality. It's like she's taking on the world, and no one damn well better try to give her a hand."

She understood. Cedar saw Marion working herself to death, as his mother had. And like his mother, the skipper refused his help—his help and his money and even his advice about danger. She caressed his arm. "Cedar, is there any chance Mike will get better? Will he ever fish again?"

He shook his head.

She gripped his arm, and through the cotton shirt his flesh felt vital and warm. Fighting a reaction that had nothing to do with her concern for Marion, she inclined her head to indicate her sympathy and turned away to drain the sink. She diverted her thoughts to the boy. Mike must have had to face the darkness in a worse way than what her mother had suffered. Two, three, maybe four times that healthy young man had had to face death, was still facing death. And what about Marion? What inner power allowed her to plow through day after day, knowing her son wasn't ever going to be the same, no matter how many fish she found?

"I'm glad you told me, Cedar," she said softly. She wiped the stainless-steel bowl and wrung out the sponge. "I don't think Marion could, not this one. Oh, she tells Tlingit Indian myths sometimes at night. Customs, too. The uncle of a child was the one who bathed a baby daily in the sea, winter or summer, Marion told me. That was because it was thought the mother or father would be too soft, would give in to the baby's wailing and spoil him. They were big on toughness, and Marion's as tough as they come, but she couldn't have explained about the bear. It's too horrible."

"I figured if she hadn't told you by now, I'd better. Knowing might give you a way to be patient with her. I was sure hoping she'd get it out there in plain daylight, though. As it is, the facts are boiling inside that tough hide, liable to bust her apart."

"If she could cry...."

"Marion? Never. Sign of weakness."

"That Tlingit training. I'd forgotten. What about her and Ernie? They seem like they're trying to get together, but too many differences stand in the way. He could probably help her if she'd let him."

He looked at her as if to say, *I'd help you if you'd let me.* She glanced away, uncomfortable.

Cedar edged her toward the wheelhouse, where he stationed her in the captain's chair and stood between her knees. After she'd spent several seconds staring around the room at the equipment jammed into every available inch of wall or ceiling, he took her chin in his hand and said, "What about us, Colleen? Do too many differences stand between us?"

Trying to maintain her equilibrium against the forces revving inside her, she asked hastily, "What about Ernie? Do you think he'd be good for Marion?"

"I do. He's got a heart from here to Seattle." He leaned back against the wheel, his long legs pressing between her knees, a cruel distraction. "It would take an act of God to bring them together, though. Literally, a catastrophe."

"Unfortunately I think you're right. But Marion's had enough pain and too much unhappiness. She deserves a little fun, not more tragedy."

"I shouldn't remind you.... I shouldn't, but I will. The same could be said of you. What gives, Colleen?"

She glanced through the windshield. "Does it have to be now? Couldn't we go on talking about other people's lives and keep things above the gut level?"

"Nope, we can't. We've got to talk."

"What about your father?" she countered.

He took her hands, one at a time, and placed them on his hips. "We're talking about you this time. My time will come. Why did you tear yourself away from that great clinch we were enjoying this morning?"

There had been only a flicker of emotion when she had mentioned his father. He had quickly resumed his light tone, obviously trying to make it easy for her to explain. It wasn't easy, she discovered. "Ask me a question, Cedar. The words are stuck inside me. Feelings have never been easy for me to express. I've always had to keep things in a little box inside my head, one part of me outwardly gay and carefree, the ugly unhappy side hidden.'' She looked up at him and saw his warmth. ''Help me begin.''

''Collie, between people who care about each other, everything they feel should be safe.''

''Are we people who care, Cedar? I mean, look at the facts—this friendship of ours is getting out of hand. It—it conflicts with what I'm trying to do here.''

''That's high school, babe. This is for grown-ups. Why did you have to keep the unhappy side hidden? What made you unhappy?''

''Everything.''

''Like what, for instance?''

''Well, not everything, I guess. I've had good friends, pretty clothes, fun times.'' Glancing at her blouse, she rubbed nervously at the lapel.

The words stuck again, the words about death and loneliness. Why? She'd learned so much about herself lately. Why did this area elude her?

Cedar caressed her hand, his fingers grazing the back of her wrist and tracing the fine bones there. Turning his hand, she bent her head and pressed her warm cheek against his open palm. ''We used to ride together,'' she said, clinging to him. ''In the summer the sun would burn our arms and bleach mother's hair nearly white. Dad's face would get red, but by dusk he'd be brown again. We'd sit in the big den, the three of us, reading and talking and telling jokes and drinking coffee. I really had a good sense of humor then. Funny, it seems to be gone.''

She felt his other hand touch her hair. She had left it loose, and the honey-red waves hung like a curtain around her bowed head, cutting out the chrome and wood of the cabin.

"Freedom, I think you're underestimating yourself. You do it all the time."

She raised her head to see his expression. It was still tender. "I don't."

"Sure do. Anyone who could relate all that nonsense about a woman on top of the Capitol and then wrestle around the deck of a grimy fishing boat—hell, isn't that a sense of humor?"

She smiled.

"N'est-ce pas?" he urged.

"Oui, mon capitaine. If you say so." She let his hand go. Glancing outside, she noted the lowering cloud bank. The afternoon was slipping away. What could she tell him to end this inquisition? The light banter was bound to wear away eventually, and then she'd be in tears or shouting out her pain again. What kept her here talking with him, trying to give a part of herself, when it was so uncomfortable? She sighed in frustration.

"Did your dad send you up here?" he probed softly, continuing that pliant caress on her hair.

"In a way. He said, 'Get ye to your man, daughter. Leave me to my memories.' I chose Alaska."

"What man?"

She heard the wariness in his question, and rose from the chair. Without looking at him, she stepped to the starboard window with the view. She studied it without seeing the mountains.

"No man," she admitted. She thought she heard a short relieved sigh from him. "At least," she added out of perverseness, sensing a solution to her dilemma, "not now. Not anymore."

"Meaning you left a boyfriend in Seattle when you came up here?"

She turned from the window to see his face. Cedar still leaned indolently against the dash, but one hand gripped the wheel with more strength than necessary. His eyes snapped with interest, or perhaps jealousy. She played on the latter.

"My ex-boyfriend is saving people in Brazil. I mentioned him to you at the ice field. I've toyed with the idea of joining him when I leave Alaska."

He leaned toward her. "But you said you wouldn't mind coming back to Marion. And you said 'ex.'"

"Right on both counts."

"I see." He folded his arms, but she wasn't disarmed. Tension filled the room. He said, "What could you learn in Southeast that you could bring with you to him? Is he in the ministry?"

"Education. Alec teaches people how to build a better life." *He failed to explain the technique to me,* she wanted to add. "What was your other question?"

"This isn't an inquisition, Colleen. We're working through some problems between us. Will you tell Alec about us?"

"Should I?"

He straightened away from the dash, and because his arms fell stiffly to his sides, she felt his anger and stepped back against the bulkhead.

"What the devil are you doing, Colleen? You know damned well I've laid my feelings for you on the line. I may be patient, but I'm not lily-livered. Do you want the damned relationship or not?"

Her feelings suddenly in chaos, she pivoted and stepped toward the aft door. The barbs had turned on her. He'd been honest and sensitive and patient with her, and she was so filled with the fear of loving him, of losing sight of her goals, that she'd walked right over his feelings. Used him. Deliberately hurt him. Her hand paused on the door, ready to pull it open and escape to the deck, but something held her in place. "Cedar, I'm sorry. I—I tried to tell you I wasn't ready. There isn't an 'us.' And no, no I didn't tell Alec. Not that it would have made a difference if I had."

She was pushing open the door when his hand gripped her shoulder. She whirled. His chest rose and fell against her breast, signaling his anger, and even now, through her desperation ran a current of need. The realization snapped her grip on patience. "Let it go, Cedar!" she cried, staring up at him. "It's no good! I can't be what you want me to be! I've been too many things to too many people who didn't really care, and done nothing about my own needs. I don't even know what those needs are. I want to know. And—and no kiss or wild embrace will change me, so don't, please. You couldn't give me enough time. I just don't fix that easy!"

"You never gave it a chance," he shouted, his cheeks reddening.

"'Chance'!" She laughed bitterly. "You never gave me the chance I came here for. You threatened to hound my every waking moment, remember, that day on the docks? And then you changed your tactics. No more threats as if I were the enemy—oh, no!" Her breath came in gasps. She clutched the ironlike hand on her shoulder and twisted it away. "The new ploy was to seduce me with crazy talk about love. Passion. Lurid propositions!"

He sucked in his breath, but cornered, she rammed home the hurt. "Chances, Cedar? The only chance I've had for freedom since I've known you is out on the *Sparrow*, and I'd hardly call that the wide-open spaces. It's a real prison, Cedar, and the jailer is as likely as you to drive me crazy!''

She turned away, but he grabbed her arm. She yanked free. ''Take me back to the *Sparrow*.'' Her chin rose, and she didn't care a hoot for his opinion of it. ''This discussion is over!''

He stared down at her, his face tight with fury. After a brief moment he snapped, ''You bet!'' He brushed by her to slam open the door.

She grabbed her coat, shoved it on. She went aft and sat with her back to the wheelhouse, while the anchor winch creaked and whined. Cedar stomped back inside to start the engine. By the time they rejoined the fishing boats, she was cold. A dismal pain had settled deep inside her. Her gaze averted, she mumbled thanks and climbed over the side rail to the cluttered deck of the *Sparrow*. She was already lying on her bunk, her face to the wall, when the *Dart* pulled away.

CHAPTER FOURTEEN

"MIGHT AS WELL put a bunch of bears in a boat, teach 'em how to troll," Blue Harry grumbled, dragging a gunnysackful of clams up over the side rail of the *Dart*, where they'd been hung overnight to rid them of sand.

"Why's that?" Colleen asked, raising her voice over the loud country music coming from the radio. It was propped on the hatch of Blue's boat, *Diversion*, tied up next door. She grinned at Doc and J.T., standing against the *Dart*'s port rail, before turning back to Blue. Now he was complaining about the weight of the clams. He hadn't heard her question. "Why might we just as well teach bears to troll?" she repeated.

"I'm gettin' to it, I'm gettin' to it. Just hold your horses a minute while I get these clams started."

He slung the dripping molasses-brown bag to a plywood board protecting the hatch, thumped it, unwound the drawstring. He shrugged out of a thick waterproof coat to work in twill trousers, rubber boots and a shaggy thermal shirt that hugged his pooched-out belly. Grabbing an old case knife, he slid the blade between the halves of a clam shell; with a twist of his thick wrist he severed the muscle, flipped the clam body into his cupped palm, cut off the neck and rinsed away the viscera in a bucket of saltwater. Colleen, J.T. and Doc watched in fascination as Blue Harry chucked the shells into the strip of bay between the sterns of the *Dart* and the *Diversion*. Lyrics about roses in a glass of wine beside someone's bed moaned out over the water, guitar strumming punctuated by shells plopping. Shiny, sand-colored clams began to pile up in Blue's enamel bowl.

Blue paused to glance across the decks of the four boats tied beam to beam for today's party. Colleen and her companions followed his gaze.

Pelican's Lady, Doc's brown forty-foot troller, rocked at the far end of the line. They all knew Josh was belowdecks, sleeping off a whiskey binge. Josh's rowdy singing had echoed across the bay for half the night, and his off-key fraternity songs had fragmented Colleen's already restless sleep.

Blue Harry's gray beard bounced and his cheeks jiggled as he explained how difficult it was to keep good trolling crews. "Bears could catch on quicker'n some 'a these young kids, come up here to—" he concentrated for a moment on loosening the contents of a five-inch shell "—come up here to be macho and get stoned and all."

"Yep," Doc said in his characteristic monosyllable. He pulled the collar of his stained yellow coat around his sallow cheeks and looked across the decks of the four trollers, his gray eyes emotionless.

"Sure." Blue waved with the grisly knife, as if Doc had disagreed. "That college kid you got this year, Doc? That Josh boy? Hell, he drinks more'n he pulls fish. If he was my puller I'd 'a fired him, made him swim to shore."

"I had fish lying on my decks most of the season."

"That may be true, but I'd have made him quit the booze cold turkey, at least." Blue saluted with a beer he'd cached next to his mess of clams.

Colleen heard the rumble of a diesel engine. She glanced toward Cenotaph Island, and felt her stomach cramp. The *Sparrow* crept through the tide toward the flotilla of boats.

Marion would tie up on the starboard side of the *Dart*, headquarters for today's get-together, and then Cedar, Ernie and Marion would come aboard. It was the Cedar part, the idea of seeing him face to face, that had tightened Colleen's nerves. The fleet loved an argument too much. They might fuss around, poke fun, egg on the battle of wills. She and Cedar would have to pretend things were fine between them, of course. For Marion's sake.

Colleen had avoided Cedar all day yesterday, and today, when he'd organized a potluck for this afternoon, she had managed to avoid being a part of his tide-pool party, searching for edible seaweeds and other marine life. Instead, agreeing to go with J.T. to pick the wide leaves of the skunk cabbage, which they would wrap around garlic-spiced salmon steaks for the barbecue, she'd postponed the inevitable reunion. But with each warble of that smoky diesel engine, Colleen's brief peace grew more fragile.

She wondered if Cedar would revert to the insults of that first day in the harbor. She wondered if she could keep from saying she was sorry she'd failed him, hurt him, lied to him. Would she ever stop letting people down?

Blue's continuing harassment about Josh's drinking was also reminding her of her failure with her father, and she brought her gaze to the man shucking clams. "You can't force someone to quit," she said. "They'll just find a way to drink secretly."

One bushy eyebrow darted up. "Voice of experience?"

She shrugged. "Not personally. I just know someone who had a problem that way."

"Well." Blue returned to his chore, his beard bobbing in profile again. "Marion's better off with you, little as you are, than Doc, here, with that blond Atlas of his. You do more'n your share, for a little bitty mite."

A rush of pleasure made her smile. Compliments about fishing skills were hard won from these men. Her smile faded when she saw Cedar standing at the rail of the *Sparrow*, a line coiled in one hand, a bulging plastic bag in the other. As the boat pulled close to the *Dart*, Marion killed the engine.

Doc sauntered over to tie off Cedar's line, and J.T. shinnied his long length beneath stay lines to secure another line on the bows. Cedar leaped aboard the *Dart*.

Beneath the black Windbreaker he wore a blue-green sweater. The brilliant color underscored his black hair and dark eyes, making him look like a Spanish nobleman El Greco had painted against a moody sky. On his right hip the black-walnut hilt of a large knife gleamed. He was compelling.

For a sizzling moment Colleen met Cedar's gaze. The deck seemed to slip out from under her tennis shoes. She felt suspended. They hadn't faced each other since the day before yesterday, when he'd dropped her off on the *Sparrow*, and now he seemed equally spellbound by this moment of confrontation.

Before either of them could speak, the door of the *Sparrow* slammed open. Marion burst through, her chest arched beneath the red wool shirt, her cheeks ruddy, her jaw firm.

"Damned Finn!" Oblivious to her stunned audience, Marion waved angrily. "Spoutin' pretties and the Bible all in one breath! Makin' himself ridiculous!"

Momentarily diverted from Cedar, Colleen took a step toward her irate skipper. Blue stopped shucking clams to watch Marion strut around the deck. J.T. rubbed his bald scalp. Cedar and Doc stared.

A blur of white jettisoned out behind Marion. Stalking in time to the drumbeat of a fast country song, Ernie caught up to her and spun her around to face him. "You've got no call to be rude when I make a statement like that!" he shouted into her face.

"Statement!" She jerked away. "Is that the name for what you just said to me? 'Marion,'" she mimed in a voice unusually high and sweet, a voice that made Ernie pale. "'A woman like you ought to be looked after. Have somebody to lean on.' Gawd! Spare me! What'd'ya take me for, a bunny in the snow without fur?"

"I meant every word of it!"

"You don't say. Who d'you think rigged that busted line up on that pole, Finn? Me, that's who!"

Sputtering, Ernie mouthed silent retorts. He worried the zipper of his white jacket, patted his sprouts of snowy hair, obviously trying to contain his temper. Then his deep pulpit voice boomed at Marion. "Look at this junkheap! You call it rigged? Painted? This barge hasn't seen a paint brush in five years! And that Jimmy under the floor boards—" he jerked a thumb toward the engine room "—she puts out more smoke than a tugboat! Why don't you get out your tools and fix her, instead of forcing her to burn herself out? You're so blamed handy all by yourself!"

"Hoo-eee!" Blue hooted, grinning.

"She runs fine for her age!" Marion yelled at Ernie. "Ain't everybody can see her way clear to takin' loan money from a friend!" She hunched her shoulders toward the *Dart* and, presumably, Cedar. "Some of us 'a got more pride."

"Pride's the downfall of man!" Ernie snapped, his face now bright scarlet.

"You oughtta know," Marion retorted.

Cedar cleared his throat, trying to divert the fishing folk standing with mouths agape on the *Dart*. "Anybody start the barbecue yet?"

Blue tore his gaze away from the altercation, his hands full of clamshells. "I never would'a figured those two. Ernie and Marion, I mean. Hot damn!"

"About the barbecue. . . ?"

"Ah. . .no, Ced. Not yet. Doc's going to see to it. Doc?"

Doc turned his dull, gray-eyed stare on Blue. "Yeah?"

"You were gonna light the coals, weren't you?"

"Forget it!" Marion piped from next door, and Doc turned toward the sound.

Blue sighed testily. *"Doc."*

"Huh?" Doc looked around. "Oh."

With a regretful stare toward the bantam Ernie and his opponent, Doc crossed the deck and climbed aboard Blue's *Diversion*, where three wrought-iron cooking grills formed a black crown behind the radio. He began loading charcoal.

"Here," said J.T., approaching Blue with his own knife drawn from a hip sheath. "I'll give you a hand with these clams. We have butter to melt?"

"Two pounds of it in the hold over yonder," said Blue, digging his blade into a beige shell, all of a sudden acting very busy, trying to ignore the hushed tense voices of Ernie and Marion. "Everybody in Sitka hates bears, you know that?"

"'Everybody'?" said J.T. with a sincere attempt to show interest.

"That's a fact. Practically every family has had somebody either killed or maimed. Good-sized Alaskan brownie can drag off a full-grown moose, you know. I heard a Fish and Game fella once tranquilized a thirteen-hundred pounder and snuggled up to her for a photograph...pretty blond brownie. The bear's head tilted sideways, and her tongue slid across this fella's face. He thought he was in love till he smelled her breath." Blue teehee'd. "She'd been munching ripe salmon in Crazy Man River."

Cedar touched Colleen's arm. "Give me a hand with this stuff?"

She glanced at the plastic sack. She could hardly refuse. "Why not? Where to with the goods?"

"Inside. Ernie's got more work space in his galley."

She glanced over her shoulder. Marion had turned her back to Ernie, and he was making some kind of plea, his hands raised. Perhaps the little guy could break through that brittle shell, after all.

Cedar went to the pilothouse and slid open the door. Colleen walked inside, and the door slid closed just as she heard Blue tell J.T. that Alaska's coastal brown bears were the largest living carnivorous land mammals in the world. She would almost rather have faced one than spend these next few minutes secluded with Cedar.

He didn't once refer to personal feelings. And that,

for some vague reason, was nearly as disappointing as having to endure a showdown. Together they washed a bright green algae Cedar called ulva. Blanched in hot water, it tasted crunchy and salty. After sauteeing soft-shelled limpets in butter flavored with garlic, they arranged the mollusks on the green bed of ulva and set the dish in the oven to keep warm. They cleaned and stripped the long muscles from some sea cucumbers and fried them in butter, then added them to a chowder made of onion, salt-pork bits, rock cod that Ernie had speared near the mouth of Lituya Bay and milk. By the time the chowder was bubbling noisily, Colleen's mouth was watering, her stomach growling. And still Cedar remained polite and slightly distant.

"Cedar," she finally bolstered her courage enough to say, "about the other day...."

"Forget it, Freedom. I'm giving you space. Let's go topside and see if everything's ready. Grab that stack of paper napkins, will you?" Bowls and plates under his arm, he led the way to the deck. Mystified, Colleen followed him.

CEDAR UNRELENTINGLY PLAYED the complacent fishing buddy. "More coffee, Doc? Marion? Colleen?"

She was last on his list for everything, including polite conversation. Doc held Cedar's rapt attention with such phrases as "sure" and "yep" and "looks like the weather's settling some."

Disgusted, Colleen helped herself to the food and, despite the quarrel with Cedar, satisfied her ravenous appetite with chewy sweet clams dipped in butter. They were delicious, the best she'd ever tasted, but the salmon was the rarest fish delicacy she'd encountered anywhere in the world. Beneath the charred skunk-cabbage leaves the pink flesh remained moist, lightly flavored with fresh garlic and mixed spices and flaky. Instantly she thought of her father. He would really have enjoyed eating seafood right out of the water, and the old Sean Conaughy would have relished the sea stories and comradery of the fishermen. Perhaps she ought to write him. . . .

Chatting idly with Marion and J.T., she went on to the chowder. Halfway through it, she gave up. It was rich and filling, but her nervousness had caught up with her, unsettling her stomach. As the sun dropped behind Cenotaph, spreading a pale magenta film across the water, easy guitar music floated through the conversations, and Colleen grew moody.

The celebration lasted another forty minutes with no change in Cedar's attitude. Josh never made an appearance, no doubt to everyone's relief. Blue spotted a grizzly on the ridge above the boats. Everyone strained through the hazy light to see a brown blur with hulking shoulders as it disappeared into the woods.

The party began to break up. Evidently recovered from her argument with Ernie, Marion offered to wash everyone's pots and pans in the *Dart*'s roomy galley. She and Ernie spent a good hour together without serious argument—surely a record—while Colleen walked the decks of the three boats retrieving soiled plates and beer bottles from unlikely places. Cedar and the others filtered down into the fo'c'sle of the *Diversion* to play poker.

A sheet of pink clouds screened the late-setting sun. All Colleen saw of Cedar were tendrils of blue smoke from his pipe. Trailing out of the poker game and run-

ning right under her nose, the woodsy scent reminded
her of happier moments with the tall, dark-haired Irishman. She heard his mellow vibrant voice lift in laughter,
and indignant that she hadn't been invited into a game
evidently reserved for traditionalists like these fishermen, she climbed over the rail of the *Sparrow* and went
to her bunk.

Marion entered the chamber some time later and collapsed on her bed with the murmured complaint, "I
never ate so much of Alaska in one meal as I ate today.
Gawd!"

Colleen, wrapped in her blankets, drifted back to
sleep. She spent the night restlessly, in the half-wakeful
moments feeling like a child sent to bed in disgrace.
Seals barked, and the howl of a wolf floated across the
lagoon; anchor chains groaned, the *Sparrow* creaked in
the tide and the breakers outside seemed to growl more
softly with the passing hours.

The *Blue Sparrow* took the ebb tide out of Lituya the
next morning. En route to the Fairweather Grounds,
Colleen tucked down into the trolling cockpit, avoiding
most of the crosswind, and watched the gleaming white
peaks of the Fairweather Range recede. The sun had
finally burned away the overcast. The mountains,
slashed with dark ridges of forest and rock, towered
over the beach. To the north, Mount Fairweather
dominated the coastline, more than fifteen thousand
feet of timber and snow piercing the cold blue sky.
Behind the *Sparrow* the bluish-green water rolled away
with a glassy shine.

Each day in Alaska was more beautiful, the scenery
more magnificent, but each hour that passed brought a
deeper regret for the distance between her and Cedar.

Whereas she had once felt confined by the tiny fishing boat and trapped by Cedar's domination of her emotions, Colleen now felt the loneliness of her life-style and the limitlessness of the ocean. Cedar hadn't the slightest idea she was hurting because of this bid of hers for freedom.

She hurt inside. It was a physical pain, constant, with occasional needlelike spears when she remembered that straight nose of his and the clefted jaw and those restless eyes. A bit of heaven in that dark-eyed gaze, she recalled thinking on an earlier fishing trip.

Why couldn't she just relax and let the relationship happen? Why was it so important that she be morally tough enough to withstand his love? She had admitted she couldn't stand to lose him, as her father had lost his wife. But now that she'd faced that fear, why did it still outweigh her will to keep Cedar? She slumped down into the cockpit, the view forgotten.

He was so strong and self-reliant. But if he ever really needed her, would she fail him? She wasn't the disloyal type, so that wouldn't be a problem. Was he a womanizer? He'd said he wasn't; still, her father's image came to mind.

Frustrated because she'd had so few of her questions answered during those captive hours inside Lituya Bay, she frowned. She should ask the skipper about him, find out how to deal with him. She glanced over her shoulder. That was the way, of course! Ask Marion. Excitement filled her. What was wrong with asking right now, while the skipper was guiding the boat into the open sea? Colleen clambered out of the cockpit and raced for the wheelhouse. She'd lost so much time!

Pulling open the door, she said breathlessly, "Marion...."

Marion dropped the magazine she'd been reading and eyed Colleen narrowly. "Where's your hat?"

"The sun's out."

"Still. With your hair up like that you could get an infection in your ears. Close the door."

"Oh. Sorry." Colleen complied, then stood beside the woman, an awkward, expectant half smile on her lips. "Marion...I've been meaning to ask you about Cedar."

Marion looked her up and down, nodding to herself. "You're taken with him, ain't ya?"

"I—" She'd been in such a daze she'd forgotten to be careful of Marion's feelings. She glanced at the rusty anchor propped on the bow. Slowly she nodded.

"Thought so."

Colleen looked at her to take a reading; Marion seemed completely unimpressed.

"You...don't mind?"

"Why should I mind? You're grown-up. Long's it don't affect your work, it's none of my affair. He's a good man, damn good. And you seem to be—" Marion's gaze cut briefly into Colleen. Then with humor tilting her mouth, she turned back to the water "—okay, for a pip-squeak."

Colleen laughed. "You've got to admit, I'm not holding you back any. I mean, for a pip-squeak."

"That's a fact."

She sounded just like Blue, but it was as close to a compliment as Colleen had heard from the skipper. She let out a relieved breath. "Well, Cedar felt—that is, he's known you a long time, and, ah, he thought you'd be upset if I got to know—'' Her voice slipping away with the awkwardness of the explanation, she breathed, ''got to know a man while I was here.''

''Yeah, he told me he warned you off guys.''

''He did? He told you that? But I can't believe he'd just throw it up in your face like that! I assumed it wasn't to be spoken of!''

''Now simmer down, Conaughy. Geez, you're jumpin' like a parakeet with a cat on his tail. What's not to be spoken of?''

''Well, Mike. Cedar said he didn't want you reminded of how Mike would have been—you know, healthy and having girlfriends and all.''

She stopped, because Marion was looking dumbfounded again.

''What the pitch pine are you talking about, girl?''

Colleen put a hand to her breast, as if that would quiet the slow regretful thud of her heart. ''Mike,'' she said weakly. ''Cedar. Me. . . .''

''Ced just wanted you for himself,'' Marion said in a hoarse tone.

''*He what?* He knows better than to try to smother me, Marion!''

''What's going on, Conaughy? Are you saying McClintock was trying to protect me? From something I might take offense to?''

Cedar had been right all along. And now Colleen had inadvertently hurt Marion. Regretting her immature handling of matters, she nodded.

''Well, for Pete's sake, he's got nerve!'' Marion's face reddened. ''What is *with* all these people around here? Do they think I'm made of glass? Dammit, I may be losing my boy, but I don't cotton to them pussyfootin' around like I killed him, or something!''

Marion's breath drew in sharply. She hadn't intended to say "killed," but the guilt was written there. Her mouth caved in, puckered. The pain hit her again, and her eyes narrowed as she bit down on the pain.

"You didn't!" Colleen gripped the woman's shoulder. "Marion, it wasn't your fault!"

Silence hung for a moment. Marion turned, her expression haunted. "Yes, it was," came the ragged reply.

Colleen gestured helplessly, whispering, "It was an accident. A terrible, terrible accident."

Slowly Marion breathed again. Her eyes widened; her fingers relaxed on the wheel. She cleared her throat. "Ah...what d'you want to know about Ced, Conaughy?" She looked away. "Where he was born? That no-good Irishman was sired in Portsmouth, New Hampshire, I think. Showed me a picture of a gravestone dated 1829 once. One of his relatives way back, involved in the building of sailing ships, was what he said."

Colleen relaxed. The storm in Marion had blown itself out. The skipper seemed to require an explosion at least once a day; now that it was over, and far more quickly than usual, she could function again. And now that Colleen had relaxed, she felt a nudge of jealousy that Marion would know so personal a detail as the McClintock gravesite in Portsmouth.

"I thought he was from somewhere on Lake Michigan."

"Was. His daddy moved down there on a project to do some building in the Lake Forest area—some wealthy people's homes—and Ced's ma had the chance to visit her sister at the same time."

"He has family still down there?"

"Yeah." The engine sputtered. Marion checked the depth gauge, fiddled with the choke on the dash, adjusting the fuel mixture. She looked at Colleen. "Hates her, though."

"Who?"

"His aunt. Alicia, I think he calls her. Without the 'aunt.' What else d'you want to know?"

"Why does he hate her?"

"He never said. There's small bits of Ced McClintock that he keeps hidden. That's one of 'em."

Her brow furrowed, Colleen thought that over. *His father, too. He keeps his father hidden away.* "Did he ever discuss his father?"

"Nope. That's another one of those small bits I mentioned. Why don't you ask him this stuff?"

"Well.... Well, I will, Marion, soon as we're talking civilly again. I'd best let you get back to your reading. Think I'll do the same. Those fish'll be thick on the lines, just like you told Cedar, and I won't have a chance again for days."

Marion nodded absently and picked up the tattered issue of *Alaska Magazine*. She began to split her attention between the waves and an article on Tlingit Indian artwork. Colleen peeked over the skipper's shoulder. Some of the ceremonial masks looked as primitive and full of aggression as the eagle mask hanging on the wall in Marion's living room in Pelican. Well, if her culture gave her strength, Colleen thought, okay.

Quietly she went below to find Hawthorne's *The House of the Seven Gables*, an 1851 edition from her mother's library. She took the book with her to the trolling cockpit, where she scooted down and opened the faded red cover.

With the breeze freshening and the white mountain peaks gathering on the horizon, she began to read of an old woman named Hepzibah, inside a gabled house with an elm rooted beside the front door—a lady whose wonderful misunderstood heart was locked up inside her aging body; whose spirit, no matter how desperately she tried, would not break free of that brittle body.

THE DAYS PASSED quickly, and when Marion took the *Sparrow* out of the Fairweather Grounds on the last of June without a word to anyone, Colleen hadn't energy left to argue about the sudden departure. The sun didn't set until midnight now, and Marion took full advantage of the extended hours to catch fish. With little hearty food and the long hours of work, Colleen's strength ebbed quickly. Today they had been up and working hard for thirteen hours.

At least the hold of the *Sparrow* was packed to the hatch cover with king salmon, eliminating the possibility of further fishing. Marion was having a difficult time holding in a smile. It reached her lips unbidden, at odd unexpected moments, as she headed south in the long twilight of full summer.

"Some coffee?" Colleen offered, wondering why Marion didn't just dance around the wheelhouse and be done with it.

A grin spread over Marion's face; wordlessly she shook her head. Colleen laughed, and for a brief moment a kind of affection lit Marion's eyes. Then she was busy with the boat again.

Angling the bow into a small cove Colleen didn't recognize, the skipper anchored just off the mouth of a
stream that rumbled out of the rocks and cedar trees. A
couple of fathoms beneath the hull the sea floor shone
golden. Curious about their mission, Colleen studied
the shore.

Tucked back into the alders that bounded the banks
of the river, a split log cabin lay graying in the evening
sun. A thin stream of smoke fed into the sky. In an adjacent clearing, knee-high green grass choked the door
of a sagging smaller structure with a black smoke ring in
the roof, presumably one of the smoke houses Colleen
had seen up and down the coast. Crows cawed, swooping from trees to stream and hopping across moss-
covered logs. The place felt lonely.

Marion off-loaded the dorg. She told Colleen to get
into it, so Colleen urged her legs to move, forced her
aching arms to support her weight as she slid down into
the wobbly skiff. She heard the hatch scrape open. Marion returned with a thirty-pound king strung through
the mouth and gills by heavy twine. She lowered it to the
bottom of the skiff. Without an explanation, Marion
closed the hold and joined Colleen. The skipper rowed
toward the log house. Colleen wondered how she found
the strength.

They landed with a bump and scratch on the rock-
lined beach, and Colleen saw a fishing net draped across
the grass, drying, filling the air with the sour smell of
evaporating saltwater.

"Stay here," Marion said, hiking the salmon over her
shoulder. "Hin Gokl can't take the shock of strangers
in her midst without proper warning."

"Who's Hin Gocle?"

"Gokl," Marion clarified, twisting her tongue effortlessly around the strange syllables. "Hin Gokl is the Tlingit word for River Swan."

Colleen climbed out of the rowboat and stood on the rocks, the bow line in her hand. What she wanted to ask was how Marion could possibly part with one of her king salmon.

"She's of the Eagle clan, same as me." Marion hiked up the salmon again to keep the tail out of the gravel. "Hin Gokl married a man from the Raven clan, as custom dictates. One day he went into the woods to hunt deer, and he never came back. She's been here by herself ever since. People stop by now and then to help her out, soon's they have a surplus. She mostly lives off the land."

Colleen glanced at the coffee-brown fishing net. "Cedar never mentioned River Swan. I've never heard anyone mention her."

"Tlingit people—I mean, her relatives—stop by."

"I see." Up in the clearing rusty hinges grated, and Colleen saw a dark slit where the door had parted from the molding. "Poor River Swan," she murmured. "Living alone out here."

"P'shaw! She's happy. A bear came in and cleaned out her root cellar the same day her husband left, but a year later. The bear was big and dark haired like her husband, and he took such a liking to the root cellar, he wintered over in it. Been other bears after that one died, some seven years later. Hin Gokl thinks it's her old man, comin' back every winter to keep her company."

"Is he there now?" Colleen asked, looking with awe and worry toward the cabin.

"Not this time of year. He'll be out around the other

salmon streams. This stream don't have a run 'a coho
till late September. Then, if the bear don't get shot by a
hunter or run into some other mischief, he'll hole up in
the root cellar again." Marion looked toward the cabin.
"Well, I better go on up. She'll be thinkin' we're trying
to steal her blind."

Half an hour later the door creaked open and Marion
came down the path, followed by a woman in patched
blue men's pants. Grace remained in the ancient Tlingit;
the silver braid lying on her shoulder barely moved.
Like Marion's, the dark face was square, the silver
brows straight above eyes slitted against the sunlight.
Her mouth had a natural pucker.

"This here's Colleen," announced Marion. "Hin
Gokl come down to see us off."

Colleen smiled at the woman. Hin Gokl's seamed face
split in a toothless grin. "You good luck," she lisped,
and then the woman turned and spoke in guttural dia-
lect to Marion, her hands shaping words that evidently
couldn't be expressed.

Marion ducked her chin in what seemed to be agreement. The old Indian woman's chocolate-brown eyes
twinkled as her gaze ran over Colleen. She pointed a
bent forefinger at Colleen's flowing reddish hair and
spoke again.

Finally the interview ended, and Colleen climbed into
the stern seat so Marion could shove the skiff off the
rocks. Hands now clasped over her stomach, Hin Gokl
bobbed her head repeatedly in farewell as Marion swung
the bow into the tide. Colleen stared over her shoulder
at the diminishing figure in the baggy blue pants. It was
unbelievable that this fragile aging woman lived alone in
the wilderness . . . with bears!

When they'd boarded the *Sparrow* and were headed toward Pelican, Colleen spoke above the uneven diesel chug, "What did Hin Gokl say about my hair?"

"She said it brought the salmon. Especially on clear days, when the sun shines right through it and charms 'em into the boat. She says that hair 'a yours is better bait than brass or silver spoons to a wandering salmon. Salmon's easily fooled by beauty. If a dominant male sees something pretty, the whole school tries to beat him to it."

It was difficult to tell where Indian lore left off and Marion's fishing experience took over. But it was a telling exchange, a cultural plate fitting tightly into the armor Marion wore to survive in this wild land. Colleen would never have gleaned fascinating insights from her friends in Seattle, who, after she'd spent so many grueling hours with Marion, seemed shallow and hedonistic. Appreciating Marion's rare good humor, Colleen replied in a voice lifting with gaiety, "We'll have to hope for good weather after the closure, Marion. I'll walk around on deck calling to those gullible kings, and they'll get so frustrated they'll take the hook."

"No kings after the closure," Marion said. "Season's closed on kings until July 25."

"What'll we fish for?"

"Cohos. In a week or two they'll be heading for several streams I know about south of Lisianski Strait." She chuckled. "I hope Hin Gokl's right. I hope that carrot top 'a yours works on cohos, too. Oh, I forgot to mention.... She said that hair could work against as well as for you."

"How's that?"

"Well, like it could attract good as well as evil. You know—storms and bad luck and such."

"That's why you're always telling me to put on my hat, Marion. You think I'm attracting evil spirits!"

"Don't laugh. Hin Gokl's been around eighty winters or more. She ain't wrong about much."

HEAVILY LADEN, the *Sparrow* practically waddled into the Pelican Cold Storage unloading dock. A light rain began to fall as Colleen and Marion filled a big aluminum tub with the fish and waited for the men on the platform above to hoist it up, unload the kings and swing the bucket down for another batch. The hold numbed Colleen's fingers, the ice on the kings and the steady rain made her sluggish and the work took the last of her strength. She and her skipper pulled around to the harbor, tied up, washed down the decks and locked the cabin. Wearily they stepped onto the float.

"Damned if you wasn't good luck this trip!" Marion allowed a jubilant smile to crinkle her face as she tucked a wad of bills into Colleen's hand. "Little bonus in there. See you don't spend it all in one place."

Colleen, her own face sagging with exhaustion, managed a smile. She closed her fist over the hard-earned cash and held it tightly all the way through the drizzle to the cottage. It was a relief to hear the brook bubbling beneath the boardwalk, welcoming. But the rooms were cold and inhospitable, indicating they had arrived home ahead of Cedar. They set about turning on the furnace and making coffee, driving away the chill.

An hour later Cedar stumbled into the warm living room, his jacket shiny with rain, a brown smudge marking his cheek and lines of fatigue underscoring his eyes. In a few days it would be the Fourth of July, but Colleen couldn't do much than exchange pleasantries with him about the coming celebration. She had no energy for accusing him of keeping other men away because he wanted her for himself.

Even Marion didn't take up the gauntlet over the issue of Mike, and Cedar said only that it was "damned rude" of Marion to leave the grounds without saying goodbye. Didn't she know Ernie was a basket case when he worried about her? Marion simply produced one of her sudden smiles.

They ate canned stew, showered in turns and fell into their respective beds.

Cedar was gone by the time Colleen got up. Rested, she felt the return of a gnawing emptiness. Cedar was clearly intending to give her more "space" than she wanted.

After breakfast, intent on wiping out her blue mood, she devoted the morning to polishing the chipped furniture and cleaning windows, while Marion scrubbed the kitchen end to end. Colleen climbed on the back of the sofa to reach a last high pane of glass, her mind flitting between images of Cedar and Marion's Indian stories. With Marion buoyed by the heavy load of salmon and the resulting payment to the hospital, which she'd mailed early this morning, she was unusually talkative.

"You said young Tlingit girls were afraid of the woods—why was that?" Colleen called, folding the cotton T-shirt to a clean spot and rubbing vigorously on the glass.

She heard the bucket of soapy water scrape across the linoleum in the kitchen. Panting with the exertion of mopping the floor, Marion said, "What scared them girls? Why, because the *Kooshd'aa K'aas* might steal 'em."

"What's a *Kooshd'aa K'aa*?"

"Land otter."

"The little furry animal."

"Technical speaking, yeah. The Tlingit never killed a *Kooshd'aa K'aa* until the Russians came, by the way. But greed for the pelts changed things. The clans began to see that nothing happened to them when they killed those little rascals."

"I'm confused. How could a land otter steal a child?"

"The little critter don't do the stealin'—it's the spirit of the *Kooshd'aa K'aa* that does it. We got legends about it. Story goes, centuries ago a young girl met one in the woods once, and she ran back to the village half-crazed and attacking everyone." Colleen could visualize Marion's mouth turned up in a smile. "To outsiders it sounds mixed up, but the Tlingits' whole existence down through time is tied to nature. Clans named after animals, animals transformed into people—you know, like Hin Gokl and her bear husband. And clans even having supernatural powers 'n all.

"If someone in a Land Otter village told you to point your canoe toward your homeland and not think of the Land Otter village you'd just left, you'd better do it. Otherwise you'd find your canoe right back in their village, and you might never get home. You'd have to do what they say. And, too, all the clans came to respect the power of the *Kooshd'aa K'aas*."

Colleen stopped polishing to listen to the uneven voice coming from the kitchen. She recalled the mossy humps and branches of spruce and hemlock near the glacier and remembered the black tightness squeezing her breath when she'd broken off Cedar's kiss. She had run from him. Her own fear and emotions had been plaguing her, but she could imagine what villagers of hundreds of years ago would have made of the experience, Indians who had never probed the complexities of the human personality in the same way as modern-day psychiatry had. She could easily see how the primitive world of the ancient Tlingit would influence the cultlike beliefs Marion was explaining.

"The girl went crazy because she saw a *Kooshd'aa K'aa*?" she asked, intrigued.

"Yep, tearing off her clothes, biting people who tried to subdue her. She even threw a stone at a *shaman* who tried to cure her by dancing before her with the drum and rattle. That just wasn't done. You don't throw stones at *shamans.*"

"That's a medicine man?"

"Right. The *shaman* was the only one who could break bad luck and drive out evil spirits."

"What happened to the girl?"

"They made a medicine from the roots of a weed, a poisonous one. Then they made four cuts on the head of the sick girl and brushed 'em with the medicine. She calmed down and eventually could recollect her experience in the woods. Then she fell asleep and woke after several hours, completely recovered."

"Amazing. What's the most powerful animal of the Tlingit, Marion?"

"*Yeitl*, the raven."

Colleen climbed off the back of the couch and came to lean against the doorway so she could see Marion. The woman was just pouring the bucketful of gray water and suds into the kitchen sink. A soft light flooded through the kitchen window, turning Marion's square red hands to lovely sculpture as she rinsed out the mop.

"I would have imagined maybe the whale or the bear would have been at the top of the list," Colleen said.

"Oh, the brown bear also has special powers and is sometimes regarded as a transformed human, like I said. The whale. The shark. But Raven's a wily fellow, and he's made up of the best and the worst human traits. He's always hungry, for instance."

"Perhaps the Tlingit of ages past understood the human personality better than I'd imagined," Colleen speculated. "The culture seems very complex."

"Stories differ about how Raven came to be so powerful," Marion continued. "Some say he existed before the world, never aged, never even died. Others say he was born to a woman who swallowed a stone, and when he got into trouble later in life, a land otter gave him a ride on his back and reunited him with his family, where he became the tribal ancestor of some of the clans."

"What do you believe, Marion?"

The woman wrung out the mop and hung it upside down in a closet near the refrigerator. She faced Colleen, her features calm. "When you're part of two cultures, the white and the Tlingit, you end up kind of a mix. I spent summers as a baby with my mother's people up north of Juneau, near Haines. And I spent one year in Sheldon Jackson High School, that missionary school in Sitka. My pa was deeply religious, like Ernie. But sometimes my mother's stories take such a God-awful hold on me, I feel like finding a way to end it all."

Colleen stepped toward Marion, her own face slack

with disbelief. "Surely you won't— I mean, you know that would be ridiculous, Marion."

"Ced would call it ludicrous, I think."

"You don't mean you would, though. Do something like that."

Marion shrugged, still implacable. "I don't imagine so. Mike's suffered worse than me, and I've got my duty to him. But the soul of a dead Tlingit is supposed to return to earth through a pregnant woman and find its clan again, maybe be born into the clan of a wealthy chief. Believe me, a little more money would be a boon about now."

Colleen laughed shakily. The notion was beyond belief. But the fact that Marion stood in her wool shirt and jeans, talking about reincarnation and a fresh start, her face calm as a protected bay, made Colleen's laughter ring with nervousness. The storm out on the Fairweather Grounds had been real, and Marion's reluctance to head for Lituya Bay had posed a serious threat to their lives.

"Now you got the time, you ought to take off for a while," Marion said, wiping her hands on her jeans. "This old place ain't gonna come completely clean, scrubbin' or no."

"I'll do that," Colleen said. "Think I'll take a walk up behind the house, maybe go find that waterfall that roars when I'm trying to sleep."

"See you don't go far, girl. The bear don't usually come out this way. They stay back around the garbage dump, out beyond the church, but you can't count on bear being where you want 'em to be. Best to stick within running distance of the houses."

Nodding, Colleen turned toward the stairs to find her coat.

"Watch out for the *Kooshd'aa K'aas*, too!" Marion grinned. "And don't make fun of 'em if you do see 'em. That's what got that little gal in trouble in the first place!"

CHAPTER FIFTEEN

LATE ON THE EVE of the Fourth of July, Colleen sat
alone on the living-room couch, wrapped in her warm
robe. A war movie from the forties droned in the background as she scanned the letter she'd written. She tried
to forget the fact that Cedar had gone to bed with barely
a civil word to her. She tried to ignore Marion's radio,
playing upstairs.

Dear Daddy, I went up to the church yesterday
afternoon. It wasn't Sunday, and it isn't a Catholic
church, but everything about Alaska is different, so
I wasn't surprised to see the doors wide open and a
few people sitting in the wooden pews. The church
isn't as grand as Father Gregory's stone, but it sits
up on a hill, its spire poking up through the spruce
branches. The windows frame this magnificent
view of the channel with the mountains rising right
up out of the water. The village kind of nestles below, with the boats tucked up to the docks and the
boardwalk just like a gray ribbon running over to
Marion Brown's cottage.

Sometimes an Alaska State ferry pulls in, and
then tourists swarm all over the place. Or the mail
plane skids up the channel in a spume of white and
docks to unload locals who went shopping in
Juneau.

Oh, remember I told you about the eagles down on the tide flats? Well, there are two more that perch in the spruce trees right outside the door of the church, stretching and checking out the meadow underneath. Esther McMillan would probably like to see them.

You'd love it up here, daddy. The people are real. They're friendly, and they care about the guy down the street. You don't think the two of you would like to visit, say, before July 10, do you? We're off until then. Fishing's been good lately, but I'm saving everything to invest in something worthwhile, as you did, so I really shouldn't splurge on a ticket home. I love you, daddy. I hope you'll be happy.

Colleen

P.S. Hug Blarney for me. He's probably going to be disgustingly fat when I get home.

She folded the letter and tucked it into an envelope. *There,* she sighed, laying the letter aside. *It didn't kill me to write to him. And if he has even two seconds of happiness with Esther McMillan, I'll be happy.*

To her right, a stair creaked from the weight of a big man, and Colleen concentrated very hard on the dancing couple on the screen. She heard Cedar enter the room.

"I couldn't get to sleep," he announced. Tucking in a red cotton shirt open halfway down his chest, he walked to Marion's favorite chair and slumped into it, his arms and legs overflowing the worn furniture. She nodded to him.

"Evening," he said, taking his pipe from the coffee table and tamping in fresh tobacco. He struck a match on his pant leg and lit the pipe, puffing softly. The smoke trailed under Colleen's nose.

"Smoke bother you?" he asked belatedly, looking apologetic.

"Not at all. It's very nice."

"Hmm." He watched the television for a moment, and Colleen tried to focus on the story. The fighter pilot in the film was telling his girlfriend he'd only be gone a year. They kissed passionately; Colleen squirmed. Cedar's timing was incredible. This was probably the only romantic scene in the movie.

"Cold?"

Colleen jerked toward Cedar's voice. "What?"

"Are you cold? Want a blanket? Your hands are all curled up into fists."

"Oh." She flexed her fingers. "Yes, I guess I'm cold at that. I'll get the afghan."

She leaned over the arm of the couch and dragged a crocheted blue-and-orange blanket onto her lap. Putting down his pipe, Cedar rose and tucked it around her. Their eyes met. Her hands were shaking, and she slid them under the blanket.

He smiled. "I was wondering if you were going down to the tide flats tomorrow to participate in the Fourth of July games?"

"I wouldn't miss it. Playing with a whole townful of people confined by the long winter and then the fishing season promises to be a rare treat."

His dark eyes gleamed with the first warmth she'd seen from him in days. "We might as well go on down there together, then."

"We might just as well." Her voice cracked with tension, and she stopped.

He patted her thigh. "Good." He stood up, moved back to settle into the chair. A subdued smile on his face, he took up his pipe. "Good," he said softly, and clamped the bit in his teeth.

COLLEEN HARDLY SLEPT that night. She got up early, putting on a blue print blouse with her jeans and brushing her hair and tying it back with a blue ribbon. Cedar bubbled with small talk at the breakfast table, until finally, exasperated, Marion said, "Ced, the two of you get on outta here and leave me in peace! I ain't heard such nonsensical pallaverin' since Mike and his pals pulled in their first mess 'a trout!"

The significance of her pronouncement wasn't lost on Cedar and Colleen. They exchanged thoughtful looks. Marion's growth had finally begun.

Grimacing in disgust, Marion heaved up out of her chair and began stacking the dishes. Cedar was the first to recover. His face creased in a smile. "We've been kicked out. If Marion wants to be a slave to the kitchen, who are we to hold her back?"

They rose from the table, and Cedar went to Marion. He kissed her noisily on the cheek.

"G'wan," Marion complained, ducking away, grinning. "Get on outta here." They went outside, letting the screen door bang and clatter, and joined the stream of villagers heading for the mud flats south of the boardwalk.

About mid-morning Colleen and Cedar won the egg-throwing contest and were awarded three dozen eggs apiece, which they could pick up at the grocery store anytime in the next year. Both of them laughed at the offer, but Colleen wondered where they'd be a year from now. *Think about today,* she told herself. *Don't expect too much from him, because when Ced comes on full strength you can't handle it.*

Ernie and Marion were sitting on a huge gray log a ways up the beach, chatting with a couple from Puerta Vallarta, Mexico, who fished all summer in Alaska. Marion had never seemed so relaxed. A happy smile softened her weathered face as children played tag and dived into the sand right in front of her. Colleen joined the couples for a few minutes, until Cedar called her over and coerced her into participating in the wheelbarrow races.

He picked up her legs. When the gun went off he yelled, "Go, go, go!" and she ran on her hands as fast as she could. At a line in the sand someone had drawn with a boot heel they switched roles. But his legs were heavy, and she tumbled across him into the sand, limbs tangled, laughing, gasping.

"Say, Ced," called a friend. "You'll use any excuse to tumble Marion's fish puller!"

Laughing, Ced pulled Colleen to her feet. "We need more practice at this partnership business." He looked at her, and her heart jerked. "Don't we?" he said softly.

"I never did much of this stuff as a kid," she said.

"I did. Every afternoon before I went to work at the pawnshop, the guys used to congregate in a vacant lot and compete at this kind of thing. We were like family. Fights and the whole bit."

She gave him a perky smile. "Oh? Street wise and a pawnshop clerk?"

He grinned. "Don't knock it, bright eyes. You learn a lot in the pawnshop business. I ended up running the place. The last two years of college I owned three of them.''

"Really. Do you still?''

"Nope. Sold them all to get my grubstake in gems. C'mon, the kids are diving for treasure. It's the best part of the day.''

He steered her toward a tight cluster of people.

"Gems, Cedar? You're a gem dealer?'' She hung back, but he urged her through the crowd.

"Later,'' he said. "You're gonna love these kids.''

The children waited with tense faces for the crack of a cap pistol, and when it sounded, they converged on a mound of wood shavings. Fifty dollars had been collected in town throughout the winter; the change was now buried beneath the aromatic pulp. The bigger kids screamed and fought for the silver. One little boy grabbed a nickel and tucked it into his baby-sister's hand. "Hold it, Tweeter,'' he shouted urgently. "Hold it tight!''

Cedar McClintock stood at the edge of the spectators' circle, his own face expectant, encouragement coming from him in low excited bursts. "Look to your left, Johnny! Betty, get in there and fight for what you want! That your youngest, Mrs. Seeger? Fine girl!''

Colleen watched him. Cedar's eyes sparkled. He waved and clenched his fist in sympathetic frustration. His deep voice carrying over the cries of onlooking parents, he called out support to a toddler more stunned by the blur of arms and legs than greedy for coins that meant nothing to her. Colleen laughed deep in her throat. Cedar was something, he really was. She wanted to hug him.

Now, as the children wandered away from the pile of

sawdust, their pockets jingling with coins, Colleen saw traces of sand still clinging to his hair. She brushed it free. Cedar turned, a happy smile on his face, and hugged her. Her feet left the sand as he swung her around.

"How about the dry-suit races?" he said. "We've got fifteen minutes to get down to the boat harbor and get suited up."

"I want to talk to you, Cedar. What's corundum? When are they going to serve the barbecue?"

"Corundum is the mineral that yields rubies and sapphires. The food is served at three o'clock. Now, c'mon, let's work up an appetite."

His gaze melted her. "Well...all, all right, but I'm starved right now."

"So am I," he said with a double meaning, bringing his lips close. He slid her body gently down until her feet touched the sand. Following her mouth without kissing her, he said softly, "But if I have to be patient, so do you."

Her eyelids drooped. She wanted his kiss and cared nothing for the fact that the beach was alive with people. But Cedar took her hand and urged her toward the boardwalk. She found herself running to keep up with him.

The gray boards had been painted in red, white and blue letters that read Freedom and Justice for All. "They as good as dedicated this day to you, Freedom," Cedar commented as they wove among the exodus of villagers. "Let's see if you can do justice to a little old fifty-degree water, huh?"

She punched him lightly to tell him what she thought of his inane play on words, and he caught her hand, spinning her into his arms. He kissed her with stark passion, parting her lips and invading her mouth, holding her shoulders still as others bumped around them. When he pulled away, her legs trembled.

"Sometimes I just can't play games," he said, his grasp on her arms like padded steel. "C'mon. We'll be late."

Firecrackers exploded in the distance, and Colleen rallied her senses enough to ask, "Dry-suit races?" She hurried to keep up with his stride. "Aren't dry suits those orange things you wear at sea when your boat's sinking?"

"Right. The races are nothing more than a quick swim across the boat harbor, really."

" 'Swim'? Cedar, you can't be serious! That water is barely above freezing. Sometimes I think the fish are even glad to get out of it. You can't mean people are actually going in that water."

"Of course people are going in. This is Alaska, my dear—not the Seattle Country Club, where the gentry brag about taking a few strokes in a heated pool."

"It's impossible." She felt that blasted fear nudge inside. "That water is a killer. People don't last five minutes in it."

"That's why it's a dry-suit race, Colleen. The suit is like a big rubber body glove. You put it on over warm clothes, and it keeps the water out."

"But even if you stay dry, the water is still—" J.T. waved from below them on the dock. He was suited in orange. "J.T.!" Colleen called, raising her hand in greeting. "The water is still freezing, Cedar."

"Not like that old country club at home, you mean?" He cut her a glance out of the corner of his eye and led

her toward a cluster of people staggering around with
dry suits half on. "Well," he added, "folks are tougher
up here."

That was why she'd come here, wasn't it? To learn to
be tough? To get rid of the hovering darkness of fear?
Her lips firm with foreboding, she gave an offhand
shrug. "What's a little cold water? I've lived through
worse just pulling fish on the grounds."

"Now you're talking like a Sourdough, Freedom.
Those old-timers who settled this wild and woolly state
swam these waters for sport. Let's go!"

IN A WHILE they were side by side on the edge of the
dock above the glassy dark green water. They held
hands, Colleen maintaining a stiff smile, Cedar chuckling with J.T. and a cluster of other contestants.

The gun blasted. As Cedar dived free of Colleen, he
shouted, "Good luck, Freedom!"

His momentum carried her into the water at an awkward sideways angle. Her face and hands numbed instantly as she curved down into the dim wet world.
Arms and legs a dirty orange color churned around her.
She felt a dull pain in her calf from a careless kick.
Down she sank, arms clawing as the darkness closed
over her, chest frozen as she fought the claustrophobia
of fear. Yes, she had only known country-club pools
and snorkling dives in clear cerulean shallows, where the
fish darted bright blue and pink through the coral. Not
this evil green underworld, this killing cold. Not this
darkness.

Colleen's fear and flailing had cost her; she had sunk
below the frenzied racers. An orange limb dragged by,
looking like part of a corpse in a Fellini film. Her chest

ached from the lack of oxygen, and she panicked because she hadn't taken the required breath of air. Arms, legs, body thrown into chaos, she pulled for the surface, her mind fighting hopelessness, her heart pumping against the fatal darkness. The orange suit was too large for her, letting the sea trickle in around her bonnet. Her terror mounted as water like chilled alcohol soaked her blouse and began to collect in one leg of the suit. She would drown in a stupid race!

The harbor was deep, and she'd foolishly struggled, fighting the natural buoyancy of the suit. The wavering ghosts of troller hulls to her left spurred her thoughts on to Marion, to Mike. They needed her. They needed her, and she'd nearly given up without helping them. Revulsion at her low self-esteem nearly choked her as she burst through the surface of the bay, gagging on the splash of salty water.

There were others doing the same, not ten feet behind her, bobbing like tops in the bulky suits. She couldn't believe it. Tough Alaskans, bested by a twenty-minute swim! Their fallability gave her courage. Her affinity to water had her stretching beyond her limit to stroke across the race course.

As she gained the middle of the pack, the bay churned white with the efforts of swimmers all around her. The dry-diving suit and the cold water of the harbor wrung the energy from her limbs. Awkward in the thick survival gear, she swam the last strokes and collapsed in the midst of gasping contestants, arms clinging to the rough dock, legs dragging in the water, chest heaving. With numb fingers she pulled the bonnet from her head; the breeze crept through her wet hair, making her teeth chatter. She'd survived. And she'd bested perhaps twenty percent of these hardy Alaskan Sourdoughs. A grim smile creased her lips.

On the dock about eye level, rubber pack boots and feet with bare bluish toes swam into her vision. Jocular conversation rose and fell as she hung there, panting. Someone named Randy from a crab boat had won the race. "Cedar tied for second," said a grating voice.

She heard gasping behind her and turned to see a woman in her fifties, at least, struggling to reach the dock. Gray hair straggled down her cheeks, and the bonnet had slipped over one eye. Colleen reached out to her, pulling the woman to safety.

"Thanks," the woman choked. She yanked off the drawstring hood. Craning her neck to look up at the line of men and women, she yelled, "Somebody get us out of here! Blue's going to catch hell for talking me into this!"

"Blue Harry?" Colleen asked.

The woman turned, gasping. "Yeah. He's going to do. . .do without conjugal rights for the rest of the season for this! I'm a human ice floe! Him and h-his wise ideas! You don't see him floundering around in one of these things, do you? Say. . .say, aren't you the gal pulls fish for Marion?"

"Yes, Colleen. . .Colleen Conaughy."

"Sadie. I hear—oh, Lordy!—" she scooped water out of her eyes "—'bout got the best of me! I hear you're holding your own out there on the *Sparrow*. Marion's a damn fine fisherman, one of the toughest. How d'you like the fishing business?"

"It's the best job I've ever had." Colleen smiled with chilled unresponsive lips. Sadie didn't need to know it was the only job she'd ever had.

"Can't stand the life myself," Sadie growled. "All that fish slime and all. Give me a house to clean and beds to make any day of the week! You going up to Rosie's Bar and Grill tonight? Going to be a shindig after the barbecue."

"Sounds great, Sadie. You planning to go?"

"You bet. Soon's I get the salt out of my hair. Damn Blue, anyway!" Sadie turned and screeched, "Will somebody *please* get me outta here!" Someone pulled Blue's wife out of the water. Her voice faded as she stumbled through the crowd.

"Here, c'mon outta there, Sprite." Cedar's face hovered above Colleen. His hair looked like black hematite, chips of it sticking up at odd angles. The insulated suit bunched around his waist. His wide shoulders stuck out of the orange tube without a patch of dampness marring his brown shirt. He pulled her up by the arms and set her on the dock. The spectators clapped like seals. Colleen's legs buckled, and Cedar grabbed her again. "Easy, there," he laughed. "Give your legs time to recover."

"I want to change," she said, leaning against him. "I think I've got some clothes on the boat. That was fun, once I got the hang of it. I wish I'd known what to expect."

"You did fine. You're a true Alaskan, now, Freedom. You've just lived through the local baptism."

"I think I prefer Father Gregory's method."

After they'd turned in their suits and Cedar had collected twenty-five dollars in prize money, he eased her through the crowd. Someone patted her on the back. "Nice going, Colleen."

She turned. "Hey, J.T.! We did it!"

He gave her his slow grin and wiped self-consciously at his head.

She grasped his damp arm, squishing the orange material, and smiled, her eyes dancing. "It was great, huh?" She turned to leave with Cedar. "Blue's wife was madder'n a hornet, Ced. I didn't know he had a wife!"

"Blue's always in trouble with Sadie. He figures everybody's got to be as tough as a brown bear, even her. Hardly anyone can measure up to his fearsome heroes!"

"Speaking of Bl-Bl-Blue...." She had begun to shiver; she could barely get the words out through her cold lips. As they approached the ramp to the docks, Colleen pointed over the heads of spectators to a troller with one pole lowered, the tip barely three feet off the water. Blue Harry, his paunch drooping over his twill work pants, stepped out on the hilt of the pole, barefooted. "What's he doing?"

"Greased-pole contest," Cedar explained. "They slathered that pole with lard and tied a red bandanna to the tip. See it...dragging in the water? Those people waiting in line behind Blue are going to try to walk out and retrieve the scarf before they fall in."

These Alaskans are gluttons for punishment, Colleen thought, shaking her head. The greased-pole contestants weren't even bothering with dive suits.

All along the rails of the boardwalk and down the ramp adjacent to the boat people were shouting and cheering. A boy with a blue T-shirt set off firecrackers at the edge of the crowd. People jerked out of the way of the snapping and smoke, then yelled good-naturedly at the boy and continued their conversations. Nearby, a man with a red nose and a wool hat in his hands collected donations for the pole walk.

"Donate a few bucks, you stingy fellas," he jeered, grinning. "You ain't out there braving that ice water! Least you can do is make it worth their while! C'mon, cough up a few bucks!"

Cedar dug into his jeans and withdrew a five-dollar bill. It fluttered from his outstretched hand. "Here, Jake. See it gets to the winner."

"Now, Ced, I been to church last Sunday. You can trust me—I'm an upstanding member of the community! Thanks, huh?"

"Sure enough."

Colleen tugged Cedar's arm, her lips blue, her teeth tapping like mice on glass. "You g-go on down to the greased-pole contest, Cedar. I'll ju-ju-just grab a sweater and some dry jeans on the *Sparrow*."

"You'd be better off getting your blood heated up." He put his arm around her, ignoring the sodden condition of her blue print blouse, and she felt as if he'd wrapped her in blankets. She snuggled gratefully against him. "You can shower on the *Dart*," he added, treating himself to a good look at the material outlining her breasts. As Cedar and Colleen filtered through the knot of pole walkers, he grinned. "Save yourself a hike back to the house. If you'll tell me what you want out of the *Sparrow*, I'll look up Marion and get the key. And if you're real sweet on the way down, Colleen, I'll even make you a cup of hot coffee."

"I yield." She sighed. "There's a navy-bl-bl-blue sweater and a pair of clean jeans in the compartment over the starboard bunk. "Ah...and a clean s-s-set of underthings—"

"Don't worry about a thing," Cedar said, pulling a key from his back pocket. "We're in luck. I didn't lose the key to the *Dart*."

"Are you really a g-gem dealer?"

He glanced down at her, his eyes merry. "Yes. Anything else about me you want to know?"

"Oh, absolutely everyth-th-thing!"

"I never thought you'd ask!" he breathed. "But right now we're risking your health, lollygagging on the docks. Here, step over the rail, and I'll unlock this white snowbird. Ernie lives aboard, so it should be warm inside."

A splash sounded behind them as she climbed to the deck of the *Dart*, and she knew Blue was now thrashing around in that cold harbor; she shivered without envy. Cedar followed her to the companionway. "You know where everything is. My robe'll keep you till I get back."

She took a short, very hot shower to conserve Ernie's water supply. The needles of spray penetrated to quickly heat her muscles. Thawed and peppy again, she wrapped up in Cedar's kelly-green robe, dried her hair and went to the galley. While she brewed coffee, faint cheers and the squeal of gulls reminded her she was in Pelican, but the walls of the *Dart* were sturdy, buffering most of the sounds.

Colleen felt separated from the celebration, and cozy. Too cozy. She shouldn't be wishing she and Cedar were anchored in some isolated bay with nothing but nights of loving ahead of them. Hours of talk, giggling like idiots—that's what it would be like with him, she imagined—if she ever got past the need to be free. He was an overgrown kid with a heart "from here to Seattle," like

Ernie. He had a way of making her forget her goals sometimes, and only deep in the passion of loving him did her mind remind her of other priorities. She had never known such frustration and eagerness, all rolled into one, as she felt now, waiting for him.

Why did one have to lose one's soul in love, she wondered. How did other women keep track of what they wanted in the face of such weakness for a man?

And that distance of his. She had wanted to plead his forgiveness, like some prideless wench in those paperback romances. Just remembering his coolness of the past week reminded her of how she'd dealt with Alec when he'd begun to forget dates and to cancel the few he managed to recall. She knew she didn't love Alec, but if she could just unravel the reasons for losing him during the time she'd thought he was a god. . . .

She turned from the built-in coffee brewer to slump into the booth, her thoughts slipping back to that last semester of college. She had used the cool uncaring treatment herself on Alec, repeatedly. It had backfired. Her false hauteur had made it easier for Alec to walk away from her. He'd give her that shrug with his stooped shoulders and say, "You've got that game tonight, anyway, haven't you? Think I'll just head over to the library and listen in on the discussion I mentioned." He would slip away, and the more she pretended she didn't care, the greater grew the distance between them.

Mystified, she shook her head. Maybe she had never really been in tune with Alec; maybe the idea of love had been stronger for them than the real thing.

She tried to imagine her and Alec working together under the conditions she had endured with Marion—the anger, the torture of overworked muscles and not enough food, the struggle of dealing alone, on a wild sea, with her fear of dying and of darkness. No, she'd never liked Alec enough to put up with such abuse, she realized. The Colleen of their last year together would have taken the first flight home. Alec needed no one, certainly not a hothouse rose he would have shriveled with his veiled contempt. She would always have been his token heiress, to be protected and scorned. And his instincts would have been right.

The *Dart* squeaked against the bumper guards, making Colleen glance outside. Cedar strode down the float, his arms full of clothes, his face a mask of... what? Colleen's hand went to her throat. He looked stricken.

She rose and went to the door. Opening it, she stepped backward and stood with her hands clenched, waiting until Cedar came through. He walked in, his face pale, strained.

He thrust the clothes into her arms. Something whispered toward the deck; she grabbed for it blindly, clutched it against her, trying to read his thoughts. Mike? Something with Marion? Colleen's father?

"My daddy...?"

"You'd...." His voice sounded squeezed in a vice. Her mouth went dry with apprehension. She tossed the clothes into the booth and searched his face. "You'd better dress," he said. His lips trembled. He ran a hand through tossed black hair. "Marion...Mike.... Mike's gone, Collie. *Dear God!*"

Grief overwhelmed him, racking his body with tremors, and for the first time Colleen realized Cedar loved the boy. He had probably helped raise Mike. Why had she never asked about his feelings for Mike?

Because he's always been the strong one. Protecting Marion. Watching over me.

She reached for him. "Cedar, love, I'm so sorry!" She put her arms around him, her eyes clouding with tears at seeing him so moved. She wouldn't cry now, she told herself fiercely, squeezing her lids shut. Cedar needed her. Marion would need her. She dragged a strengthening breath into her lungs.

He shook against her, crying in tight terrible silence. His hands flailed helplessly for a moment, grazing her back, lifting her hair, and at last he found her warmth and crushed her close. She tightened her grip. Someone actually needed her—not just someone—Cedar. The finest man she'd known.

It was only a few moments before he choked, "Poor lad—poor Marion." Then he was straightening away, pressing the heel of his palm tight to his eyes and scraping the moisture away. Colleen went into the bathroom and returned with a fistful of tissue.

He nodded thanks and turned his back. His shoulders heaved once. He picked a nonexistent piece of lint from his sleeve. She knew words were difficult. She spoke for him. "Cedar...telegram?"

Again he nodded, drew in a painful-sounding breath. He turned to her. She was startled at how brilliantly his eyes shone, the mirror of emotion. The shield of protective indifference was removed. Cedar's soul shone from his eyes, and she could see his pain. She could see how vulnerable this hard capable man really was. His anguish shook her deeply. She murmured sympathetically and touched his arm.

"Oh, babe," he said with a quietness that intensified

her own pain at his grief. "In spite of it all, I really thought he'd pull through."

"Marion...is she...?"

"Ernie's with her, hovering with blankets and hot tea and sympathy." He laughed self-deprecatingly. "She's stronger than me, that tough old gal. Not a tear in her eye, back straight as an iron poker. Just sitting in her chair in the living room, rocking herself, arms all wrapped close."

"That Tlingit heritage."

He raised a brow in agreement.

A frightening thought struck her. "Cedar! A few days ago she was talking about death. Her death! She tossed it off, said she wouldn't do anything crazy because Mike needed her, something about her duty to Mike. But if Mike's gone—we've got to watch her, not let her go off by herself."

He was shaking his head. "Ernie's with her, I told you."

"But after, Cedar, on the boat. You know what she did on the grounds."

"Ernie and I had a few minutes alone. We talked. He's going to Seattle with her to bring Mike home. He'll try to draw her out, make her open up some." He knuckled his eyes again, and she gave him a moment to compose himself.

Strong, tough skipper of the *Sparrow*, she thought, going down to Seattle to bring home her son at last. The son she'd invested the best years of her life in, her companion and friend and fishing partner. What tremendous will Marion must have not to tear through town, shrieking her sorrow. There was nothing left of Mike to love except memories. Just like Colleen's father. But Sean Conaughy had had millions of dollars worth of assets and cash to buffer his pain. Marion had nothing but a ramshackle cottage and a beaten-up boat...and her Indian heritage.

Suddenly Colleen focused on the facts: Marion would be swamped with medical bills, 'clear to the bulkhead,' as she would say; and Ernie would lose at least some time away from fishing by being with Marion. His last payment to Cedar was due in October. But if he was worried sick about Marion, he was bound to fish inefficiently. He'd probably already sacrificed thousands running after Marion all summer, heading into the cold storage to sell a pittance of the fish he could ice in that huge hold.

And if they took one of the boats to Seattle, it could be two weeks—three, maybe four, with bad weather in Dixon Entrance—before they returned. Precious weeks hacked out of the fishing season.

She searched her mind, trying to find a way to help. "Cedar, sit down while I think." She waved toward the booth, and he slid into it. She turned off the brewer and dispensed two mugs of coffee, then brought them with her to the table.

She began planning aloud. "I've got my own earnings from this season. But no, Marion wouldn't hear of a gift like that." She slipped in next to Cedar and laid her hand on his sleeve. "Cedar, are they flying to Seattle or taking one of the boats?"

He looked curiously at her. "I don't know, babe. I couldn't talk much when I was with Ernie a while ago. I got out of there as fast as I could."

She smiled at his honesty. The perfect plan was materializing in her mind. In some urgency, she patted his arm. "We've got to ask them to let us use one of the boats while they're gone."

"'Us'?"

"You 'n me, babe. We could fish as soon as the closure is off. Marion won't be fit for work for a while, and both she and Ernie have big debts hanging over their heads."

He gave her one of his rare big smiles. "Good idea! Freedom, there isn't a woman within five thousand miles that could hold a candle to you!"

Grinning, she sipped her coffee and watched him over the rim of the cup.

"She'll take the *Sparrow*," he said in sudden finality, his hand smacking the table.

"Why?"

"She hates airplanes. And she and the boy were so close. He was born on the boat, loved it, loved fishing...." His eyes threatening to mist over, he gulped hot coffee.

"Easy there, skipper," she said quietly. "There'll be a thousand more of those hot cups in the days ahead. You don't want to burn out your tongue."

He set the mug down with a splash and took her in his arms. "Freedom...Colleen...I love you." He turned her chin up to him and kissed her on the lips. His expression affectionate, he searched her face. "Don't be scared. Let me say this. I love you so much I want to give you the world." He snugged her against his chest and kissed her hair. "The world, the whole world...."

She flung her arms around his neck. "Cedar, we'll work this out—you'll see. Ernie will take care of Marion, and we'll take care of each other. It'll work out, you'll see, you'll see...."

CHAPTER SIXTEEN

"HEY, COLLEEN!" yelled Sadie, threading through the barbecue crowd toward her and Cedar as they followed the boardwalk, heading for the cottage. "Wait up!"

Spruce and hemlock marched up the mountain behind the tavern and shops, backing the festive reds and blues of the villagers' clothing with a soft moss green. The crowds were thick and noisy around the doorway of Rosie's Bar and Grill. To the tinkle of a banjo a scratchy voice sang of whaling days and "lighting your living room with oil"; off to one side of the boardwalk, on a mound of dark soil, smoke rose from four huge chunks of roast turning on a spit. J.T. wore long red suspenders in honor of the Fourth. With the carmine stripes of a bandbox hat tilting crazily over his skull, he swabbed the meat with a mop dipped in red sauce.

"Watermelon-eating contest is already over, and the roasted buffalo's great." Sadie was laughing breathlessly, patting down the yellow ruffles on the front of her blouse. "Rosie sure puts on a feast. Gee, your hair is lovely, Colleen. All red and flowing. I had to sit under the dryer for forty minutes. You ready to eat? Here, I'll show you two the plates and forks."

"Sadie." Colleen put her hand over the other woman's. Blue came up behind his wife, and Cedar half turned away, clearing his throat uncomfortably. The people of Pelican would have to be told about Mike, Colleen knew, but Cedar was in no condition to face the job now. Her role seemed clear, and Colleen led Sadie and Blue a few steps away. "Sadie, Blue, there's been a tragedy." She waited a moment, then spoke gently. "Cedar was just telling me about a telegram that came for Marion a while ago. It's Mike—something about an embolism—a blood clot stopped his heart, I think. They—they lost him. Ced's taking it badly, and Marion's...well, you know she's the strong silent type. We're going to her now. We'll all be missing the festivities."

Sadie's face softened, and she uttered a low cry of sympathy.

"Damn bad luck," Blue growled softly. "But from what little I know, the boy's better off." He glanced toward Cedar. Cedar was speaking casually to Doc and Josh, who were leaning on the railing, beers set aside and their hands busy with plates of food.

"Marion?" Sadie asked. "I should check on her—"

"Ernie's with her, Sadie," Colleen broke in. "Cedar thinks the two of them will probably head on down to Seattle as soon as they can. He'll take good care of her."

"But they fight so."

"He'll put a rein on his temper this once, I'm sure of it."

"Well—" Sadie nodded her gray head "—he does have that religious training. He's a minister, you know. The Lord has His way of bringing people together."

Blue nudged Sadie's arm. "Come on, gal. Colleen looks like she's got things well in hand." Pulling his beard in a thoughtful way, he glanced at Colleen.

"Look, we'll, ah, kind of pass the word, give you folks some time to adjust. Marion's got lots of friends in this town, and they'll be getting a few dollars together or something. We'll see to it, hey, Sadie?"

"Sure, Blue." She looked at Cedar's broad back. "Ced taught Mike to hunt, you know, fished along with him and Marion for years. He's taking it hard, I can tell."

"Sadie...." Blue tugged his wife's sleeve. "This little redhead is right on top of things. She'll give us a holler if she needs a thing."

"Thanks." Colleen smiled, stepping away. "You'll give Rosie our regrets?"

Blue saluted.

Colleen merely touched Cedar's arm and gave him a quiet nod. He took her hand, holding it tightly, and moved off down the boardwalk. He would hate to face Marion again, she guessed. All those painful memories and having to see her grief. Tough Cedar needed someone to lean on, after all, and for the first time in her life, Colleen felt she was perfect for such a job.

When they reached the cottage, there were thumping noises coming from inside. Cedar held open the screen door and waited for her to cross the threshold. Behind her, she heard him draw a breath.

The thumping sounds were from Marion's bedroom, upstairs. She was evidently pulling out drawers and rummaging in her closet. Her activity encouraged Colleen, but Cedar sat down on the couch, head in his hands. Colleen touched his shoulder. After a moment with him, she followed the basso of Ernie's voice, in the direction of the kitchen. She found him speaking on the telephone.

His complexion almost matched his pressed gray work shirt. A frost of white lashes hid his expression. "Yes, if you'll do that," he said. He glanced up and saw Colleen. "Hospital," he mouthed to her. Raising his hand in a signal for Colleen to wait, he turned back to the receiver. "What's that. . . ? Oh, yes, the cold storage at the harbor. It'll be much easier if you'll have the boy there when we arrive. Yes, I *know* this is quite unorthodox, sir, but. . . yes, I've arranged everything, and they're quite willing. All right, then. . . . I'll call you the first opportunity. And God bless you for your kindness. Goodbye."

The receiver clicked. Fiddling with the collar of his shirt, Ernie looked at Colleen. His blue eyes snapped with residual anger. "Some people are extremely unwilling to bend, do you know that, young lady? They just have to retain control!"

She smiled ruefully. "They have their rules, I suppose. How's Marion?"

"Bearing up." He motioned for her to come close and said in low tones, "She's a strong, fine woman, just a monument of self-control. I'm proud of her. It's Ced has me worried. He's never stood up well to tragedy." He scrubbed his hair. "Marion, she buries things, but with Ced, the emotions just *boil*." He stretched the word out, Southern-preacher style, raising his arms. "Just boil up to the surface and keep sputtering and bubbling till the fire goes out. It's healthier than Marion's way, but unpredictable. He took the boy's accident with the bear last fall awful hard. He's just all emotion where the boy and Marion are concerned." He shook his finger at Colleen. "And you, too, come to think of it. He damn near tore the *Dart* apart from sheer frustration when Marion stayed out on the grounds in that storm.''

"Seems to me I heard Cedar say it was you who tore out your hair in bunches.''

"He did, did he?'' Ernie shoved a hand into the pocket of his brown trousers. "I did do some mighty hard praying that night, I guess. And...I might have flung a mug against the wall or something, you know, kinda letting out my fouler feelings. But Ced paced holes in the deck, and that's a fact.''

She chuckled softly.

Ernie's white caterpillar brows darted together. "I feel bad, the two of you having to wait—''

There was a thud at the top of the stairs. He stopped and turned toward the doorway, his forehead puckered in worry. They heard Marion come down and a soft *puff* as she set something on the floor. The kitchen wall obscured the living room, however, and Marion didn't come through the doorway. Cedar said Marion's name, his voice choked with emotion, and a moment passed when Colleen knew the old friends were embracing. She swallowed the urge to cry. There were things to arrange: the fishing trip, packing up some of her things on the *Sparrow*, Ernie and Marion to see off, Cedar to care for. No time for tears. The two voices came softly from the living room, and Colleen turned to suggest she and Ernie give them a few minutes alone.

Ernie's mouth drooped. "Tough, you two having to wait a couple of weeks longer than the normal closure,'' he finished absently.

Obviously he was suffering, too. Perhaps now would be the best time to relieve his mind about financial matters, before they joined the others. Colleen touched him on the arm; the muscle felt like rock. "Ernie?"

"Yes—" he coughed lightly "—what is it?"

"About Cedar and me. We want to fish as soon as the closure is lifted, use one of the boats, take our usual cut. . .and give you and Marion the rest. Because it'll be your boat, probably, and that would only be fair. And Marion taught me what I know about fishing, so I'd like to pay her back in some way. All right?"

He scrubbed his scalp until the hair bristled like a white sea urchin. With minute concentration his pale blue eyes studied her face.

"Ernie, we'll be careful," she urged. "Cedar must be good with the gear and the boat after all these years."

Wordlessly Ernie nodded.

"Then you agree?" she pressed gently.

"Okay." He started to turn away, then swung back to her. "But what about your reputation? Normally it wouldn't be a problem. . . ."

He gestured vaguely.

She leaned toward him. "But what?"

"Well, Colleen," he said, finding his voice, "it's pretty evident you're crazy about each other. Most folks around here don't ask questions about fishing relationships. They know people have to eat. But some might, you know, make you uncomfortable. You have kind of a class about you, that pride just keeping that chin of yours pointing at the clouds. I just thought maybe this kind of thing would matter to you, is all. Preposterous as it might seem, Marion and Ced had to take it on the chin for a time—until he punched some fella in the jaw for making snide remarks. That seemed to gain them some respect."

"Oh, opinions aren't so important, Ernie. How could it be evident, anyway? We've hardly been out together."

"Colleen, that's the point. You've stuck close to home almost every day you were in town, except today, remember, when you and Ced partnered up for every game? You went off together that day in Lituya, too, and later things were strained between you. You think fishermen aren't in better tune with these things than people in the cities, who mix with millions of others without giving it a thought? This is a small community. Not enough of them—but some of them—live clean lives and practice the Word. I hear them talking...."

What right did good Christians have to turn a helpful deed into something nasty? Angry, she compressed her lips.

Ernie smiled bitterly. "Folks here don't have much to do, Colleen. They tend to busybody a bit—not all of them, mind you, just some—judging others before they even take a good look at their own faults."

"I don't care, Ernie! Let them misjudge our actions!" Glancing toward the living room, where the hushed conversation persisted, she lowered her voice. "What about you? Going off with Marion on this trip, you being a preacher and all? What kind of reputation will that leave you?"

She winced when she saw his cheeks brighten. She remembered Marion's telling her about Ernie's difficulty with the vices of California living. What right did she have to throw temptation in his face? He was a decent man. She put out her hand. "I—I'm sorry, Ernie. I'm grateful you'll be with her. And I know you care about her deeply. I'm sorry I made it sound ugly."

He released a tense breath and said half to himself, "'If they cannot contain, let them marry.' First Corinthians seven, verse nine. Don't you think I know that passage by heart?"

"Yes, of course you do. The good people here will understand why you're with her. They'll love you for it."

He gazed at her with an unspoken frustration, and she said softly, "And the unbelieving wife is made acceptable to God by being united to her Christian husband."

His snowy brows rose in surprise. "You've been reading my thoughts," he accused.

"She's not really a pagan, you know. She's just... mixed up. Or perhaps richer for her background. I don't know. The Tlingit culture stirs up inside her with what her dad believed and what she was taught in that missionary school. Ernie, marry her if you love her. She's so full of good."

"I'll admit something to you. I've tried. She just won't have it."

Colleen heard a chuckle from the living room and gestured toward the door. "Maybe now she will. It's over. Her long vigil is done. After a lifetime of responsibility to others, she has no one left to care for but herself."

Ernie put his arm around her and shook his head. "I won't rush her."

"That's what Cedar said to me. Sometimes I wish he wouldn't be quite so patient." She hadn't meant to say that, hadn't even realized the thought was in her head. Ernie's arm left her shoulders, and she turned quickly toward him. "Of course, in sane moments I don't mean that. I'm not really old-fashioned, and I've certainly not

been a prude, but I was raised with certain values.
Somewhere along the line, in Seattle with all my friends,
I lost them. I'm just realizing I want to find those values
again, but sometimes they get confused with what I *feel*.
It's such a mess. Oh, Ernie, yes. I'm worried about this
crazy plan to fish with Cedar. But it's right, isn't it? To
want to help other people even if it endangers what you
want for yourself?''

Cedar called from the other room, "Colleen, you've
got to see this stuff. What a display!''

She turned her head. Cedar sounded much stronger.
Relieved, she answered, "Yes, we'll be right in.''

Facing Ernie, she said urgently, "I'm right to go fishing with Cedar, aren't I? Just as you're doing the right
thing by Marion, even though it goes against your moral
principles?''

"My moral principles have been in far greater danger
before this, believe me. Marion's awfully prickly about
getting close. But I warn you, you don't have that deterrent where Cedar's concerned. He's emotional, and he's
in love with you. Keep your faith like a cloak and remember your goals. The hard work of the fishing trade
will do the rest.''

She grinned. "If we do take your boat, Ernie, I
guarantee that even if the fish don't bite, the *Dart* will
be whiter than she is right now.''

A smile creased his face. "Then I entrust her to you with
no reservations. Marion wants to take the *Sparrow* to
Seattle. Shall we see what's so special in the living room?''

"Indeed. And Ernie? You'd make a darned nice
preacher for that church up on the hill. Out on the
beach today I heard the minister's been called back to
Texas.''

"So half the town has told me. It's been on my mind for six months, anyway, since I first heard of the vacancy." He winked. "Been thinking about it more and more every time I have a fight with Marion. That woman will drive me back to the Lord quicker'n an earthquake under my feet."

They went to the doorway together and at exactly the same moment stopped in amazement. The living room was littered with primitive artwork, photographs and memorabilia.

Marion, her long brown hair rippling over her shoulders and obscuring most of her face, and Cedar, with his dark head bent close, were examining the black designs on a burnt-orange Indian blanket spread over their knees. The bold pattern of a primitive eagle marked it as a tribal garment. The long cream-colored fringe at the lower edge looked like the soft natural hair of a Dall sheep, and along the sides, the white tail feathers of the bald eagle nested in tufts of down.

"Hin Gokl made him this blanket when he was born," Marion was saying as she smoothed a crimped feather. "River Swan had no kids of her own, see, because she lost her husband too soon. So she kind of adopted Mike...." She glanced into the woods beyond the window. "We'll find an isolated spot at the south end of Chichagof Island...build a pyre in the Tlingit tradition. I'll wrap him in this blanket and lay his things in with him...."

With great care she lifted the eagle face mask she'd taken from the wall. She picked up a rusted spear tip that lay by her hip, and her movements rustled the reed baskets scattered among strips of red cloth. A child's handmade slingshot lay across an eight-by-ten photo of a grinning teenage Mike standing next to a halibut larger than himself. "Mike takes a two-hundred-thirty-pounder," said the blue letters at the bottom. Nearby lay a pair of brown shoes with the tips curled from long storage. A dented salmon lure hid like a beetle in a wooden bowl, beside it a small spoon, obviously a baby's. Jade gleamed dully; Colleen saw a carved seal on top of a canvas fishing vest. On its side lay a tiny metal dump truck with hardly a trace of yellow paint left...so many things, images of Mike. Colleen couldn't take them all in.

Marion laid the mask and spear aside, her hands brushing the other objects. She swung her hair from her eyes. "He'll use these things on the journey his soul makes—" She stopped, seemed to have difficulty going on. "And after," she added in the softest voice Colleen had ever heard her use, "Ernie'll say the service...."

A light scratching sounded outside the door. Marion and Cedar glanced up, pausing to take in Colleen and Ernie. Colleen closed her mouth. Cedar gave her a smile that said things were okay.

Someone tapped lightly on the screen door. Walking over to help Marion to her feet, Ernie held on to her hand, looking in awe from her long hair and black shirt and slacks to the artwork at her feet.

Cedar started to rise, but Colleen said, "I'll get it," and headed for the door, her mind swirling with images of tribal dances and burning pyres and Marion's flowing hair. *She's pretty in an earthy way,* Colleen thought in surprise. *The long hair makes her look womanly.*

Pulling open the door, she stuck her head outside. Fishing boots tramped away toward town. The thick back of Blue Harry and the stringy open stride of J.T.

were unmistakable; they were traveling quickly down the boardwalk. "What—?"

They didn't look back. Perplexed, Colleen was closing the door when she glanced at the graying boards of the porch. There, stacked in an aluminum pan, were chunks of roast meat in red sauce from the barbecue. A lemon meringue pie, half a watermelon, another pan of baked potatoes and a huge platter of steaming Dungeness crabs completely covered the small porch.

"Cedar, help!" she called, bending to sniff the musky steam from the crabs. Briefly she closed her eyes in appreciation. Without straightening, she dragged the platter backward through the doorway...and ran into someone's legs. She twisted around. Cedar.

He bent until his face met hers, upside down. "Dinner ready so soon?" His smile was a frown from this angle.

"I just realized I'm still starved," she whispered. "Do you think Marion is up to—"

"What the pitch pine are you doing, Conaughy?" Marion's voice interrupted. "What've you got?"

She straightened and spun around. Cedar stepped back against the wall, and she could see Ernie gathering baskets into a carton. Marion, her hair streaming, her normally brown face looking grayish and pinched, was folding the orange blanket. She eyed the platter of seafood.

"Food," said Colleen uncertainly.

"I got eyes, girl." There was a hint of pathos in the way Marion half turned away. Her mouth working, she hugged the folded blanket to her stomach. Finally she patted it flat and resolutely looked at the food again. "Well, Ced," she said with a small waver, "Ced, for pity's sake, don't just stand there! Help her bring it inside! But supper'll have to be quick. There's at least six hours of travel time left in the sun.''

"You're not leaving this afternoon?" Cedar protested.

"We are.''

Probably reluctant to upset her, Cedar raised his hands in acquiescence.

"Marion," Colleen began, wanting to offer something in the way of condolence. "Marion, I'm sorry—"

The skipper cut her off with an abrupt wave. "Time's a wastin'. You folks chow down, and then Ernie and you'll get them to open the grocery store and sell some grub for the trip. Ced 'n I will pack up your things on the *Sparrow*, gas up and load the boat.''

"All right.''

"All right," Marion echoed. Fitting the Indian blanket into the carton, she muttered, "Let's get this show on the road." She began to help Ernie clean up the room, but she paused with the eagle mask in one hand.

"Oh, and Conaughy...?"

"Marion?"

She turned to Colleen, her mouth working as if the words were stuck again. "Ced, uh, Ced told me...your plan to fish.''

"Yes, we....'' She spread her hands.

"See, here," Marion blustered, her tone rising in familiar command, though her voice was thicker than usual. "See here, Conaughy. You keep safety lines up around the boat the whole time you're out. And—and keep your gloves on! And your hat!" She waved the eagle mask at Cedar. "Damned gal don't ever remember to put her hat on when there's a blow! See to it, Ced. Make sure she does!''

Tears suddenly made it impossible for Colleen to stay in the room. She meant something to Marion. If she meant something special to the skipper, and to Cedar.... "Yes, ma'am," she choked. She leaned down to grope for the platter. She kept her gaze low as she hurried to the kitchen. *Dear God,* she thought as she slid the plate to the counter and straightened to stare blindly out the window. *Dear God, do I have a place in this world at last?*

CHAPTER SEVENTEEN

BARANOF ISLAND LAY off the *Dart*'s port beam, the borders of the great Tongass National Forest gouged by inlets, bays and veillike waterfalls. Thinking of the bears feeding on cohos in those streams, Cedar sighed in frustration.

This time of year a bear didn't have to fight for his living, as a man did; all he had to do was crouch on a granite boulder, watch the salmon plug the stream below him, then slap one out onto the bank. *Voilá.* Supper.

Not that he needed to make his living here. In fact, his fishing income only stepped him up a bracket so that he paid higher taxes. No, he wouldn't even miss the eighty-five thousand dollars he'd wired to the hospital in Seattle—let Marion rage at him after she got home—but this fishing trip, this trip with Colleen was everything to him. He baited another hook with herring, then glanced across the work tubs and pulleys to the trolling cockpit.

To the slim woman singing a tuneless melody while she ran the gear, this trip was a rite of passage. He'd never seen a sense of purpose so obviously dictating a person's behavior before, and it fascinated him, but it was true. Colleen was the architect of this charity ride for Ernie and Marion; the success of this trip would be a milestone in her growth. She needed to give to people. She needed to feel she had something of value to give. In that respect, Mike's death had been a blessing.

But to Cedar this trip was the keystone of his future. Life had always been a rite to him, a passage from one tough situation to another. He'd mastered the city streets as a boy, and found that if he was shrewd and quick on his feet, he could carve out what he wanted. Too bad he hadn't learned that truth soon enough to save his mother from killing herself with work, he thought with a trace of the old bitterness. But later he'd gotten better at the game. He'd bested ancient grizzled traders in the teeming marketplaces of many countries, bringing home gems and rare jewels worth fortunes. He'd learned to bargain with grasping people, both men and women—learned, really, in his youth, from his mother, to be generous to those who gave generously themselves.

Yet this land of the midnight sun—he glanced again at Colleen—and this woman—everything he'd learned until now, all the lessons, didn't give him an easy path to either of them. He couldn't master them. Every breath, every happy moment in Alaska and with Colleen was a gift.

He scanned the open channel for the white froth that would mean a school of frenzied feeding herring, and felt the irritation of helplessness. A man had to be tougher here, smarter, more sensitive to hidden forces. Colleen was relying on his years of trolling experience to meet her own goals, and so far, he was letting her down.

With a sense of desperation, he stared at the gunmetal-green water. It was as transparent and clear as plastic. "Put yourself down under the surface," he remembered Marion saying years ago. "Think like them salmon who're heading for the streams to spawn and die after four or five years of living free, travelin' the waters of Japan, Mexico, Alaska. Think like 'em, Ced. Part of them wants to remain free, but their hearts tell 'em to go back home. And they'll go. They've got no choice.''

Something grabbed at him inside as he remembered those words, something he should be able to see more clearly in his own life. But he was a man for the present. Dreams and soul searching were for folks who sat musing on front porches, the spark of vitality turned backward to shine on the best moments of youth. For him, dreams were nothing more than memories about to happen. He liked shaping each day, making things happen now. So he looked intently at the water again.

The color of the water, the temperature, the clouds of feed he'd seen on the recorder—everything looked perfect. The salmon had to be down in that cool green marineland, and they had to go for herring. He knew it. The single coho they'd brought aboard an hour earlier had had a ten-inch herring in its belly.

Cedar slipped the long needlelike shaft of the hook forward along the backbone of the herring in his left hand, snugged the hook in close to the flaps of silver skin that would serve as a mobile tail in the water—the real tail had been removed. The gold flasher, spinning through the water just ahead of the bait, would do the rest. Right, Marion?

Coiling the leader into the tray, he reached for another fresh herring and slid in the hook. Their time together hadn't started out all that well, he mused about the past few days with Colleen. In fact, they had been downright uncomfortable, what with those two days and no fish and his blue mood over Mike's death. That was Alaska, taking away a free-spirited, rugged young man like Mike and bringing Cedar the rare smiles, the beauty, the bravery and generosity of Colleen.

Oh, she'd been relaxed and busy aboard the *Dart*. But those last days at the cottage, after they'd seen Marion and Ernie off at the harbor... Colleen had pussyfooted around as if he were going to tackle her and take her by force, three layers of clothing or no. She'd faced him, the morning they left the docks, and asked him to keep to his side of the sleeping quarters while she was aboard. He shook his head. She'd turned a paradisical opportunity into an ordeal of wills, and by now he was so twisted in knots that he felt as if he'd eaten sand. Because he'd said, dammit, that he'd give her time. Cedar coiled the last baited spread into the tray and bent to set it beneath the one she was emptying.

"How're you doing?" he asked. "Arms tired?"

She looked up briefly and smiled, the sun turning her teeth to gleaming pearl. "No, fine."

She tucked a ripple of copper hair into her blue knit cap—the gesture familiar to him now. Keeping the gurdie whirring, she bent, grabbed a spread, hooked it to the line and reached for the next one, her motions fluid. It had taken him until halfway through his second season to get that rhythm. She was good. Marion's fish puller was already good.

"We'll find the fish," she said, her eyes following the black marks on the stainless-steel line, counting fathoms.

"Thought I'd duck inside and run the recorder again. Make sure that feed is still located at the turn in the drag."

"They're down there. They're going to be hitting these herring in no time."

He smiled. "What makes you so sure?"

Shoving the gurdie into neutral, she shucked off her

gloves and pulled off her hat. Her hair streamed, dancing and catching gold lights and sending a jerk of desire so suddenly through him that his body curled toward her.

She stood in her navy-blue sweater, jeans hugging her slim thighs, just stood there, grinning at him. In unstudied provocation she raised her arms high over her head. "Well?"

"Well, what, Colleen? Damn, but you make it difficult to keep my promise."

"The sun finally came out!" She laughed, looking truly happy for the first time since he'd met her. She ran her hands through her hair, lifting the feathery strands, playfully fluffing it so the breeze took it like a kite and whipped it into a mass of gold threads. "It'll work! I know it will!"

"Colleen...." She must know what she did to him when she played around like this. "For heaven's sake, what's your point?"

"Hin Gokl says it'll draw the salmon."

"What, your hair?"

"Uh-huh. Better than these." She picked up a six-dollar flasher and tossed it back into the box, where it tinkled and blinked like a mirror. "She says when the sun's shining my hair is good luck with the fish. Yesterday was overcast. Today it's not. Go on, Ced. Find the patches of feed." She winked. "I'll do the rest."

Chuckling, he shook his head. "You're something, you know that? I want to give you the world, the whole damn world...." He turned away, meaning it, wanting her, wanting to find the fish and get the season over with so they could go back to Seattle. Not for marriage, of course, but for the first steady, long-term relationship he'd ever wanted. In Seattle, at least, there'd be time to court her the way he knew she should be courted. With champagne. Flowers. Moonlit dinners at his condominium. . . and to hell with the conference in Düsseldorf. His executive director, Mack, could go in his place. Unless Colleen said, "Cedar, I want to go to Germany with you." But that was dreaming. . . .

"Hey, Ced."

Almost to the wheelhouse, he turned, waited.

"Know how to wash a fish?"

"No, tell me, salmon-trolling woman with the salmon-lure hair. How do you wash a fish?"

"You throw it in a washer with a little Lux Liquid. . . ."

He laughed, and still laughing, went inside to flip on the recorder. Outside, the gear started humming again, and the flashers tinkled as she snubbed them to the line.

He watched the paper roll off the recorder's spool. The lead drew a crater, one they'd passed over nearly forty minutes ago. Still a while yet before they'd go by that shallow spot where he'd seen the cloud of feed, where they'd snagged that coho.

A small red double-ender and a sleek gray crab boat cruised on the horizon. He switched on the VHF radio. Couldn't hurt to pick up any odd gossip, he thought.

A fisherman was talking about "catching" a new door for the house. A young voice came on and said, "gonna catch me one of those fancy redwood hot tubs this trip." "Nuts!" Cedar growled. Nothing happening for them, either. He turned down the volume. Restlessly he riffled through a stack of cassette tapes, selecting a homegrown recording by a young crab fisherman in

Pelican's summer crab fleet, the slim guy who had taken first in the survival suit race.

Randy Welch had pulled salmon and worked in canneries and hand trolled all along the coast of Alaska. He wrote songs and sang them in that scratchy baritone that was a mix of Willie Nelson and McCartney, spanning decades, half bluegrass, part country and western, gettin' down with the loneliness and passion and spirit of the fisherman. Maybe Randy would change their luck.

As he was slipping the cassette into the player, Cedar glanced at the recorder. *Feed. They were right above the biggest hot spot he'd seen in years.*

He spun around to lock the wheel into as tight a circle as he dared, poked the on button on the player and deserted the cabin, heading for the trolling cockpit.

"Colleen!" he called, climbing in beside her and grabbing a tray of baited spreads. "Shake that pretty hair, baby, because we're over the hot spot!"

The strains of a guitar sprang from the wheelhouse. Colleen jerked toward it, gave Cedar a quick smile and tossed her head. The grating youthful voice joined that fast-rhythm guitar, and the *Dart* came alive with Randy's song.

> He's a Fairweather troller
> on the East Bank on the grounds
> Watchin' the fathometer
> and loran to make his rounds.
> He's got the Jimmy turnin'
> a six-hundred-rev speed,
> Keepin' an eye on the recorder
> for some patches of feed....

"Pat-ches of feed," echoed Colleen, counting fathoms, bouncing to the beat.

Cedar ran the port-bow pole line first, his arms and shoulders grateful for the sprint, his blood beginning to pump as he sang along with Welch.

> The puller's on the back deck
> cleanin' fish and baitin' hooks
> Then he jumps down in the fish hold
> where he ices those Chinooks.
> You soon get your sea legs
> amidst the ocean rolls
> Your adren'line starts to runnin'
> when you see those dancin' poles!

"Come on, poles!" Cedar shouted, enjoying himself. Colleen's elbow grazed his back, and he glanced toward her, saw the fitted jeans moving as she moved in unconscious sensuality. He forced himself to turn away, singing,

> If the wind should pick up
> and the tides are just right
> We'll take the flood into Lituya
> where we'll anchor for the night. . . .

Lord, he'd better stand in this cockpit for the next two days, he told himself, snubbing up a spread. Because if he heard one more soft moan out of Colleen as she turned in her sleep, sloshing the water in Ernie's bunk, he was going to leap across that companionway and do something he'd wanted to do since the middle of

May—make her moan and cry out with the pleasure of making love.

How the devil was he going to breach that fear that kept her from him? She'd be gray-haired and brittle and a little crazy with disillusion, unless she broke free. All that life and beauty going to waste—

"Cedar!"

And then he heard it, too, the clatter of the pole and the ringing of the starboard-bow pole bell. She had a fish on. Two, three, five strikes shook the pole.

One hand on the gurdie, the other full of snubber with the leader trailing, she froze, her gaze questioning. "What should I do, finish baiting this line or bring the other one up?"

Amused, delighted, he threw back his head. The laughter rattled from him. "Put the line in the water, Freedom, and shake that golden hair. We want them all!"

TWELVE HOURS LATER the setting sun spread magenta from one side of the wheelhouse to the other, burning a pink tinge across the white paint. They drifted off the coast of Baranof, fifteen miles from Sitka, the evening breeze sighing to the strains of Cedar's best Tchaikovsky.

Cedar flopped belly down on the hatch and propped his head on his arms, his mind filled with the music.

"I hate salmon," Colleen declared, slumping against an upturned bucket near the wheelhouse. She nudged a silver coho with her boot. "They're so greedy. Look at them, lying there with their bellies emptied of our herring, piled on one another like lemmings."

Cedar looked around at the litter of gleaming salmon

and smiled. "I love the little beggars. Folks after my own heart."

"How do you mean?"

"Living for the moment. Going down with a fight. What's that song. . . 'Live fast, love hard, die young'?"

"Like that thing on the wall in your locker? That poem that says, 'Tomorrow is nothing until you live it'?"

"Something like that."

"I guess it doesn't sound half-bad, celebrating life. I've been doing a lot of thinking about that. 'Tomorrow is only a dream. . . .'" Her voice fell away.

He sighed. It was so gratifying to have a hold full of iced cohos, the deck swamped, the sun going down—and this woman with the red-gold hair sharing the moment. "We did it, Colleen. They're going to fall down laughing at us, call it beginner's luck, the two of them, but we know we did it."

"Do you suppose they're in Seattle yet?"

"Sure. With this weather?"

She sighed wearily. "Marion would have loved today."

He glanced at her. Colleen's hair looked wild; blood from cleaning fish stained her jeans. But the red backlighting in her hair and the warmth it gave her skin made her look like a wanton in one of those waterfront movies. He felt a stirring for her and closed his eyes. His shoulders felt numb, his legs ached, but his caveman instincts never let up. He groaned softly.

"Ced?"

"Mmm?"

"We really did it, didn't we? Together."

He opened his eyes. She was leaning toward him, her eyes wide and violet. He nodded.

"What are we going to do with them?"

"After this cat nap we'll run into Sitka. Cold storage will grab up every last one of them."

"Keep one of them, will you?" Her voice dropped an octave, resonating through him. "For tomorrow?"

He sat up and swung his legs over the hatch, his heart pumping with a slow new energy. "Sure, Freedom," he said guardedly. "But why? What's happening tomorrow?"

A long pause. And then into the magenta evening she said, "Us."

He had to make himself stay where he was. She could mean anything by that. Almost anything. Huskily, because he didn't trust his full voice, he whispered, " 'Us'?"

"Yes."

Then he was kicking the fish out of his way, wading through them to get to her. She stood up. He came to her, gripped her hands and looked down into her face. Violet pools full of longing and vulnerability met his gaze. Still he was wary. "Why?" he asked hoarsely.

"Because you've loved me and been patient and a joy to work with," she said. "Because I want to give back to you. Because we belong together."

Tchaikovsky clicked off. The wind sighed in the rigging. The flutter and cry of swooping sea gulls pierced the silence.

Cedar felt a happiness akin to what he'd felt as a child careening on an inner tube down that fast stream in New Hampshire, the water splashing in his face, the breeze whipping his shirttails as he slid over the falls and crashed into the pool below. Unable to believe Colleen, but filled with that same heart-stopping joy, he crushed her close. She felt so small. She'd worked beside him for sixteen hours; she had to be practically out on her feet. Yet she leaned against him and slid her arms around his waist, her grip sure and strong.

He stood there in shock for several moments. Then her body brought him to life, and he shook slightly as he buried his face in her shoulder, seeking the warm white curve of her throat.

She chuckled low and softly, her head falling back.

The salt of work mingled with a natural sweetness that he remembered tasting before, and he kissed her hungrily, his pulse jumping. "Colleen," he murmured, fevered. "To hell with selling the fish tonight. Let's get cleaned up and roast that coho now."

"No." She unwrapped her arms and pushed some space between them.

Suddenly on guard, he gripped her arms. "'No'?"

"Cedar, listen to me." She moistened her lips, and his breath raked the stillness. "This is Ernie's boat. He trusts us." She glanced at the mud-red water.

She was right. Ernie was a preacher at heart, and their sleeping together on his precious *Dart* would be rubbing his nose in the very life-style that had driven him from the ministry. The fishermen were his congregation now; he gave them his example because that was all he trusted himself to give. She was right.

"He trusts *me*," she added in an urgent tone. Her eyes came back to him, and he could see her resolve. "But what he doesn't know is that you and I will be together for a long, long time. And for the beginning of our loving, Cedar, we need. . . ." She waved toward the dark shadow of the island.

And then he understood. He smiled, relieved. "Virgin territory, so to speak."

She laughed. "Yes."

"You're a genius, Freedom, and I'm going to give you the world."

"I want you, Cedar. Only you."

He leaned close and caressed her lips with his own. "That, my love, would be more taking than giving, from my point of view. But I'm fully prepared to offer myself as a down payment on the world at large. What say we shower and head for town? We'll sell the fish, ply some sleepy maître d' with our cash, eat a good meal, then turn in. Tomorrow, Freedom, is only a few hours away."

HE DIDN'T KNOW WHERE she'd kept it through the fishing season, but she came out to breakfast with him wearing a summery dress that reminded him of pale blue opals. A short white sweater caped her shoulders. The sleek material of the dress wrapped low over her breasts and tied snugly at her waist, falling in loose feminine swirls around her knees. It would be easy to free her of that light cloth, he thought, watching her walk beside him beneath the shadow of false-front stores and offices. Her high full breasts moved beneath the material, and he groaned inwardly. She wasn't wearing a bra.

She wore the type of flat-heeled blue shoes he'd seen on women in Hong Kong, her toned honey-gold calves and slim ankles looking shapely in the low canvas.

"You look yummy again," he said, trying to keep from sweeping back her tantalizing curls so he could kiss the pale curve of her shoulder...and her throat... and her lips. "Oh, to hell with it!" Stopping on the sidewalk, ignoring the more roughly clad residents of Sitka, a bustling fishing and lumbering town, he swept her hair away. He cupped her chin in his hand. Her eyes shone as clearly as an English summer sky, not a flicker of uncertainty in her gaze. The excitement poured through him. "You always look yummy," he said, brushing her lips in a kiss.

She gave him a bright happy smile. "Not when we're in the fish."

"Even then. For a few weeks, there, you were looking pale, but now there are sunsets in your cheeks, and your eyes look like that blue diamond I was telling you about."

"And yours," she said, playfully tapping his nose, "yours are like that volcano, Mount Edgecumbe, over there across the channel from us, or like it used to be, anyway—all fire and smoke and mysterious intent. We at least have to eat breakfast, Ced."

"And for dessert . . . ."

She grinned. "Early blueberries?"

He took her arm and steered her down the street. Breakfast had better be a quick affair. He was hungry for more satisfying fare.

"I like that blue-green sweater you're wearing," she said conversationally. "We'll call it your Alaska sweater and have it framed and mounted behind glass someday. It'll remind me of the forests and channels and rugged people I met here. . .during the best year of my life."

"Why 'the best'?"

"I grew up."

"I'll give it to you as a graduation present, then, how's that? I bought it in Ireland three years ago. It'll keep you warm for years to come."

They crossed an intersection. Cedar nodded to a burly Tlingit man with his arms full of groceries, his thermal

shirt and jackboots marking him as a lumberman.
"Morning."

The man's gaze cut to Colleen. He perked his eyebrows and grinned at Cedar.

Cedar gave him a subtle shrug that said, "Yeah, ain't
she something?"

A car honked, and a tour bus pulled to the curb ahead
of them. Cedar felt a wave of irritation wash over him.
The city. He'd come to Alaska to avoid the bustle and
confusion, and here he was on a day he'd probably remember for the rest of his life, stuck back in a town that
hummed with activity. He began to think of a cove where
he could take Colleen after breakfast, somewhere where
the grass grew thick in the clearing and they could spread
a blanket; no other people, no exhaust fumes, just a clear
cold pond a stone's throw away, where they could swim
and play.

Colleen was saying, "No need to give the sweater to
me, Cedar, when we'll be—" she paused to stare at
someone in the crowd disembarking from the tour bus.
"That woman, Cedar, she looks like—she's waving to
us! To you. Cedar, I think she's waving to you."

Cedar refocused his thoughts, scanning the crowded
sidewalk. His heart plummeted. "Dear Lord, it's
Alicia!"

The old revulsion filled him. At seeing her furs and
jewelry and graying coiffed hair, here in a roughshod
town like Sitka, the bile rose in his throat. It was as if
she defiled the town. Fury tightened his lips. "Let's cut
across," he said shortly, gripping Colleen's elbow.

"But, Cedar!" She resisted, glancing at the tall
woman in the tailored brown skirt and matching fur-
trimmed jacket. "She knows you. She's waving us over.
She's coming this way."

"Trust me, it's only because she wants something. Now let's go find a nice quiet café where Alicia's type wouldn't be caught dead."

"All *right*, Ced, but don't drag me across the street. These aren't exactly the woolly days of the West!"

"Sorry." He loosened his grip. Brakes squealed; Cedar jerked Colleen back from the blur of a passing station wagon. He had to wait as three more cars sped down the tarmac. Colleen kept looking at him as if he were Sasquatch.

"Cedar Cleary!" Alicia's sickly-sweet tones wafted from behind.

The street cleared, and he brought his arm around Colleen, who was glancing over her shoulder. "Cedar," she protested again. "I've never seen you so rude. She looks nice."

As he was stepping away, Alicia appeared at his left, her brown eyes flicking over him, glancing off Colleen. Tightening his arm protectively around Colleen's slender waist, he stepped back out of traffic and glared at Alicia. "Alicia," he said in cold, level acknowledgment.

"Why, Cedar Cleary, imagine finding you in the middle of my Alaskan safari!"

"Hunting again, are you?"

The peach blush on her cheeks faded a little, but the ingrained phony smile rapidly brightened that taut skin. She must have had four face lifts to keep that youthful face, he thought in disgust. She was approaching sixty-three, the age his mother would have been.

"Cedar Cleary, let me look at you!" Gushing and oohing, his aunt ran a frail hand laden with gold and diamonds down the sleeve of his Windbreaker. He shrugged her away. "Well, but you do look fit," Alicia crooned, nonplussed. She shifted her gaze. "And who's this lovely young thing in your arms? Chip off the old block, Cedar, you really are. Your daddy all over again.''

Cedar heard the breath leave Colleen's lungs, and he smiled privately. Abruptly Colleen snuggled against him and purred petulantly, ''Ced, darling, I'm so-o-o hungry. Do we have to stand like heathens in the middle of the street, talking to strangers, when you promised to buy me breakfast?''

When he looked down at the would-be wanton at his side, he saw the angry gleam in her blue eyes. *Good for you, Freedom. Alicia didn't score on you, after all.* He patted her arm, playing the role of sugar daddy. ''Of course, pet.''

Raising an arrogant brow to his aunt, he said, ''If you'll excuse us, Alicia. You'll miss your safari— Oh, and have them take you by the Pioneer's Home. It's the watering hole for all those virile Alaskans who tamed this land.''

''Splendid!'' Alicia didn't have the vaguest idea that he meant for her to visit the most famous retirement home in Alaska. She beamed. ''I'm sure that's on the itinerary. Oh, but we should visit after almost fifteen years apart. We're all the family we have, dear. Have you settled here, or are you just—'' her gaze assessed Colleen ''—having breakfast? After your mother died, we rather lost touch, didn't we?''

A cold hate gripped him to hear Alicia speak of his mother. ''After you broke her heart, you mean.''

Speechless, Alicia stepped away from him.

He smiled. ''Who did you go after when you were through with him—my father, I mean—after you wrecked our lives? Use your first husband's fortune, did you, to trap another and suck him dry?''

Although Colleen went rigid beside him, he couldn't spare her a glance. He felt blinded. The rage and despair of seeing his mother work herself to death, supporting him, welled up to cloud his vision, but he could also see that burgundy-lipped mouth in front of him. Those hands weighted in jewels—hands that had never known the washers full of clothes and the lipstick-smeared beer glasses her twin sister had ruined her own delicate hands on.

"Well, Alicia? Still glad to see your only surviving relative?"

A silver-haired man called from twenty feet away, where the tour group had lined up and was slowly disappearing into a hotel dining room.

"Cedar, you—"

"Go on." He waved abruptly. "I'm sure you'll manage to eat. A conscience like yours doesn't falter over a few ghosts from the past!"

Straightening her back, Alicia choked. "You're so right." She recovered jerkily, years of pretense coming to her aid. She smoothed her hands down her stomach and relaxed them against her thighs.

"He was a weakling," she said, smiling maliciously, degrading his father. She stared pointedly at Colleen. "For anything in skirts. It didn't matter if they could offer him better than he could earn on his own, building houses like a peon. He was a grasping, weak-willed excuse for a man. He could be bought, though. *I* bought him, and when I was through with him, I threw him out! Does that destroy the tower of steel you carried around in your mind, Cedar Cleary? Does that shatter all those images a boy cherishes of his father?" She laughed.

"How could it?" he said, a pulse jumping in his

cheek. "You haven't told me anything new. You told it all to my mother, too, you heartless vamp!" He gasped, the hatred so intense he could barely breathe. "You told it to her that last time you came visiting, your fancy Caddy parked in front of our two-room walk-up, your arms full of conscience presents. You were full of half-truths that day, aimed at healing your guilt. You didn't give a damn about her!

"You haven't hurt me today, Alicia." He let go of Colleen. The silver-haired, portly man broke from the tour and came toward them, looking perplexed. "You've done nothing but remind me that you're still the lowest creature on earth, a greedy, grasping person. Go on." He waved toward Alicia's silver-haired companion, hovering behind her. "Alaskan safari! More like a manhunt, and you'll leave the bodies for the crows!"

"Now, see here!" blustered the tourist, putting his arm around Alicia, peering with concern into her face. "Who is this guy? Do we need the police?"

"Oh, John...." Alicia spoke faintly, consoling herself by rubbing the fur on her collar. "No, just a local I was asking directions from." She glanced at Cedar, her dark eyes hard. "Just a rude stranger."

"Be sure you check out the Pioneer's Home." Cedar smiled, feeling wintry. "Although, Alicia, I doubt you'd fit in with them—those Sourdoughs had to have heart to carve out a life in this country." He nodded briefly to the stranger. "No offense. You'll want to get her off the street, though. She just doesn't fit in."

Chuckling hollowly, Cedar pivoted. "Ah, Freedom! I know of a nice restaurant up the street where the air's not polluted. Shall we?"

Her expression strained but sympathetic, she murmured in mock sarcasm, "You didn't introduce us," and hurried with him across the blacktop. Tires thrummed nearby; brakes squealed. He hated the city.

Behind them, Alicia was moaning about insufferable blackguards and the tourist was saying, "We'll get you a nice hot cup of coffee and some of those huge Haines strawberries, won't we, my dear? And we'll see if we can't find an Indian totem pole or a fur parka from the Eskimos to take back home?"

That's the ticket, fella, Cedar thought bleakly. That was the language his aunt understood. Alicia, hiding the fact that she'd come from a childhood of poverty. *Damn you, Alicia! Play the helpless widow, marry him, drain him, leave him.* The litany droned like a dirge in his brain, souring the day, filling his heart with misery until he couldn't bring himself to even touch Colleen, though she didn't bear the faintest resemblance to the gray-haired vulture they had just escaped.

CHAPTER EIGHTEEN

THEY HAD SEEN the onion dome and white spire of St. Michael's Russian Orthodox Cathedral and the Sheldon Jackson Museum, with its Russian relics and Tlingit tribal collection. Now they stood in the gloomy spruce grove of Totem Bight Park, adjacent to the campus where Marion had spent one year of high school.

Still Cedar wouldn't discuss the Alicia incident with Colleen. His normally sensuous lips pursed, and his mood rivaled that of the shadowed forest. The carved totem loomed above Colleen. The bear's ferocious grin was painted bright red; the green frog stared at her. A killer whale and a number of other primitive animal shapes wound up the pole, and through the branches, the black eyes of an eagle glared across the trees to Sitka Sound.

Each Tlingit symbol she'd seen this morning reminded her of Marion, building Mike's funeral pyre in the woods somewhere up north; Ernie, standing with his red Bible, booming out the service in his Southern Baptist voice. But the fierce glare of the eagle reminded her of Cedar, facing his aunt.

"Tell me about your mother and father," she said softly, still gazing at the totem. She knew Cedar was frowning toward a broad path of pine needles overhung with spruce. She tugged her white sweater closer around her. "I mean, it's obvious by this time that you need to talk."

"Is it?"

"Yes, Cedar, it is. Finding virgin territory, as you put it last night, is the last thing you want to do today."

"I guess you're right."

She closed her eyes over the prick of hurt his agreement gave her. But they had a lifetime for loving. He needed her now, needed as much unselfish understanding as she could give him. "Cedar?"

"Mmm?"

"Tell me about them."

When a twig crackled, she turned and saw him studying her, his face creased with unhappiness. "Let's go to the water," he said.

In minutes they were sitting above the tide line, the gray blue sweep of Mount Edgecumbe's volcanic cone and the circular clouds above it breaking the hazy line where the sound met the sea. A crow hopped among bulbs of army-green kelp, looking for insects. The water lapped between the stones, bringing the salty scent of the ocean to Colleen as she sat on her rock.

Cedar had chosen a flat ledge of stone two yards from her, making the hurt arrow through her again. She had to remind herself Cedar was troubled. She watched the black raven flutter up off the beach and settle again as a gentle wave collapsed on shore. She stared at her blue canvas shoes. She smoothed the folds of her dress. She waited a long while, feeling the burden of his memories.

At last his hand swept upward in a futile gesture. "They were sisters," he said bitterly. "Can you even imagine it? One couldn't have any more children, and the other never wanted any."

"Your mother couldn't have more?"

He nodded.

"She couldn't... for health reasons?"

"Correct. She would have died."

"Go on...."

Abruptly he stood up. He was restless, and he began to walk over the stone rubble toward town. She fell into step with him, walking on the uphill side of the beach.

"Oh, my father understood for a few years, I guess," he said, giving the water his fierce attention. "I mean, that she wouldn't sleep with him again."

"Wouldn't sleep...?"

"She was Catholic. Same as you."

It was an accusation. Confused, she asked, "Why did she have to stop sleeping with him, Ced? Even back then Catholics practiced the rhythm method of birth control, didn't they?"

"It wasn't foolproof. If she'd gotten pregnant, she wouldn't have had the option of one of those convenience abortions. If you got pregnant then, the church favored the life of the child, and to hell with the mother. She was devout."

"I see."

His eyes found her. "Do you? It was because of me that she refused to sleep with him again. She was devoted to me. Eventually I was all she had. After—" he waved "—Alicia."

"Yes," she said as gently as she could. "I see that you've been dragging the guilt around yourself—for years, and it's difficult for you to realize now, as a man, that none of this was your fault. None of it, Cedar, just as you told me."

"She said they loved each other. A lot."

"Cedar, let it go."

He bent, picked up a stone, lobbed it hard into the channel. It plunked with a splash. He picked up another.

She took his hand, wrapped tightly around the stone, and held it against her stomach. The fist trembled. A muscle ticked on the side of his jaw.

"Cedar, I almost let my father's problems destroy my life. You told me I had no control over his suffering, and I believed you. I—I wrote that letter, Ced. Now let me help you."

He let go of the stone. "Don't misunderstand, Colleen." He gently grasped her arms, but when she saw his eyes, they still seemed troubled. He arched back to look up at the sky, trying, she suspected, to find words. "I'm—I love you. I want very much to find this spot I know about and very gently—"

She murmured, relieved, and he glanced down at her again, his eyes softer. "Very gently and completely get to know you. It's just—you're right, yes, I need to get rid of this bile in my throat over Alicia. It'll take some time."

"I know...." She touched the cleft in his chin, traced the shape of his full lower lip, caressed his cheek. They had forever. Once she'd realized she and Cedar could work out their problems together, that they needed and could help each other through anything, the decision to commit herself to him had come suddenly— across a deck crowded with silver salmon. She loved him. She was capable of giving, and he wanted her to give. And they had time.

Oh, she was full of fears, yes. But the sheer peace of sharing a cabin with him, working beside him hour after hour with the music blaring and the poles dancing—she had never felt so powerful. So full of love. She had never liked herself so well as the days following that sad telegram from Seattle. She had never loved anyone as much as she'd loved Cedar during those three days on the *Dart*. The love flowed through her eyes to him now, and she whispered, "Cedar, my love, I understand."

He drew her fingers to his mouth and kissed them, then brought her hand through the crook of his arm. They began walking again. Three ravens cawed from the spruce trees. Frowning at the birds, Cedar asked dryly, "Alicia seems like a proper, upper-middle-class midwesterner, doesn't she?"

"With a nasty tongue, yes."

"She's a whore."

Colleen flinched. "You're not pulling punches today. No wonder you've kept your thoughts about the past hidden."

His boots crunched loudly on the stones; he was moving faster. He said savagely, "All Alicia cared about was a change of bed partners! My father was convenient. Neither one of them gave a hoot for the others they hurt."

"What happened to her?" She meant his mother, and he seemed to know it.

"She expected him to find release at times—I'm sure of it. But with her own sister? He left my mother for Alicia, and their betrayal took the spirit out of her. Over a period of seven years, she just got paler and more weary, until one day she took this medicine the doctor gave her for an infection. They should have tested her, Colleen," he appealed to her, kicking stones out of his way. "Tried to find out what was really wrong with her.

But she had neither the time nor the money for proper medical care, and she didn't seem to care that she was ill. She was run-down, and the drug killed her.''

He stopped. Colleen's momentum carried her a few steps beyond, and she turned and came back to take one of his hands. He pulled away, stuck his cold hand into his Windbreaker pocket and started walking again. His hate for Alicia and his father had obliterated his sensitivity to Colleen. She felt the anger directed not at her but at the world in general. She dug into the shallow reservoir of confidence she'd gained and held on to the knowledge that she loved him. He needed time. Her own fragile relationship with him was fine, she told herself, practically running to keep up with Cedar as he climbed to the blacktop road that wound through town. Things would be fine between them in a few hours.

Cedar didn't speak again. When they reached the boat harbor, he sighed in disgust at the tourists and fishermen and women who wandered along the swaying docks. He helped her aboard. As he was reaching for the stern line to cast off, she suggested, ''We could go below and have some coffee. You want some coffee?''

''Sounds good,'' he replied without enthusiasm. He bent to check one of the fenders that protected the hull from the dock. He glanced at her. ''You brew it while I get us out of this traffic jam. I really don't like cities, Colleen.''

''Right. Right, Ced, we'll talk out on the water.'' She headed for the wheelhouse.

''Colleen, don't push me about this, okay?''

A gull squealed overhead. She glanced up, wondering how long he'd stay withdrawn. Yet who was she to point a finger about that? She'd been as closed as a clam about her own problems. She turned, smiled at him, then repeated his own words to her. "I'll give you time. We have lots of time."

Instead of responding with a smile, as she'd expected, he straightened. The wind lifted that lock of hair that looked nice on his right temple. His uncertain expression worried her.

"Really," she said nervously. "We've got...years."

He took a step toward her. "You keep saying that. What's behind it, exactly?"

"This really isn't the time, Ced...."

"Colleen, I've wanted you for a long time. My feelings for you are intense. They grow deeper every day. But that doesn't mean...." He shrugged, growing more uncomfortable by the minute.

The adrenaline leaped through her bloodstream, but she felt fear, not joy. "What are you saying, Ced? That doesn't mean...what?"

"Marriage."

The word hung in the early-afternoon air. The sea gull dropped out of the sky and clung to the stern rail, searching for scraps of fish that might have been left. The *Dart* rocked. The rubber bumper guards scraped against the dock. All the details of Colleen's surroundings lodged rigidly in her mind, frozen, like her heart. She had been right about him all along. Marion had even repeated, 'Ced wants you for himself.' But not, oh, God, not for marriage. Not even someday. Not even a flicker of uncertainty in his eyes when he had said it didn't mean marriage.

"Colleen, for heaven's sake!" His tone was exasperated, surprised. "You're talking marriage when we haven't even slept together?"

Her defenses came up. Her chin rose, and she pinned him with her eyes as he stood across that polished deck from her. "The point of marriage, Cedar, is not that you sleep together first, necessarily, but that you sleep together forever afterward. That's the point of marriage! That's what 'till death do us part' means!"

She saw him shift awkwardly. She saw him begin to turn away. She felt the blood leave her face. "Cedar... what awful mistake have I made?"

He pivoted. "Mistake—I don't know what you're thinking! One minute I'm telling you about my family, and the next you're talking marriage!"

"Yes! Yes, I thought that's what you meant when you said you loved me. When you said you wanted to give me the world. That's the kind of thing a sensitive man says to his future wife. The world, Cedar. You said you wanted to give me the whole damn world! Oh, sweet Mary, what did you mean?"

His face went cold, unbelievably cold, as it had when he'd faced Alicia. "Colleen," he said harshly. "Marriage was never what I meant."

She backed a half step, then whirled. All she could see were docks and trolling poles and the rough-hewn implements of fishing. A man in green waders was scrubbing his deck. A buff cat stretched on a hatch cover, then leaped into a basket. *If he'd hit me,* she thought, *it would have hurt less.* She lifted her trembling hand, a last gesture of hope, and choked out, "You don't mean this. You're just angry and full of hate about Alicia."

His boots thudded up behind her. The hope renewed, she turned to him. He grasped her arms in that way he had of getting her attention, skimming her sweater from her shoulders. "I don't want to mislead you," he said

urgently, shaking her a little. His gaze went to the lov
vee of her dress, and a tremor went through her as hi
eyes darkened. He ran his hands up her arms, massag
ing, urging, "I'm crazy about you, please believe that
Yes, Alicia's coming here reminded me of all my family
lost because of her, of all my father was."

She moistened her lips. "And you? Are you a chip of
the old block, as she said?"

She saw him almost deny it. He shook his head slightly
But in mid-moment his jaw slackened, and the reckonin;
came to his face.

"Oh," she murmured. "No, Cedar, no."

"I—I've always been with whatever woman I wanted
I never considered marriage. . .children." Something
like self-disgust curled his lip. Letting her go, he said, "
never look at the future, Colleen."

"But I saw you watching them," she argued, pleading
with him.

"Who?"

"Those children, kids at the Pelican Fourth of July
games. You loved them!"

"Other people's." He stood aside, gripping a stay wire.

Again he'd turned from her. In desperation she
grated, "Liar!"

He was pivoting toward her when she whipped
around to grab his sleeve.

"You love children! You love me! You'll give it all up
because your father left your mother? Because your
aunt uses men, then junks them when she's through?"
She shook him. "Come off it, Cedar! Two examples in
your childhood. Are they so powerful a deterrent that
you'll sacrifice your own happiness to remain single?
Safe and single?"

Angry creases whitened in his cheeks. He jerked away. "You've got style, Colleen, I'll give you that! Talking about my hang-ups. You're as grasping as the rest of them! Look at you! Yes, your chin goes up!"

"Damn right!"

"Yes, and now you've put walls around the first really decent relationship you've ever had. You were a shell of self-pity when I met you. I'm the one who waited out your insecurities."

She gasped. He laughed shortly. "You're the one who's giving up something of value. You need some priest and the state's approval for what I do because it's natural and right. You're no better than me, Colleen. Your terms are just different!"

She'd come to Alaska to change views like his—views she had once held herself. She rushed toward him, hitting his chest with both raised palms. Grunting at the impact, he twisted and started toward the stern line. The sea gull squawked, whirring away. Colleen yanked Cedar's arm. She came up under his face and shouted, "You're damn right my terms are different, bud! Thank God I remembered in time!"

"WE HAVE A CHOICE to make," he said two nights later. He held to the galley doorjamb, steadying himself against the roll of the sea. Forward of the kitchen, the rain spattered on the roof of the trunk cabin, as it did against the window near Colleen. Aft, a cleat in the staying sail pinged somewhere along the boom mast.

Colleen rose from the kitchen table; she had closed her book when she heard him coming down the companionway stairs. From the cassette player behind her drifted guitar strains and marimba chimes and the flute-like golden Mangione horn. Decision about what, she wondered. He had already made the only important choice between them, back in Sitka-by-the-Sea, where she'd made a fool of herself proposing to him.

She hadn't looked at him yet. She folded a tan towel over her wrist and picked up her satin makeup case. She unzipped it and peered inside. Her soap was there. She began to close it again.

"I said we have to make a decision."

Steeling herself as she had for three days, she glanced at him, telling herself he was just her everyday partner in the salmon business, like Marion. His eyes were burning with anything but weather matters, though. Nervously she picked up her book. Keeping her voice matter-of-fact, she asked, "What kind of a decision?"

He jerked a thumb upward. "Weather's closing in. Forecast for late tomorrow for Sitka and vicinity calls for gusting to thirty knots. On the outside, here, that could mean eighty, maybe more."

"I knew it would storm soon."

"Oh?"

She looked at the varnished wood ceiling and remembered the gust-driven rain stinging her face as she'd pulled cohos today. At least cohos were lighter than kings, averaging eight pounds, but the current and the wind had shoved the boat around, making it miserable to fish. Cedar had pulled aboard most of the large halibut they caught—the season was open on the wide, white-bellied fish for the next eight days. If Marion weren't so prickly about physical contact, she and Ernie would dance a jig when they saw the earnings. The hold was more than half-full again. It was probably good timing to head home now. Yes, a storm was brewing—both outside and inside this cabin.

Bracing her feet as the deck tilted, she nodded. "It felt the same way up on the Fairweather Grounds, that day the wind started to blow."

"Well, you're right. It'll be nasty tomorrow." He went to the stove and dispensed a cup of coffee. "Want some?"

"No, thanks. Think I'll get my shower and turn in."

He turned from the range, gesturing with his mug, giving her the impression he wanted her to stay put. "We could fish in the morning and then head into Sitka—take us about four hours. Wait out the storm there."

"Or?"

"We could get an early start and try to make it all the way to Lisianski Strait before the storm breaks. Once we're inside it won't matter much. Except for that right-hand turn at the inlet, it's practically a straight shot into Pelican."

She thought of the dangers; she thought of the possibility that Cedar would notice her fear. It wouldn't have mattered as much if they'd reconciled, but things were back to normal, she thought dryly. She was back in her cocoon and hoping the world didn't crash in on her. "Will it blow bad before we get to Pelican?" she asked lightly.

"Not until late tomorrow night, probably. What do you want to do?"

"If Ernie's in Pelican, he'll want the boat back."

"That's what I figured. I just didn't know how much more fish you wanted to try to bring in before we went back home."

Home. The word rolled off his tongue as if it meant something to him. She turned toward the sleeping quarters. "Home, I guess. If you think we can make it."

"We could hole up on the other side of Khaz Peninsula if things get too rough on the way up Chichagof Island."

"Fine."

His smooth baritone stopped her as she was opening the door. "Twenty thousand dollars is enough, then?"

"Yes, I'm sure Marion didn't expect a thousand. She'll be grateful."

"So will Ernie." His voice grew velvety. "It was a nice gesture, Colleen."

She nodded and started forward.

"Colleen?"

Again she stopped without looking at him. "*Yes,* Cedar. What is it now?"

"I love you."

Her eyes snapped shut.

"I had to tell you," he pleaded, and she could hear his restraint. "It wouldn't stay inside any longer."

A shudder went through her. Tears squeezed from her tight eyelids. She was off guard. The deck pitched, and the molding of the doorway slammed into the side of her head. The tears trickled down her cheeks from the pain. She held her head, rubbing the sore spot, the tears falling *splot splot* on her towel.

Cedar came up behind her. His hands, the hands she'd watched for a week, hard capable hands, clasped her arms with gentle pressure. He turned her to face him. Gently he probed the bruise as Colleen looked up into his face with the tears streaming from her eyes.

She gave a half shrug. Her lips trembling and pressed together to hold back a sob, she straightened the collar of his black Windbreaker as he murmured over her injury. She'd come so far this summer in her bid for self-respect to have him destroy her so easily now.

The fishermen respected her despite the fact she was tiny; her tough toned body hadn't let Marion down, and the skipper had actually grown fond of her; even her father might be happy again, and his happiness didn't depend on Colleen's pleadings. But she had been the most vulnerable in one area, the giving and taking in a love relationship. The relationship had disintegrated even before it had bloomed.

With the realization that Cedar didn't love her enough to marry her had come the gut-wrenching return of fear, the dreams at night, the terror of failing. She wasn't worth his respect. He used Alicia and his father as an excuse. He was far too sure of himself to let his relatives' weaknesses keep him from what he wanted. He wanted her body, but she didn't deserve his commitment. He was like Alec.

Alec had used her until the real work of his life began; she hadn't been valuable enough to take along even to carry his briefcase. And again she would be used—by Cedar, the same man who'd helped her realize she was of value to those around her. The irony was rotten. The lesson had cost too much. Was she supposed to throw away those values she'd told Ernie she wanted back? Her scruples, her pride, her chance for children and a loving marriage? Was she supposed to repay Cedar by having an affair with him?

And then she remembered her goals. Her passion for freedom returned. Happiness was still a long way down the road. When she finally found it, it wouldn't be called "sleeping with Cedar." She took a deep breath and shoved his hand away. "It's all right," she said thickly, wiping her eyes with the corner of the towel. "It's—I'm fine."

"Oh, Colleen," he whispered. "I do love you." He wrapped her close and said hoarsely, "The other reason I wanted to head for Pelican is that I can't stand another night on the boat with you without—"

"Cedar, don't!" she said raggedly.

"I miss you."

"Cedar."

"I can't help saying this, Colleen!" He caressed her back and ran his hands into her hair, his touch fevered. His sure, firm hands tilted her head up, insisting she look at him. "We're like two eagles clashing because we want the same nesting site. We dive-bomb each other's vulnerable spots, claw out a space where the other can't follow. Colleen, every time I see you scrubbing a clean spot on Ernie's boat or staring for twenty minutes at the same page in that book you're reading, I want to hold you. It's breaking my heart to see you so lonely. And I'm lonely. Colleen, we love each other. Don't throw it away!"

"Sweet Mary!" She struggled, dropped the makeup kit and the book, speaking over the cloying thickness of tears and desperation. "Get out of my way!" She pushed him back through the door. Panting, she grabbed the kit, turned to snatch a clean pair of thermals from her bunk and ran toward the bathroom. Inside, she slammed the door and leaned her back against it.

Cedar came down the aisle and rapped on the door. "Give it a chance. Give us another try. We'll work it out, Colleen!"

Crying silently, she reached toward the shower and slid the door open along the tracks. She jerked off her sweat shirt.

"Colleen!"

Her hands shaking, her face wet, she shed her socks, jeans, underthings. Stepping into the shower, she slammed the curtain closed. She put her head under the stinging stream of hot water, and drowned out Cedar's deep voice.

CHAPTER NINETEEN

COLLEEN MOANED and came awake. The blackness of the old nightmare clung, the fear foul tasting in her mouth, and she gripped the wood frame of the bed. The boat jerked, pitching her against the bulkhead. She cried out. They were underway, she realized, the panic of the death dream receding behind a new fear. The Jimmy diesel ground like a chainsaw through the storm; the wind slapped rain against the outside of the trunk cabin. On the *Sparrow*, Colleen would have had difficulty staying in her bunk, but the shallow water mattress and wedges of foam support served to balance the monotonous pitch of the boat. They were wading through a nasty storm. How long, she wondered. How many hours had she lain here fighting imagined monsters while Cedar fought the sea?

She scrambled out of the warm waterbed. Rubbing her eyes, removing the evidence of last night's tears, she glanced across to the other bunk. Cedar's reading light illuminated a balled-up pillow and twisted sheets.

Instantly the wound of sorrow for their estrangement returned to the pit of her stomach. The brown blanket slashed with orange lay crumpled at the foot of Cedar's empty bed, and from its condition, Colleen realized he hadn't fared well through the night, either.

"We'll work it out, Colleen." His words came back

for the thousandth time, urging her against her will to trust him. But she was leery. Leery and gun-shy, like a Sitka black-tailed deer who bore the scars of an old bullet wound.

Stumbling down the aisle to the bathroom, she hurriedly washed up. The wind moaned outside. Waves warbled through the backbone of the hull, big waves, waves that coursed beneath them at twenty-five, thirty miles per hour, slewing the *Dart* sideways and rocketing it down into the troughs. *His shoulders must be killing him,* she thought, pulling jeans and a thick aqua sweater over her thermals. The southeasterly was throwing them around as if the *Dart* were a toy boat in a bathtub. She donned socks and boots, then made her way to the galley.

He had thought of her. He'd left scrambled eggs and toast in the oven—and a note. She pulled it from the oven door: "Give us a chance. Love, Ced."

The *Dart* pitched to port, and she crushed the note as she grabbed for the table, steadying herself. She glanced worriedly through the polished-wood window frame. Stretching away was a sloping valley of water that blended with the slanting grayish rain, before the *Dart* plowed diagonally up the crest, then rocked to starboard as the wave hissed beneath the hull. Sliding into the trough, the boat's stern fishtailing, Cedar gunned the engine...then cut it back as they rose again. Blown by gusts, spume and rain rattled like buckshot into the window. The waves looked enormous; the rain and the southeasterly peppered the sea to a froth.

Colleen felt buried in water. Apprehension rose to the surface of her skin in goose bumps. *Cedar is at the wheel,* she told herself. *Calm down.* Unlike Marion, he was far too exuberant about life to consider suicide. He would be careful with their lives.

She loved him, but she tossed the note into a container fitted under the counter. Too big a risk. He'd leave her for someone better. Chip off the old block. He'd admitted it.

Awkwardly in the twisting, rolling galley, she dispensed coffee into a mug, added honey and washed down a breakfast she had no appetite to eat. It was a messy chore to wash dishes with the water slopping everywhere, but she finally put the last dish away and faced the door to the wheelhouse. Her stomach gurgled with tension. Storm inside, storm outside. They had so little time left together, though. She'd be civil, at least. She'd offer him coffee.

Taking a deep breath, she opened the companionway door. The sounds of the sea snarled down at her, wind clawing at the raised steering room, tons of water rushing against the hull—and all of it broken by the crackle of the radio.

"Damned engine again." The voice was Ernie's. Amazed, Colleen strained to hear what he was saying over the burring sounds of radio and weather. "Seas might overrun us, I'm afraid. We'll try to make it as far as Khaz, maybe get a tow from a boat in the area."

"Good luck, skipper," Cedar said. "You understand, under any other circumstances I'd try to get to you. If it was just my own life. . . ." Cedar's voice faded, and then he finished strongly, "But there'll be other boats trying to get home before she really breaks. I'll alert the Coast Guard to your location, and then you keep me informed. Roger me on that."

Static. "Ah, roger. We'll be in—"

Colleen scooped a breath of air into her lungs and burst up the stairway into the wheelhouse. Chrome and wood gleamed everywhere, with radios and sonar and fishing instruments tacked to the ceiling, the walls, the dash. To her right, Cedar held the wheel in one hand and the black radio transceiver in the other. She narrowed her gaze at him. "What the devil do you mean, leaving Ernie and Marion to fight out trouble alone!"

Cedar snapped around. He almost dropped the transmitter, and the wheel spun in his loosened grip. He righted it, growled in disgust, adjusted for the next swell.

"What's wrong on the *Sparrow*?" she demanded, fists bunched.

Cedar lifted the mike. They rolled in a trough; Colleen held on. He pressed the transmitting button. "Ah, Ernie, you still on the horn?"

"Roger."

Cedar smiled grimly. "Hang on for a sec. Got a little conference going on this end."

"Will do, Ced. Marion's having a cat fit, so make it quick."

"Right."

Colleen leaned close to him and demanded again, "What do you mean, 'if it was just your own life'? What's going on?"

"Trouble with the *Sparrow*'s engine." Evidently uncomfortable in the face of her outrage, Cedar gestured vaguely. "She's sputtering and knocking. Won't hold steady power."

"What does that mean in weather like this?"

Haunted dark eyes met hers. "It means if they don't find shelter, they may get overrun by the seas— broached, swamped, Colleen."

Her lips drew into a tight *O*. Cedar might be sacrificing the lives of his closest friends to keep her out of danger. "Ced," she gasped, holding to the lip of the portable chart table near the wall. "Cedar, we can't *do* this."

"We can and we will!" He half rose from the captain's chair, his eyes brilliant with intent, his jaw tight and jutting. "I've made the decision for us."

"But they might die!"

He turned away to take a hard grip on the wheel. They pitched down a wave.

"Cedar, for the love of God!"

The radio barked. "Ced, you got anything to add?" asked Ernie.

Colleen leaped toward the controls and jerked the radio out of Cedar's hand. "You're not doing this to them!" she shouted. "I don't care if I die in this—" she waved at the rain-plastered sea "—this hellhole. We're not abandoning Marion! She's had it, Cedar. She can't take any more. She's a good woman and she deserves to live, and we're going to help her!"

As she fumbled for the button, Cedar shouted, "All right! We'll go to them, but you'll do as I say. Go below and get the four survival suits."

Nodding, her face white, she handed him the microphone.

"And haul all that cable up from under the bunks. All of it. The light line, the heavy rope and the blunderbuss."

" 'Blunderbuss'?"

He clicked on the mike. "Ernie, stand by. We're heading your way."

Ernie's reply was buried beneath Cedar's answer to

Colleen. "Blunderbuss, Colleen. Looks kind of like a short cannon—used for shooting cable from one boat to another. Get it, unpack the extra blankets, dig out the slickers and warm clothing. And pray, baby. We'll need it all."

Again she nodded. As he was bringing the mike to his mouth, she leaned over and flung her arms around his neck. She squeezed until she cut off her breath. He sat there, unmoving, his jaw hard against her cheek.

"In spite of everything," she whispered tensely, "I love you, Cedar. Somehow we'll work it out."

He turned to her. The anger and frustration in his gaze made him look dangerous. He wrapped a possessive arm around her waist, snugged her hard by and growled, "You cost me my pride, Freedom."

Stunned, she tried to leave him. He jerked her back, his arm crushing her. "You cost me my pride, but losing you would cost me my sanity, too. We'll have that wedding, dammit!"

"Cedar, Sweet Mary, God!" Happiness, surprise and insult raged through her.

"In you is every hope I've never dared to acknowledge," he thundered, as if the realization had been torn out of his heart. *"All right?"*

"Yes. Yes, all right, Cedar! But this is a little abrupt!"

"I know this lacks romance—" He had to glance away, ease more power out of the boat. Then he scowled at her. "You gave me no chance to do it more gracefully, that's all. You shut me out like a steel door, forced me to choose between your way or losing you. And once I'd made that choice, I couldn't risk your life. Men get this macho feeling in their gut when a woman's with them at sea. They do stupid brave things they'd never attempt on their own, and they do cowardly things like leaving their friends to fight out trouble alone when a woman they care about could be—"

"You don't have to explain," she said more gently. She paused. Lightning flashed behind them, glowing in the chrome. Thunder rumbled overhead. "I know you did it for me," she said then. "But Cedar, you've got to ask me what I want out of things if we ever get marr—if we live through this."

"Right now there's no time for manners. Now get below, Freedom, and do everything exactly as I tell you until this day is done."

"Aye, captain," she said softly, and slipped from his arms.

TWO HOURS LATER the gray green blur of Chichagof loomed like a whale in the distance. The *Dart*'s struggle against the sea had worn away Colleen's brief happiness, till the possibility of dying seemed more real than the chance of living happily with Cedar. When they hovered at the crest of a wave, she strained toward the island, trying to spot the troller, praying the rescue would be quick and successful—praying she and Cedar would have that chance to discuss marriage plans.

A ruby light ticked in the distance.

"Cedar...."

She waited while he maneuvered the boat. The waves were dropping off slightly. The big water hadn't come inside yet, she knew. Perhaps they'd make it....

Thunder grumbled somewhere to the south. The hull creaked. They rose, rose, hovered...she spotted the salmon-pink wheelhouse, the black-and-blue hull of the *Sparrow*.

"There!" she cried, pointing.

The seas hurled against the shoreline, shooting spray gainst the misty spikes of spruce, carrying it like a sheet ehind that low-slung troller. Her stern took each wave ke a boxer, rock jawed and shuddering with the impact. Poles lowered, stabilizers cutting the water like hark fins, the *Sparrow* clung tenaciously to a northwest ourse. Grimy smoke poured from her stack.

Cedar swore. "They're too close to shore." He rabbed the mike, broadcasting over a channel they'd elected to give them free air space. "Ernie, I've got a ead on you. I'm off your port side about fifteen hundred yards. Do you read?"

"I can read fine long's the print ain't too small," Marion's dry voice came over the air. "What're you doing swooping into my trolling drag like a white vulture, Ced?"

"Marion!" Cedar grinned in relief at Colleen. Although she knew he was shaken by the battering the *Sparrow* was taking, he kept his tone light. "Ah, look, ou're hugging mighty close to the island, ah, what're ou going to do—try to ski home cross-country?"

"I got a bone to pick with you, McClintock."

"Later, Marion. Where's Ernie?"

"What were you doing throwing your money around Seattle last week?"

Colleen looked at Cedar in confusion. Today was Monday. He'd been with her last week, from the time of the news of Mike's death. He winked at her.

"Habit, Marion," he laughed. "Seattle's my home ort. What else is a single sailor supposed to do with his money?"

"Yeah, and you're taking back every lousy cent of hat eighty-five grand, McClintock."

He had paid money to the hospital. Colleen gave him a distorted smile, part fear, part admiration.

He went back to Marion. "We'll talk about finances later. How—I mean, yeah, how'd the funeral go? You feeling okay?"

The static stretched for a long pause. Marion said, "What do you take me for, Ced—a lightweight? Tha boy 'a mine is done with hurtin'. He's sleepin' real peaceful down on the tip of this island, spruce trees keepin' the rain off him, ravens keepin' him entertained, hell—' The button still pressed, she shouted, "Ernie! Where the devil's that coffee you promised?" They could hear her bossing the "Bible-totin' Finn" just as she'd bossed Colleen when Marion was upset about something. "This here call's for you!" Marion bellowed.

In a moment Ernie boomed into the *Sparrow*'s transmitter, "Yo, Ced. You reach the Coast Guard?"

Cedar explained that he'd reached the Guard, but that they were involved in another rescue farther north. They'd break the cutter free as soon as possible and send it over to assist the *Sparrow*. Cedar had tuned the marine radio overhead to the Guard's transmission channel, and he monitored the station every quarter hour. All the details lined up, Colleen thought, relieved.

"Ernie, you've got to get out a ways from the island," Cedar said. "Otherwise, if I throw a rope across your deck and you bobble and go broadside, you're liable to drag us into the rocks."

"Right, hold on a sec."

The radio went silent. Lightning blanched the southern sky. A bright flash drew Colleen's attention to the island. A spruce glowed like the tip of a match, and she knew the tree had grounded the bolt.

Ernie came on. "Ced, Marion's going to hold course. The tip of the peninsula is only fifteen minutes ahead. We're going to try to make it around to the inside."

Cedar's gaze slid to Colleen, and she knew this was the decision point. She bent and picked up the heavy blunderbuss. It was cold. The fear palpable, she took a breath and held it toward him. "Ced, you know we've got to give them a tow. They'd be ground to dust on shore if their engine conked out."

His gaze darkened with uncertainty.

"Do it! We've got to!"

"Ced, did you read me?" Ernie interrupted. "We're holding course."

He let out his breath, picked up the mike. "Ernie, tell Marion we're coming alongside. We're going to try to tow you in."

Marion's voice crackled. "Ced, you idiot! We could swamp you! Foul your propeller with the line. Ernie's just a worrywart. This bird ain't doing nothin' worse 'n she normally does. I got things under control. You got Colleen aboard. Just let the Coast Guard know where we are and then get the hell out of here."

"I can't do that, Marion."

"Why the hell not?"

"Because your fish puller says so! And I'm good and sick of arguing, so just quit bossing people for once in your life and let somebody give you a hand. We're sending the rope across your bow!" He started to hang up the mike, then shouted, "Out!"

Still gripping the wheel, he rose from the captain's chair. "Take the wheel, Colleen. I'll tie the cable to the stern and then fire the rope."

"Okay." Handing him the gun, Colleen slid into the

chair. Her hard callused hands felt the yank and pull of
the shiny wood. The bow tipped up, showing sky and
slanting rain, and her heart jerked with sudden panic.

"Cut power!" Cedar yelled.

She complied. She began to shake. The *Dart* dived
down the belly of the wave, landing with a *whoof*.

"Power!" he demanded. "Easy! Don't charge full
blast over the crest. You'll bury the nose going down."

She worked at smoothing the process, her shoulders
locked, her arms stiff, her eyes wide as the stern skidded
sideways. She corrected. The engine dug in, roller-
coaster rolling, climbing, skating down again.

"Good," he said. He rubbed the knot of muscles on
her shoulders. "Easy, easy. You can't outrun them.
Just keep enough speed to surf the boat over the waves
as they roll by."

She nodded. The fear lodged in her throat, preventing
words. She could feel the tremendous push of the water
astern. Glancing out the window in the aft door, she saw
the wood deck slick with seawater and rain. The ocean
rose around the *Dart* like snowcapped peaks around a
skier. Cedar was going out there, she thought, burying
her own terror. He slipped into his yellow slicker, shoving the orange survival suits out of the way so he could
push the ropes against the door.

Blinding light x-rayed the clouds—white striated like
veins through the charcoal flesh of the storm. Thunder
rumbled, snare drums humming until the great crash of
a base drum opened the sky. Another bright flash. a
fresh torrent deluged the *Dart*. Cedar, out there in the
tearing wind and the thrash of the sea, she thought. The
old familiar blackness hovered in her mind— shadow of
an eagle crossing the sun. Her breath drew tight. She

wanted to fling open the windows, the door...let that wind howl through the cabin, bringing her oxygen, tearing out the terror.

She fought the fear. She forced herself to glance ahead to the salmon-rose-and-blue shape growing larger in the frame of the windshield.

She gasped, her eyes widening...a crawler rose up and crashed on the *Sparrow*'s deck, rattling the trolling gear. Another wave climbed behind the boat, pushing, pushing. And then that eighty-year-old stern rail cut into the swell, breaking it in two, and the sea poured down in a fury of gray, green and white. The smokestack coughed black char. One of the trolling poles buried itself in the sea, bowing like a bird's wing, then snapped to. The stabilizer cut cleanly once more. A galvanized support in the hayrack gave way. The rigging askew, the dory pulled sideways by the water, the *Sparrow* spit the seas from her scuppers and labored up the crest of the wave, clawing and scrabbling for headway. Colleen quickly turned away. They must hurry. Marion and Ernie were in danger of slipping forever into that black limbo beneath the water.

The *Dart*'s engine was more powerful, the hull more sturdy against the punishment of wind and angry sea. Forging, slacking off, manhandling the wheel, Colleen headed steadily toward a midpoint in the *Sparrow*'s bruised-looking hull. Colleen steadied her breathing. They would make it. She had to keep her wits, had to believe God and the saints would be merciful.

"You okay?"

She jerked sideways. "What?"

"Colleen, what's the matter?"

"Matter? Nothing, Cedar." She glanced away from

his concern, hiding the fear. He couldn't be effective out on that pitching deck if he was worried about whether she could hold the wheel steady. She took a tighter grip. "Okay. Now what?"

"You'll have to ease up behind and alongside them. But don't get any closer than about fifty feet from their hull. That'll give you fifteen feet between us and their pole. It'll be tight. If you feel us drifting too close or getting swamped, just hit the air horn, heel hard to the west and gas it. I'll hang on. Otherwise, when I yell, that'll mean the rope's out across their deck. Ernie'll need time to secure the line to something on the bow, so hold steady. When I yell again, ease a knot or two more power out of the *Dart*. Take up the slack as gently as you can. But I'll be back inside by then. Questions?"

She looked hard at him, the fear thick in her throat. "Cedar, be careful. "I—I don't want to lose you. The waves—"

He held up a thumb. Then he leaned to her and swept her lips with a hurried, urgent kiss. "Dammit, Freedom. . . .'

"What?"

"You and Marion have gone a long way toward destroying the myth that women are helpless and weak out on the water. Stubborn, yes." He smiled faintly. "But I'm damned glad you're with me."

He had told her before that she was strong. *But you don't know, Cedar. You don't know how terrified I am.* She nodded vaguely.

"Hey, are you sure you're okay?"

"Yes." She worked the controls. Then she reached to his sleeve, drew him close. She looked up into his face. "You'll be careful, Cedar? You won't do anything stupid or brave?"

The slicker crackled as he brought her abruptly to his chest. Even through the layers of clothing she could feel the rocky ribs. She sighed in relief and closed her eyes, drawing from his strength, his sureness. He was the strong one. The wave of black uncertainty slipped back a ways. *Saint Joan of Arc, protect him.* The wheel jumped in her hands, and she pulled away. Keeping her eyes trained toward the brighter northern horizon, mimicking Marion's brusqueness, she said, "For crying out loud, Ced, put on your hat! There's a blow out here!"

He laughed. He cuffed her lightly on the shoulder. "Just keep her steady on northwest once you're up on the *Sparrow*'s beam."

The wet moaning wind swirled into the cabin. Cedar dragged the gun and coils of rope outside, leaving Colleen with her shaky grip on the wheel and the gusts whipping her hair into her eyes.

CEDAR SLAMMED back inside, his face dripping and his hair gleaming. Pulling off the slicker, he flung it behind the chair. "I'll take the wheel!" he shouted.

He slid into the seat as she came out of it. She was white from the strain of holding the boat steady while he and Ernie secured the ends of the cable, but one glance at the lines in his face and the bright flicker in his eyes told her Cedar had come close to terror himself. She gripped his shoulder for an instant, felt the iron-hard muscles, and lurched to the chart table, where she hung on. She hadn't lost him. Over and over her brain repeated that. He was here with her, still safe, safe as either of them could be.

The whole boat jolted, pulled up short by the umbili-

cal attached to the *Sparrow*. Colleen fell against the dash
Cedar's arm blurred out, and he grabbed her shoulder.
"I'm okay," she said, flashing him a terrified look. She
rubbed her elbow. She'd bruised it, but the pain radiated
away as she stumbled to her feet.

She glanced behind them. Ernie lay sprawled under the
lee side of the *Sparrow*'s cabin, clinging to the stays, one
leg dragging dangerously over the rail.

"Ease off!" she cried to Cedar. "Ernie's down!"
Running to peer out the window, she watched Ernie
crawl into the gutter between the rail and the foredeck.
"Thank God!"

"Can I take up the slack?" Cedar called.

"Wait." She saw Ernie round the wheelhouse and disappear inside, to appear again as a shadow beside Marion. "Yes, okay, easy."

She breathed shakily, grasped the lip of a locker at the
back of the wheelhouse and held on. Cedar gently increased power. Her ears ringing from the chortle of the
Dart's engine, Colleen stared outside.

Lightning speared the rain-shrouded sky.

Outlined briefly as she reared up the crest of a wave,
the *Sparrow* reminded Colleen of a bruised warrior stallion snorting in fury, one green eye and one red blinking
back the rain, hindquarters dug in for the final charge.
The cable caught her up short. She came down with her
staying-sail luffing, stabilizers skimming the water, nose
lowered as she barreled toward the *Dart*. The *Dart* pulled
away, and the tug-of-war continued up the coast, with
the cable sawing against a piece of gear out back.

"Almost to the tip of the peninsula," she heard Cedar
say absently.

Small islets blurred in and out of the rain. Colleen

forced herself to look away from the rampaging storm. "Finally," she murmured in relief. They would head into Khaz Bay and hole up in the lee of one of the islands or the peninsula. She crab-stepped across to the captain's chair and rubbed Cedar's neck, feeling him shift his shoulders in an unconscious gesture of appreciation. His hair shone like wet coal. *Almost there.* Aloud, she asked, "How long?"

"Five, maybe ten minutes."

He sounded weary. She patted his shoulder and glanced at the fathometer. Again she felt the chill of fear. "Cedar, you're too shallow! You're in five fathoms!"

His head jerked toward the screen, toward the windshield, back sharply over his shoulder. "Get on the radio! Tell them we're cutting left."

She grabbed the mike. "Marion! Shoals ahead. Cut left. Repeat, hard to port! Do you read?"

Cedar spun the wheel, glanced at the screen, muttered.

Ernie said, "Roger. We'll head due west. Take her easy on the turn. The towline is trying to yank out half our bow. She's not going to tolerate much—"

Static. The jerk and groan of the line. . .the grumble of the engine and thunder, the rush of waves, rain, wind. And suddenly the *Dart* surged forward, free.

"We're off!" Ernie's deep voice rasped, the fear thick. "We've lost you!"

Cedar started to rise. "Cedar!" Colleen shrieked. "The island!"

One second away from the wheel, and the *Dart* had careened to the right, a stubby cluster of trees and surf dead ahead.

After a half glance of helplessness toward the floundering *Sparrow*, Cedar dived for the wheel and spun it hard left. The fathometer read three fathoms, three and one-half, four, six. The island slid by the windows.

"The ax!" he shouted. "Down in the galley, under the sink. We can't let the line snag the prop."

She dived below, scrambled through soap and brushes, dragged out the long-handled wood ax. She ran back to the wheelhouse and reached toward the aft door.

"Take the wheel!" he thundered.

She ignored him. This was her battle, not his. He'd paid his dues. When she slid open the door, the wind pushed her back.

"Colleen! Take this wheel!"

She ducked low, fought her way along the pitching slippery deck, one hand grabbing sections of rail, the rain beating her forehead, soaking her sweater. The tremendous force of wind and sea sent her headlong into the holding boxes. As she struck her head, spasms of pain racked her, and the ax toppled away.

She shook her head, fought blindly until she felt the blade of the ax. She spun it away, grabbed the handle. Cold and frightened, she slid over the holding boxes into the trolling cockpit. Icy seawater swirled over her boots. A wave like a mountain rose behind the stern, lifting the cable as it whipped in the wake. The wall of water towered over her. Those Swiss Alps looming over a skier. She waited, terrified, the ax held high, until the stern rose beneath the wave. In that moment, when the boat hung over the steep peak with its stern free and the prop churning for a hold, she gathered every speck of strength in her body for that downward stroke of the ax. The rope parted, jerking the ax out of her hands. It flipped into the wake. Miraculous! Sweet Mary!

The stern dropped out from under her boots. As the nose of the troller plunged, she fell against the back wall. The only thing that kept her aboard was the wind pushing her back into the boat. She screamed, though it was after the fact. Weak, panting, she clung to the rail as they spun sideways in the trough. Timing, she thought. Time the mountains. Timing is everything! Adrenaline spurred her to crawl into the nearest bin and reach for the hayrack. It came at her again, that green, snow-capped mountain of water, hissing and throwing spume in her face. It rose, steep-sided canyon, lifting the stern, and she dived into the gully between the hatch and the rail, scurrying forward until she flattened on the deck and locked her hands on the molding of the wheel-house door.

She saw Cedar glance back. His mouth opened in a silent shout. The water sheeting off her face, her hair plastered across her cheek, she raised her head and grinned at him. His eyes had that bright gleam she remembered from days ago, when he'd been crying. He kept his hands on the wheel as the ocean came up under the boat, kept his gaze locked to hers as the force of the wave strained her grip on the wood. The *Dart* wallowed in the trough. Colleen rose, staggered into the wheel-house, shut the door. Leaning against it, she closed her eyes. She took a moment to make the sign of the cross. Then she fell against Cedar's arm and buried her face in his shoulder. His hand came to her back. They held each other for a fierce silent moment.

"Mayday!"

They both glanced toward the radio.

"Mayday!" Marion shouted into the radio. "Repeat, Ced, this is a mayday! Call the Coast Guard. We're taking water through a hole in the bow. Rope tore out a chunk of wood."

"Got to keep them in sight," Cedar muttered, hauling on the wheel, spinning the bow directly into the oncoming waves. Mountains again. The whole boat creaked and shuddered as tons of twenty-five-mile per-hour seas battered them, pale-green water and froth pounding the foredeck, hammering the windows. The roar muffled the engine.

"Answer my mayday, damn you! Where are you?"

Colleen ground her teeth to keep them from chattering. She jerked the mike off the radio and shouted, "We have your mayday. We'll call them, skipper, hold on!"

She glanced at the mike they were using for communication with the Coast Guard. As she was reaching for it, Cedar grabbed it and depressed the button. He gave call numbers and the name of vessel, repeated the information, then said hoarsely, "We've just lost the *Sparrow*. They've got a big hole in the bow, and they're taking on water. You guys have got to get here fast. I can't do any more, don't have the gear. Just lost our towline. You guys are the pros—get here!"

"Ah...roger, *Dart*," came the complacent reply. "Our cutter is half a mile west of your position. We'll see if we can't hurry 'em up...."

"I've done all I can!" Cedar shouted, as unnerved as Colleen by the lack of emotion in the man's voice. "You guys come in here! Get here fast!"

Colleen depressed the button and spoke to Marion. "Cutter half a mile west and coming, Marion. Where's Ernie?"

"Below! Trying to plug the hole."

The fear was gone from Colleen. A crisp cold logic

had replaced it. That fact had barely registered when Colleen said sharply, "Marion, where are the survival suits you keep in the fo'c'sle? Do you have them on?"

After a moment Marion said, "Lord, the suits. They're below. Ernie!"

Cedar hung up his mike, his face gray with strain. They heard Marion shout orders to Ernie to get on his survival suit, for crying out loud. Didn't he know they were taking on seas?

Colleen met Cedar's grim smile.

The *Sparrow*'s running lights appeared. Cedar moaned, "Oh, God, her bow's tipping."

It was true. The blue-and-black bow rode low, nosing dangerously as the swells bullied her stern. She had power, but not much. They circled around the dying craft, and Colleen was reminded of a whale hovering behind her wounded calf.

"Marion!" she cried into the mike. "Marion, hold on."

"You bet," Marion laughed, a touch of hysteria making her voice high. "Hey, that old Finn finally got his way, didn't he?"

"What do you mean?"

"Well, he's been hounding me, ain't he? Gripin' about us being together till death do us part?" She chuckled. "Like I said, Conaughy, we ain't got no choices about the way things turn out."

Colleen clung to the dash as a wave pushed the stern up around their ears.

"You know somethin', Conaughy?"

"What's that, skipper?"

"This preachy-mouthed Finn sure gives a pretty sermon. Standin' out there in that peaceful clearin', that

big voice boomin' out the Lord's word...." Static
scratched. Colleen felt a poignant wetness blur her vision. "You know what else, Conaughy?"

"No—" Colleen swallowed. "No, what else?"

"Gave me a lump in my throat, that's what. Almost
convinced me to do him a favor and marry him."
Marion laughed her coughing laugh.

While Colleen was staring hard at the *Sparrow*, thirty
yards to starboard, the eighty-year-old troller broached.
The seas hit her port side, ripping away the dory, the
hayrack of gear, pushing her sideways toward a small
island. "Marion!"

"Conaughy, this is mayday for sure! Get that
damned cutter over here, because we're hitting the
beach!"

The radio went dead. Water poured over the
Sparrow. A pole tore away, flipping like a javelin into
the rain.

Cedar was on the marine radio, demanding action,
giving conditions, his voice hoarse with sorrow. Colleen
stared in disbelief as her former skipper and the boat
she'd sweated on and cursed for its faults rammed into
the shoals, surf pounding her, smothering her, beating
her into the rocks. The crack of timber shot through the
storm.

Colleen screamed; Cedar grabbed her arm. He
brought her hard against his chest and held her as her
screams reverberated around the cabin.

He said something to her, shook her. But her heart
broke with the *Sparrow*, and Colleen wailed, her face
jammed into his Windbreaker, her shoulders shuddering.

"Colleen!" Cedar's voice penetrated finally. Gasping, she looked at him. "Off the port bow! The cutter!"

A huge white Coast Guard cutter loomed out of the rain, her decks lit with strong lights, guardsmen scrambling. A great anchor splashed into the water. A helicopter lifted off the deck, soared out over the water and hung, teetering, in the thirty-knot wind. Searchlights played over the area. From the bottom hatch a steel cable began to snake down toward the surf, its tip weighted by a heavy stirrup.

"They're too late!" she ground out, staring with bitter fury at the copter.

She turned to look at the crushed *Sparrow*, gleaming in the searchlights—and looked again. A spot of orange, two...clinging together on the tilted wheelhouse. Ernie and Marion were saved from the battering of the sea by the upended stern, wedged among the rocks.

CHAPTER TWENTY

"MR. ESAU?"

Ernie smoothed down his blue tie and looked at the balding minister. "Yes, brother Dixon?"

"Do you take this woman, Marion Brown, for your wife?"

"I do," Ernie said promptly, grinning at Marion.

Marion, wearing a conservative beige suit, fiddled with a wisp of hair that had come loose from her crown of braids. She half glanced, nervously, toward the wedding guests, packed to the walls of the tiny church. Ernie kept grinning at her as she elbowed him in the ribs and hunched her shoulders toward the preacher, implying that he keep his mind on the ceremony.

Ernie's grin only widened. Marion sighed in disgust and turned away.

The minister pivoted, his pate gleaming in a ray of sunlight from the window. "Mr. McClintock?"

Cedar cleared his throat. He glanced at Colleen, his face serious, his gaze a mixture of devotion and consternation. He nodded slightly as if to tell her they'd work it out, whatever it was he still feared about marriage. Her eyes misty, she smiled and squeezed his hand.

"Er...Mr. McClintock?" the minister said again in a soft Texas drawl.

"Oh, sorry. Yes."

"Do you take Colleen Conaughy for your wife?"

Again Cedar looked at Colleen, and her heart jerked at the lengthy pause. The smile trembled on her lips. She wanted to tell him he looked stunning in his navy-blue suit, but this wasn't the time. She wanted to tell him he'd never be sorry he married her, but it was too late. He was a man who took from the world what he wanted, and she knew that would never change. Whatever Cedar McClintock was thinking now would determine their future.

His eyes traveled slowly over her blue dress and canvas shoes, the outfit he'd asked her to wear, and back up to her rippling sunlit hair. The familiar knee-weakening current bonded them for a moment. And then he nodded. "Yes," he said in that mellow baritone that echoed from the walls. "You bet I do."

"Thank you," drawled the minister, his voice relieved. He made one final quarter turn. "Now...Mr. Conaughy, is it?"

"Sure and it is, man. Conaughy. Sean Conaughy."

The crowd murmured, amused.

Colleen looked past Ernie and Marion to her father... and to the Widow McMillan, standing in her ivory lace dress, her graying chignon just touching her collar as she gazed happily at Colleen's father.

Her father, Colleen noted with a nudge of admiration, stood stiff-necked in his brown suit, silver hair thick and curly like her own, green eyes clear and focused dead ahead.

"Mr. Conaughy," said the preacher, "do you take Esther McMillan for your wife?"

"Sure 'n I do, now," said her father. He glanced at Colleen, gave her a sly wink and faced forward again, somber faced as before.

"Well, then," the minister summed up, raising o᳑
hand above Ernie's red Bible. "The women have take᳑
the men to have and to hold, until death doth part the᳑
and deliver them to God's kingdom, and the men ha᳑
duly added their voices in agreement to this holy vov᳑
As my last duty to this congregation. . . ." From his st᳑
tion on the altar dais, he gazed out over the fisherme᳑
and their wives and children. He raised his arm to ad᳑
drama to the ceremony he and Ernie had arranged ov᳑
the past week. "As my last duty to you before turnin᳑
my flock into the capable hands of brother Ernest Esa᳑
I accept the pledges of these, God's children, and in H᳑
name pronounce them wedded, husbands and wiv᳑
until the end of their days."

Applause and hoots filled the church, drowning o᳑
Sadie's piano playing and the guitar strumming of cra᳑
fisherman Randy Welch. Arms linked, Colleen an᳑
Cedar filed out of the church, followed by Ernie an᳑
Marion and Mr. and Mrs. Sean Conaughy. They startle᳑
a pair of eagles from the ancient spruce shading the yar᳑
and the great birds used a branch as a runway, launchin᳑
into the breeze blowing off Lisianski Inlet.

"Smart birds," Marion pronounced as she and Erni᳑
joined Colleen on the grassy hill above the village. Sh᳑
scowled at her new husband. "My clan gits when the gi᳑
tin's good."

They chuckled as Blue Harry, Doc, J.T. and Josh, a᳑
looking uncomfortable in dress shirts, with the cuff᳑
rolled, ties and city shoes, converged on the wedding com᳑
pany. Sadie bellowed from the church doorway for Blue t᳑
wait for her, but Blue was already thumping Cedar and E᳑
nie on the back, chuckling, "You old bear cubs, you᳑
Never thought I'd see the day, and that's a fact."

Cedar grinned at Blue. Then he turned to Colleen, his expression fading to seriousness. He took her slowly in his arms. Deliberately he drew her hands to his crisp collar and slid them around his neck.

An eagle soared across the sun then—a brief blinking shadow—and she smiled.

"What are you thinking, Mrs. McClintock?" Cedar asked, his voice husky and low against her lips.

"How free I am," she said softly. "How many choices we have ahead of us...all of them free, none of them scary, because we decided to make them together."

He hugged her. "Freedom...I'm so glad you made me marry you." Chuckling, he kissed her gently.

She returned the kiss, but her mind finally grasped his words, and she pushed him slightly away to demand, "What do you mean, *made* you marry me?"

Someone coughed behind Cedar. "Package arrived for you, Mr. McClintock."

The young voice urged Cedar to crane his neck over his shoulder. He looked down. "Is it here?"

"Yes, sir," said the boy Colleen couldn't see.

"Cedar," she said. "What do you mean, *made* you?"

He turned to face her, hugging her until the breath was squeezed out of her. He took her left hand and held it up in front of her. "You see this hand?" he asked, a gleam of laughter making his eyes merry.

"Yes, I see it. What did you—"

"You see this gold band on your ring finger?"

"Yes, but—"

"It's just a down payment. Go get changed! I'll explain everything to you once we get to this spot I know that's perfect for wedding nights."

"Well, okay, but I want to know—"

"Colleen," he said with mock exasperation.

"Yes, Cedar?"

"If you don't get changed and then come back here and make your goodbyes, like a proper wife, I'll be a *very* improper husband to you... right here in the church yard." He leaned close and trailed hungry kisses along her throat. "Very improper, indeed," he whispered.

She laughed and broke the embrace. Glancing over her shoulder, a questioning smile flirting around her mouth, she went to find her father. *Some things can' wait, husband,* she thought. *Family is family.*

"Colleen, lass."

She turned. "Daddy...."

He held his arms open, and she went to him, hugging him and feeling very grown-up and awkward.

"It's a fine man ye married, Colleen," he murmured stroking her hair in the old way. "Your mother would be pleased, she would."

She leaned away and sought his gaze. He looked at her with steady affection. "You're... over her, daddy? At last?"

A brief mood passed over him. He said, "No, lass, could never be that, now, could I? But I'll tell you one thing. I'd be right sorry if I lost you, too."

"Oh, you won't." She hugged him. "We'll be spending winters in Seattle, only thirty miles from you and Esther. She's lovely, daddy. Oh, I'm so happy for you... for me. We'll be traveling some, Cedar and I, and fishing here in the summers. But we'll spend time with you and Esther and Blarney's Blood, too." She winked. "Sure 'n you don't expect me to give up me rightful kin, daddy!"

He returned her warm embrace, held her tight and

ong. Then he patted her back and let her go. "Run
along, lass. Your man has asked ye to ready yourself.
The missus and I will be down at the *Dart*, havin' tea
with the Reverend Esau. And, daughter. . .?"

"Daddy?"

"Ye'll come to Seattle for a proper weddin', like ye
promised? You're not forgettin' your faith?"

"We'll be there, you can count on it. As soon as we
see Ernie and Marion settled and off on the *Dart*. Besides, Father Gregory would be immensely hurt if we
didn't let him make things 'proper' for you and me."

"Good lass." He smiled. "You were always such a
good, capable young woman, Colleen. I don't marvel
that ye made it through without me these past three or
four years."

How wonderful it felt to hear her father say those
words. "It's your toughness, daddy," she said, tucking
his collar under his brown lapel. "Your good tough
Irish blood. It got us both through some hard times.
That and a little Irish luck!"

"And your faith, daughter. Don't be forgettin'
that!"

"Aye, daddy. I'll not be forgettin'." She gave him a
thumbs-up and slipped away to change her clothes.

COLLEEN WAS nearly naked. Nearly his.

Only moments left of freedom, she thought. The hot
springs bubbled, squirrels chirped and a raven cawed
somewhere in the woods outside the bathing shelter.
The raucous enthusiasm alienated her. Her navy lace
lingerie felt inadequate—out of place—in this wet tepid
rook of moss and cracked stone. She was feeling jittery
here on the ledge.

As it rose from the White Sulphur Springs, the steam clung to her bare arms and legs. At her feet lay jeans, sweater, shirt and white tennis shoes. Two yards to her right, her husband's clothing rustled to the ground. She glanced as far from the purring sound of his zipper as she could. . . to the dull green gleam of the bottle tucked into a bucket of ice near the wall. French champagne. . . two crystal goblets; Cedar had had them sent up with the ring from Seattle. The delicate flutes represented sharing. Pairing. Unity. She'd wanted this moment all her life, and now she felt like running.

Through the rough wood window came a salty breeze from the sea, that crisp wind that stood more for freedom than any single cell of life, and with it came lemon bands of sunlight. But the rays didn't warm her. Like duelists they struck and danced in the facets of the marquise-cut blue diamond from Seattle. She gazed detachedly at the ring.

Cedar had been nearly dancing, too, when he'd slipped it on her finger after they'd arrived on shore. It must be very special, this ring that said they were united. But the symbol was a mockery. Her mind and body refused to join in welcoming this moment of giving. Instead, scenes from the ice cave in Lituya Bay sent shivers along her shoulders.

The float plane had long ago left them to settle into the secluded cabin back in the woods. They'd explored the beach, chattered about the Pelican fleet, kicked bits of charcoal from the firepit near where she'd first met Ernie. Finally they'd impulsively agreed to bathe together in the hot springs.

The moment had arrived; silence hung between them. Slowly, reluctantly, she slipped out of her bra and added it to the clothes at her feet.

Her misgivings about this moment, her mental withdrawal made her feel she was barely out of high school. She was reminded of the Colleen who had arrived in May, single, uncertain, searching. She'd come north. For what? Hoping to find moral and mental strength— courage. Had she grown all that much? Today she'd married Cedar McClintock, a man she loved but didn't know, after only two months of stormy courtship. It smacked of immaturity.

Had she hoped the ceremony this morning would make this last hurdle easy? She should have considered these questions in the frenzy of preparation last week, after the rescue, and put off the wedding. She bit her lower lip. *Child! You gave up the personal quest too soon. Sold out to marriage.* And yet something deeper than fear said she wanted to spend her life with Cedar.

"Are you sorry, Colleen? Is that what your frown is about?"

Cedar's voice coaxed. She turned to him, her gaze glancing off the corded arms and broad shoulders. Riot of black hair over his temple; she'd always loved it. Dark eyes a mixture of need and concern; that, too, was Cedar. Husband. Strong enduring man.

"Cedar...."

He read not the reasons for it but the substance of her fear, and stepped quickly to her side.

His lower body grazed her thigh, and her gaze jerked back to the water. The brief touch told her his need was already obvious—more obvious each second. She held herself stiffly, watching bracelets of silver widen toward the edge of the pool. *Help me, husband. I'm frozen.*

With a light touch he tickled her arm. "You're afraid?"

"Silly, isn't it."

"Of what?"

"Myself," she said without looking at him. "That's always been the case."

"But after that huge take of salmon down by Sitka...you were so willing."

"I was near physical exhaustion, Ced."

He turned slightly away. His voice gained an edge. "Not the next morning. Until Alicia, we had big plans for after breakfast."

She shrugged. "We might have faced this then, as well."

"So the phantoms are back."

"Yes."

After a moment he moved to her side and slid an arm loosely around her waist. "We'll switch lanes, Freedom. Have some champagne, wait a while—"

"No!" Her gaze darted to him. "Ced, no, we can't. *I* can't. For God's sake, don't let me walk away from this!"

Frowning slightly, he studied her face. "We've both done enough of that."

"Are you sorry, Ced? Sorry you stopped running?"

A shadow flickered in his eyes, enough hesitation to make something twist inside her, awakening a response, at last, to the warm touch of his arm and side against her own flesh. She'd gambled so much to marry him; had he cause for regret, too? He ran his right hand through his hair, dismissing the brief mood, and said, "The good we'll share will cast out any of my ghosts, Colleen."

"Sweet Mary!" Her breath left her. "You, too."

He tightened his arm reassuringly. "Alicia might flit in and out of my thoughts once in a while, but I won't look back, Freedom, because I'll have you to help me bury her ghost. I'll have you to look up to. . .her to forget.''

"I might disappoint you," she said.

"Impossible."

"Cedar," she urged, swiveling to face him, "don't put me on a pedestal!"

At her sharp tone he scowled. "Give me more credit!"

"For what?"

"For judging your character, for choosing the right woman. Dammit, Colleen—" his hands closed on her arms "—don't ever try to take away my right to choose. After what we've been through this summer, don't ever tell me I'm wrong about you. Freedom—" he drew her close, every plane and hollow pressing into her and beginning to burn "—Freedom, we'll make mistakes, but we'll just patch them up again, that's all. What did you think we were going to do with ourselves 'till death do us part'?"

Her lips curved up at the corners. "Go fishing?"

"At the very least," he said more softly, intimately.

"You fish so well, Ced. You really do."

A grin, very wide and confident. "There's something else I do well, love. . . ."

Encouraged, she snuggled closer, arms weaving around his neck, breasts teasing, a thigh pressed to his loins. As he blossomed, hardened against her, she felt a deeper excitement, longing. Perhaps this time all of her—mind, heart, body—would welcome him. She was his wife. Surely that made a difference.

"I've drawn your bath," came a husky murmur near her ear. He nibbled delicately. "Mrs. McClintock. . . ."

"Thoughtful roomy," she replied softly.

"Mmm. Mind if I join you?"

Rhetorical question. As he stepped away, glancing over his shoulder to find footing in the pool, warm steam enveloped her. He eased her into the moving heat of the springs.

The immersion was a baptism, a rite by which her separate warring selves accepted what was to follow. Pending unity; she understood that. A mutual exchange—freedom for the fortune of shared existence.

She sighed silently in relief.

He slid off the remaining lace, a sensuous unveiling. That, too, she understood. . . and wanted.

Thighs tightening, she slid back to rest her head in the cradle of his arm, near the stone. The move was deliberate. She would give him pleasure.

Her body floated out past his chest, breasts buoyant above her narrow waist, hips curving mysteriously into the water, thighs and calves glowing far below. She waved her legs. Her torso rose, gleaming breasts bared briefly, and as she settled he chuckled softly, knowingly, and brought her hip against him. A nudge. Water dancing. Their glances met.

As he began a caress over her left hip and down her thigh. . . the heat of the springs made hotter by the slow search. . . his eyes watched her face.

Her lips parted involuntarily, moist with the natural steam of the springs. *Pending unity*. The phrase began to hammer at her senses.

"Pillow," he said unexpectedly.

"What?"

"You need a pillow."

"I have one."

"My arm is honored, but it has other business."

She smiled quizzically. "Fancy business?"

Gently he slid his arm between her shoulders and the rocks. Inevitably, as her toes touched the bottom of the pool, their bodies floated into contact.

"Lord," he groaned distractedly as he leaned across her, diamonds of water glittering in the shadowed places on his chest and beneath his raised arm, and brought back two thick towels. Rhythm thrummed through her.

Cedar eased her against the terry-cloth pillow, spreading her hair over the material and up over the rocks. To hold herself steady, she found nooks in the ledges, leaving her arms open, torso half-submerged, legs drifting.

He braced his arms on either side of her head. "Comfortable?"

Words were out of place. She nodded, eyes wide.

"Good, because I...."

His own words faded as he swept her body with his gaze. *Possessive,* she thought. *He's always been possessive. It's his nature.*

"Lord, Colleen, the wait has been worth it. A lifetime of loving...."

Again their gazes met, current linked, the invisible force they'd both felt before. She drew him closer with an expression that said, "The waiting is done. Let the lifetime begin."

With grace and control Cedar leaned toward her. The damp hair on his chest grazed her nipples, then her stomach. The need expressed in his eyes was suspended by will, a deliberate prelude, the waiting. Then something, a small movement, a partly held breath finally expelled—his dashed his will, and he kissed her suddenly.

For a moment she retained the distance, knowing instinctively the slight tease of restraint would spur his pas-

sion. But he gathered her up, stomach tight against
stomach, and deepened the kiss, sending her blood
pounding. This was no tentative exploration. He knew
her mouth as perfectly as she knew his. His tongue was
expert, demanding invasion. A demand to yield.

Instead of yielding, she surged against him, confident, flinging her arms up around his neck, her own
tongue dancing and retreating and making demands to
match his.

The abandoned kiss drove her once more against that
cushioned ledge, but this time her thighs found purchase
around his hips. His hands cupped and massaged like
the water, a moving sea of sensation.

A freedom of movement, a flow of strength and impulses, came to their bodies. They clashed as warriors,
merged as lovers. Sinuous dance. Zeus and Hera. Shy
virgin rejecting his virile strength. Wanton crying his
name, crying her need, opening to him, stalling full
penetration and yet throbbing from within, responding
from a need so driving, so basic, she couldn't reject
him. He entered—warm full relief to her craving—and
began to move.

Now Colleen's brain and body knew unity, pleasure,
peace. And yet not peace, not yet. There was still a rushing, rushing toward fulfillment, toward oneness. It
came to them, water thrashing, splashing, as they
merged, instants of oneness, of love, of completeness—
expressed in guttural cries and high primal wails.

THEIR RETURN was a lethargic drifting.

His dark head was slightly above hers, his breath
pulsing against her cheek. They remained locked
together, the ripple of water and the chatter of birds

oming full upon them as if the world had only now
upted into life.

Her hand molded to the slight dip in his waist, a
atural fit. His left hand cradled her head, neither of
em remembering the moment he'd done that, and his
her supported her back.

He spoke, a rasping reminder of deep passion. "A
fetime of this. Imagine it, Colleen."

She touched his cheek, his lips, his eyebrows, and
urmured, "We're blessed."

They didn't leave the pool then. Champagne in crys-
l glasses followed, chicken sandwiches from a basket,
isp celery, olives, an apple split and shared. They ate
venously, fed each other and punctuated the fare with
timate caresses, with laughter and with growing affec-
on.

HE FLOATED ACROSS the White Sulphur pool until her
reasts nudged against his chest. When his eyes dark-
ned, she smiled with an inner understanding and asked,
Are you going to invite any of your old girlfriends to
ur Seattle wedding, Cedar?"

He splashed water on his arms, letting it warm his
kin as it slid down the curved gleaming muscles and
ickled into the hot springs. He cupped his palms and
oured water down the valley between her breasts, then
aid with studied diffidence, "I hadn't thought about it.
Marion says she doesn't know if she and Ernie can spare
e time away." He looked up, not a sparkle of humor
n his eyes.

With a pretense of anger, she splashed him. "Marion
asn't your girlfriend!"

His mouth tilted kind of funny, the laughter lurking.

He asked blithely, "You going to invite old boy friends?"

"Naturally. I want them all to see what a gorgeous fisherman I married."

He gathered her against him, letting her learn with her lower body how seriously he was thinking of ceremonies in Seattle. She laughed softly, her own longing making her voice low. "Marion was never your woman," she repeated.

"Never, Freedom. . . I just want to keep you on your toes."

"Well, you managed to keep me guessing, at least about our honeymoon spot. How did you get our cabin?"

"Forest Service. I rented it for ten years."

"You didn't! I told daddy we'd go to Seattle in a few weeks for the wedding."

"Hey, relax, I'm kidding. I rented the cabin for ten days. Long enough to get paid back for marrying you— for starters, at any rate."

"So that's it! That's what you meant when you said you were glad I made you marry me. But I didn't hold out favors for marriage, Cedar. You *are* a black Irish swain."

"Sure 'n I am, lass. Never denied it, did I?"

He held up her left hand. The marquise blue diamond flashed fire. She gave him a cocky grin. "I suppose, Cedar. . .oh, I suppose you'll manage to barter a few favors now and then." She grinned wickedly and slid her body along his until she locked her bare legs around his thighs. He groaned in pleasure.

"But we can't make love every second, Cedar. You've got to teach me about gems." She said this with

lse severity. Then she giggled. "Those gem fields you
) to in Brazil and Australia and Burma. What great
in to travel while you work!"

He caught her left hand again, brought the diamond
her eyes. He studied both intently. At last he smiled.
'hile she watched him quizzically, he brought her ring
nger to his lips and kissed it. "What great fun—" he
ghed "—to look for gems that match the parts of your
natomy I adore."

He kissed her finger once more and let her hand go.
And what great fun to see plays again and read books
gether and look at boats and—"

"What'll we call her? When we find the one we want,
mean."

"*Willing Sprite,*" he said with certainty.

"For a work boat?" she asked incredulously. "A
outheast troller?"

"Why not?"

He seemed a little hurt that she'd rejected the name.
Well," she appeased. "I thought maybe something sea.
unding. *Pelican's Reach* or *Storm's Lady*, or some-
ing."

"*Freedom's Catch* is the only other name I'd con-
der," he said, beginning to kiss the inside of her wrist.

Diverted, she murmured, "It doesn't really matter,
ve. We'll do well together, won't we?"

He'd reached the soft pale flesh of her inner arm. He
ibbled delicately, chuckling when she tightened her legs
round him. "Together, yes, but you're going to make
s lots of money, you know that, Mrs. McClintock?"

"Am I, now?"

"Aye, lass," he said in a raspy brogue. "As my inter-
ational business associate, you'll bedazzle the clients

with stories of the Freedom statue and make dea
that'll give 'em nightmares. And as me fishin' partner—
well, ye'll be mesmerizin' the fish aboard with that su
set hair ye have. It's good luck, ye are, lass, and I fanc
keepin' me luck runnin' true forever.''

"Agh—ye talk fancy, ye Irish swain! Ye'll be teachir
your children to wiggle the hearts of every lass or la
who sets eyes on 'em.''

His gaze slid over the wet curves of her body, and h.
breath tightened and held. He lowered his head to he
breast. His lips moving against her skin, urging her ey
to close and her head to fall back in abandon, he said
"I've a hankerin' to be lovin' ye...pleasurin' ye..
makin' ye call my name in that low cryin' way ye hav
when you're needin' me touch....''

He nuzzled tenderly, and the fires spiraled throug
her body. "Cedar....''

"Aye, lass." His lips traced her breast. When she sli
her fingers into his hair, bringing him closer, and sighe
again in gratitude for the happiness she felt, he whis
pered, "That's the sound I've been hearin' in m
dreams.''

"Love me, Cedar.''

"Aye, Freedom lass. I'll love ye forever.''

ABOUT THE AUTHOR

Because she grew up "filled with the trauma of pulling up roots and the exhilaration of seeing new vistas, new peoples," Louella Nelson has experienced the most diverse aspects of her country. Living and working in New England, Alaska, Hawaii, Arizona and California has given her a love of adventure and wild things.

Appropriately, readers can look to her Superromances for lively endearing characters, for drama and passion. But Louella relied on more than her own wide experience to write *Freedom's Fortune*; one of her brothers is a salmon fisherman in Pelican.

Today the author lives in Southern California, where she is a magazine editor and single mother to 15-year-old Stacee. With a background in marketing and promotion for the trade, Louella has won several awards for photography, magazine design and writing.

Postscript: she's a romantic at heart—and she loves to dance.